Stuart Harrison

STILL WATER

HarperCollins*Publishers*

HarperCollins*Publishers*
77–85 Fulham Palace Road,
Hammersmith, London w6 8jb

The HarperCollins website address is:
www.**fire**and**water**.com

Published by HarperCollins*Publishers* 2000
1 3 5 7 9 8 6 4 2

A catalogue record for this book is
available from the British Library

ISBN 0 00 226153 7 (TPB)
ISBN 0 00 710751 X (HB)

Set in PostScript Linotype New Baskerville by
Rowland Phototypesetting Ltd,
Bury St Edmunds, Suffolk

Printed and bound in Great Britain by
Omnia Books Limited, Glasgow

STILL WATER

Stuart Harrison lived in New Zealand for many years, where he met his wife. They now live in Dublin with their two young sons.

For Dale, Mac and Robbie

Part One

CHAPTER ONE

Ella cut the motor, and her boat drifted silently towards the shore. With no running lights to guide her there was only the pale moonlight to illuminate the rocks that lay ahead. She was tense, her grip tight on the wheel. Tall trees loomed above throwing her into deep shadow as she searched for a safe spot to tie up. Not for the first time that night she questioned what she was doing. A mixture of remorse and the fear of being discovered threatened to overwhelm her, but she pushed her doubts and misgivings aside. They were a luxury she couldn't afford. With a quick gesture she wiped her eyes as unbidden tears blurred her vision.

'Not now Ella. Don't lose it now,' she told herself quietly.

Ahead of her loomed the large outcrop of rock she'd been looking for. She spun the wheel quickly to avoid running aground, and the boat glided quietly broadside. Ella stepped out of the wheel-house, and rope in hand, she judged the moment to jump ashore, landing on a soft carpet of pine needles. Quickly she tied off around the trunk of a tree, and then, in the dark shelter beneath its branches, she paused to get her bearings before setting off back through the woods.

A group of killer whales swam in from the deep slope waters at the edge of the shelf, moving towards an unwary prey ahead of them. The moon vanished behind drifting cloud and the water was, for a moment, as black as pitch.

Overhead the sky was lit with faintly pulsing stars, and as the cloud passed, the moon once again cast its silvery grey light on the waves. The gulf air off the coast of Maine was thick and humid. The orcas maintained a loose formation, arching their powerful, glistening bodies through the troughs created by the three-foot swell. There were ten in all, adult males and females with several juveniles. The pod was led by an old bull who measured thirty-two feet in length and weighed eight and a half tons. He had the heavy set, thick build of male orcas, and his six-foot dorsal fin was characterized by a wavy pattern along the inner edge, like a double-toothed notch. The rest of the pod, including the females whose dorsal fins were about a third as big, bore similar patterns which spoke of a common genetic ancestry.

The sounds reaching the bull from a source that was still some distance ahead were at first faint and irregular. The swish and hiss of movement bore the signature of some warm blooded creature. The bull made clicking sounds that travelled through the water, and from the returning echoes he formed a map of the surrounding area which he compared to the storehouse of knowledge he'd built up over many visits to this part of the gulf in previous years. The ocean was relatively shallow, the seabed marked by fissures and valleys, and a deep channel ahead that ran from north to south off the coast of a large island. It was from this direction that the sounds originated.

The bull slowed and swam back to join the matriarch of the pod. She was smaller than he, perhaps twenty-six feet in length, but like him she bore the scars and marks of her advancing years. To keep up with the pod she was being partially supported by two females as they swam alongside. The bull gently sonared her body and the returning echoes told him that the rattling, watery sound of her breathing had become worse. She was growing weaker. She had been sick for many weeks now, and during that time her blubber had become dangerously thin. He stroked her with his flipper, and she responded by rubbing gently against him, but only briefly as even that minimal effort was too much for her. He remained with her for a short time before resuming his position at the front of the pod.

4

The faint swishing grew louder and more distinct. The bull stopped, and raising his head out of the water he looked towards the dark mass of an island silhouetted against the sky.

He dipped beneath the surface again, and turned towards a cove that was separated from a harbour at the southern end of the island by a broad, forested headland. The cove was partially protected by a submerged reef that curved out like a long crooked finger from the base of sheer cliffs on the northern side of the mouth. Here the heaving mass of the sea was made treacherous by conflicting currents that swirled about the underwater rocks. In the darkness, on a receding tide, the surface was marked with a brush stroke of white foam, while at the cliffs the sea pounded the rocks relentlessly and flung spray eighty feet into the air. Amid the sucking and churning water, another sound lured the orcas forward. It was the hiss made by a mixed school of bluefin tuna speeding through the water as they hunted mackerel. The tuna were of differing sizes, mostly twenty pounders, but there were also a good number of four-year-old fish weighing around sixty pounds and even some eight- or nine-year-olds that weighed up to three hundred pounds. It was for the rich succulent flesh of these migrating predators that the orcas had travelled inshore.

They approached in a line. It was a hunting formation they used often, with each animal having its allotted place. The smallest, a young female, took centre position, with successively larger animals on either side. Only the sick matriarch, with one female remaining at her side, stayed back, unable to take part. The bull took his position at the extreme left flank and with great sweeping motions of their powerful flukes the orcas rapidly picked up speed. As they gathered pace the larger animals at each end of the line were faster, which had the effect of creating a natural double-sided pincer movement. Travelling at almost thirty knots they bore down on the bluefin that were feeding around the mouth of the cove, still unaware of the approaching danger.

The bull was the first to utter a piercing scream, which was immediately taken up by the rest of the pod. The tuna reacted as if a bomb had burst among them, scattering in terror. Many tried to escape by fleeing in the opposite direction, and so found themselves unwittingly herded inside the cove, just as the orcas had intended. The water reverberated with a loud series of staccato clicks interspersed with solid booms, and the range of the orca vocal sounds further panicked the tuna. Only some of the older, more experienced fish understood what was happening and tried to escape towards the open sea.

One of them, a hundred pounder, flashed past the bull, but he changed direction with amazing speed and agility and with a single bite severed its tail. As the hapless fish spiralled down he seized it and shared it with the female closest to him, leaving only the head to sink to the depths. Other tuna tried to go deep, but along the line they were intercepted, until eventually there remained only those that had fled into the cove. The orcas patrolled the entrance, continuing to make their terrifying clicks and screams, and banging their flukes on the surface of the water to deter any of the fish from trying to escape. Then taking turns, they swam into the cove in pairs to feed.

At its widest point the cove was a mile across and the water was deep. On one side steep rocky cliffs fringed the shore and it was from here that the reef extended more than halfway around the entrance. On the other side the woods reached to the water line. A thin strip of beach marked the inner shore, and a small wooden jetty protruded like a gnarled finger into the bay. The beach reflected back the pale light of the moon, appearing as a whitish ribbon stretched along the edge of the dark water.

The bull and one of the females were the last to enter the cove. Swimming towards each other from opposite sides they herded the tuna into an ever tightening mass in the middle of the bay. Then they turned towards shore and drove their prey into shallower water to prevent them from diving deep. The female chased a three hundred pound fish that broke the surface in a flash of silver. The bluefin twisted in mid-air as it tried to escape, but it was intercepted by the bull, who took a chunk from its belly. The mortally wounded fish crashed to the sea again and was finished off by the female. All around them tuna were fleeing in blind terror. The orcas manoeuvred with incredible agility, disabling as many as they could, severing tails and caudal fins with swift bites before leaving their victims to sink. Only when the water was calm again did they seek out the wounded fish.

When their hunger was satisfied, they returned to the entrance to the cove and together they escorted in the sick matriarch. Her breathing was laboured now, and she swam with weak motions of her flukes. The bull led her into the shallows, and seizing a tuna as it flew past him he bit off its tail and took it to her, feeding her half the fish which she managed to swallow. A moment later, however, she brought it up again, as she had everything that she'd eaten over the last few days. The bull swam alongside her, gently rubbing her sides and listening to the increasingly distressed sound of her breathing. He patted her with his flipper, and she responded with a half-hearted gesture. They were both half in, half out of the water in the shallows, the bull's massive notched fin completely clear. He backed up a little and encouraged the cow to do likewise.

Just then a loud report shattered the quiet of the night, and the bull turned and spied towards the shore where the sound had come from.

Ella put her hand to her forehead and felt the warm stickiness of blood. The pain was sharp, like tiny needles repeatedly stabbing her and it brought her round quickly. She sat up, trying to figure out what had happened. Her foot had snagged on a tangled root near the foot of a live oak, and she'd fallen, striking her head against the trunk. The rough bark had grazed her skin enough to make it bleed. She figured she'd been unconscious for maybe half a minute. A dull ache inhabited her skull. When she moved it felt like something sliding around in there, squeezing her brain, and for several minutes she had to rest with her head in her hands, leaning forward with her elbows resting against her knees.

Her gaze fell to the bundle beside her, and she looked away suddenly feeling that she would be ill. The scents of the warm,

7

thick night air were oppressive. The soft, sweet loamy smell of earth and rotting leaves mingled with something even earthier, something corrupt. The smell of death.

'Jesus,' she said quietly, her voice desolate.

She sat still for a moment longer, trying to muster the strength of will to go on. Blood trickled down her face but she recalled from somewhere that head wounds always bleed heavily and look worse than they are. Shakily she got to her feet. She took a deep breath or two, then bending down, she grasped the bundle at her feet, and slowly resumed dragging it backwards a step at a time.

It took her another ten minutes to reach the path that led through the woods to the point. The houses out that way belonged mainly to summer people. She was sweating now, and her breathing was laboured. Her arms and shoulders were aching, and while she rubbed her sore muscles she stared upwards through the leafy canopy to the sky. It was a clear night, and though the forecast had promised thickening cloud and squalls later on, neither had materialized. Ella peered along the path, which was deeply shadowed but lit here and there with patches of pale moonlight. She didn't expect anybody else to be out at this time of night. An owl hooted somewhere close by, and a deer shrieked way back in the woods.

The nape of Ella's neck prickled uncomfortably. The deer had sounded eerie, like a cry from beyond the grave. A shuddering breath escaped her. She half expected to see a pale visage, a silent accusing face hovering in the trees, but there was nothing there. Then she heard the snap of a twig, and the unmistakable sound of a footfall from along the path. Ella froze. She was close to a tree, her outline broken and absorbed in its shadow. Her heart pounded and her mouth was dry. She waited, wondering who else besides herself would be out there this late, but there was only the soft rustlings of some creature among the undergrowth, and the barest tremor of leaves caressed by the breeze. She counted to thirty, then another thirty, her senses straining. Finally, no longer sure of what she'd heard she cautiously peered around the tree.

At first there was nothing but shadows, but then a shape to

her right gained substance. A figure stood motionless on the path, no more than six or seven feet away from her. A gust of wind moaned softly in the branches of old trees and moonlight seeped into a revealed space. Ella recognized Kate Little and drew in her breath.

For an instant they stared at one another, then a cloud passed across the face of the moon and the path was cloaked in darkness again. Ella heard footsteps fading, and once again the path was empty.

Seconds passed that seemed more like minutes. Ella remembered to breathe and she exhaled in a soft whoosh of breath. Her heart was beating like a hammer against her chest. At last, not knowing what else to do, she reached for the bundle at her feet and once again commenced dragging it through the trees towards her boat.

The *Osprey* was making seven knots through the swell, heading north-east from Sanctuary Harbor. She was a dragger, one of several that worked from Sanctuary. She was an old steel hulled vessel, forty-eight feet long and built on the Cape in the fifties for working the once rich cod fisheries of Stellwagen Bank. Now she fished mainly for bluefish and stripers, working in the waters ten to fifty miles off the island. Her sides were rust streaked, and her forecastle was so coated with grime it was hard to tell what colour she had once been painted.

Her skipper, Carl Johnson, was in the wheel-house listening to a radio station playing country music down low. Suddenly, over the twang of steel guitars and the mournful voice of Tammy Wynette, he heard what sounded like a rifle shot above the steady but muted thump of the diesel engines. He looked towards the island, and the faint white smudge of the reef that protected the entrance to Stillwater Cove. He reached for the throttle to drop the engine revs, but as he did so, Billy Pierce started up the winch on the deck and for nearly a minute Carl couldn't hear a thing except the clank and grind of machinery. When it was over, the *Osprey* was riding the swell, the engine just idling.

9

'How come we stopped?' Billy shouted from the deck.

'Thought I heard something.'

Billy looked across the water where Carl was gazing. 'What was it?'

'Dunno. Nuthin maybe.' Carl shrugged.

He turned his attention back to their heading, and as he did his eye fell to the bottom sounder. A cluster of black dots showed that a large school of fish was moving eastward off their bow. He cranked up the throttle, watching the screen while he altered course.

'We got somethin' down there,' he called out.

Billy looked up at him. 'What is it?'

Carl frowned, his eye on the screen. 'Could be mackerel.' He wasn't certain. The readings looked as if the fish might be big. It was all mixed up. Maybe mackerel and something else.

The *Osprey* was at full throttle now and she ploughed through the water, the bow waves glowing in the dark. Carl had completely forgotten about the shot he'd heard earlier. He called down to Billy to start putting out the net. He glanced at his watch. It was a little after two.

At three seventeen Ella took the *Santorini* out of the cove. She was in complete darkness, running without lights against all sense and marine codes. Overhead the promised cloud had at last begun to thicken and drift in from the east, and now and then the moon was obscured. Ella hugged close to the southern shore, moving slowly, her eyes on the white foam of the reef. On a night like this, with the weather clear and calm, she was safe, but even so she was aware of the muted crash and roar of the ocean as it pounded the reef and the distant cliffs. A memory of her father's boat flashed in her mind, wrecked on the rocks here six months ago during a storm. It had broken up, battered by ferocious seas. She gripped the wheel tightly, and bit down on her lower lip, shoving the memory of that night from her mind.

Once clear of the cove she picked up speed. She watched the lights of a fishing boat briefly, but it appeared to be heading away from her. The looming mass of the island receded, though when she looked Ella could see a faint yellow glow from a house on the point. Maybe it was Kate Little's house. When she was a quarter-mile out from the island, over the channel, Ella cut the engine and the night settled into silence. Her eye fell to the shape lying in the dark shadow of the railing, and dismissing all thoughts of Kate, Ella went to work.

It was some time before she became aware of the sound of an engine. She snapped to, aware she'd been lost in thought. A dragger with its running lights on approached out of the darkness off her bow. She wiped away tears that had run silently across her cheeks.

The note of the dragger's engine changed pitch and slowed and Ella knew that she'd been seen. As it came closer she recognized the *Osprey*, and she could even see the silhouette of Carl Johnson in the wheel-house. In her own wheel-house the radio crackled.

Ella hesitated, then ducked inside and switched on her mast light. She picked up her radio mike.

She took a breath and hoped her voice wouldn't sound shaky. 'Hi Carl. Is that you there?'

'Yeah, Ella. Everything okay with you?'

'Sure, no problem.'

There was a pause. 'You weren't showing any lights. Thought something might have happened.'

His curiosity was edged with concern, and she did her best to lighten her tone. 'It was just a loose connection. I fixed it. Everything's fine now.' She clicked off the mike, watching the *Osprey* drifting closer. She glanced towards the davit and the hauler, and waited to see what Carl would do. A couple of seconds went by and then she made a decision and clicked on her mike.

'See you later Carl.' She started up the engine and turning the wheel brought the *Santorini* about as if she was heading back towards the harbour. Carl held his course for a couple more seconds, then the pitch of his engine altered and the *Osprey* turned eastward.

'Have a good night,' Carl said.

'You too.' She clicked off the mike and released her breath, her heart thumping. Only when she was sure that the *Osprey* was well away did she cut back her engine.

This time she worked quickly. She took a knife and severed the line that ran to the hauler, and there followed a splash, and then silence, and the water was black and still again.

CHAPTER TWO

The smell of wood smoke drifted over the fence. Henry came out on his porch, and called over.

'You there Matt?'

Henry was Matt's neighbour. He was around seventy, a little dark-skinned guy with Portuguese roots. The day Matt had moved into his house three months earlier, Henry had come over with a present of a bluefish he'd caught from the little fifteen-foot crabber he went out in most days, and ever since he'd been convinced Matt liked fish as much as he did himself.

'Got some mackerel smokin'. You want one for your breakfast? They're good eating.'

'I already ate,' Matt said from his porch.

The two houses occupied a clearing on a steep part of the hill overlooking the town. Henry appeared where the fence ended. A strip of grass separated the two properties. A dusty road led down between the trees and eventually came out on to Valley Hill which was the main route into town.

'I'll save a couple of fat ones for your supper.'

'Thanks Henry. You want anything from town today?'

'Maybe some tobacco if you've got a minute.'

Henry rarely went into town himself. He kept his boat in a rocky bay on the southern tip of the island, and when he wasn't fishing he was tending to his orchard and the new cider press he was building, which was mostly funded by the investment Matt had made in the venture. Though the amount was small it represented pretty much all the money Matt had. Henry's cider was the best Matt had ever tasted, and together they planned to bottle it and sell it on the mainland. From small beginnings, as the saying goes.

Henry joined Matt on the porch. He was wearing jeans and the same shirt with its long faded pattern that he wore on most days. He had kind of a bandy legged gait, and friendly eyes. The lingering whiff of fish and smoke accompanied him wherever he went.

'There's coffee on the stove if you want some,' Matt said.

Henry went inside and reappeared with a mug. They both looked out on the harbour, and the gulf beyond. The sea was coloured aqua, mottled in shades of light and dark, sometimes approaching emerald, until in the distance it changed, becoming a deeper almost midnight blue where the temperature changed. Already there were boats dotted about, some from St George and others from nearby islands or the coast. Bass Harbor and Penobscot Bay lay to the north; to the far south; the Cape.

'That's a nice suit,' Henry observed.

It was dark blue, one of half a dozen usually hanging in the closet from Matt's days as a prosecutor for the DA's office in Boston. It was the first time he'd worn a suit since moving to the island and he already felt self-conscious about it.

'I have to see a client today,' he lied.

'Uh huh.' Henry sipped his coffee. 'You goin' to that meeting tonight?'

'I thought I might.'

'Guess you'll be seeing Ella Young there.'

'I guess I will.' Matt wondered if the suit had been such a good idea after all. If it was so apparent to Henry that his intention was to make an impression on Ella, then he supposed she would see through him as well. 'It's going to be hot again,' he said changing the subject.

'Yep.' Though Henry made no other comment his eyes shone with mild amusement.

The woods behind them were mainly oak and maple, with some firs further up. To the west, over the ridge, it was mainly cedar. Much of the island was covered with woods and cranberry

14

bog. Though there were several villages and a sprinkling of farms in the north, Sanctuary Harbor was the only town of any note. The island attracted a few summer people, some of whom had built big houses on the point. Matt's own family had once owned a place there, where they had spent summer vacations. The rest of the year home had been Boston, where Matt's father had run a successful law practice and his mother had occupied herself playing tennis and getting herself elected to the boards of various charities.

The island hadn't changed much. Its economy was based on fishing and the service industry around it. It was a working town. Unlike some other islands in the gulf, St George attracted few tourists, and those it did attract came for that very reason. The few hotels and guest houses were clean and comfortable but they were rarely full. The stores in town catered primarily to the local population, and there was an absence of tourist trinkets and home crafts except for some scrimshaw, an art which was still practised, but these days by few. The bones they used to carve their sailing ships and intricate figures were from the occasional dead minke that beached itself somewhere around the island. The cottages on the hillside seemed to sag under the weight of their years and many could have used a lick of paint. Matt's mother would have preferred a vacation home on the Vineyard or Nantucket or Cape Cod itself; but his father had disagreed. Once a year he liked to get away from it all, he said. To be someplace where he didn't have to shave every day or worry he was going to meet up with somebody in the yacht club bar who'd want his opinion on some business problem or other. Matt and his brother Paulie had sided with their father, and in the face of so much opposition their mother had capitulated, on condition they build a decent house on the point. And so it had been, and they had joined the small community of summer people who came every year.

Fifteen years had passed since the house had been sold, two more than that since Matt had last set foot on the island, until three months ago when he'd found this house, owned by the estate of a woman who'd died a year ago. Henry claimed she'd been a miserable type and a poor neighbour, though since she'd died he'd missed having somebody to talk to. The house with its views and the woods behind, had appealed to Matt, it was a good place to start over. Somewhere he could try to bury the ghosts of his past.

He tossed his coffee grounds into the bushes. 'I better get going,' he announced.

'You have a good day,' Henry called. His eye dropped to Matt's polished shoes and it seemed he was trying not to grin.

As he drove down the track Matt looked in the mirror at the fine dusty cloud he had raised in his wake, and saw Henry on the porch shaking his head with evident mirth.

Once he hit the blacktop it was a ten minute ride into town to his tiny first floor office on a street off Founders Square. Two paths bisected the square, cutting across the yellowing grass from corner to corner, and bench seats had been placed at regular intervals where people could sit and pass the time of day. Around each of them the grass had been worn away to bare earth which in winter became mud before it iced over. The building that housed the town council was opposite the police department, and the fire department lay on the south side, the library and courthouse on the north. These, like most of the buildings in the town looked vaguely shabby, and the flag that fluttered above the courthouse was faded. Everything about Sanctuary looked a little down at heel, like an old dog lying panting in the shade.

For most of the morning Matt read the paper and drank coffee. He was the sole employee of his newly opened practice, and in two months he'd made almost enough money to cover his groceries. It was a slow start, but then he hadn't expected to make a fortune. Maybe Henry's cider would pay the rent. During the afternoon he made some calls and settled a land dispute between two farming neighbours in the north.

'I guess you'll send me your account,' Norton, who was Matt's client, said grudgingly, implying that he considered Matt's role in the settlement had been slight and was hardly worthy of payment.

'Maybe you could just let me have some bacon.'

There was a short silence as Norton figured he probably wanted a whole pig. They agreed on a side of ham, but even when Norton hung up he sounded suspicious, as if he thought he was somehow being cheated.

'Don't mention it, you miserable old bugger,' Matt said after he heard the click.

He was relieved when the day drew to a close. He walked across the square towards the town offices. The mayoral election was due to be held in a few weeks' time, dominated by a proposal to develop land on the south shore. The issue was a hot one, and had been debated long before Matt's arrival on the island. The community was almost neatly divided half and half, for and against.

Matt waited by the steps, nodding to one or two people he recognized as they drifted into the building. Outside, a few groups stood around talking in low voices and smoking. A bunch of guys from the docks from whom the odour of fish wafted fell silent and watched a woman walk across the square, their expressions sullen with resentment. As Ella drew near Matt went to meet her, and she smiled when she saw him.

'Hi there.'

'Hi,' he said.

'I'm glad you could come.'

'Hey, I wouldn't miss it for the world.'

Their looks lingered, each of them aware he wasn't referring just to the meeting. Ella possessed a curious feature in that she had different coloured eyes. One was grey, the other green. In a certain light Matt thought they appeared similar, both kind of smoky, but when she smiled or when her passions were aroused the difference was more noticeable, and for some reason it was this feature that, to Matt, made Ella rise above being merely attractive.

They climbed the steps and their arms touched as Ella brushed her pale yellow hair back from her face. She was slim, and maybe five-five or six, but she possessed an air of strength that belied her size. Determination was evident in the jut of her chin, hinting at stubbornness. Though they'd only known each other a short time Matt already admired her. She made a living running her own lobster boat, a tough enough life for anyone, but tougher still for a woman working in what was very much a man's world. But unlike the men outside, Ella didn't carry the smell of her work around with her. She was scrubbed clean, her skin almost glowing pink, and on the air in her wake he caught a hint of some scent she used.

The action of sweeping back her hair exposed a band aid at her hair line, and the nasty looking discoloured flesh around it, swollen and dark with a yellowing flush at the edges.

'That's a hell of a knock. What happened?'

Self-consciously she allowed her hair to fall forward again, largely concealing the bruise. 'I slipped. It's okay.'

'You should have somebody take a look at it, just to be sure.'

'Maybe I will.'

They went inside and squeezed by people in the hall. The meeting chamber itself was almost filled. Many of the seats were occupied and people also stood at the back against the wall.

'Good turnout,' Ella said.

A grizzly looking guy with a shock of white hair approached.

'Ella. Come on over here.' His eye rested on them both, a faint speculative smile creasing his face. 'Seems you two are always together these days.' He shook Matt's hand, and guided them over to a group he'd been talking to. As Ella went to meet them Matt noticed the flush of colour at the back of her neck.

'How's it looking?' Matt asked, finding himself left with George Gould.

'Oh, it's hard to tell. But I think it's going to be close.' George gestured towards the group of fisherman Matt had seen outside who were now standing at the back of the room. 'Those fellas over there, they're all for Howard. Jake Roderick, you know him? He's the ugly one looks like nobody ever taught him to smile. Him and his brother are kind of the ringleaders of that happy bunch. Can't see his brother at the moment.' George scanned the room and checked his watch. 'Funny, thought he'd be here by now. Anyway, those two own some land where

18

Howard wants to build this development of his, so there's no question which way they'll vote when the time comes. That land will probably triple in value inside a year. Maybe more.'

'Money talks,' Matt observed.

'For some. Jimmy Noon, he'll vote for Howard too. Jimmy runs the hardware store on Independence and there's no doubt he'd be happy to see more visitors on the island. But it doesn't always follow. See Joanna over there, that's her wearing that blue dress, she owns the café just across the square, and she'd probably stand to do well if Howard wins, but she's on our side.'

George went on pointing out where people's loyalties lay. At the front of the chamber was a podium and strung across the back wall were two banners. One proclaimed 'Prosperity For The Future', and on it was a picture of a marina berthing lots of gleaming white boats. People walked along promenades past stores and restaurants. The scene created the impression it was designed to impart; one of affluence and a different kind of life, more like Bar Harbor than St George. Underneath was the legend 'Vote For Howard Larson'. Beside it another banner said 'Vote For Ella Young And Protect Our Island'. There was no picture, and the contrast between the two couldn't have been clearer. Howard Larson's with its promise of wealth and change, and Ella's with its simple message of appeal.

George excused himself and Matt found himself standing alone. A few people cast curious looks his way. He was still new enough around town to be vaguely interesting. He knew a face here and there, people he remembered from his adolescent summers, and he said 'hi' to a couple of them. He looked towards the front of the room, and unwittingly caught Howard Larson's eye. Howard said something to the person next to him and made his way over.

'Matt. Good to see you.' He clasped Matt's hand. He wasn't a tall man but his bulk made him appear larger, more imposing. He had fleshy jowls and small bright eyes that were hidden for a moment by the flash of reflected light on his glasses. His smile stayed in its well practised place. 'I guess we're about to start.'

He looked around the room appraising the crowd, and it

seemed he was calculating his support. There was a faint note of strain in his tone and Matt wondered just how much Howard had riding on the outcome of the vote. Though he owned the processing plant out towards the heads, the fishing industry had long been in decline, and rumour had it that Howard was in trouble.

'So, have you made up your mind where you stand?' Howard followed Matt's automatic glance across the room. 'I guess Ella's had an unfair advantage in getting her view across, huh?' He laughed, but there something mean spirited in the sound.

'To tell the truth I didn't take much persuading,' Matt said.

Howard's smile slipped a fraction. 'You ought to keep an open mind until you've heard all the arguments, Matt. Hell, I don't need to tell you that, you being a lawyer.'

'I've lived in the city most of my life, Howard. I came back here because I wanted to live somewhere peaceful and unspoiled, but you want to change that.'

'Well, people can't eat pretty scenery, Matt. It isn't ourselves we have to think of, it's the young people. Old George over there, now he'd as soon dig up his mother's grave as have me win this election and see this project go ahead. He'd have things stay just the way they are around here for ever. But people need jobs, a future for themselves if kids aren't going to up and leave the first chance they get. Old timers like George can't see that things have changed. It isn't like the old days, we can't rely on fishing anymore.'

'I wouldn't say Ella's what you'd call old, Howard,' Matt pointed out. 'And she makes her living fishing.'

'Well, Ella means well, but the fact is, the way things have been going these past years, she'll be as glad as anybody else if this marina gets built in the end. We're talking about bringing more visitors here, Matt. That means money, jobs. People are going to want houses, they'll tell their friends, and the whole thing snowballs. Everybody's a winner.'

Especially if you happen to own a lot of the currently worthless land on the south shore, Matt thought.

'You should think about it,' Howard said. 'This'll mean opportunities for smart people. How's that practice of yours doing anyway?'

'It's slow, but I guess things'll pick up.'

'You know, this could be good for you. All those people coming here to start businesses and build new homes, I guess they'd need a lawyer to handle all those contracts. They'd probably be more comfortable with someone from the mainland who talks their language, but someone who knows the island as well. I could steer them your way, Matt.'

'Isn't Doug Keillor a buddy of yours?' Matt asked, mentioning another practising lawyer on the island.

Howard waved a hand in casual dismissal. 'Doug doesn't have your experience. Anyhow, there'd be more than enough for the two of you. Think about it. Maybe you could talk to Ella.' Then with a conspiratorial wink he turned and went back towards the podium.

As Matt watched him go he wondered if Howard was so willing to offer him such an obvious inducement, what would he be like if he was elected as mayor?

Joanna Thompson got the meeting started, and Ella was up first. She spoke with passion for the island where she'd lived her entire life. As she became more animated she radiated a kind of sparky energy that made Matt's heart thump. She talked about the way of life they enjoyed on the island, the lack of crime, how people still talked to their neighbours and got along, and about how she and many others still made their living from the ocean that surrounded them, and both defined and dominated their lives. He wished he'd met her a long time ago.

A voice spoke up from the audience. 'Yeah, I get forty cents a pound for a lobster and then some tourist down state goes out to eat and pays twenty-five bucks for it. I oughta be in the restaurant business.'

The room broke out into good-natured laughing, and on the stage Ella smiled too. 'You do okay Bill Harris. I saw that new tyre you bought for that truck of yours the other week.'

There was more laughing since everybody knew that Bill Harris's truck was about fifteen years old and was kept going

21

with huge quantities of oil and the occasional prayer, and his boat wasn't much better. A lot of people were in the same situation.

'Course if you've had enough of fishing I guess you could always go punch in at Howard's plant,' Ella added with a sly swipe at her opponent. 'Or maybe you could get a job in the new gas station Howard wants to build.' She paused, and her tone became more serious. 'The thing is, don't we live here because we like it, because we choose this way of life? I guess if I'd wanted to live in a place that gets overrun with tourists every year I would've left a long time ago. Sure, it's not always easy to make a living here. I should know, I fish for lobsters and nobody needs to tell me how hard it is these days. There aren't as many of them as there used to be. But things will get better again if we all just hang in there and don't take more than our share.' At this, she fixed her look pointedly at someone at the back of the hall and Matt swivelled around and saw Jake Roderick staring resentfully back at her.

'Maybe Howard's marina would bring in people and money, and more jobs. But what kind of jobs? Waitressing or bartending or gardening for people who'd build big houses and drive real estate prices out of our reach? And maybe we'd have new stores for all these people, but they'd be selling stuff we couldn't afford to buy. And what else would we have? How about drugs? I hear there's a lot of that kind of thing wherever the yacht crowd go. Is that something you want your kids around?'

Ella paused and looked around the room, and a lot of people appeared thoughtful. Howard scowled unhappily. Then Ella smiled, and spread her arms, hands palm up in a winning gesture that softened a speech that might otherwise have come across as a little strident. 'But what do I know? Thanks for listening anyway.'

She went back to her chair, and for a moment there was silence, then somebody clapped once, hesitantly, and Matt took it up and a smattering of appreciation ricocheted around the room. As the noise died down Matt heard a voice mutter behind him.

'Damn bitch.'

He didn't need to look to know the voice belonged to Jake Roderick.

After the meeting ended Matt walked Ella to where she'd parked. They took the long way round, walking slowly, ending up passing the docks where the moon cast its light on the water. The night air was warm and close.

'You did well,' he said.

She smiled. 'Thanks. Howard won them back a little though didn't he? He's not stupid, I'll give him that.'

It was true, Howard had scored a few points for his side. He'd prepared graphs and charts that projected income streams from the increase in visitor numbers the marina would bring. He'd promised that the new stores and restaurants that were part of his plans would be reserved for island people first. 'This is about making our lives better. Not somebody else's. Ours,' he'd said, and a lot of people had nodded in quiet agreement.

'I think you still won the night,' Matt said.

'Maybe.' Ella frowned.

'Something wrong?'

'Just . . . I don't know. Things have gotten dirty. I suppose I wasn't expecting it.'

'Politics will do that.'

'Or money.'

'Usually they're the same thing. Howard has some unpleasant supporters. Jake Roderick for instance. I got the impression he doesn't like you.'

'You're right he doesn't. Him or his brother.'

'Have they been giving you trouble?'

'You could say that.' She made a gesture dismissing the subject as they reached her truck. 'Anyway, thanks for coming. I'm glad you were there tonight.' She hesitated. 'I'm glad you're here, too. On the island I mean.'

Barely pausing to think, he bent towards her and their lips brushed. It was tentative, and slight, and he sensed her uncertainty before she pulled back, gently.

23

'Matt . . . I haven't had a good run with the men in my life.' She tried to make it sound light, and kind of smiled.

'Listen, I don't want to rush you. I got carried away with the moment. We've got all the time in the world. I'm not going anywhere.'

She smiled again, and nodded, though her eyes seemed hooded with doubt or uncertainty, or perhaps just caution.

'Well, goodnight.' She started to get in her truck, then paused. 'By the way, nice suit.'

He grinned and closed her door. 'Goodnight Ella.'

CHAPTER THREE

Dave Baxter had worked for the St George police department for more than twenty-five years, the last seven of them as chief. He was forty-seven years old and came from a long line of Baxters on the island, of which he was the last. He had a sister who lived in New York State, but they hadn't seen each other for six years, though they talked occasionally on the phone and exchanged cards at Christmas. Baxter lived alone, as he had done for most of his life. Once, when he was younger, there had been a woman who he'd seen regularly for almost three years but eventually it became apparent to them both that she wanted more than merely the pleasantly amiable relationship they enjoyed. Marriage had been discussed, but when it hadn't gone any further than that, the woman had given him an ultimatum. She gave him six months to decide what he wanted, and when that time was up and he hadn't reached a conclusion she made her own decision by upping and leaving the island. Baxter had considered going after her, as he suspected she had wanted him to, but he decided to think it over for a while first, and then the next he heard she had married a grocer from Bangor. Since then he had pretty much been content with his own company, and that of friends. He didn't understand women, and to be truthful was even a little afraid of them.

On the Wednesday morning after the meeting, Baxter was sitting opposite Jake Roderick who had come to file a missing persons report concerning his brother. Baxter scratched behind his ear after Jake had finished talking.

'You haven't seen Bryan since Monday night. And you haven't heard anything from him. No calls or anything like that?'

'I told you. He's just gone.'

'Well, maybe he's visiting somebody.'

Jake shook his head once, emphatically. 'His truck's at the house. I went over there.'

Baxter picked up a pencil and tapped it thoughtfully against his teeth. The clock on the wall showed that it was about the time when he usually went over to the coffee shop for a late breakfast. Just thinking about it he could smell the bacon cooking. He contemplated telling Jake that he should give Bryan another day. Probably he just went off somewhere and decided not to tell Jake where he was going, or else he forgot. Baxter had to admit it was unlikely though. Bryan didn't normally do much that Jake didn't know about. Unless it concerned women of course. Bryan went his own way in that regard. Judging from the dark expression Jake wore he wasn't about to be put off so easily anyway. Baxter sighed and rose to his feet.

'Okay, we better go out there and take a look.'

They drove to the house in Baxter's cruiser. Bryan lived in a clearing set back in the woods in Stillwater Cove, reached by a track that came off the main route north. As Jake had said, Bryan's truck was in the garage. Inside, the house was clean and orderly, nothing out of place.

'Your brother keeps this place pretty good,' Baxter observed. 'He have someone come in or something?' He thought of his own place, which was a mess in comparison.

Jake looked around, and his brow furrowed a little. 'No, he doesn't have anyone.'

'Girlfriend maybe? Someone he's been seeing?'

'Bryan sees a lot of different people.'

Baxter could see how that would be. He wondered if Jake ever got to thinking about how he'd drawn the short straw when it came to looks. The younger Roderick bore little resemblance to Jake, other than a certain dark, brooding quality. Jake was kind of squat and lumbering, whereas his brother was tall and muscular. Bryan had a kind of rough charm which he could turn on if he wanted, whereas Jake was more the monosyllabic type. Baxter guessed women liked all that thick black hair, the wide shoulders and the flashing smile. He sucked in his gut a little, catching sight of himself in a mirror.

He opened the door to the living room. Inside there was a gun rack behind the door. One of the racks was empty and he ran a finger in the groove and it came away free of dust.

'There something missing here?'

Jake looked. 'Yeah. A rifle. A Remington.'

'Maybe it's in his truck.' They went outside to check. On the way Baxter paused by a stand in the front hall where a couple of sets of keys were in a bowl. 'These Bryan's?' he asked, picking one set up.

'Yes. There's a key for the house and barn, that one's the cold store and the other's for the *Seawind*.'

'What about this other set here.' Baxter picked them up. There was just a key for the house and the barn.

Jake shrugged. 'Spares I guess.'

Outside they looked in the truck, but there was no rifle. Baxter closed the barn door and looked up at the house as if it might tell him something. 'The door was open when you got here?'

'It wasn't locked anyway.'

'And you took a look around?' Baxter peered through the trees around the clearing, as if Bryan might appear. 'Maybe he went hunting and something happened.'

'I took a look, but I didn't find anything,' Jake said.

'Well, I guess we better get some people out here.' Baxter headed back to his cruiser. He started thinking about how many men he would need, and how to organize a proper search. The woods went back into the middle of the island, and rose high up into the hills. If a man hurt himself out there, if he couldn't signal for help, he might never be found. Such things had been known to happen, though not on St George that Baxter could remember. It was Wednesday. If Bryan was out there somewhere, maybe with a broken leg or worse, how long had he been gone?

'When did you say was the last time you saw him?' Baxter asked.

27

'On Monday night. After he left Ella.'

'Ella?'

'They had a fight.'

'Yeah? What was it about?'

'I didn't hear it all. She said we fouled her gear or some damn thing.'

Baxter could believe that. It wouldn't be the first time the Rodericks and Ella had clashed over her accusing them of cutting traps or deliberately dragging buoy lines. Nor was Ella the only one to have had problems with them. The Rodericks were rogues. They had come to the island maybe six or seven years ago, and simply muscled their way into the harbour lobster gang. There were traditional places where people fished, where a family had sunk their traps for generations, and these were generally respected. Kind of unwritten rules. But the Rodericks had made it clear right from the start that the only rules they played by were their own.

'Where'd this fight happen?' Baxter asked.

'At the dock. Crazy bitch pointed a goddamn rifle at him.'

'Ella did that? She threatened him?'

'I said so didn't I.' Jake narrowed his eyes suspiciously, as if he thought Baxter didn't believe him. 'You don't have to take my word, there was others saw it too.'

Baxter didn't say anything. He looked at the empty house again, and unwrapped a stick of gum which he popped in his mouth. 'You want some?' he offered.

Jake scowled. 'I got work to do if we're all finished.'

'Yeah, we're all done.' Baxter got back behind the wheel. He was thinking about Ella pointing a rifle at a man it was well known she disliked, to say the least, who had now vanished. It was probably nothing. All the same, Baxter experienced a vague unease.

CHAPTER FOUR

Ella manoeuvred the *Santorini* alongside the dock as her stern-man jumped ashore and she cut the engine. She threw Gordon the bow line. Out of the corner of her eye she saw Dave Baxter at the end of the dock. He was leaning against a shed, chatting with one of the other guys who worked from this dock, but he was watching her. Their eyes met and she raised a hand in greeting and he waved back and smiled, but all the same Ella experienced a quickening sensation inside.

She and Gordon unloaded their catch, which didn't take long since they'd had a poor day. Almost every trap they'd hauled had contained a couple or three lobsters, but most of them were undersized.

'We'll do better tomorrow,' she assured Gordon when they were finished. She hoped they would, this time of year they ought to be bringing in plenty of big ones. She saw Baxter approaching from along the dock. 'You go on, I'll clean up.'

'It's okay,' Gordon said, already dragging over a hose.

'Go on,' she urged.

He straightened and shrugged. 'Well, if you're sure. I'll see you in the morning.'

'Bright and early.'

Baxter said hello to Gordon, and paused to exchange a few words, then came over and grabbed an overturned crate to sit on. He squinted up at the sun, still hot at the end of the day and beating down from a clear sky.

'Ella. Good day out there?'

29

'I've had better. What can I do for you, Chief?'

Baxter wiped his forehead. 'It's probably nothing, but Bryan Roderick's gone and got himself lost or something.' He waved vaguely towards the point. 'Nobody's seen him around for a couple of days. I've got some people searching the woods back there in the cove. You haven't seen him have you?'

Ella shook her head. 'Me? Why should I have seen him?'

'I'm just trying to pin down when he was last around, you know. Got to figure out how long he's been gone. Thing is, I heard you had some kind of a run in with him on Monday.'

'That's right, I did.'

'I talked to Jake and a couple of other people, Ella. They said you threatened Bryan with a rifle.' Baxter spoke almost apologetically, and the way he squinted from the reflected light off the water gave him almost a pained expression.

'They told you the truth,' Ella said. She grinned. 'Chief, you don't think I shot him do you?'

Baxter's laugh sounded a little hollow. 'Course I don't, Ella, but you know, I have to ask these things. That's what they pay me for.'

'I was kidding, Chief.'

'Yeah, I know you were,' Baxter said, but he appeared uncertain. He looked out across the harbour, then back at her. 'So you want to tell me about this fight you had.'

'Bryan came by looking for a little fun at my expense. He'd been drinking I think. Anyway I had some trouble with my traps in Little Shoal Bay a few days ago and the *Seawind* was out there the day before. We got into an argument.'

'Well, I can see how that might happen,' Baxter said. 'Threatening him with a rifle though Ella, that's a little extreme isn't it?'

'I didn't do that because of my traps. He tried to come on board my boat. I don't like people on my boat unless I ask them first.'

Baxter looked at her, and at the distance between him and the *Santorini* as if he was committing this information to memory.

'Come on Chief, you know what he's like. The Rodericks and

30

Howard have this marina thing cooked up between them, and I guess I'm not their favourite person right now. I didn't like some of the things Bryan was saying. I was just making a point. The gun wasn't loaded anyway.'

'What kind of things *was* he saying?'

'Just personal things. I don't need to repeat it word for word do I?' Ella was used to the comments some people made around her, and sometimes about her on the dock. She'd practically grown up with it, and she'd learned a long time ago to let it go over her head. Those that made them wanted her to react, expected her to because she was a woman. She never did, even when they stepped over the line, which only happened occasionally. She'd had to accept that not everybody was crazy about a woman owning her own boat, and some people let their resentment of her show. They were a minority however, and she ignored them because she knew they hated it that they couldn't get to her. But Bryan was different. He had a way of looking at her. She could read every thought in his mind, and he knew it. His mocking smile made her flesh creep.

Baxter shook his head. 'No, I guess not. So what happened after that?'

'Nothing. He left.'

'And you didn't see him again?'

'No, not at all.'

Baxter stood and smiled, then spread his hands. 'Okay, we're all set then, I guess. See you later Ella.'

'Bye Chief,' she said, and watched him amble back the way he'd come.

Along the waterfront, Howard leaned against the side of his Cherokee and thoughtfully watched Baxter get in his car. Across the street, on a wall, one of his election posters that bore the same image and slogan as the banner he'd used at the meeting the night before had been ripped down, leaving just a fragment of torn paper. One of Ella's had been put in its place, and a picture of her smiling wholesomely at him set his teeth on edge. He felt sweat from the heat of the sun running down his neck,

31

making his collar wilt. This fucking election was going to be the death of him. He watched Ella as she washed down her deck and entertained a brief fantasy about her and that goddamned boat of hers sinking to the bottom of the frigging ocean. Despite his bad humour, and the ulcer he thought he was developing that was eating away at his insides like battery acid, he saw her bend over and appreciated the curve of her ass in her jeans.

It was a temporarily pleasant image. The dark blot of the processing plant which he owned out towards the heads drew his eye to remind him of the corner he was in. His father had built it before the war. There were fish in the gulf then, more than you would believe judging by the numbers that existed today, and the plant had made a fortune. Howard had urged his father to expand the business, maybe start a wholesale operation on the mainland but the old fool had believed St George would one day rival Nantucket and Martha's Vineyard as the summer playground of the wealthy, and so he'd poured his money into buying up as much land as he could until he owned vast tracts of the island. But fish stocks had declined, and the once prosperous island economy had foundered. The island existed now as a beautiful uncut gem, undiscovered and unspoiled. And Howard hated it with a vengeance.

A passer-by cast him a curious look and belatedly Howard remembered to smile. 'Beautiful day isn't it?'

'Yeah, it is,' came the laconic reply.

Howard saw the plant again, an oily curl of smoke rising from its chimney. The place was killing him, sucking him dry. He couldn't afford to close it down, and he sure as hell couldn't sell it. Everywhere he looked he saw it and smelt it, the pungent stink of fish oil. If he was voted in he had plans to turn it into a hotel one day after the marina had been built, and the right people had started coming here. Then maybe he could leave this lousy island forever. In his dreams he lived out in California or maybe New Mexico. Anywhere but St George.

He looked at his watch and wondered where the hell Bryan Roderick was. He hadn't seen him for a couple of days. The election wasn't far away and it seemed like it would be a close

32

run thing. Too damn close for comfort. He needed Bryan and that brother of his to do something about it, tip the odds a little more in their favour. Howard frowned, thinking about the parcel of land he'd almost given away to the Rodericks. He'd seen right off that he needed them to have a stake in his plans. Howard had always been confident that he could handle the political side of his fight with Ella, but he'd recognized it was foolish to leave anything to chance, and he'd figured if anyone could make Ella think twice about standing against him it was the Rodericks. So far they hadn't succeeded. He hoped he hadn't sold them that land for no reason. But then if Ella won it wouldn't matter. That land would be worthless and he would be ruined. Despite the heat an icy finger scraped along his backbone. Jesus. Where was Bryan?

In the end he couldn't wait any longer, and he decided to go and look for Jake. He went into the *Schooner* and peered around the room. Jake was sitting alone at a table, staring morosely at the beer on the table in front of him. Howard bought him another, and a bourbon for himself and went over. He sat down, wiping the dusty seat first, making sure he didn't put his arms on the table which was covered in a layer of cigarette ash and a puddle of beer. The place stank of cigarettes and some underlying smell Howard wasn't keen to identify. Maybe puke.

'Where's Bryan? I was waiting for him,' he said, sliding a beer across to Jake. 'You know, things aren't looking so good.' He leaned in closer and dropped his voice. 'If you two don't do something about Ella, she could win this election. You want that to happen?' He shook his head in exasperation at the thought. 'Bryan said he could take care of her. Seems to me as if he was wrong. Looks like he hasn't taken care of anything.'

Jake simply looked at him as if he hadn't heard. Howard sometimes wondered if Jake was all there. Talking to him was like trying to get sense out of a goddamned ape. Come to that maybe an ape would be easier. He'd heard they were teaching chimps sign language these days. At least if that was true he could communicate with a chimp. He preferred to deal with

33

Bryan. Maybe he wasn't exactly a rocket scientist either, and it got on Howard's nerves the way Bryan thought he was some kind of stud or something. Jesus, he thought every woman on the island creamed her pants when he walked past. But at least he understood what this was all about. Money. The universal language. Where the hell was he?

'He's gone,' Jake said.

'What?' He waited for Jake to repeat what he'd said, but Jake just looked at him. 'Gone where? Who's gone? You mean Bryan?'

'Haven't seen him since Monday.'

Howard's rising irritation got the better of him. 'What is it with you two? You know if Ella wins, you can kiss goodbye to any marina. You've got as much to lose as I have if that happens, just remember that.' He jabbed a finger across the table. 'You were supposed to persuade her to stand down and time's running out. I suggest you get hold of your brother and remind him of that.'

'Bryan's dead.'

Howard blinked. 'Dead? When? How?'

Jake just stared at him, a light burning in his eyes that made Howard think uncomfortably of the glow from some otherwordly furnace.

CHAPTER FIVE

The clock on the wall which Matt had inherited with the office, told him that it was a quarter after six. He checked his watch. The clock had gained twenty minutes since the day before. He figured it was time for him to leave anyway and he rose and stretched. Outside he heard footsteps climbing the stairs, and somebody knocked at the door. When he opened it Ella stood outside looking uncertain

'Come on in.' He stood aside, delighted to see her. He'd been contemplating calling her that night, though he didn't want to appear over eager. Slow down boy, he'd cautioned himself. He'd begun to think a great deal about Ella, but he didn't want to push things too quickly, for either of them, so having her turn up at the office was a pleasant surprise.

'I didn't know if you'd still be here at this time.' She looked around with a faintly curious air.

'Swamped with work.'

She looked doubtfully at his desk where a moment ago he'd been doing a crossword puzzle.

'Okay, so I lied. Actually I was just thinking about leaving. How about you and I get a drink someplace?'

She shook her head. 'I can do better than that. Why don't you come to the house for supper later. Unless you had something else planned?'

'Not a thing,' he said. 'Just tell me where and when.'

She told him where she lived and said to come by around seven. They walked down the stairs to the street together. He thought she seemed distracted, as if there was something bothering her and he wondered if there had been some other reason for her visit to his office.

'Is everything okay Ella?'

She looked at him and for a second she appeared to hesitate, then she nodded. 'Everything's fine. I'll see you tonight.'

'You can count on it.'

He arrived a few minutes early, showered and dressed in a clean shirt and jeans, clutching a bottle of white burgundy in one hand. He'd briefly considered wearing a jacket and maybe even a tie, but just imagining the look Henry would give him had changed his mind. The fact he'd even considered it, however, had brought home to him that like it or not, Ella had found her way under his skin. He wasn't complaining. She was intelligent, good company, and lovely, not to mention that he liked her a lot. He guessed he just hadn't been expecting to feel this way about anyone. At her door he acknowledged a faint nervousness, like a kid on his first date, and he smiled at his own foolishness. He knocked and when the door opened Ella stood framed by the soft light of a lamp behind her.

'Hi. I'm not too early?'

'No, come on in.' She led the way down the passage to the living room. 'I hope you don't mind but my mom is going to eat with us. I thought it'd be nice for her to meet you. She doesn't get out much these days.'

'I'd like to meet her too,' Matt said. 'Especially if she's anything like you.'

She smiled at the flattery and took the wine when he offered it. 'Make yourself at home.'

There were photographs on the mantel. The room was comfortable, even if the furniture was worn. It had a pleasant lived-in feel, and the cooking smells coming from the kitchen made his mouth water. Ella went to open the wine, and while she was gone he looked at a picture on the wall. A child stood with two adults. The child appeared to be a boy though the image was a little blurry and it was difficult to tell. The man was tall and lean, his eyes shadowed. Ella came back and handed him a glass of wine.

'My parents.'

Matt looked again. 'This is your father?'

She sipped from her glass, her eyes on the picture. 'Yes. He died last winter.'

'I'm sorry.' There was sadness in her eyes, but something else too, something he couldn't interpret. 'What happened?'

'There was a big storm. His boat was wrecked and he drowned.' He thought she might add something else, then whatever it was, she let it go. 'Shall we sit down? I hope you like beef.'

'Beef is great. To be honest I thought we'd be eating lobster. The truth is I've never really liked them.'

'Me either,' Ella confessed. 'When you make your living catching them, they kind of lose their appeal.'

'I guess so.'

'You know,' she said hesitantly. 'I remember you coming here for the summers. Your family had a house on the point. Pointers.'

Matt was surprised that she'd known him. 'Pointers?'

'That's what we called you summer people.'

'We had a name for you too. Lobbies.'

For a second she looked affronted, then she laughed at herself. 'Actually that's good.' She hesitated. 'I wasn't going to tell you this, but the truth is I had a crush on you when I was a kid.'

'You did?' He was frankly amazed. She was maybe thirty-one or two now, which made her four or five years younger than him. The last time he'd been on the island he'd been approaching twenty, so she would have been fifteen or sixteen. He couldn't believe he wouldn't have noticed her even then. She laughed at his expression.

'I won't be offended if you don't remember me. I looked different then, and when we mixed with you pointers it was usually to fight.'

He looked back at the picture then, at the child he'd mistaken for a boy, and a memory stirred. 'That's you?'

37

She grinned, obviously enjoying herself. Matt thought maybe he did remember her after all. An image came back to him. A girl around thirteen years old. Short, sun-bleached hair, her fists clenched at her side and her face set angrily. Some kid in the dirt at her feet, wiping blood from his lip with a stunned look on his face, wondering how come a girl had put him on his ass. Other kids had looked on, and suddenly aware of them all, a flash of uncertainty and confusion had leapt in the girl's expression.

'That was you?' he said. 'Short hair, skinny?' She nodded, smiling at the look he wore as he tried to reconcile past and present.

Now he'd placed her he recalled other incidents. Passing her on the street once and as she hurried by Paulie shook his head. Thin in her jeans and looking like a boy with her chopped hair and a smattering of freckles on her nose. Weird kid, he'd said. Mostly, though, Matt remembered seeing her on the dock, helping someone he guessed was her dad as they unloaded a day's catch from a boat.

'I wouldn't have known it was you.' He tried to recall if he'd ever had an inkling that she'd had a crush on him, and was certain he hadn't.

'Ella was a tomboy then,' a voice said.

Matt rose as a woman appeared in the doorway. She walked with a limp, and held her left arm awkwardly in the manner of somebody who'd suffered a stroke. He recognized Ella in her immediately, though their colouring was different. The older woman's hair was almost entirely grey, but it was streaked with remnants of the black it had once been, visible in the picture on the wall. The most obvious similarity between them was a sense he had of inner strength and he saw where Ella got her spunk. From the slight accent in her speech and her features Matt guessed she was of mid or south European heritage. Greek maybe.

'This is my mother, Helena.' Ella introduced them. 'This is the man I told you about Mom. Matt Jones.'

He shook her hand. She was thin, and frail, her skin dry

textured, but she gripped his hand firmly, if briefly. Her smile was like her daughter's. It transformed her.

'I'm very pleased to meet you Mrs Young.'

'Please, call me Helena.' She looked fondly at Ella. 'You know I don't think she wanted to be a girl when she was young. She didn't even own her first dress until she was sixteen, and she followed her father around everywhere, right from when she could first walk. Pestered him to take her on his boat. He pretended that she was a nuisance, but secretly he loved it. She could strip an engine by the time she was fourteen and she knew the waters around the island as well as anybody.'

Ella reached over and covered her mother's hand with her own, and for a second the two women shared something that Matt was excluded from. Some deep bond that existed only for them. He sensed that it went far beyond the normal mother-daughter relationship. The moment passed and Ella rose.

'Let's eat,' she said.

Over supper they talked about the island. Helena related how she'd come there as a young woman to marry Ella's father. Briefly they touched on the election, Helena glowing with pride as she contemplated the idea of her daughter becoming the next mayor. At the mention of Howard's name she waved a hand in dismissal.

'I remember when he came home from college, that was before his father died. Howard always had a look on his face like he'd sucked on a lemon,' she laughed. 'He doesn't care about the island.'

She asked Matt a little about himself and he told her that he was divorced and had a son, that his parents still lived in Boston, and that his father was retired now. Ella knew he'd been married, though he hadn't told her much beyond the fact that Kirstin had left him and had remarried.

'Ella tells me that you were a prosecutor in Boston?' Helena asked.

'Yes.'

'And so what brings you here to the island? You can tell me I'm a nosy old woman if you like.'

39

Matt smiled. He wasn't sure he could have explained all of his reasons easily, so he kept it general. 'I just decided I needed a change from the kind of life I was living. I always loved this place when we came here when I was a kid.' He didn't want to get into the sense of failure his wrecked marriage had engendered, the fact he'd worked so hard that he had a son he barely knew.

'You had a brother didn't you?' Ella said.

'Yes, Paulie,' Matt said cautiously. 'He was a couple of years older than me. He died, when I was still in law school.'

'I'm sorry.' Ella shook her head. 'I remember him. He was so full of life.'

'That was Paulie. He did everything at a run. Seemed like he had enough energy to take on the world.' He faltered, unsure whether he wanted to go into what had happened, but it was something he knew he had to get to grips with. He felt like his brother's death had plagued his life, and he ought to get used to confronting it. It was partly the reason he'd chosen to move to St George.

'Paulie was just starting out as an architect when he was killed. It was one of those dumb, pointless things that happen. He walked into a grocery store one morning during a robbery. The guy with the gun was high on something and he panicked and Paulie got shot.'

Helena's eyes widened. 'That's terrible. And your poor parents.'

'It was pretty tough,' Matt admitted. 'My folks took it hard.' He picked up his glass, suddenly keen to change the subject. 'But it was a long time ago, and it shouldn't spoil such a terrific meal. To the cook.' He raised his glass, and Ella smiled, though the way she scrutinized him he didn't think she was fooled by his pretence at being unaffected.

After the meal Matt helped clear away the table, and then Helena made her excuses and went to bed early. 'I get so tired these days. I hope we meet again.'

'I hope so too.'

Ella went to see that she was all right, and when she came back she closed the passage door.

40

'I like her,' Matt said. 'How did I do?'

'We don't make snap judgments in this family. But I guess you did okay.'

Over coffee they talked, discovering a little more about each other. Matt told her about his ex-wife and son. They lived near Salem now.

'Alex is seven now. I'm hoping he'll come up here in the fall for a visit.'

Matt already knew that Ella had been married once and when he asked her about her ex-husband she seemed to talk about him easily enough, though there seemed little to tell. She'd married young and it had lasted for less than a year.

'I don't even know where he is any more,' Ella said. 'Last I heard he was in Mexico.'

'Kids make things more complicated,' Matt said. He was sure Kirstin would have been happy for him to drop out of her life entirely, but that wouldn't happen, because of Alex. After a while the conversation came around to Paulie again, though Matt didn't think he'd raised the subject this time.

'Did you becoming a prosecutor have anything to with what happened to your brother?' Ella asked.

'Why would you think that?'

'I don't know. Something about the way you sounded earlier. You were close weren't you?'

'I guess we were. He was your everyday all-round-athlete-cum-academic older brother. You know the type, good at everything. But I never felt as if I lived in his shadow, I looked up to him. I guess I was angry when he died. Becoming a prosecutor seemed like a way to hit back.'

In fact Paulie's death had consumed him for a long time. He found himself opening up to Ella, admitting that he'd buried himself in zealous, maybe obsessive, pursuit of his work, to the exclusion of almost everything else. He'd been on a mission to put the bad guys away and throw away the key. To avenge Paulie. In the end though, he lost his family, and one day he woke up and thought he hadn't achieved anything with his life that was worthwhile.

41

'I wanted to do some good,' he explained, 'but I felt like I was banging my head against a wall sometimes. The system got to me. Lawyers cutting deals to get their clients a reduced charge on a plea bargain, or else they'd go to trial and convince a jury to believe whatever story they came up with: it was an accident, or self-defence or else the defendant had a lousy childhood so that was supposed to make it okay that he pushed his wife in front of a car. That happened by the way. The guy who did it was having an affair, but his wife had a drug problem and the defence claimed she was turning tricks to pay for her habit. The jury bought it and accepted the guy's plea that it was temporary insanity because his mother was a hooker and had abandoned him as a kid, and that was why he went nuts and accidentally pushed his wife under a car. He walked.'

Matt shook his head, aware that he'd started to sound bitter. He looked at his knuckles clenched tightly around his coffee cup and he put it down. 'I'm sorry, I didn't mean to get into this.'

'No, it's okay. Is that what happened to the man who shot your brother? Did he get off?'

'They never caught him.'

Ella was silent for a moment, contemplative. 'Can I ask you something?' she said hesitantly. 'I know what happened to your brother was terrible, but don't you ever think that sometimes people do things that might seem awful, but if you knew everything about them, maybe things aren't always the way they look? It doesn't always mean they're bad people does it?'

'I suppose I've seen too many guilty people escape their responsibilities. People forget about the victims.'

He'd seen himself as some kind of white knight, chasing down the bad guys. At first Kirstin hadn't complained that he could've made more money working in some other branch of the law, even though when her car sometimes wouldn't start in the supermarket parking lot she had to cope with a baby and bags of frozen groceries melting in the trunk. But she resented the fact that he was never home. There were fights, Alex crying in the background. When Alex had taken his first steps, it had taken

Matt six days to notice. He remembered the stony silence when he had, and Kirstin's accusing stare that had pierced him far more deeply than words of anger might have.

'But don't you think the facts can't always tell the full story?' Ella insisted, leaning towards him, her gaze intent on his.

'I don't know. It's hard to answer a hypothetical question like that without getting into specifics. I'm probably not the best person to ask. I screwed up my marriage and I have a son I barely know over this.'

Ella fell quiet, reflective, and once again he had the same feeling he'd had outside his office earlier, that there was something on her mind.

'Is there some particular issue you're thinking of Ella?'

'No. I was just interested to know why you came here to live, that's all.'

'The answer is to start again. To get away from a life that almost destroyed me. And you know what, right now I'm glad that I did. I'm glad I'm here with you.'

Ella smiled, but there was a distant quality in her eyes he couldn't fathom.

'More coffee?' she asked.

'Thanks.'

She went to the kitchen and when she came back with a fresh pot they changed the subject, and talked about other things, but it seemed to Matt as if their conversation had robbed the evening of some of its lightness. Ella appeared quiet and a little withdrawn and in the end when he eventually saw that it was getting late, he took his cue to leave. Ella showed him to the door.

'Thanks for inviting me,' he said. 'You're a great cook.'

'Thanks.'

'I'd like to return the favour. Maybe cook you a meal at my house one night. Though I can't promise the same quality. I can just about manage spaghetti.'

'I'd like that, sometime.'

He'd been about to suggest a day, maybe towards the weekend, but there had been the faintest suggestion of hesitation in

43

her response which made him think he should leave it for now, and ask her another time. He remembered her comment about having had poor luck with men in her life, and he had the feeling Ella wasn't somebody who could be rushed. Something in her manner made him decide not to try and repeat the kiss of the night before, appealing as the idea might be.

'Goodnight,' she said.

'Goodnight Ella.' As he walked to the gate he heard the door close softly behind him.

CHAPTER SIX

The sun flamed in the blue vault of the sky. The *Santorini* rode a three-foot swell half a mile off the island. She was a thirty-eight-foot lobster boat, built in Portland nearly thirty years ago. She was painted light blue, a job Ella had done herself, and the wheel-house was at the stern, her deck wide and clear for carrying bait and traps. Behind the wheel-house a hatch led down to the engine compartment and a tiny galley and cabin. Ella had bought the boat when she was twenty-five years old, with her own hard-earned cash and a loan from the bank that had also covered her traps and a truck. When she'd started fishing the bays and coastal waters of the island, a lot of people had stood by waiting for her to fail. Some grumbled it wasn't natural or right for a woman to work her own boat, even if her dad was one of the best fishermen on the island. She'd silenced them all by proving them wrong. In the winter she went shrimping, in the days when there had still been shrimp to be had, and for the rest of year she caught lobsters. For a few years she'd done well, better than most, which had caused some resentment, but then the government had started raising the legal size of lobsters that could be taken, and introduced other measures to protect declining stocks. In some areas of Maine the lobster population was just a fraction of what it had once been, and St George was one of them. Times had gotten tough for a lot of people, and though Ella had hung on where others had gone under, the last couple of years hadn't been easy.

She and Gordon were working a string of traps they'd set two days earlier. They'd left the harbour an hour before dawn after

Ella had managed just four hours' sleep, and even during that short time her rest had been fitful. Whenever sleep pulled her down and she sank gratefully into its embrace, her personal demons emerged to haunt her. Her dreams were mixed-up images of her brother who had died as a baby, her father's only son, and the storm in February, her mother's frantic phone call in the middle of the night.

Gordon connected the surface line of a trap to the hauler, having already removed the buoy which the line had been attached to. Ella's buoys were painted the same colour as the *Santorini*, but with alternating yellow and white hoops, a combination that identified them as belonging to her. Gordon was seventeen, and had been her sternman for a year now. They took turns to operate the hauler that brought the traps up from the seabed while manoeuvring the boat among the buoys on the surface, while the other emptied and re-baited each trap. He started the hydraulic motor, and the line came up, raising the trap from ten fathoms below.

They waited anxiously. Gordon glanced at her and attempted a smile. He resembled his father, with his red hair and slightly squashed features, though he had his mother's eyes. Gordon sensed that the line was coming to an end and he peered over the side as the trap emerged from the sea, dripping streams of water. The bait was gone, but the pot was empty. He swung it on to the rail.

'How many is that now?' Ella said.

'Twenty-four.'

'Dammit!'

She turned away so that he wouldn't see the tears of rage that pricked her eyes. She blinked them away, and her mouth set in a determined line.

'Okay, let's re-set it.'

Gordon hesitated.

'What is it?'

'What if it happens again?'

'Then we'll set them again. And we'll keep on setting them.'

She spoke with more resolve than she felt. Every trap they'd

46

hauled had been stripped. The loss of income from just one day would hurt her, but the same thing had happened on a string they'd hauled late the day before. If it went on, after a week, maybe a little longer, she'd be forced to lay Gordon off, and without his help she would struggle to continue alone. The payments on her truck and the boat, as well as the mortgage on her mother's house, would soon mount to a debt she could never repay. It was frightening how susceptible she was to even a little bad fortune. Except that fortune had nothing to do with this.

Ella reached for bait. On these traps she was using dabs which cost seventy-five dollars for a barrel of frames, the filleted remains of the ground-fish. She punched the iron through the eyes of three frames and looped them onto the string in the trap, working quickly with short aggressive actions, then closed the hatch. Gordon stood watching her. She thrust the trap at him with enough force that he staggered off balance.

'We haven't got all day. I'll take the hauler,' she snapped, changing positions with him.

He looked surprised, and a little hurt, but he moved out of the way while she gunned the throttle and spun the wheel to manoeuvre the boat into position.

'Okay,' she said.

Gordon slid the trap along the rail and it hit the water with a splash and rapidly sank, the line snaking after it.

Ella headed for the next buoy, turning in a tight circle against the current. The roar of the motor rose and fell as she expertly lined the boat up and they drifted past. Gordon leaned over the side and with one seamless action hooked the buoy with a gaff and dragged it aboard and wrapped the line around the hauler. He worked in stony silence and Ella wished she hadn't taken her frustration out on him.

'I'm sorry, I didn't mean to bite your head off. Don't mind me.'

'Why are we letting him get away with this?' he said suddenly.

'Who?'

He gave an impatient shake of his head. 'Jake. You know this is his doing.'

'We don't know that for certain.'

47

'Who else would it be?'

He was right. She knew it was Jake. It was four days since Bryan had gone missing and there was talk that the search was being called off. There were other rumours going around the docks. People were mentioning Bryan's name and how she'd threatened him in the same breath. It was no secret that she hated the Rodericks. Especially Bryan, and nobody had seen him since.

They went back to work and hauled up the next trap. It too came up empty, and Gordon looked at her pointedly, but he didn't say anything. He re-baited it and dropped it over the side. Ella gunned the motor, and spun the wheel to take them to the next buoy. She worked automatically, controlling speed and direction with practised ease and as each trap came up empty she tried not to let it get to her. She willed herself to think of other things, and as she worked her thoughts ranged backwards through her memory.

Ella would have been maybe twelve or thirteen when she saw Matt sitting on the beach in the cove, reading a book. He was lean and loose-limbed, tanned from the long summer. His brother and the other kids they hung out with were swimming or sailing. She never saw Matt swimming. When some kid shouted from the water as he turned turtle and dived beneath the surface, the look Matt wore made him appear strangely vulnerable.

As a kid she'd had little to do with the pointers who came to stay in their summer houses each year. St Georgians were insular. Summer families were just people from away, like they belonged to another planet. It was ironic given that the island might yet vote Howard in as mayor, and his marina would be the beginning of a flood of newcomers who would ultimately change life on the island for good.

Matt was the first boy Ella had really noticed. He'd aroused feelings in her that previously had been foreign to her, and the result had been confusing. Sometimes when she saw him on the street she had wished she could just go up and talk to him, but she'd been unable to think of a word to say. He was older than her and barely noticed she existed. She had no idea what his life away from St George was like, any more than he would have understood any-

48

thing about her daily existence. Sometimes she saw him talking to a girl his own age, another pointer who'd be wearing some pretty flouncy dress and lipstick, and Ella would want to puke out of jealousy and disdain. At that time she hadn't even owned a dress and she wouldn't have been seen dead wearing lipstick.

Then one summer, when she was almost sixteen she'd gone to a dance for the first time. She was wearing a dress her mother had helped her choose, and that year she'd started to grow her hair out. At the dance she felt out of place even though there were girls she knew there. She felt like candy on a stick, all prettily wrapped up and put out on display. Boys she knew looked at her, their surprise plain. Matt was there too and she'd waited for him to notice her, to come over and speak to her, but whenever she dared sneak a look he was looking at somebody else. Eventually a local boy had come and talked to her, and she had felt strange because he was acting differently around her than he ever had before and it made her feel uncomfortable. As soon as she could she escaped outside, into the comforting darkness and the cool air. That was the last time she'd seen Matt until he'd turned up back on the island a few months ago.

Now she found him intruding into her thoughts throughout the day. Whatever it was that had begun to develop between them had started slowly, layers of feeling building almost imperceptibly each time they met, and steadily the layers grew and formed a perceptible thickness. When he'd kissed her after the meeting Ella had experienced a stirring in her breast, a realization that she had developed feelings for him that almost caught her unaware. It had made her think. It had been a long time since she'd felt close to any man. It had been her mother's idea to ask him to supper, perhaps sensing what she felt. She recalled how relaxed he'd seemed at first but a shadow had fallen over the evening after her mother had gone to bed, when he'd talked about how he felt about the career he'd left behind in Boston. It was clear that his brother's death had affected him deeply, and that it had left a legacy of bitterness in him. He might have exchanged his career as a prosecutor for that of small town lawyer, but he still viewed the world through a narrow lens, seeing issues as either black or white. That worried Ella. No relationship between two people could flourish when one of them harboured secrets. Perhaps she'd hoped that she could confide in Matt, that he would understand what had happened, but as she'd listened to him talk she'd reluctantly admitted to herself that she couldn't take the chance. The knowledge saddened her.

All that day she and Gordon worked, hauling the traps they'd placed along this stretch of shelf, and then more that they'd set close to a finger of rock that protruded from Seal Bay on the rugged western side. In all, they brought up two hundred and eighteen traps, and in each case though the bait was gone the traps were empty. Ella wondered why Jake hadn't simply cut off her trap lines from the buoys, costing her a sixty-dollar trap as well as the catch, but she guessed this was his way of extending her misery. He was taunting her. He wanted to see her return to harbour each day, after working ten hours, for nothing.

It was late afternoon by the time they headed back towards Sanctuary. They were a mile off the island when a movement in the sea several hundred yards to their port side, brought Ella back to the present. A fin broke the surface of the water, and then another. As she watched, entranced, a pod of killer whales moved in a northerly direction, rising and dipping in the swell. She called out to Gordon and pointed, and they watched them pass. Orcas were regular visitors to the gulf around this time of year, but not in great numbers and Ella was always fascinated when she was lucky enough to see them. They came in from deep water to catch migrating fish, but these days pickings were lean for man and orca alike and it didn't help that some fishermen, like the Roderick brothers, would shoot at them on sight, claiming they competed for fish. She had seen Bryan Roderick once, standing on the deck of the *Seawind*, aiming his rifle at a pod of orcas which had veered away and picked up their pace. When the *Seawind* had changed direction to pursue them she'd hailed them on the radio and threatened to report them. They would have denied it, but at least on that occasion the threat had been enough to stop them. She remembered looking through her glasses and seeing Bryan, appearing disturbingly close, staring back at her.

Returned to the present, Ella experienced a vague sadness as she watched the orcas pass by. In their diminishing forms something irretrievable was vanishing from the gulf.

Overhead a lone kittiwake soared, following their path.

The bull noted the sound of the small boat's engine as the pod cruised past. He saw the two figures on board and heard the sound of a winch and the hiss of a trap being raised from the seabed. He was used to the sight and sound of man and the way in which they hauled vast catches of fish from the sea by net or hook. He understood also that some vessels could be dangerous, and was cautious when the pod were in their vicinity.

The pod turned westward later in the evening and eventually came close to the mainland shore. The bull heard the sounds made by a large school of feeding shad directly in their path. Three of the orcas swam in a long, wide sweep around them, and when they were in position the others, led by the bull, advanced on the fish. Two more of the orcas dived deep to prevent the shad escaping once they became aware of what was happening. The rest maintained silence to conceal their approach. As they drew near to their prey, they began making audible sounds, and the sea reverberated with a range of clicks and shrill screams which had the purpose of echo-locating the shad, and both frightening and disorienting them at the same time. The shad immediately fled, kept close to the surface by the orcas that had swum underneath them, and gradually they were herded into an ever tightening mass all streaming in the same direction. Ahead of them, the three orcas that had swept wide waited as the unwitting fish approached.

At a signal from the bull they attacked, making terrifying sounds as they swam at speed towards the school. The shad immediately panicked, the front runners turned against those behind and the surface of the sea became alive with a mass of terrified fish. The orcas began breaching, rising from the waves and crashing down again with huge splashes that sent shock

51

waves through the water, partially stunning their prey. Then one by one they took turns to swim into the school to feed.

A small dinghy with an outboard motor was anchored close by, and two men on board were fishing with rods and lines, unaware at first of what was happening. As the orcas began their initial approach towards the shad many of the school broke off and tried to shelter close to the dinghy.

The men noticed that their boat was suddenly surrounded by fish of about three pounds in weight.

'What the hell . . .' one of them said, and looked to his companion in bewilderment.

Both men immediately brought in their baits and dropped them over the side, but none of the swarming fish were biting.

'Looks like something's spooked 'em.'

The other man looked around. About two hundred yards behind them a mass of water was boiling at the surface, where thousands of fish were thrashing in panic, and he caught sight of the dorsal fins of several approaching orcas.

He pointed, white faced, and his companion followed his fearful gaze.

'Oh shit,' he said quietly.

An orca erupted from the sea fifty yards away, its great, black body and snowy white chest clearly visible as it rose twenty feet into the air before crashing down to the surface with an enormous splash.

'Jesus,' one of the men breathed, awestruck.

His companion immediately dropped his rod and scrambled to the back of the boat where he began trying to start the small motor. The waves created by the orcas were rocking the little boat precariously. Suddenly the other man shouted and pointed frantically. Heading straight towards them at about twenty-five knots was a five foot dorsal fin rising from a bubble of water beneath which could be seen the massive body of an orca.

'Christ, it's coming right at us,' the man at the motor breathed.

The two men gripped the gunwales, their eyes wide in fright as

52

a six ton killer whale bore down on them. At the last moment the orca changed course, but the wave he created rocked the boat badly and one of the men was pitched into the water. His companion shouted to him, leaning over the side with his arm outstretched. What the man in the water couldn't see was that behind him the orca had turned and was surging straight towards him, the great fin towering above the surface as the animal drew closer.

The man swam as fast as he could, but he was weighed down by his clothes and shoes, and he was beginning to panic. He guessed from his companion's terrified expression what was happening.

'Hurry,' the man in the boat shouted.

The man flailed his arms in panic. He knew that the orca was coming for him. He felt himself lift as the front of the pressure wave hit him and he cried out in pure terror. Any moment he expected to be engulfed in vast jaws that would crush his bones and flesh to a bloody pulp. In his horror of being devoured he screamed and took a mouthful of water which started him choking. Bizarrely he could feel his hands brushing the panicked shad in the water, then he fell again and was carried on a wave to the side of the boat where his companion grabbed him.

For still another second he didn't comprehend what had happened, until at last he realized that his companion's gaze was focused beyond him now, his expression slack and pale rather than terror stricken. He turned and saw the orca's dorsal fin dip beneath the waves, and he thought he heard a high pitched sound, and then it was gone. Suddenly the sea was once again calm and still, disturbed only by a breath of wind.

The shad that hadn't been eaten had dispersed. Further pursuit of such small prey was counter productive and the pod re-grouped to continue on their way. The young male who had swept by the boat joined the flank. He had never considered the man in the water as potential prey, any more than he would consider killing one of his own kind for food. Though the man had been totally helpless the orca had ignored him. Even a juvenile animal such as he, had long since learned to recognize the brain impulses of a highly evolved predator, equal in intelligence to himself.

CHAPTER SEVEN

The *Santorini* entered the harbour late in the afternoon without having taken a single lobster. Jake Roderick stood among a group of men alongside the *Seawind*. As they talked quietly among themselves they cast hostile glances towards the *Santorini* as she docked, and it seemed to Ella that Jake wore the trace of a grim smile.

She did her best to ignore them. Gordon stepped on to the dock to tie up and then without warning he picked up a short gaff and started towards the men. When Ella saw him and guessed his intent she called out, but he paid no attention and she scrambled to go after him. He reached the men and stopped in front of them, feet apart, hefting the gaff in one hand at his side.

'Which one of you bastards has been at our traps?' He looked from one to the other, and each of them seemed surprised to be confronted by someone they all thought of as not much more than a boy. They looked uncertainly at one another.

'What's wrong? Nobody got the guts to take me on face to face?'

'Watch what you're saying,' one of the men warned, but he eyed the gaff and kept back.

'Or what will you do?' Gordon mocked.

Jake pushed his way forward, and the men parted to let him through. He appeared unconcerned. 'You better get back to your mother's tit, before I give you a hiding you won't forget in a hurry, boy. What are you planning to do with that thing? You think you've got what it takes to use it?'

Gordon glanced at the wicked steel point of the gaff. The quiet threat in Jake's tone caused him a flicker of uncertainty.

'You could kill a man with that thing. Split his head right open. Think you could do that? Because if you come at me with it, you better be ready to.' Jake cast his eye around and went casually to the side of the *Seawind* where he reached over and grabbed hold of a gaff stained with fish blood. He hefted it in his hand, testing the weight, then without warning he swung it against a plastic fish crate on the dock. The point blurred with the power of the motion, then smacked into the crate and shattered the plastic with a loud crack.

Jake yanked the point free. 'Think you could do that to me?'

Though Gordon stood his ground, he was unnerved. The other men looked on, waiting to see if he would back down.

'The only reason you're on your feet now is that you're still wet behind the ears, and because I know your dad,' Jake said. 'Wasn't for that I'd make you sorry you picked that thing up. Now get the hell back where you came from and mind your manners, before I forget myself.' His voice was low, almost languid, his apparent lack of concern a calculated insult.

Gordon wavered, his face flushed, the handle of the gaff felt slick with his sweat. He felt the pressure of the men all watching him, saw a couple of them grin. He started to take a step forward.

As Ella reached him she saw the muscles tighten across his shoulders and knew he was about to do something stupid. 'Gordon don't.'

She grabbed him, and as he hesitated Jake yanked the gaff out of his hand, almost pulling Gordon off his feet, then with a casual gesture Jake flung the gaff towards the harbour and it sailed through the air, made a splash and sank without trace.

'You shouldn't send a boy to do a man's job, Ella,' Jake said.

She ignored him, turning her back to position herself between them while she appealed to Gordon.

'Don't listen to him. I know you're trying to do what you think is right, but this isn't the way to handle it.' She tried desperately to think of some way to defuse the situation, to allow Gordon to salvage his pride without being goaded into a fight

55

he could only lose. She didn't want to feel responsible for him getting hurt. He was tense, his fists gripped tightly at his sides and his expression was rigid with anger.

'Please, Gordon, don't do this. If you get hurt who's going to be my sternman? I need you. I can't manage the *Santorini* without you. That's what he wants.'

She prayed that he would listen, that his stupid male pride would allow him to see sense.

'He shouldn't get away with it,' Gordon said tightly.

'He won't. We'll beat him. But not like this. He isn't worth it.'

'Better listen to what she says, boy,' Jake said. 'I guess your dad must be too damn soft on you. Maybe I should teach you a lesson anyway. If you were mine I wouldn't let you work for this damn bitch.'

Ella held Gordon's gaze, and spoke calmly. 'He's just trying to goad you. Don't listen to him. I need you in one piece.'

He resisted, but she could see he was thinking.

'Please Gordon.'

At last she felt some of the tension ease from him and seizing the moment she guided him by the arm back towards the *Santorini*. As they walked along the dock Jake shouted after them.

'This isn't the end of it Ella. I'll see you in hell before I let you get away with what you did.'

She didn't look back. 'I want you to get your things and go home. I want you back here bright and early in the morning.'

'I'm not afraid of him . . .'

'I know you're not.'

They reached the *Santorini* and she helped him get his things together. 'See you tomorrow, okay?'

He looked back towards the group of men, all grinning now and nudging each other.

Slowly Ella drew his gaze back again and he nodded.

She watched as he left to make sure he didn't get it in his head to go back and pick another fight. Along the dock the group broke up, sensing the drama was over, and Jake went back to his boat. She tried to concentrate on hosing down the deck, but she kept thinking of all the empty traps they had raised to the surface one by one that day, and the day before. She started off-loading the busted traps they'd brought back for repair, and hauled the now empty bait barrel on to the dock. Though she refused to look she could feel Jake watching her. All the while the back of her neck burned. She heard coarse laughter, a sound she knew well.

Her eye fell to a three-foot length of wooden four by two lying on the dock and barely aware of what she was doing she picked it up and holding it so it was partly hidden behind her leg she strode towards the *Seawind.* When Jake saw her he looked surprised, but then he jumped down to meet her.

'I want you to leave my traps alone you goddamned bastard, or so help me I won't be responsible for my actions,' she told him, her voice quivering with anger.

His black eyes glowered. 'Bryan always said somebody ought to fix you Ella.'

'I bet he did. Bryan's pretty good when it comes to fixing women isn't he?'

'Watch your damn mouth.'

'Or what?' Ella said. 'What will you do Jake? Well come on then, you big sonofabitch.'

Jake hesitated and then suddenly he came at her and Ella reacted without thinking. She swung the length of wood in an arc towards his head and though Jake saw it coming and tried to step back out of the way the blow caught him a glancing chop to the side of his skull. The impact jarred through Ella's wrist. Blood flowered brightly at Jake's temple, then his stunned expression folded as he crumpled to the ground.

CHAPTER EIGHT

Dave Baxter had never kidded himself that he was any great catch. His hair was greying at the temples and his pants got tighter every year. He guessed he was in okay shape otherwise. Thickening maybe, but still solid. He looked as if he might have done some boxing in his youth. His nose was bent out of shape and a little squashed from having been broken a couple of times. But the only thing close to boxing he'd ever done was to bust up bar fights when things got rowdy in the *Schooner*.

He pulled over to the side of the street and climbed out of his cruiser. He'd spent the day as he had most of the week, combing the woods around the cove along with twenty other guys, looking for Bryan Roderick. Baxter didn't think they were going to find him and he'd decided to call the search off. He paused in the shade of a cottonwood growing out of the sidewalk beside the market, and fished in his pocket for a stick of gum. He'd given up smoking three years ago, breaking a lifetime pack-a-day habit, but now he was addicted to Wrigley's instead, and he went through a couple of packs a day. He'd also gained about twenty pounds, which he'd never been able to shift.

A Mercedes wagon was parked across the street. Baxter recognized it as belonging to Kate Little, and he looked around, wondering where she was. He knew she bought her groceries at the market, and figuring she might be inside he went on in.

'Hey Dave,' Julie Eggert said. 'Usual?'

She reached for a ten-pack of Wrigley's spearmint flavour. Baxter had known Julie ever since they were kids. She'd been the prettiest girl in school, but now she weighed about a hundred and eighty pounds and wheezed if she walked more than a hundred yards. She was married to a fisherman and they had six kids between them, which partly accounted for the fact that she looked about ten years older than she really was.

'Thanks,' Baxter said.

'You all set now?'

'I guess.' He handed her a bill and while she rang up the sale he looked down the aisles for Kate Little. 'Maybe I'll get something for supper while I'm here.'

'Sure.'

Baxter went past the freezer cabinets at the back of the market, and picked out a pack of hamburgers just so he wouldn't look too obvious, then he wandered past each aisle, checking them all, but there was no sign of Kate. He went back to the checkout, and she was there, unloading her cart while Julie ran the packages past the scanner.

Julie glanced up at him. 'You can take those over to Lisa, Dave, so you don't have to wait.' She put his gum where he could reach it on top of her register.

'That's okay.' Baxter picked up a magazine from the rack and flicked through it, occasionally glancing towards Kate. She took the last item from her cart, and started looking in her bag for her wallet. Her hair was jet black and reached about halfway down her back. Baxter wondered how her hair would feel. It looked so sleek and shiny, it reminded him somehow of fine misty rain on a summer's evening. Her nails were painted a bright red that went with her lipstick, and the cuffs of the white linen shirt she wore were turned back once over her slim wrists. The shirt looked expensive, as did her pants and shoes. She wore a couple of big rings on her fingers that Baxter guessed were diamonds.

Julie rang up a total for Kate's groceries and told her the amount. She took a credit card without smiling and while it processed she turned her back and started talking to Lisa who was on the next checkout about something one of her kids had done. If Kate noticed the subtle insult she didn't show it. She

59

just looked calmly out of the window to the street outside. Baxter frowned.

After Kate had left, Baxter replaced the magazine and paid for his gum and packet of burgers.

'You see that?' Julie said, looking at Kate as she left the store. 'Two bottles of vodka in her groceries.' Her mouth turned down disapprovingly.

A week ago Baxter had seen Dan Eggert, Julie's husband, lying outside the *Schooner* moaning quietly beside a pool of his own vomit, and he'd had to drive him home, but he didn't mention it.

'I guess we have to get used to plenty more like her if Howard Larson wins the election though,' she added resignedly. She looked at the posters on the window. One of Ella's, and one of Howard's.

'I guess you'll be voting for Ella then.'

Julie frowned. 'I don't know. Dan was talking about maybe opening a little place to sell chowder and lobsters and such. He says all those summer people are going to go crazy for that kind of thing.' She looked thoughtful, as if she were picturing herself behind the counter of her own business. 'Then there's all the talk about Ella and Bryan Roderick going missing like that.' She brought herself up sharp, and flushed, remembering who she was talking to.

'You should know better than that,' Baxter said. He took his purchases and went outside. He tried to picture Dan Eggert running any kind of business. Dan worked on a dragger called the *Rose Marie* and when he wasn't working he was often drunk. He shook his head. Some people just had no sense.

Kate was loading her car, and for a moment Baxter thought about going over to ask her if he could give her a hand, but by the time he'd tried to figure what he'd say it was too late and she'd finished. He watched her drive away, a wistful look on his face. He'd never been confident around women. He was distracted from his reverie by the sound of the radio in his car. He leaned through the window and picked up the mike.

'What is it Martha?' he said.

'Chief? I just had a call from Tom Spencer. There's been some trouble at the dock. I think you better get down there.'

'What kind of trouble?'

'It's Ella Young. She and Jake Roderick had some kind of fight.'

Baxter frowned, though he wasn't surprised. He'd been afraid of something like this happening. 'Okay. I'm on my way.'

Anne Laine had been one of two doctors in Sanctuary Harbor for nine years. Originally she'd come to the island for a vacation, wanting to really get away from it all, and St George had been about as far away as she could get without leaving the country altogether. She'd liked it, and had decided to stay, and though sometimes she got a little tired of the long winters, all in all she'd never regretted her decision. She made less money here than she would somewhere else, but the island and its endless views of the gulf, and the quiet solitude of the woods, more than made up for it. Sometimes the people were a little clannish, but in all the time she'd lived there she had never locked the door to her house, and she'd never once felt afraid to walk a dark road alone at night, and that meant something these days. She finished wrapping Jake's head in a bandage, and gave him a prescription, which he accepted without looking at.

'Get this filled and take a couple of these every four hours. You're going to have a sore head for a few days but there's no serious damage.' Her tone was matter of fact.

In the outer office Baxter was waiting while Howard Larson did his best to sound outraged about what Ella had done.

'And she expects people to vote for her,' he said, shaking his head.

Baxter hadn't really been listening. He was relieved when Anne appeared and it gave him a chance to cut Howard off. He got up to meet her. 'How's the patient?'

'He'll live. He took a fair hit, but there's no sign of a fracture.'

'Yeah, well, he's got a pretty thick skull,' Baxter said, and Anne raised her eyebrows and smiled.

Howard pulled a sour face. 'Seems to me you're not taking

this thing very seriously, Chief. You should've seen him when I brought him in. Jesus, there was blood everywhere. It was just luck that Ella didn't kill him.'

'I doubt she meant to do anything like that, Howard.'

Anne said they could go on through and Baxter went in to see Jake for himself while Howard followed behind, still talking.

'I don't know. That woman's got a hell of temper, you can't deny that. Maybe this isn't the first time something like this has happened,' he added with dark insinuation.

Baxter stopped, figuring where this was headed. 'Let's not get ahead of ourselves here.'

'Come on, Chief. Everybody knows Ella threatened Bryan. And you haven't found him out there in the woods yet, have you?'

Howard actually looked pleased, Baxter thought, and it wasn't hard to figure out why. Anything that would make Ella look bad would be a bonus for Howard. The talk had started pretty quickly on the docks, people drinking and putting two and two together and coming up with ninety-eight. 'He'll probably turn up,' Baxter said, though his voice lacked conviction. The truth was he was starting to get worried about this whole thing.

'You ought to lock her up before she kills somebody else. Jesus, look at him.'

Jake sat in a chair, gingerly feeling his head.

Baxter wondered if Howard was deliberately stirring up trouble, and how much he had to do with this. 'That kind of talk isn't helping anyone, Howard.' He drew up a chair and sat down in front of Jake. 'You want to tell me what happened?'

'That bitch, Ella, blind-sided me, that's what. Could've damn well killed me.'

Baxter opened a gum wrapper. A faint blood stain had seeped through Jake's bandage and he watched it with fascination. He couldn't help wondering how Ella had managed to get the better of a man who was twice her size and about ten times as mean. He had to admit a grudging admiration for her, though he was also vaguely disturbed. He wondered what else she might be capable of if somebody really made her mad.

'How'd this start?' he asked.

'Why the hell don't you ask her?'

'I'll talk to her later, but right now I'm asking you.'

'You gonna talk to her about Bryan while you're at it? It's been four fucking days now.'

'We've been all over this,' Baxter said. Jake had been in his office twice a day since Wednesday. Baxter wondered if Howard had been putting a bee up his ass, and concluded that it was highly likely.

'She pointed a gun at him for Christ sakes,' Howard interjected. 'Plenty of witnesses saw her.'

'Yeah, and they all saw him walk away afterwards. Come on Howard, you know better than that.' He turned back to Jake. 'You starting some kind of feud with Ella isn't going to help matters, Jake. I talked to Tom Spencer and he reckons the last couple of days somebody has been stripping Ella's traps. You know anything about that?'

'You trying to say this is my fault?'

'No, I'm just trying to figure out how this started. My guess is Ella had a reason for what she did.'

'Seems to me you ought to be asking her that,' Howard said.

'Ella's already been taken in. I'll be getting to her, don't you worry about that.'

Howard actually smiled. 'She's under arrest?'

'Don't get too excited, Howard. Jake, you want to press charges of assault?'

'Of course he does,' Howard said without waiting for Jake to answer.

Baxter acted as if he hadn't heard. 'If you do,' he mused, 'it'll mean we'll have to look into both sides of the story. And I guess we'll have to get into detail about how Ella did that damage to your head. Might even make the *Island Herald*.' He allowed Jake to ponder the idea of everybody reading over their breakfast about how a woman got the better of him.

Jake scowled.

'I'll take that as a no, then.' Baxter got up to leave. 'I'll see you later Howard.' He smiled to himself as he left.

*   *   *

Matt was in the coffee shop when he overheard a couple of guys talking about what had happened. When Ella's name was mentioned, he thought there had to be some kind of mistake, but when he got back to his office he called the police department and discovered that Ella was there.

'Is she under arrest?' he asked.

'You'd have to speak to the chief about that,' Officer Williams told him. 'He ought to be back any time.'

Matt hung up, and fixed a 'back in ten minutes' sign he'd made up himself on the office door. By the time he reached the police department Baxter had returned from the doctor's office and when somebody went to fetch him he emerged wearing a faintly curious expression.

'Chief.' Matt offered his hand and the two men shook. They had met soon after Matt had moved to the island. He'd made a point of calling in to introduce himself, and the impression he'd formed of Chief Baxter was that he was fairly typical of a small town policeman, inasmuch as he knew just about everybody on the island, and everything that was going on. They'd had coffee and Baxter had told him that crime on St George didn't amount to anything more serious than the occasional piece of vandalism or pilfering, a lot of which went unreported anyway. Often it was the symptoms of long running feuds between rival fishermen, which were dealt with by those involved in their own way. Though Baxter had appeared to have a fairly relaxed attitude to policing, Matt had figured that he kept his finger on the pulse and knew when to step in to prevent trouble getting out of hand.

Now as they shook hands, Baxter appeared guarded. 'Russ told me you called. You representing Ella, Mr Jones?'

'Does she need representing?' Matt countered. 'And by the way, it's Matt.'

'Well, Ella isn't under arrest if that's what you mean. She didn't mention she'd called you.'

'She didn't call, I overheard some talk in the coffee shop and I thought I'd come over and see if there was anything I could do.'

64

Baxter eyed him with faint suspicion.

'I'm not here looking for a client, Chief, if that's what you're thinking. Ella's a friend, that's all.'

'I wasn't thinking that,' Baxter said, but Matt would have bet otherwise.

'So, what exactly happened? I heard something about a fight on the dock?'

Baxter looked thoughtful, even worried. 'Yeah. I should've seen it coming I guess. Ella and the Roderick boys have never been exactly what you'd call on the best of terms, but looks like things have gotten worse. Jake and Ella got into an argument today. Ended up with Ella taking a chunk out of Jake's skull with a length of wood.'

'Ella did that?' Matt tried to picture it. He knew that she was tough, and he could easily see her standing her ground in an argument, but it was a giant leap from there to imagining her braining somebody in a physical fight.

'Ella doesn't deny that she hit him,' Baxter said. 'But I spoke to the doctor and Jake's going to be okay. He's not going to press charges either. He kind of lost enthusiasm for that idea when he thought about how it was going to look when people read in the paper about him being beaten up by a woman.'

Matt was still trying to figure out what could have happened. 'She must have had a reason if she hit him. She must have been protecting herself.'

'Ella was defending her livelihood if you want to look at it that way. Somebody emptied the traps she hauled today, every last one of them. That's a lot of work for no result.'

'Jake did that? He admitted it?'

Baxter shook his head. 'Didn't need to. It was him all right.'

'Why would he empty her traps?'

'Happens sometimes. People get into disagreements about who ought to be fishing where, or else it's some personal grudge getting settled. Usually it's just a couple of trap lines that get cut, or maybe a small string stripped. Doesn't normally run to this kind of thing. There's a kind of code the fishermen stick to. They have their own set of rules. A little messing with another man's traps is one thing, it's not going to send him to the wall so the bank sells his boat and he can't make a living. Something like this is stepping way over the line.' Baxter frowned, and his worried expression deepened.

'What made Jake cross the line?'

'You were at the meeting the other night, weren't you? So I guess you know all about this marina plan of Howard Larson's. The Rodericks and Ella have been butting heads over that for a while now. There's been a fair bit of bad blood between them, and now Bryan's missing. People are starting to talk.' Baxter saw that he'd lost Matt. 'You did hear about that?'

For the past couple of days Matt had been helping Henry dig the foundations for the shed to house the cider press, and he'd only been into town a couple of times to check his messages, of which there had been none. He'd heard about Bryan being missing, and that there was a search going on in the woods, but he hadn't connected it any way with Ella.

'What kind of talk?'

Baxter sighed. 'I thought you'd know. Seems like that's all anybody's talking about on the docks.' He related how Ella had threatened Bryan with a rifle during an argument the night Bryan had vanished. 'She doesn't deny any of it.'

'She threatened him?' Matt echoed incredulously. 'What does that mean exactly?'

'The way Ella tells it they were arguing, and Bryan looked as if he was about to get on her boat. She got her rifle and told him he ought to think about it first, as it would be the last thing he ever did. Or words to that effect anyway. Though she says the gun wasn't loaded,' Baxter added.

Matt shook his head. 'Wait a minute, you're not suggesting that this has anything to do with Bryan's disappearance are you?'

'It isn't just a case of what I think. I'm saying that people are talking, and Jake isn't the kind to stand around and do nothing when he gets an idea in his head. Ella said that was the last she saw of Bryan, and there are witnesses who saw him walk away. Right now I don't know what happened to him.'

66

'I think I better talk to Ella now,' Matt said.

'Help yourself.' Baxter pointed towards a door. 'She's in my office right over there.'

Ella appeared surprised when she saw Matt. He drew up a chair in front of her and sat down. Though he was disturbed by what Baxter had told him, especially the part about Ella threatening Bryan with a rifle, he determined not to let her see it. He told himself he didn't know what kind of pressures she'd been under lately with the election and harassment from the Rodericks, and he dismissed the idea that Ella knew anything about Bryan's disappearance. He smiled, guessing that she would welcome the sight of a friendly face.

'How're you doing?' he said.

She managed a wan smile in return. 'I'm okay I guess. Why are you here?'

'I heard you had some trouble, and I thought maybe I could help. I just talked to Chief Baxter. Jake isn't pressing charges.'

Ella didn't seem surprised, but she peered at Matt as if she was trying to figure what he was thinking. 'I shouldn't have hit him. I guess everything that's been happening lately got to me more than I thought.'

'Baxter told me about your problems with the Rodericks. How long has it been going on?'

Ella shook her head in a weary gesture. 'Months. Three, four maybe. I've always had trouble with them, but since I decided to stand for election things have been worse. I've had phone calls when there was nobody there. Once my truck wouldn't start and when I opened the hood I found the battery had been taken. Footsteps behind me at night once or twice, but nobody there when I called out. That kind of thing.'

'Did you report any of this?'

'What? A wrong number, a couple of hang-up calls. Somebody walking in the street at night?'

Matt could see her point. Individually none of the incidents amounted to more than petty theft and nuisance value. Collectively intimidating perhaps, but difficult to prove.

'I think somebody tried to break into the *Santorini* a while

67

back. Maybe they were planning to foul the engine or something,' Ella said.

'And you think it was the Rodericks?'

'I'm pretty sure. I think the calls and the footsteps following me were more Bryan's style, but they're both as bad as each other one way or another.'

'Is that what you and Bryan were arguing about on Monday?'

Ella met his eye with a level gaze, the different shades of her eyes a little disconcerting. 'Yes.'

'Baxter said you threatened him with a rifle.'

'It wasn't loaded.'

'But you pointed it at him?'

'Yes.'

'You know there's talk about this now that he's missing.'

'I heard.'

Matt waited, half expecting her to add something, though he wasn't sure what. Was he expecting her to deny her involvement? He was reminded of the feeling he'd had over supper with Ella and her mother, that Ella had something on her mind. Had it been this she was thinking of? He recalled how later that night she'd questioned him about his feelings over what happened to Paulie, and his attitude toward the justice system. He wondered if there was a link. She was watching him, and from her expression he thought she had guessed what he was thinking.

'You should have told me about this before,' he said, knowing he sounded like he was admonishing her.

'Before what? Before I took things into my own hands you mean? You think I was wrong to do what I did?'

'I just don't think pointing a gun at somebody is the answer.'

For a second she was furious, it showed in the light in her eyes which seemed to harden to a fine point, and then it was gone and she just looked weary.

Matt wished he'd kept his mouth shut. He imagined she didn't need somebody to censure her right now, what she needed was his support. There was an awkward silence. 'Listen, you've had a tough day. You don't need to stay here any longer, let me take you home.'

68

She hesitated, then at last nodded. 'Thanks.'

On the way out Baxter asked Ella if she was okay. He warned her that if anything else happened with Jake, she should come to him before she started handling things the way she had that day. Ella promised that she would.

'You take care,' he said.

At the door Matt glanced back inside. Baxter was watching Ella, wearing a thoughtful, vaguely troubled expression.

CHAPTER NINE

It had been a long day, and Baxter was getting ready to go home when Russ Williams told him there was somebody to see him. It was past eight, and Baxter was hungry. The incident between Jake and Ella had left a bad taste in his mouth, and a residual feeling of unease. He thought if Bryan didn't show up soon there was going to be trouble for sure. He didn't feel like handling any more problems that day.

'Can't it wait until the morning?'

'It's Carl Johnson, Chief. I think you're going to want to hear this.'

Baxter sighed. 'Okay, bring him in.'

Carl Johnson was wearing jeans and a sweat-stained T-shirt, and he looked as if he'd come straight from the dock, or maybe the bar. Mingled with his fishy stink, Baxter could smell liquor on his breath. They shook hands. Carl's were bony and callused, his eyes watery blue.

'What can I do for you, Carl?'

'Well, the thing is Chief, we've been away for a couple of days. Just got back this afternoon and I heard about what's been going on.'

Baxter didn't follow. 'What's been going on?'

'About Bryan. I heard he was missing.'

Baxter perked up. 'You've seen him?'

'Well no. Least not exactly.'

'Not exactly Carl?' Baxter wasn't in the mood for any cryptic puzzles. 'If you know anything about this, just get it out, all right?'

'Well, we . . . that's Billy Pierce and me,' Carl explained. 'You know Billy works for me? We were leaving the harbour on Monday night. Isn't that the last time anybody saw Bryan? Anyway, we were heading north-east towards Coffins Shelf and we saw Ella's boat out there. The *Santorini*.'

At the mention of Ella's name Baxter held up a hand. 'Wait a minute.' He waved Carl to a chair and sat down himself. He wasn't sure where this was heading, but he wanted to make some notes anyway. 'Russ, do you have a pencil, this damn thing's busted.' Russ Williams looked in his pocket and passed him a pen. Baxter took a sheet of paper from a drawer. 'So, you saw Ella. What time was this?'

'Around three fifteen a.m.'

'Tell the chief what you heard,' Russ interrupted, and Baxter shot him a look to let him know he was the one asking the questions.

Carl frowned. 'Oh yeah, that's right. About an hour or so earlier I thought I heard something. A rifle shot.'

'A shot?'

'That's what it sounded like. Maybe more than one but I'm not sure 'cause Billy was using the winch and I couldn't hear anything. I remember I slowed down the boat to listen because I wondered who was out shooting at that time of night.'

'And this is when you saw Ella?'

'No that was later.'

'So where were you when you heard this shot?'

'Off Stillwater Cove, about a quarter of a mile out I guess.'

'So you heard a shot, what happened after that?'

Carl shrugged. 'We picked up a school of mackerel on the fish finder. Usually we don't get so lucky just coming out of the harbour like that and it seemed like too good a chance to pass up, so we started to set a net. It took us a while but we got a few of 'em. Seems like they'd scattered as if something had spooked them. Maybe sharks. Anyway, by the time we'd hauled in the net we were coming round past the cove again, only further out this time. That's when we saw the *Santorini*.'

'This was around three fifteen you said?'

71

'About then. She was running without lights. I thought maybe she was in trouble, so we slowed down.'

'You're sure it was the *Santorini*? You said she wasn't showing any lights.'

'Sure,' Carl said. 'We were pretty close and I was using glasses. Besides, I spoke to her on the radio.'

'You spoke to Ella?'

'Yep. Like I said, I thought maybe something was wrong. Anyway, when we slowed down Ella went back to the wheel-house and put on her running lights. I asked her if everything was okay, and she said she was fine. Something about a loose connection. Then she came about, and started heading back in the direction of the harbour.'

Carl fell silent. Baxter pondered what Carl had told him, which as far as he could tell didn't mean a thing. He wondered if he was missing something. Russ Williams was practically squirming in his seat, itching to butt in.

'Is that it?' Baxter said at length, a little irritably.

Carl scratched his chin. 'Well, she had something hanging off of the davit.'

'What was it?'

'Couldn't see it properly. It was kind of long and narrow. Looked like some kind of bundle or something.'

There was another silence that went on for several seconds. 'You mean like a trap?' Baxter prompted.

'No, it was too big.'

'Well, how big was it, this thing?'

'Five, mebbe six feet. It was hard to tell.'

'About six feet?' Baxter said, aware that he was starting to sound like a damned parrot.

Carl nodded slowly. 'Yeah. About your size.' He hesitated. 'At the time I didn't think much of it I guess. I mean, I was a little curious that's all. But later, I started wondering what she was doing. She was acting kind of strange having her lights off and all.'

'I thought she had a loose connection?'

'Well, that's what she said.'

'You didn't believe her?'

'I don't know. I got the feeling she didn't want to be seen.'

Baxter sat back in his chair, and tapped Russ's pen against his teeth. 'What happened then?'

'Well, nothin' I guess. It looked like she was heading back towards harbour.'

'What about this thing you saw? This bundle or whatever?'

'Well, I can't be sure. But I think it was still there. Her hauler was on the other side of her boat from where we were.'

'That's it?'

Carl hesitated. 'Like I said, at the time I didn't think too much about it, so we headed off ourselves. But I remember looking back a few minutes later and it seemed like Ella had stopped again.'

'Why do you think she would do that?'

'Could be all kinds of reasons I suppose.'

Baxter waited patiently, guessing there was more and wondering if Carl was going to volunteer it.

'Like I said, I can't swear to nothin', but maybe she was dropping whatever it was she had over the side,' Carl said at length.

'You saw her do that?'

Carl shook his head. 'It was dark, and she was too far away by then. I'm just saying maybe that's what she was doing.'

For a long time nobody said anything. Baxter rubbed his temples, feeling the start of a headache coming on. He wondered how much of what Carl had described was what he'd decided had happened since he'd returned and heard all the talk on the docks, and how much he'd actually seen. He leaned forward resting his arms on the desk and fixing Carl with a serious look.

'Carl, I want you to think carefully about this before you answer. Are you saying you didn't actually see Ella put anything over the side, is that what you're saying?'

Carl took a moment. 'No, I didn't actually see it. That's just what it looked like.'

Baxter thought some more, then stood up. 'Thanks for telling us this, Carl. We're going to need to get all this down in a statement, okay?'

'Sure.'

'Oh yeah, and we're going to need to talk to Billy too. Tell him to come by in the morning will you?' As Russ showed him to the door a thought occurred to Baxter. 'By the way, Carl, who are you planning to vote for in the election?'

Carl shrugged, but looked a little puzzled. 'Howard Larson I guess. The way he talks about that marina bringing people here, jobs and such, I'm all for it. Fishing is shot to hell these days. Why? What's that got to do with this?'

Baxter waved a hand. 'Nothing probably. One other thing. Have you told anyone else about this?'

'I might have mentioned it to a couple of people.'

'That's what I figured. Thanks again Carl,' he said, only this time he didn't sound as if he meant it.

CHAPTER TEN

The sound of hammering and sawing next door woke Matt early. He dressed in jeans and a T-shirt and went outside. The sun was up, starting to heat the moist August air over the gulf. It had been sticky during the night, and Matt had slept naked with the single sheet on his bed crumpled to one side, a film of sweat against his skin.

A pile of lumber had been delivered outside Henry's house, and he was in the process of building the shed that would house the cider press. Matt went around to help, and for a couple of hours he worked in the relative cool of the early morning, though he was soon stripped to the waist as he and Henry put up the framing. Henry worked without talking much. He was wiry and strong, the cords on his arms standing out from skin as brown and weathered as a nut.

Matt was thinking about Ella, as he had all night, questions without answers parading across his mind. After leaving the police department the day before he'd driven her home, and during the ride they hadn't talked much. Outside her house he'd told her that she should call him if she needed anything.

'Thanks, I will,' she'd said.

There had been a brief moment of awkwardness before she'd got out of his car. He sensed that the subtle change he'd detected in her mood the night he'd been to her house for supper had become a tangible distance between them. It bothered him when he'd thought they were getting on so well. Either he'd been fooling himself, or they had both been on the verge of something more than just a mutual attraction. He didn't think he'd been wrong to sense that Ella shared his feelings, though maybe she'd been approaching the issue more cautiously than he had. That was understandable, and in truth he wasn't against the idea of slowing things down a little. They had both suffered ruinous relationships in the past, and he'd wanted to take the time to get this one right. He knew that he could easily allow himself to fall in love with Ella, but he'd made a promise to himself once that next time it would be for ever.

Now as he worked, holding up a cross beam while Henry nailed it, Matt wondered what had changed to make Ella back off. He thought again about how she'd threatened Bryan with a rifle, and he felt uneasy about it. How did that old saying go? Don't point a gun at a person unless you intend to use it. He couldn't avoid the suspicion that Ella's attitude towards him, and Bryan's disappearance were somehow linked.

A little after eight the phone rang in the house and Matt went inside to answer it. He picked up the receiver and Ella was on the line. She sounded strained. She told him she was at the police department.

'Chief Baxter wanted me to come in and answer some questions. I told him I wanted to call you first.'

Matt was confused. 'Has Jake changed his mind about bringing charges?'

'I don't think this is about Jake.' Ella sounded cautious. 'Matt, I wouldn't ask for your help, but you said if there was anything, that I should call.'

He felt the hand of trepidation on his shoulder, but when he spoke he tried to keep it from his voice. 'You did the right thing. I'm glad you called.'

'Thanks,' she said, her relief obvious.

'What has the chief said to you?'

'Nothing much, but I think it has something to do with Bryan.'

Matt tried to sound confident and put her at ease. He could hear the worry in her voice. 'Whatever it is, we'll get it sorted out,' he assured her, but his disquiet was growing by the second. 'Put Chief Baxter on.'

He waited while the phone changed hands and Baxter came on the line. 'What's this all about, Chief?'

Baxter hesitated, and Matt guessed that Ella was standing right next to him. 'I think you might want to come down here and hear this in person.'

Matt said he was on his way and asked Baxter to put Ella back on the phone. 'Don't say anything until I get there, okay?'

'All right.'

'And don't worry,' he added before he hung up the phone.

He went outside and told Henry he had to go into town, then quickly changed into a shirt and pants. On the way to the police department he made a hurried stop at his office. From his window he looked down on the street below. There were a few people about even though it was early. Across the street, Catherine Lunt who ran the little fruit store was coming out of the door to the apartment she lived in over her store. Most mornings he went in there to buy peaches or maybe a melon. He used the coffee shop along the street where he had begun to chat with the regulars, and people had started to stop and pass the time of day in the street. He knew that to a lot of them he'd always be a pointer, somebody from away, but he hoped in time the islanders' reserve would break down to some degree. His life here had already taken on a whole different rhythm from his previous existence. Just sitting on the porch at night playing chess with Henry and watching the sun go down while the lights came on in the harbour gave him a good feeling. He'd come to believe that moving to the island had been the right thing for him to do. In Boston his life had been empty. Since Kirstin had left him and taken Alex with her, he'd gone through a slow awakening, questioning the way he'd been devoured by some need to avenge Paulie. His life had been an empty shell, devoid of any true meaning. He'd begun to think he'd turned a corner since moving to St George. In his day-dreams Alex came to stay, and he got to know his son again, and had a chance to make up for the time that they had already

77

lost. He admitted that Ella had figured in fantasies he'd enter-tained where the three of them got on like a house on fire, and for once the future had seemed welcoming.

But now he felt the irresistible pull of forces about to wrench his dreams apart.

When Matt arrived at the police department, Baxter was sitting on the edge of a desk in the outer office. He looked as if he hadn't slept much.

'Ella's in my office,' he said. 'We gave her a cup of coffee. I offered to get her a doughnut or something but she said she wasn't hungry.'

'That's a nice gesture, Chief. Let me have a word with her, then you and I can talk and you can tell me what this is all about, how's that sound?'

'Fine by me.'

As Matt headed for the office Baxter called out and Matt turned back to him. 'And Matt? It wasn't a gesture. I've known Ella just about all her life.'

Matt nodded, chastened by the mild rebuke. There were good cops and then there were cops like Baxter, who lived and worked in small towns where they had grown up and lived all their lives, and who cared about the people it was their job to serve. 'Understood. No offence meant, Chief.'

'None taken.'

He went through to the office. Ella looked up from her un-touched coffee, and she appeared ill at ease. She met his gaze, then her eyes slid away, but a stubborn set to her mouth remained.

'You okay?' He drew up a chair in front of her. 'This is getting to be a habit. So what's this all about, any idea?'

'Not really. All I know is it's something to do with Monday night. Chief Baxter wanted to ask me what I did after Bryan left the dock. That's when I told him I wanted you here.' She paused and looked uncertain. 'Does this mean you're my lawyer now? You being here I mean.'

The same question had occurred to Matt. It seemed as if their relationship was about to shift again, and he wasn't entirely

78

comfortable about the change, but for now he let it go. 'We can worry about that later. Right now I'm going to talk to the chief, then I'll come back in here and you and I can talk and we'll take it from there.'

'Okay.'

'Good.' He got up and went to the door, and turned, about to ask her if there was anything she thought he should know about, but somehow he couldn't bring himself to ask the question. He guessed if there was she would have told him. 'I'll be right back,' he said.

Outside, Baxter related everything that Carl Johnson had told him. As Matt listened he could guess at the questions that were turning over in Baxter's mind, probably the same ones that were occurring to him, but which he thrust aside, reminding himself that he had to think of Ella as his client.

'So, you have any ideas about this, Chief?'

'Well, I'd like to hear what Ella has to say before I think too much about it.'

'But you're making something of this, right? I mean I guess there's no law against Ella being out on her boat as far as I know?'

'There's no law against it,' Baxter agreed. 'Listen, I don't like this any more than you do. But you know as well as I do that I have to ask Ella what she was doing out there. Just about the last time anybody saw him alive, Bryan and Ella were arguing and she was pointing a rifle in his face. Everybody knows they've been banging heads over one thing and another lately. So when somebody comes in here with a story about hearing gunshots in the cove where Bryan happens to live, and seeing Ella out in the middle of the night acting a little strangely, and maybe dumping something over the side of her boat, you have to admit it looks a little suspicious.'

'Doesn't matter how it looks,' Matt said. 'Bryan was alive and well when he left the dock that night and there's nothing to tie him with Ella after that. You said yourself Carl Johnson didn't know what he saw exactly. There's nothing in any of this that would hold up in court. It's all circumstantial.'

79

Baxter appeared a little taken aback. 'Nobody's talking about any court here. I just want to hear from Ella what she was doing, that's all.'

Matt had the impression that Baxter, whatever suspicions he had, was telling the truth about not liking any of this, and that so far at least he hadn't drawn any firm conclusions from what Johnson had told him.

'Okay, but give me a minute with her first.'

'Take as long as you need. You have to wonder though,' Baxter added, 'if Ella doesn't have anything to hide, how come she called you?'

Matt had been asking himself the same question. Before he went in the office he composed his features, trying to disguise the fact that what he had just heard had unsettled him deeply, but the second Ella saw him he felt as if she'd read the uncertainty in his expression as if it were an open book.

'What is it?'

He sat down, and briefly went through what he'd learned. 'Carl Johnson reported hearing gunshots,' he concluded. 'And you've already admitted threatening Bryan with a rifle earlier that same night.'

'I had no reason to deny it.'

'What exactly happened? Can you remember what was said?'

'He tried to get on board the *Santorini*. I told him if he put a foot on my boat it'd be the last thing he did.'

Inwardly Matt winced. He pictured her, holding the rifle as she warned Bryan off and he found he could envisage it quite easily, and then he saw her wielding a length of wood as it split open a man's skull. He put the incident with Bryan to one side for the time being to concentrate on what Carl Johnson had seen and heard, and opened the page of notes he'd made when he'd spoken to Baxter.

'So, you were out there near the cove? It was your boat Johnson saw?' She nodded. 'And he spoke to you on the radio?' She nodded again. 'What time was it?'

'I don't know. Maybe around three if that's what Carl said.'

He made a note. 'So what were you doing out there?'

He watched her carefully and she hesitated just a fraction before answering.

'I was fishing.'

'And what time did you go out?'

'About nine, maybe nine-thirty.'

'Which was how long after your fight with Bryan?'

'Half an hour, thereabouts.'

Matt made another note. 'Were you alone?'

'Alone?'

'Were you fishing alone? Was there anybody with you?'

'No. I mean yes, I was alone.'

'You fish a lot at night by yourself?'

'Sometimes. Not often.'

'You catch much that night?'

'A little.'

'Johnson said you had your lights off. Is that true?'

'Yes. I had a faulty battery connection.'

'Right, that's what he said you told him. You remember talking to him?'

'Of course.'

He made another note, he now had a series of ticks on his page. So far Ella hadn't denied anything Johnson had said.

'Was there a moon that night? I mean how was the visibility?'

'There was a moon, but it was partly cloudy.'

'Could you see Johnson's boat clearly, I mean how far away was he?'

'It was dark. He was, I don't know, a hundred and fifty yards away. Maybe a little more.'

'But you could see his boat clearly?'

'I could see it.'

Matt took a second to make another notation, and while he did he asked his next question without looking at her. 'So you were out there fishing that night. Carl Johnson said he thought you had some kind of big bundle rigged to your davit when he saw you, and to him it looked like you were dumping it over the side. What was in that bundle Ella?' He tried to ask the

81

question in the same tone he'd used for all the others but he wasn't sure if he'd pulled it off.

'There was no bundle,' Ella said. 'I don't know what he's talking about. Maybe he saw a trap or seaweed or something. I think I remember bringing something like that up that night on one haul.'

Matt had heard a thousand witnesses on the stand, and he knew the sound of the truth when he heard it, and he knew right now that Ella was lying. It affected him. He was saddened to think she would hold out on him, that she felt she had something to hide, and partly for that reason he experienced a flash of anger. He looked up at her and locked his gaze with her own.

'I want to help you Ella, but I can only do that if you tell me the truth.' He paused to allow his words to sink in. 'Because you know how this looks don't you? You have a fight with a man everybody knows you don't get along with. A man who has a lot at stake over this marina, which you oppose, and you threaten him with a gun in front of witnesses. Next thing is he disappears and it turns out you just happened to be seen that same night near where he lives, dumping something over the side of your boat. And then there was the shot Johnson talked about. Did you hear any shots that night Ella?'

She glared at him. 'No, dammit, I didn't hear any shots. Why don't you just say it?'

'Say what?'

'Just come out and say you don't believe me. It's what you think isn't it? It's written all over your face.'

'You're surprised if I'm a little doubtful?' he said incredulously. 'Come on Ella. You pointed a goddamn rifle at a man.' He couldn't erase that image of her from his mind. It was Matt's experience that people who pointed guns at other people were usually about a hair's breadth away from pulling the trigger.

Ella's voice was controlled but brittle when she answered. 'I told you the kind of trouble I've been having with Bryan and Jake. You think that's nothing? Maybe it doesn't sound like very much, but that's only a part of it. I grew up on the docks, around the boats and the men who work on them and in case you

82

haven't noticed I'm the only woman down there. And in case you haven't noticed this either, I'm around people every day who aren't always the most liberal minded people in the world. Since I was fourteen I've had to put up with guys who put me down every chance they get, guys who don't think a woman ought to be doing what I do for a living. Some of them resent me because I'm good at what I do. Better than a lot of them. How do you think it feels when somebody watches me walk by when they're cleaning their nets and thinks it's hilarious to sniff their fingers and leer at me? Like they're even original! That kind of thing isn't just poor taste, it's vicious, Matt. That's the kind of thing that would amuse the Rodericks. Bryan especially. You don't know all the remarks and innuendo, all the dirty tricks I've had to put up with from them. But you know what? I never let those sonsofbitches get to me, and if they did I never let them know it. I always stood up to them, and so when Bryan thought he could come on to my boat without being asked I let him know he couldn't. And you know what else? It damn well worked. So if you think I over reacted when I threatened him, or that I shouldn't have hit Jake yesterday after he tried to steal my living away from me, then you don't know anything about what it's like to be in my shoes and maybe you don't know anything about me!'

For a while neither of them said anything. Matt admitted to himself that perhaps, as she said, he didn't know much about the things she'd endured in her life. Perhaps he was judging her by standards that didn't apply here the same way they did where he came from, though he wasn't sure he believed that. What he did know was that for the moment their arguing about it wasn't going to help any.

'The thing is Ella, it doesn't matter what I think,' he said. 'Chief Baxter is going to ask you the same questions I have. He's going to look at you and see somebody who threatened a man, for whatever reason, and then he's going to put that together with what Carl Johnson told him and he's going to want to know what you were doing out there by the cove that night. So tell me again what were you doing?'

'I already told you, I was fishing.'

Looking in her eyes as they blazed green and grey was disconcerting, like seeing two separate people. He wondered if he was wrong to doubt her. She said she was fishing, and why wouldn't she be?

'And now I have a question for you,' she said.

'What is it?'

'You want the truth? You want to know if I killed Bryan? Here it is. I did not shoot Bryan Roderick. I did not kill him. I never saw him again after he left the dock.' She enunciated every word clearly, her eyes never swaying from his. 'So now you tell me this. Do you believe me?'

His answer was in the time it took for him to reply. He wanted to believe her, that much was true, but the sense he had that she wasn't telling him everything still lingered.

'If you say that you didn't, then I believe you,' he said, but he knew he hadn't been able to completely disguise his lack of conviction. Her reaction surprised him. He expected anger, but instead she simply looked at him, and both her eyes appeared closer in colour, a smoky grey. She nodded once, a subtle confirmation of something she'd expected, and that affected him far more than her anger could have done.

Baxter questioned Ella for forty minutes. He went over everything Johnson had seen, or thought he'd seen, and he went back to Ella's fight with Bryan, and though there were a couple of times when he paused and looked thoughtful as he wrote down her answers, and he went over some things a couple of times, in the end it was apparent that there was nothing to link Ella with whatever had become of Bryan. One thing he asked her when she said she'd been fishing that night, was if she'd caught much. Matt picked up a subtle note in his tone that made him instinctively wary, but he didn't know what to make of it. Ella repeated what she'd said earlier, that she'd done okay.

'I might want to see your rifle, Ella,' Baxter said when it appeared he was about finished. 'Maybe Russ could come down to the *Santorini* with you now and fetch it.'

'My rifle?'

'It's just a routine thing.'

'I don't have it anymore. I lost it a couple of days ago.' Baxter glanced at Matt, who maintained a neutral expression.

'How'd that happen, Ella?' Baxter asked sounding frankly disbelieving.

'I had to shoot a shark and somehow I dropped it over the side.'

He frowned, but because he had no choice, Baxter let it go, though he looked unhappy about it. 'One other thing Ella. You ever been to Bryan's house?'

'No. Why would I?'

He shrugged. 'No reason.'

Eventually Matt asked if he had any more questions, and Baxter shook his head.

'I guess not. You're free to go Ella.'

As they left, Baxter signalled that he wanted to talk to Matt alone. He waited until Ella was out of earshot.

'I thought you might like to know that I talked to Ella's dealer this morning. He told me she didn't sell him any lobsters on Tuesday morning, and she didn't have many when she came back in again that afternoon.'

'Meaning?'

'Ella says she was fishing. So what did she do with her catch?'

'Don't fishermen keep what they catch in a tank sometimes?' Matt ventured.

'Yeah,' Baxter said, as if he'd already thought of that too. He unwrapped a piece of gum, and Matt had the feeling he had something else on his mind.

'What is it, Chief?'

'I wanted to ask you if Ella would agree to us taking her prints while she's here.'

'What for?'

'Elimination. We dusted Bryan's house. Actually we didn't find much. We've matched Bryan's to some we took off the *Seawind,* but other than his we only found one other on a faucet in the kitchen.'

'That's all?' Matt asked.

'Yeah. It's kind of like somebody did a pretty good job cleaning up in there.' He didn't say anything else but the look he fixed Matt with made it clear what he was thinking. Why would anyone clean up unless to hide something?

'I don't want you to take Ella's prints. Even if you got a match it wouldn't prove anything except that she'd been in the house some time recently.'

Baxter shrugged. 'Ella said she's never been there. I could still charge her over that fight she had with Jake, and get her prints anyway, but I'd rather she agreed voluntarily. Can't hurt if she doesn't have anything to hide.'

Matt didn't like Baxter's request much, but he didn't see that Ella had a lot of choice.

'Let me talk to her.' He went over to her and explained what Baxter wanted. 'You don't have to agree, but if you don't he can charge you with an offence over the run-in you had with Jake and take them anyway.'

'Would he do that?'

'I don't know,' Matt answered honestly.

'He can take them,' she said.

Matt felt a quick rush of relief which he tried not to let show. The fact that she was willing, questions of principle aside, indicated she had nothing to hide. Baxter called over Officer Minelli, and he took her over to a table where he produced a kit. It just took a few minutes.

'Okay, Ella, you're all set,' Baxter told her when Minelli was finished, and he showed them to the door.

'You'll let me know if anything else comes up and you need to talk to Ella?' Matt asked.

Baxter nodded. 'I'll let you know.'

After they left the police department Matt and Ella walked towards where she had left her truck. They were silent, the gulf between them now felt like it was a mile wide, Matt thought. He wasn't sure exactly how he felt any more, and he wanted time to think. They reached Ella's truck and paused on the sidewalk.

'Is that it?' Ella asked.

'Unless they find more evidence.'

'Evidence?'

'A body,' Matt said. 'That's why he wanted your rifle. If they found a body and it had a gunshot wound, they would have looked for a bullet to see whether or not it came from your weapon.'

Ella looked away, and smoothed the hair back from her face. As she did, Matt caught sight of the bruise at her hairline which he'd noticed on the night of the meeting. The swelling had gone down, but it was still visible. He recalled her telling him that she'd slipped. The way she'd reacted, averting her eyes and changing the subject when he'd mentioned it came back to him, and jarred. Ella seemed to sense what he was thinking and she started to raise her hand to the spot, a reflex action, but then she stopped herself.

'Well, thank you. You'll let me know what I owe you?'

They shook hands and the formality of the gesture emphasized how far apart they were. 'Forget it. Anyway you didn't actually retain me. Let's just see if anything else develops,' he said.

She looked at him steadily, her expression unreadable.

'While you were talking to Chief Baxter, I was thinking that maybe this isn't such a good idea. Perhaps we ought to just leave it at this.'

It took Matt a moment to absorb what she was saying. 'You don't want my help?'

'I just think it's better this way.' She paused. 'I want to thank you for what you did, though.'

Then before he knew what else he could say, Ella opened the door of her truck and climbed in. He closed the door and stood back, and as she pulled away from the kerb without looking at him he could only watch as she drove away.

When he got home later, Matt saw that Henry had finished the framing on the cider shed and had started on the walls. He went over and they stood on Henry's porch and drank a beer together. The air was close and still. Matt's gaze drifted down across the trees to the southern side of town. In the half light the place looked about as tranquil and pretty as it was possible to be. The ocean glinted with flashes of gold from the setting sun, white frame houses emerged from the emerald foliage of high summer, and the spire of a church added a symbol of wholesomeness. There was no sound of traffic, no steady throb of trucks rumbling by, not a glass skyscraper to be seen.

'What's on your mind Matt?' Henry asked.

'Just thinking.'

'About Ella?'

'Yeah.' He explained what had happened that day.

'You don't think she killed that fella, do you Matt? From what you said she told you flat that she didn't.'

'No, I don't think that,' Matt said at last, though he recalled his conviction that she'd lied to him when he'd asked her what she was doing that night.

'Did you tell her that?'

'I don't know if she believed me.' Even as he spoke, he admitted that the revelations of the past couple of days had thrown him. He didn't feel as if Ella was the person he'd thought her to be.

'I don't know, Henry. Ella won't say what she was doing out there by the cove, but I don't think it was fishing. When you do what I did for a living for long enough, you get a sense for when somebody's not telling the truth about something.'

'Well, maybe she has her reasons,'

Matt thought about Paulie, dead because some crackhead had pointed a gun at him. He knew Ella had a temper, and she had shown she could resort to violence. He guessed she did have her reasons. He just wondered what they were.

Part Two

CHAPTER ELEVEN

The orcas had swum south-west through the gulf in their search for food. They were following a flow of colder water, encountering mackerel, hake and other fish on which they fed opportunistically. As they swam, two of the immature males were chasing each other in play, working back and forth across the path the pod were taking. One erupted from the waves and as he came down he almost landed on top of the other young male, startling him. Once again the two of them rushed off, continuing their game.

By evening the bull was again concentrating on finding food. He led the pod over the banks he knew and remembered from previous seasons, searching for fish. Occasionally they heard the sound of humpbacks feeding at depths of eighty or ninety fathoms, and once or twice they passed close to minke whales, which sped off quickly when they heard the orcas approaching.

Food supplies for the past few days had been sporadic, but each day the numbers of smaller baitfish the pod encountered seemed to be greater, and with them the larger species that preyed on them. But the bull was searching for something in particular. The numbers of tuna like the school the pod had herded into the cove almost a week before were increasing, and the bull was expecting that with them would come the giants. These fish, some up to twelve feet long and weighing up to fifteen hundred pounds, were too fast and wily for the orcas to catch in deep water, but over the shallower banks, where there was more likelihood of surprising them, the orcas stood a better chance.

Each year the bluefin, including the giants, migrated north from Mexico, following the warmer currents in over the banks to feed. Over the past few years the seasons had followed unnaturally warm cycles brought about by changing weather patterns. The warmer water had resulted in a decrease in marine life, and that, combined with the activity of so many fishing boats in the gulf over the years, had depleted fish stocks. Many species had spent more time in the slope waters far off shore, including the bluefin, and consequently the orcas too, as well as whales that fed on sand lances and herring. But this year cooler temperatures had once again prevailed in the gulf. The oxygen-rich water over the banks had seen an explosion of life, and once more the numbers and size of fish were increasing. Though nothing like earlier years, it was enough to tempt in voracious feeders like the giant bluefin, which followed bands of warmer water that flowed beneath the surface.

That evening the orcas approached a point several miles off St George where the shelf rose so that the sea was no more than thirty fathoms deep across a broad plateau. The bull and the now eldest female in the pod, along with another adult male had separated from the main group and were swimming some distance ahead. It was the female who first heard the sound of powerful, fast-swimming fish pursuing smaller prey. She analysed the sounds she picked up, and compared them to her vast store of memory. A school of giants was hunting about a mile ahead of her and moving roughly parallel to her course. Immediately she and the other two orcas changed direction to rejoin the pod.

The bull had also noted the sound of a vessel approaching from the north, its engines at full throttle.

The *Seawind* was a fifty-two-foot, steel-hulled fishing boat, built during the early eighties in Portland. She was originally designed as a dragger, and still able to be rigged for nets, but Jake's preferred fishing method was by long line, though he also fished for lobsters at the height of the season. The *Seawind*'s wheelhouse superstructure was atop her forecastle where the cramped crew quarters and galley lay towards the bow. The long deck behind was cleared for working and at her stern was a gantry and davits and a drum midship from where the main line was laid out over the stern. Jake and Bryan had made some improvements to the boat after they'd bought her, installing new twin Mack diesel engines to give her a speed that could match many sports boats. They had also fitted a long bowsprit with a small platform at the end where a man could stand with a harpoon ready to spear the swordfish that in some seasons they pursued.

Jake stood in the wheel-house watching the crew. He'd done his time on deck, snapping on short lines called leaders that bore the baited hooks as the main line went over the stern. He'd hauled catches aboard in all weathers, freezing and half soaked from the spray as the bow plunged into great troughs between waves. On a boat where the deck was behind the forecastle it wasn't so bad since the superstructure provided some shelter from the elements, but then there was the oily stink of diesel that the crew breathed hour after hour, and in rough weather, after a while, protection or not, it didn't make a lot of difference. The fish were taken from the hooks as they came aboard and thrown to the deck, the hooks and lines coiled neatly in boxes ready to be re-set. The fish were then gutted and put into the hold.

Down on the deck, the crew had brought in the main line and were busy cleaning the catch. Many of the hooks had been returned empty, and the catch had been poor. Most of the fish were stripers, though there had been several small porbeagles as well as the odd bluefish. Jake brought the *Seawind* around and wondered in which direction to head to make another set. He glanced at the fish finder, and read the temperature read-out of the surrounding sea. There was no evidence of fish in the vicinity. He thought about heading out to deeper water to search for a temperature break where the warm gulf stream and the cooler waters over the banks collided. Jake, like most other fishermen who worked out of Sanctuary lived a financially precarious existence. The *Seawind* carried a large bank loan, and after paying the crew and covering expenses even when times were good there was never much money left over.

Calder Penman, who was acting as first mate in place of Bryan, joined Jake in the wheel-house. The door was open to let the fresh breeze inside. Overhead the sky was pale blue, smeared with high cirrus cloud. The sea was coloured shades of green and blue and deep aqua, and the *Seawind* rode easily on a slight swell, making a steady eight or nine knots.

As Jake stared at the moving mass of the ocean his thoughts turned to Bryan, and his hands tightened on the wheel. He was convinced that Bryan lay in the channel somewhere where Carl Johnson said he'd seen Ella that night. But Ella was still walking around as free as a goddamned bird, thanks to that fancy lawyer of hers.

He felt the bandage on his head. He wished there hadn't been people around to stop him from getting his hands on her after she'd hit him. Maybe that was the only way he was going to get any justice for Bryan, since it looked like Baxter wasn't any match for a city lawyer like Matt Jones.

'Fucking bitch,' Jake muttered aloud.

'Who?' Penman said, looking puzzled

Jake looked at him. 'Ella, that's who. How come Baxter hasn't arrested her yet?'

'I guess they have to have evidence Jake.'

'What more fucking evidence do they need? Carl saw everything that happened.'

Wisely, Penman said nothing.

Just then one of the crew shouted and pointed towards something off the starboard side where a flock of gannets wheeled above the sea. Now and then one of them would fold back its wings and dive to the surface like an arrow. Jake picked up his glasses and focused for a closer look.

'What do you see?' Penman asked.

Jake didn't answer right away. The gannets were feeding on fish at the surface, but what kind of fish and what size he couldn't tell. Often baitfish were herded to the surface by dolphins or some other predator, and occasionally this could mean an opportunity for fishermen. Just then a silver blue flash leapt from the water, struck by the rays of the sinking sun in an explosion of light.

'Jesus!' Jake dropped the glasses and started spinning the wheel to bring the *Seawind* around and at the same time he pushed forward on the throttle. The Macks roared into life, then the boat seemed to pause in the water for a moment before her twin screws bit deep, churning the sea into foam at her stern and thrusting her forward.

'Bluefin. Goddamned giants.'

Penman ran outside to the rail to get a better look. Even after thirty years as a fisherman in the gulf, this was a sight he'd rarely seen. Excitement coursed in his veins. 'Damn,' he said. 'Ain't that somethin'?'

The bluefin were at least ten feet in length, which meant they had to weigh at least a thousand pounds. They were moving at around seven or eight knots as they hunted some school of much smaller fish, now and then leaping from the waves in pursuit.

'How many do you count?' Jake said.

Penman watched for a while as they drew nearer. 'Maybe thirty. Forty even.'

'Rig the harpoons.'

Quickly Penman ran to the ladder, shouting instructions to the crew. Jake kept his eye fixed on the giants as he closed the gap on them. In all his years at sea he had never before seen a school of fish this size. Once they had been a more common sight, but in those days only sports fishermen were interested in catching them. The processing plant might have bought the carcass for ten cents a pound back then, but these days it was a different story. Giants were highly prized for the sushi market. Just one fish in good condition and dressed out could fetch anything from twenty to as much as forty dollars a pound at the market. For a thousand pound fish that added up to a lot of money. The flesh had to be perfect, the fat content just right, but such fish were air-freighted to Japan overnight where they were a prized delicacy. A chance to catch one might only come once in a lifetime.

On deck the crew made frantic preparations, all of them infected with the same excitement. Each of them was paid a share of the catch as the main part of their wages and one giant could mean hundreds, even thousands of dollars extra for each man on board. As the *Seawind* drew nearer they gathered at the rail to watch. Suddenly one of them shouted a warning.

Jake followed where he was pointing. A pod of orcas were approaching from the southwest at an angle that would intercept the tuna. They were coming fast, their great black and white bodies appearing in the troughs between the swell.

In the wheel-house Jake's expression turned grim as he counted at least eight of the predators.

'Black bastards,' he said to himself.

Close by, a tuna leapt from the water, a huge twelve foot monster. It was fat and round, like a torpedo, its head bullet shaped. On top it was dark blue but underneath its belly flashed silver. Beneath the waves Jake glimpsed the streaking shapes of several others. He swung around several degrees, having found his target, one eye still on the approaching pod.

The bull had recognized the pitch and tone of the *Seawind*'s engines. The pod had encountered this boat at other times, and he knew it was dangerous.

The orcas approached in silence so as not to alert the bluefin to their presence until they were almost upon them. The sound of powerful bodies hissing through the water grew louder. The bull heard the pounding of massive hearts and the beat of muscular tails. All at once a bluefin streaked in a flash towards the surface in pursuit of a ten pound striped bass. The bull heard it coming, and swiftly turned through a hundred and eighty degrees, and leapt from the sea to intercept it. Orca and surprised bluefin met in mid-air. The bull bit off the giant's tail as they both crashed back to the waves and blood spread quickly in a widening stain. Even as the stricken giant began to sink, alive but helpless, the bull moved on. They were among the fish now, and as the bluefin realized what was happening they panicked. The orcas attacked ruthlessly, severing the tails or caudal fins of the tuna as they attempted to flee. They worked in pairs, one going deep to prevent the bluefin diving, the other attacking near the surface. In just the space of a minute half a dozen of the giants had been dispatched and allowed to sink for the orcas to retrieve and eat later. Their priority was to kill or disable as many as possible before the school fled. Already some of the bluefin had escaped, gathering immense speed with just a few quick thrusts of their massive tails. Into this melee the *Seawind* surged, with Penman on the bowsprit, his harpoon poised to strike.

A female orca dived to intercept a fleeing fish. She cut it off and it veered away, rocketing back towards the surface, erupting just a few yards from the hull of the *Seawind*. The female followed, too late registering the warning the bull sounded.

Penman's first throw missed the fish he was aiming for as it veered at the last moment to evade a pursuing orca, but even as it did so it was hit by another from below. From the wheelhouse Jake witnessed twenty thousand dollars' worth of bluefin all but bitten in half. He glanced around at the gun locker behind him, but he couldn't reach it without letting go of the wheel, and Penman was signalling that he had another target.

'Dammit!'

He altered course. An orca rose from the sea fifty yards off their port side, its snowy white belly flashing, a bluefin struggling in its jaws. Fish and orca crashed back to the surface in a vast spray of water faintly smeared with pink. All around, the sea had erupted in a fierce explosion of carnage. As Jake watched the slaughter his teeth were gritted in rage. The giants had broken off their feeding now, intent only on escape, and in a few more seconds they would be gone.

Down below Penman took aim. A fish leapt and he threw, but the bluefin swivelled in mid-air and the harpoon narrowly missed and pierced the fin of a pursuing orca. Penman reached for his knife to sever the line.

'Leave it,' Jake shouted.

The line tightened as the orca found itself caught and began to be dragged by the momentum of the boat. It struggled to keep up to prevent itself from drowning, but Jake knew it would soon tire. Even an orca wouldn't be able to match the *Seawind*'s speed for long, and then the animal would drown, or be towed helplessly at the surface until the bluefin had dispersed and Jake could deal with it. He would simply put a bullet in its brain, then cut it loose. Blood from the wound was flowing freely. Soon sharks would be attracted to the area, and maybe as the orca would be unable to defend itself, they would save Jake a bullet.

Out on deck a shout went up as one of the crew threw a harpoon and speared an eight-foot bluefin as it flashed past the hull a few feet below the surface.

The bull heard the female's distress call and as he swam after her he tasted her blood in the water. He stayed clear of the boat as a bluefin was slowly hauled towards the stem. The stricken orca wallowed in the sea thirty yards off the side. On board the boat the crew were busy as they worked to bring their fish in close. The bluefin was struggling, swimming on a forty foot line, trying to go deep, but being dragged inexorably closer to the boat. The remainder of the tuna had escaped, scattering in all directions.

The bull dived twenty feet below the surface and swam to the female's side, rubbing close and making soft clicks and squeals to comfort her. Further back the rest of the pod had heard her distress calls and had broken off their attack, but the bull warned them away. The shaft of the harpoon had pierced the female's dorsal fin, and its barbed tip held it fast, the line stretching through the air back to the boat. The boat's engine note abruptly altered pitch and the screws churning the water slowed down. The bull spied towards the deck as a man emerged from the structure at the front of the vessel, holding something cradled in his arm.

Jake loaded the rifle as he walked to the rail.

'There's two of 'em,' Penman shouted, pointing.

Jake recognized the shape of the bull's dorsal fin with its distinctive double notch. He'd run into this pod before, and he knew it was the lead male.

He grinned. 'Come to see what's happened have you? Well I guess I can get the both of you now.'

He worked the bolt on his rifle and raised it to his shoulder. The bull went under, but no matter, he would get rid of the one they'd harpooned, and wait for the bull to surface again. He found the dorsal fin in his sight, and travelled along the body to the head, then aimed at a point just above the eye. Pulling the stock into his shoulder he started to tighten on the trigger.

Suddenly the surface of the water exploded and a vast shape filled his sight. There was a sound like a high pitched thwack, and it took him a second to absorb what had happened. Cursing, he quickly sighted again and fired.

The bull swam to a depth of fifteen fathoms and looked back towards the surface. He could hear the wildly beating heart of the distressed female. Again he made comforting sounds, and then with several rapid swipes of his flukes he rose upwards, travelling with surprising speed for such a large animal. He hit the surface and shot from the water, and in mid-air he grasped the harpoon line in his great conical teeth and bit down. The line severed with an audible snap of tension, and the bull crashed to the sea again. The female immediately dived, even as the sound of shots from the boat reached them and thin streaks penetrated the water like silver arrows, where they quickly died.

Both the bull and the female swam back to join the rest of the pod. Once clear of the boat they stopped, and the bull examined the female's injured fin. He seized the harpoon by the barb in his teeth and drew it and the remainder of the line out. Blood flowed from the wound freely, but it would heal in time, and the blood would quickly clot. The female swam close to him, rubbing against him affectionately, and when they joined the rest of the group, one by one the others made close physical contact to comfort her and renew the pod's bonds.

The orcas found and shared all of the bluefin they had killed, enjoying the rich firm flesh of the fish. When they had finished, the bull swam back towards the *Seawind*.

Jake cursed the orcas when they'd escaped, but the bluefin that was being brought alongside prevented him from giving chase, and so he went to watch. The value of the fish was affected by its condition and it was important not to allow it to struggle so hard that the spinal temperature rose to the point where the flesh would begin to cook from the inside. The sooner the fish was killed and dressed, the more it would fetch. The giant was at the surface now, just a few yards off the boat, and two of the men were ready with gaffs and lines. Jake let out a low whistle. Maybe if hadn't been for those damn orcas he might have caught another giant, maybe two or three, but he figured this one would fetch at least fifteen thousand. Maybe a lot more.

'Bring it in steady,' Jake warned. 'That's your bonus you're looking at there boys.'

The tuna was a beautiful fish. Perfectly streamlined in shape, sleek and shiny with grooves for the pectoral and first dorsal fins to fold into, and lateral thickening keels to strengthen the tail and improve water flow. As it was manoeuvred alongside, the crew prepared to slip lines around head and tail to connect to the hauler and bring it aboard. Jake leaned against the rail and peered down.

'Careful with that line dammit!' he growled to the man next to him.

Something in the water caught Jake's attention. He squinted against the glare, wondering if he'd imagined the dark shape he thought he'd seen. All at once, the surface of the sea erupted in a mass of spray. A huge shape rose with the force of a freight train and the terrified men fell back with cries of alarm as the orca, its massive jaws agape, leapt towards them with terrifying speed. The men had a sudden swelling vision of black and white, and rows of lethal teeth, a mouth big enough to sever a man in two with a single bite, and then the orca seized the bluefin and bore it down. A second later the line went slack.

It was over in a second. Then the surface of the water calmed again, and only the wildly beating hearts of the crew were proof of what they had seen.

Jake was too stunned to speak. He simply stared in disbelief. Then he yelled out a roar of pure rage like some animal bellowing its fury. The crew and Penman looked at one another with nervous, sideways glances.

CHAPTER TWELVE

It was early in the morning and the coffee shop was quiet. The only other customer besides Matt was a man who sat by the window reading a book and making notes while he ate bacon and pancakes and drank coffee. He glanced over and nodded as Matt took a seat. He looked like a tourist, maybe a college teacher on vacation. He was around thirty or so, and he wore a close-cut beard, round silver-framed glasses and was dressed in jeans and an REM T-shirt.

Matt chose a table near the window and when Sally Brewster brought him his order she slid into the seat opposite him and took out a pack of Kools.

'I'm on a break. You don't mind do you?'

'Help yourself.' He was glad of the company. Sally was in her thirties, a divorcée with a friendly manner and the kind of face that was beginning to show the first early signs that her pretty looks were fading.

'So, when are you going to take me out, Matt?' she said, eyeing him across the table as smoke drifted from her cigarette.

'There's nowhere I can think of in this town that's good enough to take a woman like you Sally, or I'd have asked,' he told her.

She cocked her head to one side. 'Is that true?'

'Of course.'

She sighed. 'Well, you're a liar like all men, but that's a sweet thing to say. Why don't you just show me that house of yours? I'd like to see what you get up to all alone up there.'

'I'm not alone. I've got Henry to keep me company.'

She leaned forward, pressing her breasts against the edge of the table. 'I think I can compete with ol' Henry,' she said, and winked.

Matt grinned back and sipped his coffee. He never really knew if Sally was serious since she flirted with half of her customers this way. He guessed she did it partly to make her day a little more interesting.

Sally smoked, and from the kitchen came the clatter of pans and the sound of Boyd's cursing. Boyd and Sally were partners. He was fat and had grey hair he tied back in a ponytail and was rarely caught smiling. He did the cooking, and generally stayed clear of the customers, having long ago recognized that his natural talents didn't include being nice to people on a daily business.

'So, how're you enjoying the quiet life Matt?' Sally asked with a trace of irony. 'Bet you didn't expect to find yourself in the middle of a murder when you decided to come back here.'

'I haven't heard about any murder, Sally.'

'Then you must be going around with your ears closed. That's all I hear about these days.' She took something from her pocket, and when she smoothed it out Matt saw it was one of Ella's election posters. Where it read 'Vote For Ella Young', somebody had added 'Or She'll Kill You'.

'Jesus,' Matt said. 'Is this what people think?'

'Well, let's just say there's a lot of talk about what Carl Johnson saw that night.'

Matt stared at the poster. Maybe it was meant as a perverse joke, but somehow he suspected whoever was responsible had a more sinister motive. 'Tell me something Sally, you must know Bryan pretty well. What kind of guy is he?' He was careful to use the present tense, not acknowledging the likelihood that Bryan was dead.

Sally sucked on her cigarette. 'Oh, he was kind of good looking I guess,' she mused, unintentionally slipping into the past tense. 'But then the competition around here isn't up to much. Present company excepted of course. He was like most guys, he only wanted one thing.'

'I heard he could be pretty unpleasant.'

Sally raised her eyebrows. 'Ella tell you that? Well she's right, he could be a gold-plated bastard all right. If he is dead, I don't know why everyone thinks it must have been Ella that killed him. If you ask me she would have had to join a pretty long line of people ahead of her willing to do the job.'

'That the voice of experience, Sally?'

She put out her cigarette. 'Well, I'm not about to cry at his funeral if that's what you mean, but I didn't kill him either.' She got to her feet. 'But if you want to know about this, here's someone you could ask.' She jabbed her finger at the poster just as the door opened and Howard Larson stepped in.

He saw Matt, came over and slid into the seat Sally had just vacated. 'You don't mind some company do you Matt? How about some coffee here Sally?'

As she went back to the counter his glance lingered for a second where her uniform was stretched tightly over her rear. When he saw the poster on the table he picked it up and shook his head and grinned until he saw Matt's expression.

'What? Come on, you have to admit it has a funny side.'

'I must have a poor sense of humour.'

Howard made a gesture as if it was nothing. 'Listen, you can't blame people for talking, and this kind of thing? It's the price of playing politics, Matt. I don't approve personally of course, but I guess if you want to play with fire you have to be prepared to get a little burned.'

'This goes a little beyond just politics,' Matt pointed out.

'Yeah, well, whatever.' Howard gave the appearance of wanting to drop the subject. He folded the poster and pushed it to the side of the table. 'Thing is, Matt, just because Ella and I are on different sides in this election, that doesn't mean I don't like her. But you can't expect me to pretend I'm broken hearted if this means I have a better chance of winning. This is the real world, Matt. Shit happens, and if I'm honest I'd rather it happened to Ella than me. And anyway, I happen to think the marina will be good for the island. It'll be the first step in a whole future of development around here.'

'You're all heart Howard. I suppose you wouldn't have had anything to do with this.' Matt indicated the poster. 'Like you said, all this gives you a better chance of winning doesn't it?'

'Listen, you think that was ever really in doubt? I would've won anyway. I mean, I don't deny Ella has her supporters, though I guess not as many as she had before, but they're going to thank me in the end. The fact is a lot of those peckerheads wouldn't know a good thing if it came up and bit them on the ass, but this development is going to be the best thing that ever happened to this goddamned place. It'll mean tourists, houses, business. Things will change and most people know that. They see a chance to get ahead. I thought you'd be able to see that Matt. It's all very well wanting things to stay the way they are, but people have to eat. You know how many people left the island last year because they couldn't find a way to make a living? A lot let me tell you.'

Howard gulped at the coffee Sally set down in front of him, his eyes flicking like a lizard's tongue over her cleavage.

'All I'm trying to do is make things better for everyone on this shitty little island,' Howard went on. 'Half these people don't know a thing about the real world, Matt. What we need is more people like you. People who've been around a little, who don't shit their pants at the first sign of a little change.' He paused and his expression took on a sly slant. 'You should think about what I said to you the other night. There are going to be a lot of opportunities around here. You ought to come over to my office, take a look at some plans. We could talk. This world needs leaders, men of vision, to show people what's really good for them.'

Matt finished his coffee. 'Howard, you know what the difference is between you and Ella? To her this is home. You think you know what's best for people, but all you really want is to make a profit on the land you own. But then what? My guess is you'd be gone within a year. You'd find somewhere more to your taste. Somewhere that isn't just a shitty little island.'

He rose to leave, unable to stomach Howard's company any longer. His barely disguised glee at the suspicion that had fallen

105

over Ella made it tempting to shove the poster down Howard's throat. Matt would have bet everything he had in the bank, which admittedly wasn't much, that Howard was behind the defacement of Ella's posters anyway.

Howard's smile vanished. 'You know what else is different about me and Ella, Matt? I didn't kill anyone, that's what.'

Matt ignored him but as he reached the door Howard called out.

'Don't say I didn't give you a chance. You're as bad as the rest of them. Ella's going to lose anyway. You think people are going to support her now? You better think again, Matt.'

As he left Matt nodded to the man in the REM T-shirt who looked up at him with mild curiosity.

The road crossed a ridge, then dropped down to run through woods that fringed a cove as dark green and smooth as glass. The woods that rose high on either side, a mixture of firs and maples and oaks, were reflected on the surface of the water.

Bryan's house was set back amongst the trees. Out past the entrance to Stillwater Cove there was a smear of white beyond the heads where the sea churned into foam on the reef. A cold knot formed in Matt's stomach. Over the years a lot of boats had been wrecked on the reef and people had drowned there. The currents and undertow were treacherous, especially in bad weather. Even fishermen who knew the local waters well were wary. Matt knew first hand how the cove could turn ugly. Right now it appeared tranquil and picturesque, deceptively calm. He imagined the surface grey and foaming, whipped by winds and the surf crashing on to the rocks. He thought of a man thrown into the water, sinking, the fight going out of him, and being overtaken by that feeling of inertia.

He passed the turning to the point where the big houses owned by summer people were hidden in the trees. The road dropped and levelled out and he looked for a track that headed through the woods in the direction of the water. When he found it, he emerged into a clearing where there was a wooden house with a screened-in porch. Alongside were a garage and a small barn. The scene was quiet. Matt turned off the engine, and absorbed the stillness that descended around him.

It was quiet, just the sound of birdsong. The house and clearing were bathed in golden light that slanted low across the trees. The house itself was painted white, though the colour was faded. Parts of the grey slate roof had been patched and there was a new frame in one of the front windows. Perhaps, Matt reasoned, it was Howard's undisguised pleasure at the feeling that was running against Ella in the town that had brought him to the cove. Perhaps he didn't want to see Howard win the election, and that was why he had started to wonder what had really happened to Bryan. Or maybe it was self-interest that motivated him, because it seemed clear that until the issue was settled one way or the other, the distance that existed between himself and Ella wasn't likely to be bridged. He wanted to believe her when she claimed she hadn't killed Bryan, and for the most part he did. But she knew something, and she wasn't telling him. He thought he could get used to the idea that perhaps she wasn't exactly the person he'd thought she was, that she could hold a rifle to a man and threaten to shoot him. But not while this enigma of Bryan's disappearance remained between them. He thought that for her too it was as much of an obstacle, though he was uncertain why. Perhaps if he knew that, he would know everything.

Whatever his motivation, he decided he had to discover what had happened to Bryan Roderick.

He walked around the house, but it told him nothing. At the edge of the clearing a path ran for fifty yards before it emerged from the trees to a strip of stone and sand beach that curved right around the edge of the bay. On the southern side the trees appeared to reach almost to the water's edge, and the beach petered out to rocks. The ground rose gently, and further out on the point Matt could see the roof of a house here and there. In the other direction, three quarters of a mile away, the beach curved around to the foot of sheer cliffs that extended all the way along that side of the cove, reaching out to the entrance where the surf pounded the rocks. Something flashed in the sun, and shielding his eyes from the glare, Matt saw a sports boat moored a little way out from a large black rock on the beach, but there was nobody around that he could see.

An old boat shed stood at the water's edge. The door was partly ajar, and when Matt looked inside he found it was empty. The air smelt of mould and towards the back was shot through with shafts of light where the sun poured through missing boards in the walls. At the other end a wooden ramp led down to the water, which at the edge was dark green and appeared deep. A wooden jetty extended twenty yards out into the bay.

Neither the shed nor the jetty had been there when Matt and Paulie had once come here with their little sailboat, though that was more than twenty-five years ago. He hesitated at the end of the jetty, looking out across the water. It was warm, but cold sweat prickled his brow, and his heart beat climbed a notch or two. There was barely a breath of wind, and the surface of the water rippled gently, deceptively calm. He put his foot on the first board of the jetty and tested his weight. It creaked a little but seemed firm. He took another step. Looking down through the boards he could see the bottom fall rapidly away. The water was clear, but looking ahead it was dark where the ground dropped steeply. Matt paused, his hands were slick and he wiped them on his pants. There was a roaring sound in his ears. The long ago sound of kids laughing rang in his ears. He told himself not to look at the water, and stared ahead to the end of the jetty which seemed as if it was a long way off. With each step he took he tested his weight on the boards, and each creak and groan from a rusty nail made him sweat harder. When he was fifteen feet out he stopped and looked down. He couldn't see the bottom. He felt dizzy, spinning with vertigo, and for a moment thought he would drop to his knees. Taking deep breaths he counted slowly to thirty. Just in front there were several boards missing and he knew he wouldn't be able to cross the gap, though it was no more than eighteen inches across. He turned and went back, concentrating on where he placed each step.

For a while he listened to the gentle suck and draw of water on the shore, rattling pebbles on the slope so they rubbed against each other, inexorably smoothing their edges. He squatted at the water's edge and scooped up a handful of stones. They felt smooth and wet in his hand, their sharp angles dulled and worn away. He remembered Paulie, pulling him from the water, how he'd laid gasping on the beach that day, how Paulie had water streaming across his face, his hair plastered to his skull. He stood up and threw the pebbles into the water.

Something flashed in the sunlight again a half mile away. Along the curve of the shore, a figure moved near the black rock where the boat he'd noticed earlier was riding at anchor a short distance off the beach. Curiosity drove Matt towards it and as he drew closer he saw that what he'd mistaken for a rock, was in fact something else. Its shape and texture seemed too smooth, but vaguely familiar, though what it could be he didn't know.

He was still two hundred yards away when a stench carried on the breeze made him pause. The smell was redolent of fish, but there was a stronger, more powerful smell that assaulted the senses, something rotting and fleshy. He'd rounded the curve of the shore now, and as he hesitated, unsure if he wanted to get any closer, a figure appeared and seeing Matt, raised a hand in greeting.

The thing on the beach was half in, half out of the water, and rather than being black all over it was in fact marked with pale patches. When they were fifty yards apart Matt recognized the man he'd seen at breakfast that morning. He also saw that the thing lying on the shore was in fact some kind of animal, and by its size and markings he thought it was a whale of some sort.

The man smiled as he approached and held out his hand. 'Hi, I'm Ben Harper.'

'Matt Jones.'

They shook and Matt gestured along the beach. 'What is that?'

Harper looked back, and took off his glasses which he polished on his shirt. He squinted, screwing his eyes against the light bouncing off the water. 'That,' he said, 'is the most magnificent creature living on this earth, in my opinion anyway. At least this one was. It's dead now. It's an orca.'

'A killer whale?' Matt knew they were seen in the gulf now and then, but he'd never seen one himself, except on TV. The image that sprang to mind was of captive animals performing tricks at Seaworld. Somehow, even dead, the animal on the beach was far more impressive. For one thing it looked bigger in the flesh. He could make out its flippers now, and the shape of the head. 'What happened to it?'

Just then he caught a whiff of the stench of decay on the breeze, and he gagged, swallowing bile.

'You get used to it after a while.' Harper seemed unaffected by the foul odour.

'You're used to this?'

'I'm a marine biologist down at the oceanographic institute at Woods Hole. I see a lot of dead animals in my work. Actually I'm on vacation right now, but I found this orca last week and I've been trying to figure out what happened to it. Near as I can tell it died from pneumonia.'

They walked back towards the orca, Matt's curiosity overcoming his reluctance to get any closer to the source of the putrefying stink. He saw a pile of greyish coloured material on the sand and moved around to get a better look, and then he understood what Ben Harper had been doing. Alongside a pair of muck covered overalls and an open bag were what looked like oversized surgical instruments. The whale's underside had been slit open from close to its head right back to near the tail, and part of its guts had been pulled out. Aside from the mass of intestines it seemed as if some of the animal's other organs had been removed.

'The lungs were clogged with mucus,' Harper explained, apparently oblivious to the shade of green that Matt had turned. 'My guess is that it beached itself here before it died. It's a female. Pretty old I'd say from the state of the teeth. Maybe sixty or seventy years.' He paused, and only then seemed to take note of Matt. 'You okay? You look sorta pale.'

In response Matt turned and rushed with stumbling steps

back along the beach, making a line for the trees. He bent over and retched, vomiting into the undergrowth. The smell from the dead whale felt as if it had attached itself to the soft tissue in his mouth and throat, and no matter how hard he tried he couldn't get rid of it. Each time he thought he'd finished, another violent spasm would grip him.

'Here, drink this.' Harper appeared at his side and offered a flask which Matt sniffed suspiciously. 'It's lemon juice,' Harper told him. 'I find it helps.'

Gratefully Matt took a drink. The juice was sour and strong, but it seemed to do the trick.

'Try gargling a little,' Harper advised.

Matt did. He spat once he'd rinsed his mouth, then handed the flask back. 'Thanks.'

They walked back along the beach, to where the smell wasn't so overpowering.

'I guess I forget how it can get to you when you're not used to it,' Harper said.

'What are you going to do with it?' Matt asked. He was thinking about all the stuff on the sand.

'I'll take some more samples, some of the teeth, but I'll just leave the rest to nature.'

Already the carcass was dotted with a mob of seabirds that had been waiting nearby for their chance.

'Nature's very efficient at cleaning up after herself. In a month there'll be nothing but bones on the sand. It's unusual,' he added thoughtfully.

'What is?'

'To find an orca like this. Normally they die at sea, and just sink into deep water.'

'But this one beached didn't you say?'

'Yeah. But these animals don't usually strand themselves the way some species do. I don't know what it was doing in this bay in the first place. Normally orcas travel in groups of around a dozen or so. I've spent time studying them in Newfoundland and off the west coast up around Vancouver Island. They're not that common around these waters, though sometimes we see

111

them down off the cape. I guess it's possible this one got lost and disoriented because it was sick.'

They had walked back some distance now, to where the beach curved back around towards the jetty in the distance.

Matt was thinking about something Harper had said. 'How long ago did you say you found that whale?'

'Orca,' Harper corrected him. 'Strictly speaking they aren't whales. They belong to the dolphin family.' He thought for a moment. 'It was Tuesday. I came out here early to do some fishing.'

'You happen to see anyone? A guy.' He gave a rough description of Bryan as well as he could remember him.

'Sorry.'

Matt shrugged. 'It was a long shot.'

'I did see a woman that morning though,' Harper said. 'If that helps at all.'

'A woman? Here?'

'About where that jetty is.' Harper pointed. 'Is it important?'

'It could be. What time was this?'

'A little after six maybe. There was some early mist, and I was anchored further along the beach, maybe fifty yards out. I wasn't expecting to see anyone out here. Gave me a start when I saw this figure come out of the trees on to the beach, then she stopped for a moment and stared out across the bay. I don't think she even knew I was there with the mist and all. To tell the truth it was a little strange. It was quiet, and very still, and suddenly there she was.' Harper shrugged a little self-consciously.

'Where did she go, this woman?'

'After a little while she went off along the beach that way.' He gestured towards the point.

Almost unwillingly, a tight feeling in his gut, Matt said, 'Can you describe her?'

'Slim. Good looking, thirties maybe.'

'What colour was her hair?'

'I couldn't tell. She had a sweat top on with a hood, and jeans I think.'

It could have been Ella, Matt thought. But it could have been anyone. 'You said she was on foot. You didn't see a boat?'

'No.'

'Could you have missed it because of the mist?'

'I don't think so. I would have heard it if there had been one. I didn't move from where I was until the mist lifted, and there was no boat then.'

'This woman,' Matt said. 'Would you recognize her if you saw her again?'

Harper thought for a moment, then nodded. 'Yeah, I think I would.'

CHAPTER THIRTEEN

The house where Howard lived had been built by his father nearly sixty years before. In the study, a portrait of the older Larson hung from the wall over the desk. Howard kept it there to remind him that his father had wanted him to stay on the island and dedicate his life to the damn fish plant the old man had built in the thirties.

'This wouldn't be happening if you'd listened to me,' Howard said as he stared up at the wall and took a sip of bourbon. The door was open, and his wife paused on her way past.

'Howard, are you talking to that picture again? He's been dead nearly fifteen years.'

'He's still around, trust me. I can feel the old buzzard looking down on me. I think he gets a kick out of seeing me go under.'

Howard had received bad news from his accountants that afternoon, warning him that if the plant continued losing money at its current rate he would be broke within a year. 'I told him to sell that damn plant fifteen years ago, but he wouldn't listen. You could see then the industry was going to go all to hell one of these days. And I was right wasn't I?'

Angela Larson came into the room and smiled. 'Howard, that isn't why you wanted him to sell and you know it. You just never liked it here, that's all.'

'Yeah, well, who can blame me? I'm forty-seven years old Angela, and look at me. Stuck in this crumbling ruin, sweating and worrying myself into an early grave to keep that plant going. I swear that place will be the death of me. I tell you, one morning you'll wake up and I'll be lying next to you stiff as a goddamned board.'

'You shouldn't worry so much,' Angela murmured absently, already losing interest in their conversation. She placed her hand on his cheek and her eyes drifted towards his desk and the plans for the marina that were spread out across it.

'Come and look at this,' Howard said. 'I want to show you where the yacht club is going to be. And see here, what do you think of that?' He showed her the drawings he'd commissioned. An artist's impression of a supermarket and a parking lot, and then a gas station. 'Know where that is? It's that block of land where the old man wanted to plant pine trees, only he never got around to it. See here, this is all waterfront. I've sectioned it for housing. Twenty-five one acre plots. They should be worth a hundred thousand each the day I win the election. A year from now maybe twice that.'

Howard beamed at the drawings, envisioning them made real, and as he conjured images of buildings and development he saw himself controlling it all, negotiating deals with contractors, building mansions for the wealthy clients who would come to St George for the summer, berthing their yachts and cruisers in the marina.

'You're right, Angela, I never wanted to live here. I mean, look around, what the hell is there here for us? A town that's dying a little more every year. Fishing's all gone to hell. I tell you, without my plans this whole island will be a ghost town one of these days. But you know what? Once things start to change it might not be so bad. Course it'll take a couple of years, but soon as people hear about what we're doing we'll start to attract investors, then it'll really take off. We could build a new house, on the hill looking down on the marina. I've already got the site picked out. The best on the island. There'll be new people to mix with. A whole new crowd hanging out at the yacht club I've got planned. Maybe we'll meet people we could go and visit in the winter.'

Howard paused, the excitement for his vision of the life they would have running away from him. He grinned a little self-consciously, and then he noticed the expression Angela wore. Her smile masked vague boredom, but worse than that she looked pitying.

'It all sounds wonderful,' she said. 'Well, I think I'll go up to bed. I'm kind of tired.' She leaned towards him, brushing his cheek with her lips.

Howard put his hand against her hip, resting it there briefly. The feel of her body, the scent she wore, made his flesh cower. A spasm of intense irritation leapt through him. He knew that Angela had long ago lost her faith in his ability to make his plans real.

'Goodnight,' he said.

'Don't be long.'

'I won't.'

He watched her go, and knew that in five minutes she would be reading some novel, lost in another world, other people's lives, and fifteen minutes after that she would turn out the light. Howard rarely went to bed these days until she was sleeping. He sometimes wondered what she thought of him, of their marriage of eighteen years, of what her life had become. She was from old Massachusetts money, though her family had fallen on hard times when he met her. He'd always felt as if he didn't deserve her, as if he wasn't good enough. She was still beautiful, even after all these years, whereas he had grown fat. He didn't kid himself. He looked in the goddamned mirror sometimes and he hated himself for what he'd become, though he blamed the lousy island for being at least partly to blame.

He'd looked like a good prospect once. Nobody knew then that fishing was a dying industry, that soon the fish would all be gone. He thought she had always liked him, and that in the beginning she'd imagined she could grow to love him one day, but instead, as the money had run out and his aspirations and plans had turned to dust, her feelings for him had become clogged somewhere between like and affection. He didn't move her. In the end she merely felt sorry for him.

Howard had come to realize this gradually, the truth finally taking full shape and settling like a weight over him more than

116

a year ago. Since then he'd been unable to make love to her. She'd always been reserved when it came to the physical side of things, strait-laced even. In the early days when they were in bed together he felt as if she indulged him, remaining largely unaffected herself. She'd never once commented on the fact that they no longer had sex. It was as if she hadn't noticed. Or if she had, she welcomed it enough not to risk upsetting things by drawing attention to the fact.

As she left the room, Howard experienced a familiar hollow absence of feeling in his groin. He turned disconsolately back to his plans. If he failed to make them happen it would be the end of him, he knew. The plant would eventually bankrupt him, and another failure would sap his spirit beyond redemption. He would never be able to make Angela proud. There would be no dinners with wealthy friends who would build houses on the waterfront on land they had bought from him, people she would feel comfortable with. They would never stand together on the terrace of their new home, looking down on the lights below, on everything he had made happen. They would never go inside together, Angela taking his hand as she led him with a smile towards their bedroom.

Howard poured himself another drink and thought about Ella. She aroused conflicting feelings in him. On the one hand he admired her. She was attractive. More than attractive, she was stunning in a way, and she had balls, he'd give her that. He'd even mused, once or twice, that had he been married to somebody like her, perhaps his life would have been different. She would have supported him, encouraged him, rooted for him all the way, unlike Angela who merely smiled without conviction at his ideas. Wasn't that a fucking hoot?

But Ella could be his downfall. She'd made people scared about letting in the big bad outside world if the marina went ahead. Howard couldn't understand why people were afraid of change. That was the whole point. Nothing stayed the same for ever. All of Ella's talk about the islanders themselves ending up as second class citizens in their own back yard, delivering pizza and pumping gas for rich people had hit a sensitive spot.

St Georgians were touchy about such things. She had them thinking that the newcomers would take over and start running things. She was probably right, but so what if the islanders mostly ended up doing some service job, what was wrong with that anyway? At least it was regular work.

Howard reached into a drawer and took out some sheets of paper that were clipped together. Each sheet had two columns of names. Those who he knew would vote for him, and those who would vote for Ella. The names were a cross section he'd canvassed, enough to give him a feel for the way the election would go. On Ella's side some names had been crossed out and written in on his own side. People were switching horses. Small towns were a funny thing, and Ella's support had always been tenuous. The people who backed her were the young and the old, and the old resented change, but they resented women fishermen almost as much. Ella had lived here all her life, long enough to counter that prejudice, but now with all the talk going around, people were starting to turn against her. His little trick with the posters had helped, set tongues wagging. If the election had been tomorrow he guessed he'd have won. But the vote wasn't for another ten days, and even in Sanctuary that was a long time in politics. Maybe by then people would give her the benefit of the doubt, or they'd simply begin to forget about Bryan. Enough of them anyway. The bottom line, Howard concluded, was that there were a hell of a lot of ifs and maybes; way too many for him to feel comfortable. And there was too much riding on this vote for him to take any chances.

For a while he pondered this fact, and then he looked at his watch and emptied his glass. As he left the house he paused, struck by the notion that he was about to step over a line. It caused him to hesitate. He wavered, and then he thought about what would happen to his life if he lost the vote, and he decided that sometimes the stakes were simply too high to flinch from a little unpleasantness.

Jake was sitting in front of the TV when someone came to the front door. His wife answered it, and when she came back she said it was Howard Larson. Jake got up, wondering what had brought Howard here.

'I felt like I should come and see how you're doing,' Howard said. 'I heard about Carl Johnson.'

'What about him?'

Howard blinked uncertainly. 'I mean I heard what he saw. It's a terrible thing.'

Jake didn't say anything. He didn't like Howard, never had. It had been Bryan's idea to buy the land on the shore where Howard wanted to build his marina. Jake hadn't been so sure. Making a fat profit on the deal was fine, but the downside was it meant getting into bed with the likes of Howard.

'I just wanted you to know I'm right behind you,' Howard said, filling the silence. He looked as if he was waiting to be asked in, and reluctantly Jake showed him through to the kitchen. He opened a beer and threw a questioning look at Howard.

'Want one of these?'

'Thanks.'

'Sit down if you want.'

Howard sat on one of the old chairs by the table. Jake gave him a beer and leaned against the counter and drank from his bottle. He waited.

Howard took a sip from his beer. 'Like I said, I'm with you on this. Ella ought to be in jail if you ask me.'

Jake took a mouthful of beer, and wondered what the fuck Howard wanted. He was starting to get a headache. Lately he'd been having them a lot. He massaged the back of his neck absently.

'I guess there's no point in relying on the law around here.'

'What?' Jake's headaches had been getting worse. Sometimes his vision started to blur a little, everything going a little dull and grainy. Howard was talking but he hadn't heard everything he said. 'Come again,' he said.

Howard blinked, and a flash of irritation marked his expression, but then it was gone. 'I was just saying I don't know if anyone could blame you if you took things into your own hands.'

Jake was struck by an odd note, and Howard looked kind of

nervous. What the hell was he talking about? The pain in Jake's head had become a dull throb. It affected his hearing, so that Howard's voice sounded strange, unnatural. He wished Howard would leave. He needed to lie down somewhere dark.

'If it wasn't for that lawyer friend of hers she'd probably be in jail.'

'What lawyer?'

'Matt Jones. They're pretty friendly those two. You know how these lawyers are, show them a smoking gun and they'll try and convince you it's a cigarette lighter.'

Jake drank some more beer. He had no idea what Howard was talking about.

'It's come to a fine thing when a man's brother is murdered and nothing gets done about it, that's all. Like I said, I doubt anybody could blame you for wanting to fix things yourself.'

Howard's voice sounded husky, as if his throat was dry. He took a drink and licked his lips.

'What the hell did you come here for?' Jake said at last, his patience exhausted. 'Is there something you're trying to say to me, because if there is why don't you just come the fuck out with it.'

Howard looked startled. He didn't say anything, then he got up. 'Maybe I should leave.'

Jake wasn't about to argue and he showed Howard to the door. When he'd gone he slammed it shut. In the kitchen he saw that Howard had barely touched his beer. He went upstairs, and lay down in the dark. Downstairs he could hear the drone of the TV. His headache pulsed. He thought of something Howard had said. Nobody would blame him if he took things into his own hands.

Howard drove back towards his house, unnerved by his meeting with Jake. The man wasn't right in the head in his opinion. He doubted Jake had heard more than a fraction of what he'd said. Howard frowned. Maybe that wasn't such a bad thing anyway. He experienced a vague relief. Perhaps there were better ways of fixing Ella.

CHAPTER FOURTEEN

Ella signed the receipt that Art Turner handed to her. He watched her, his thin face looking more pinched than normal, and when she handed back his pad and pencil he tore her off a copy and grinned, showing yellowed teeth.

'Can I get a cheque now?' Ella asked.

'Right now? I don't know Ella.'

'I'd appreciate it, Art.'

He hesitated, then shrugged. 'What the hell. Sure you can.' He opened a drawer in his battered old desk and took out a cheque book.

While he wrote out the amount Ella looked out the window of his office to the dock beyond. Art was one of four lobster dealers on the island. He acted as a middleman, buying the fishermen's catches, which he then packed up and sent off to the mainland wholesalers who again sold on to the stores and restaurants. Normally Art paid out at the end of each week, but Ella had been dealing with him long enough now that he was willing to make exceptions. He tore off her cheque and handed it over.

'There you go.'

'Thanks.'

Ella looked at the amount on the cheque, and thought she would at least be able to pay Gordon, and settle her account at the store, but that was about it. She had already missed a payment on the *Santorini* and her credit was stretched at the bank.

'Everything okay?' Art asked.

'Sure. It's fine. I was just thinking about something.'

'The market's good right now. That's top dollar you know.'

'I know that Art.' She smiled. Never in all the time she'd dealt with Art had he tried to cheat her out of a cent. 'I guess I could always use more, that's all,' she added ruefully.

'I can take everything you can bring me,' Art said.

'Yeah,' Ella said frowning.

'I heard about your trouble with Jake. There's talk he's been messing with your traps.'

'Well, somebody has.'

Art looked at his feet. He shifted uncomfortably and when he spoke again he did so without meeting her eye. 'Don't you worry about the talk that's going around. That's just people who don't know any better. I did business with your dad for a long time. I remember when you were just a little girl.' He broke off, his face colouring. 'If there's anything I can do, Ella. I mean, I could maybe see my way to an advance or something like that.'

'Thanks, Art. I appreciate it. But I'll get by,' Ella said, surprised and touched by his offer.

'Well, anytime.'

'I really appreciate it.'

On the way to the bank Ella paused at the corner of the square. Matt's office was close by and she wavered uncertainly. Just a few weeks earlier she had felt that her life had begun to take a new course, one she welcomed, albeit cautiously. It had been a long time since she had felt anything for a man. After her marriage had ended she had dated a few people, but none of the men she'd been out with had stirred anything within her. She'd gone through the motions, not wanting to be thought of as unapproachable, but though she'd waited to feel something, some spark that went beyond merely friendship, it hadn't happened. St George was a small place, and as time passed there were fewer eligible men. She began to wonder if she would be alone for ever, which was partly why she'd started seeing somebody who lived on a nearby island. He was a widower, and had two young children, and their affair had lasted for several months until he had asked her to marry him. She'd known immediately that she couldn't, that she didn't love him enough, and he had seen it in her eyes and had never asked her again. In a way it had hurt her almost as much to think that she might never be in love, as it had hurt him to realize she couldn't share his feelings. Shortly afterwards she had stopped seeing him, and there had been nobody since then.

Meeting Matt again had made her see that perhaps she had not yet used up all her chances. At first she hadn't known if her quickening pulse when they were together was just an echo of a young girl's crush. But as they got to know each other she found that in his company time passed quickly, and that she had a good time. They seemed to have that connection which so rarely happens, when conversation flows easily. Afterwards she would try to remember what they had discussed and it would seem as if they'd talked about everything and nothing; snippets of the past both general and personal, of observation and opinion, exchanging anecdotes that often made them smile, but sometimes were sad too. And all the time, over coffee, or as they walked together after a chance meeting, or when Matt turned up at the dock, a slow realization of possibility had begun to awaken within her. It was the knowledge that she could fall in love, that her future didn't have to comprise a cold bed at night and an empty wishful longing that left her feeling that one day, when her mother had gone, she would be all alone in the world.

But events had dashed her hopes like the callous sea would a storm-tossed wreck. Rifts between them had been exposed, differences that couldn't be explained, and once again she faced at best a lonely future.

And now even the rest of her life was threatened too, everything she cherished, that she had never imagined would change. No matter what happened in her personal life she would always love the sea and the island. The landscape was her refuge, the solitude of the woods and the bays and coves that dotted the coastline, the ocean that gave her a living and wore a thousand different costumes, changing colour with the seasons, with the days, the passing of a cloud even. She respected the ocean, the cycle of life both in it and around it, and she had always known that if she treated it well, if she took only what it could afford to lose, it would protect her.

She had never been tempted to leave St George. For all its faults, the insularity of small communities where families all knew each other and all about each other, the good things outweighed the bad. Nobody ever went hungry on the island. If a man lost his job and couldn't find another, his neighbours would help him out. There might be disputes over fishing rights, and sometimes these turned into petty feuds, but if a man lost his boat in a storm, if he couldn't make his living and there was no money to buy another, then people would help him build one and the debt would be paid off over as many years as it took.

Howard Larson wanted to bring change to the island. His marina and the houses and developments that would follow would bring the world to St George. No matter how he tried to sell it, money was at the root of it. And with money came greed and envy, and close behind that came crime and drugs and all the other ills of modern society where people cared about themselves and nothing else. The meadows would be dug up for roads and housing, the woods cut down to build mansions, the coastal waters clogged with pleasure craft and the pollution of wet bikes. Ella had thought she could stop Howard and his supporters like the Rodericks. People who took and never replenished. It was ironic, she thought now, that when he was alive Bryan had tried to wreck her chances of winning the election, and had failed, but in death he might succeed.

Even his intimidation hadn't swayed her from her resolve. A month ago, she'd been walking home in the dark, when she heard footsteps behind her. It wasn't the first time it had happened, but that night she was taking a shortcut past the church, down an alley with a wall on one side, and the overhanging branches of dripping trees on the other. It had rained earlier, and plumes of vapour rose like gas from the ground in the yellow pool of a streetlight. She hurried on through the darkness and the footsteps hurried with her and as she rounded a corner and stopped, instead of stopping too they kept coming. Her heart beat like a drum, and she turned to run but before she could a hand was clasped around her mouth and she felt herself dragged backwards.

She'd struggled, but an arm encircled her body, pinning her arms. He didn't say anything, but he hadn't needed to. She could smell him. She knew it was Bryan. He increased the pressure until she thought he would crack her ribs and suddenly she understood and she stopped struggling. He relaxed his hold, just a little, but still she was pinned to him. She could feel the length of his body pressed into her back, his arm against her breasts and she felt helpless. His male smell, his size and strength overpowered her, and she knew that was the point. He was warning her. She felt an urgent hardness. A wave of fear and revulsion swept over her.

Then abruptly he pushed her away and as she stumbled to her knees he turned and vanished and by the time she was on her feet, trembling with the aftermath, he was gone. But she was sure it had been him.

The memory of that night made her shudder. Somebody brushed past her and apologized, and she wondered how long she'd been standing on the corner. On the wall beside her was a poster she hadn't noticed before, the remnant of one of her own campaign posters. Somebody had done a poor job tearing it down, but it was still possible to read some of the words scrawled in ink along the bottom 'She'll Kill You'. She reached out and ripped it down, then walked off in the direction of the bank.

After Ella had deposited her cheque she went back to the *Santorini*. When she returned, Gordon was finishing cleaning down the deck. She handed him the money she owed him, and he looked at the bills, then took half and offered the rest back to her.

'What's this?'

'I don't need it right now.'

'You take it. It's yours.' She closed his fist around it, and when he looked as if he would protest she held his hand tight around the money. 'I appreciate what you're doing. Really I do. But there's no need. Take the money.'

He glanced towards the empty berth where the *Seawind* was normally tied up. The day before, as a precaution, Ella and Gordon had moved some of their traps further out on the shelf than normal for this time of year.

'Don't worry,' she said, guessing what was on his mind. 'Listen, why don't you get going. I'll finish up here and I'll see you in the morning.'

He started to object, but then focused on something behind her and he started to get up in a hurry. 'Okay. I was about finished here anyway.'

Ella looked back along the dock, and saw Gordon's father approaching, on his way home from a shift at the processing plant where he'd worked since selling his boat a few years ago. She and Alan Neelon had always been on reasonable terms, though since he'd given up fishing to work at the plant for a regular wage, he'd changed. He seemed embittered by life, and she wondered if he resented the fact that she had managed to keep going where he had failed. Perhaps doubly so since Gordon had come to work for her.

'I'd better go.' Gordon clambered ashore and went to meet his father.

Ella called out and raised her hand. 'Hello Alan.'

The older man barely nodded to her, then abruptly jerked his head at Gordon. 'Come on. Your mother will have supper waiting.'

Gordon glanced back at her, his embarrassment clear.

'I'll see you tomorrow,' she called, as if she hadn't noticed anything amiss.

Alan Neelon glared at her, then came back towards her. 'I won't have Gordon working for nothing, Ella. You still owe him for last week.'

'I just paid him everything I owe him,' Ella said.

'That's right Dad.' Gordon showed him the wad of bills.

Rather than satisfy Neelon the sight of the money seemed to

antagonize him. 'You paid him this week. What about next week, and the one after that?'

'I've never let anyone down that I owed money to in my life.'

'I could get him work at the plant. It's regular money. Maybe you won't be able to keep him on with you for ever.'

'I'll admit things haven't been easy,' Ella said, 'but we'll get by. But it's up to Gordon. If he wants to leave I won't stop him.'

'I'm staying,' Gordon said without hesitation.

Neelon glanced at his son, then looked back at Ella. He seemed to be struggling with something he wanted to say. In the end he let it go and turned wordlessly away. Gordon threw her an apologetic look. He caught up with his dad and as she watched them Ella saw Gordon say something that made the older man pause. They started arguing, and Alan Neelon looked angrily back in her direction. She watched until they were out of sight. She could guess what they were arguing about. Alan Neelon didn't want his son working for somebody who might have killed a man.

Later, she locked up the *Santorini* and walked into town. She picked up some groceries in the store on the way home. At the checkout in the market, Jenny Pope smiled and took her money.

'How are you Ella?'

She looked up and caught sight of her reflection in the window. Her expression was deeply lined with worry. 'I guess I've had better days.'

Jenny handed back her change, and for a fraction of a second Ella felt a subtle pressure on her hand.

'Don't let the bastards get you down,' Jenny said in a low conspiratorial whisper, and she winked.

'I won't,' Ella said, buoyed by a small gesture which neverthe- less meant a lot. 'Thanks.'

Outside, she crossed the street and went to the post office across the square. At the bottom of the steps she paused for a moment, looking in her bag for the letter she wanted to mail. When she found it she looked up, and almost collided with somebody coming down the steps.

Ella started to apologize, but the words died on her lips as she found herself face to face with Kate Little. For perhaps a second or two they stared at each other, surprise being overtaken by other, more confusing emotions. For an instant Ella was back in the woods beside the cove where she'd glimpsed Kate in the darkness. A jumble of words collided and refused to form a coherent phrase in Ella's mind.

Kate recovered first. 'Excuse me,' she said quietly, then passed by.

Ella stared after her for a moment, her heart beating wildly while the blood drained from her face. At last she turned and went up the steps and vanished inside the cool dark space of the building.

Across the street, Matt sat in his car. He was struck by the tableau he was witnessing, the expressions on the faces of both women. It was unexpected, and somehow jarring, as if for an instant everything stopped still. Then it was past, and the two women parted and went their separate ways. Ben Harper sat in the seat next to him and peered intently through the windshield.

'Is that the woman you saw in the cove?' Matt asked.

Ben nodded. 'That's her.'

'You're sure?'

'Positive.'

Matt told himself that it didn't prove anything one way or the other, but he couldn't quell the rush of doubts and the sinking feeling that overtook him. Just the fact that Ella had been in the cove the morning after Carl Johnson had seen her raised questions. He recalled what Baxter had said about Bryan's house, the lack of prints, how it seemed as if somebody had cleaned up recently. Is that what Ella had been doing?

Ella had gone, and the other woman was getting into a Mercedes wagon. From the way she looked Matt guessed she was a summer resident. She seemed out of place, in her faded jeans and designer shirt, her swept back, raven coloured hair. He noticed Ben was watching her too.

'You know her?' Matt asked.

Ben shrugged. 'I just saw her that one time.'

It took Matt a moment or two to realize what he meant. He looked back as the woman in the Mercedes drove away. '*That* was the woman you saw in the cove?'

'Sure,' Ben said. 'Who did you think I meant?'

CHAPTER FIFTEEN

Matt took the turn off the main road that led out along the point. He slowed as he passed the house his parents had once owned. It was set back among the trees, and there was a car out front and a child's bike lying on the grass. He drove on, following the road as it ran close to the top of the ridge, dipping and curving with the contours of the land, edged with woods of maple and cedar that sometimes grew in close and cast the road in perpetual shadow. But now and then the woods fell back to make clearings where sunlight filled the open spaces with drowsy midday heat. At one such clearing Matt pulled over and walked to a knoll where a wooden bench faced the view. The ground fell away steeply to woods below, and then to Stillwater Cove. The water in the bay reflected the myriad greens of the trees all around, ruffled by an offshore breeze. It looked like a water-colour, splotches of paint on a canvas. The cove was deserted, devoid of any evidence of human life. On the far side of the bay it was possible to just about make out the dark shape that was the beached orca, and specks of fluttering birds greedily mobbing the carcass, but there was no sign of Ben Harper's boat.

The air carried the faint taste of salt. Out beyond the entrance to the cove the line of white foam that marked the reef was clearly visible. Beyond that the ocean glittered, seemingly endless. It seemed like a lifetime ago that Matt and Paulie had roamed these woods looking for squirrels, lying on the coarse sand in the cove during the summer. For a while Matt was lost in his memories. Snapshots of incidents. The long ago echo of childhood.

He went back to his car and pulled back on to the road, and several minutes later he drove through an open wooden gate and followed the driveway to the house owned by Kate and Evan Little. The house was wooden, built in Victorian style with turrets and ornate trim, four storeys high and freshly painted white with black shutters on all the windows. It stood in maybe an acre of lawns studded with oaks and maples. Parked outside was the Mercedes station wagon Matt had seen the day before. He pulled over and looked up at the house. He'd spent a few hours asking around about Kate Little, and what he'd quickly discovered was that her reputation preceded her. Her husband was some kind of wealthy businessman who was disabled and rarely if ever appeared in town. They came to the island each summer, the husband sometimes going back for weeks at a time to New York where they normally lived. His wife had a reputation for drinking, and more besides. When Matt asked Jane Nelstrum at the bakery if she ever saw Kate Little in there, Jane had glanced towards her husband serving along the counter.

'She comes in a couple of times a week. But he always serves her. Seems like he moves faster when she's around for some reason.'

'Don't listen to her, Matt,' Arnold Nelstrum said. 'She's a nice woman, that's all.'

Jane Nelstrum sniffed. 'Depends what you call nice.'

He got more, similarly oblique comments the more he asked around. It seemed that Kate Little was less popular with the women in town than with some of the men.

He got out of his car and went to the front door and pressed the bell. When Kate Little appeared, she offered a faint quizzical smile.

'Hello?'

She was wearing tan pants and a cream shirt tied above her waist. Her hair was pulled back and held in place with a wide black band and she carried a bunch of flowers in one hand and a pair of scissors in the other. There were faint lines at the

131

corners of her eyes, but it was the colour of them that was arresting. They were deep blue, almost violet and the contrast with the rich darkness of her hair made a startling feature.

'Mrs Little?'

'Yes?'

'Hi, I'm Matt Jones. I'm a lawyer. I wondered if I could speak to you for a few moments?'

She took his proffered hand, and her grip was firm but brief. 'A lawyer?'

'That's right.'

She hesitated, as if waiting for him to elaborate, then she stood aside. 'Come in.' She led the way through to a large airy room. Open doors led out on to a terrace at the back of the house. She put down her flowers on a table next to a half empty glass of what looked like orange juice.

'So, how can I help you Mr Jones?'

'I'm looking into the disappearance of a local man who lived in the cove not far from here. He was last seen a week ago and I'm kind of checking to see if anybody remembers anything that might be useful.'

Kate picked up a pack of cigarettes and lit one. She inhaled and blew a stream of smoke towards the open door. 'The police have already been around asking about that. A few days ago.'

'I know,' Matt said. 'And I don't want to take up any more of your time than I need to, but I'd really appreciate it if you could spare me a couple of minutes.'

'All right. Though I can't tell you much.'

'Thanks, I appreciate it Mrs Little. Is your husband home? I'd like to talk to you both if I could.'

She studied him for a moment, then inclined her head fractionally. 'Come this way.'

He followed her back to the hall and down a passage. Matt noted the scent she wore, the deceivingly casual but no doubt expensive clothes. Her hair reached past her shoulders, and framed her smoothly planed cheeks, partly masking the long curve of her neck. He tried to guess her age, and figured maybe mid-thirties to early forties. It was difficult to tell.

'You don't sound like an islander Mr Jones,' she said conversationally.

'I'm not really, but when I was young my family spent summers here. My parents had a house on the point. I just moved here a few months ago.'

Kate stopped at a door. 'This is where my husband works.' She knocked and a voice answered from within.

Inside was a large room that had been converted for use as an office. At a desk sat a man in a wheelchair working at a computer. There were several other computers on a long table, along with printers and a fax machine and a scanner. The man had close cropped grey hair, and hollowed cheeks. At the sound of the door he looked over, pausing in his work. His face was pale, and his eyes dark and sunken, though they glittered with intensity.

'Who the hell are you?'

'This is Mr Jones. He's a lawyer. He'd like to ask us some questions.' To Matt she said, 'My husband, Evan.'

There was a pause, then Evan Little approached, the whine of his electric chair loud in the silence. He stopped but didn't offer his hand.

'You'll have to forgive my manners. We don't get many visitors up here.'

'I'm sorry to interrupt you,' Matt said.

'I'm a little unsociable these days. I get absorbed in my work. As you can see, this is where I spend a lot of my time.' He gestured around.

Matt noticed a bed in one corner with an elaborate pulley positioned over it. The sheets were pulled back as if it had been recently slept in.

'What kind of work do you do?' Matt asked.

'I own a software company. These days I pay people to run it for me, but I like to keep in touch with what's happening. The business side of things has never really interested me. I'm more into the design aspect. What kind of questions is it you want to ask anyway, Mr Jones?'

'As I explained to your wife, I'm investigating the disappearance of a local man, Bryan Roderick. He lived in the cove, which means he was practically a neighbour of yours. I know you've already spoken to the police but I wondered if there was anything you might have remembered since then.'

Little turned his chair and went to a table where there was a glass of what looked like whisky. He picked it up and took a mouthful. He looked at Kate as he spoke.

'We don't mix with our neighbours, Mr Jones. I'll tell you the same thing we told the police. We never heard of this man. As you are no doubt aware, we're summer residents here. We keep pretty much to ourselves.'

Kate stood by the window, gazing outside with the distracted air of somebody half listening to a conversation that didn't concern her.

'Were you both home last Monday night?' Matt said.

'Was that the night he went missing, this Roderick person?'

'That was the last time anybody saw him. Did you hear anything unusual that night? Or see anything at all?'

'What kind of thing?'

'There was a dragger out beyond the cove that night. The skipper thought he heard a shot around two fifteen.'

'We would have been asleep at that time.'

Matt glanced at the bed across the room and Little followed his look.

'Sometimes I sleep here if I'm working late. But I didn't that night if that's what you're wondering.' There was an edge to his tone.

'You didn't hear anything either then, Mrs Little?' Matt asked. She turned away from the window, and she and her husband exchanged glances. Matt thought she appeared uncertain, while Evan Little had a sardonic gleam in his eye, as if he was privately amused.

'No.'

'Do you mind if I ask if you sleep in this room often?' Matt said, turning back to Evan Little.

'Yes I do mind Mr Jones. What does that have to do with anything anyway?'

'It's just that you seem certain that you didn't sleep here on

Monday night, I wondered if there was any particular reason you remember that.'

'I don't need a particular reason. Not that it's any of your business Mr Jones, but being confined to this chair hasn't affected my brain in any way. You think because my legs aren't much use the rest of me isn't either?'

'That isn't what I meant.'

Little stared at Matt. He drained what was left in his glass, then abruptly turned his chair and went to a drawer in his desk where he scrabbled around and took out several bottles of pills. He counted out a handful and tossed them back. Kate watched, but though Matt wondered if the pills, whatever they were, ought to be mixed with alcohol, she didn't make any move to stop him.

'You know what people think?' Little said, sounding strained though calmer. He'd started to sweat and he gripped his chair with both hands. 'They think being in a chair has turned my mind to mush. Like it's my brain that's useless rather than my damn legs. They talk about me as if I can't understand what they're saying. Even when I'm in the same room they ask Kate how I'm doing.' He uttered a short derisory laugh. 'Even the doctors do it. "How is he?" they say. Ask me dammit! I'm sitting right here!'

'Evan . . .' Kate said, sounding concerned.

He waved her off. 'I'm okay.' He looked back at Matt. 'There's nothing else we can tell you about this man,' he said curtly, then he went back to a screen and started typing on a keyboard as if Matt had already left.

Matt figured he'd outstayed his welcome. 'Well, thanks for your time.' As he followed Kate to the door, Little called out to him, his tone abruptly civil again.

'Sorry we couldn't be more help, Mr Jones.'

Matt thought about the scene he'd witnessed when Kate and Ella had met outside the post office, and how he'd been struck by the looks they had exchanged. There had been something about them that had seemed off key. He couldn't put his finger on it now, but it was as if each of them hadn't known what to say or do. Like people who normally avoided each other, suddenly meeting unexpectedly and not knowing how to deal with the situation.

'You have to forgive my husband,' Kate said at the door. 'He's often in pain and he has to take a lot of medication. Sometimes it affects his moods.'

'That's okay, I understand. Mrs Little, can I ask you something. Do you happen to know a woman called Ella Young?'

There was a flicker of recognition in her expression, but then it was gone. 'I don't think so.'

'Maybe you've run into her without knowing it. She's blonde, in her thirties, she owns a lobster boat called the *Santorini*?'

Kate shook her head. 'I know very few people on the island, though the name does sound familiar.'

'Perhaps you've seen posters around town. She's running in the mayoral election.'

'That must be it.'

'But you've never met?'

'Never.'

'Well, it was just a thought.' He started to leave, but once out the door he stopped as if something had occurred to him. 'By the way, do you ever walk in the woods around here? Maybe down to the cove?'

'Sometimes.'

'How about last Tuesday. Were you in the cove early that morning, say around six?'

She hesitated, and Matt had the feeling she was weighing up which way to answer.

'Yes I was.'

'Did you see anybody that morning?'

'No.'

Matt studied her for a second or two, trying to decide whether he believed her. She met his gaze calmly and said nothing more.

'Well, thanks anyway for your time, Mrs Little.' He shook her hand.

On the drive back to town he pondered Kate and Evan Little.

He decided that he didn't like the husband, and he didn't believe either of them.

At the police department Matt asked to see Chief Baxter and when Baxter appeared they went through to his office, where Baxter indicated Matt should take a seat. Baxter himself sat down behind his desk.

'What can I do for you, Matt?'

'I wondered if anything new had turned up in this Bryan Roderick business.'

Baxter took a pack of gum from a drawer in his desk, and offered Matt a stick. While he chewed he tilted back his chair and tapped a pencil against his thumb nail. 'Well, I called off the search, for now anyway. I can't keep men out there looking for ever.'

'You don't have any new evidence then?'

'I did get a report back from the lab on the mainland on the prints we sent in.' He picked up a faxed sheet of paper among the mess on his desk. 'Ella's didn't match the one we found on the faucet.'

Matt was relieved to hear it, though he'd guessed as much. Had there been a match he imagined he would have heard about it before now. 'So where does that leave you?'

'Good question,' Baxter said. 'Nowhere much as far as I can tell.'

Matt thought Baxter looked unhappy about the situation. 'You think he's dead don't you?' he ventured.

'Uh huh. I guess I do. Bryan wasn't the type to just up and vanish without a word to anyone. Plus nothing's gone from his house. Clothes are still there, toothbrush, shaving gear, his truck. Doesn't make sense he'd just leave without any of those things. Plus his bank account hasn't been touched. The only thing I can say for sure that we can't account for is his rifle.'

'Which points to the possibility that maybe he went out hunting and had some kind of accident.'

Baxter got up and went to a map on the wall. He pointed out the areas that had been searched, which extended way beyond

137

the cove. 'I don't think he could've gone any further than this on foot. Even if he had a reason to. Course, even with dogs we might've missed him if he wasn't able to make himself known. But I don't think so. Bryan wasn't much of a hunter, but when he did go out he went back in these hills here. There's nothing much around the cove.'

'You're saying you think somebody killed him.'

Baxter spread his hands. 'Unless you've got a better theory.'

Matt shook his head. 'I don't.'

'The next thing I guess you're gonna ask me is if I think Ella was the one that killed him.'

'Is that what you think?'

Baxter frowned, and leaned forward, his chair legs hitting the floor with a thump. He leaned on the desk, and started tapping the pencil against his chin.

'I'm not asking as her lawyer by the way. Ella kind of fired me.'

Baxter raised his eyebrows. 'If you're not her lawyer, what are you?' he asked.

'A friend.'

'She know you're here?'

Matt shook his head. 'I don't know what she'd say if she did.'

'Well,' Baxter said after a while. 'I'll answer your question. I don't think Ella would kill anybody in any kind of premeditated way. She's got a temper, and she's pretty tough when she has to be. I guess she'd never get by doing what she does otherwise. But she's a good person.'

Matt waited, guessing there was more.

'I've been thinking about this a lot,' Baxter went on. 'It could be whatever happened to Bryan was an accident. Him and Ella didn't exactly get on, we know that much. And we know they had a fight that night. We also know that Ella went out on her boat not long afterwards. Let's say that she was fishing around the cove, and for some reason she went in there and went ashore. There's plenty of places around the point she could tie up. Maybe she found some of her traps cut or stripped that night and she figured it was Bryan who did it. They get in

138

another fight, and somehow or other Bryan ends up getting shot. I don't know how. An accident, who knows? Ella panics, and she gets his body on to her boat and takes him out to the channel and weighs him down and puts him over the side.'

As Matt had listened he'd admitted to himself that he'd imagined a similar scenario himself. But after Ben Harper had said it was Kate Little he'd seen in the cove that morning he'd started to wonder what other possibilities there might be. What had Sally Brewster said, about Ella needing to get in line if she'd planned to kill Bryan? It had been a flippant remark, but perhaps behind it lay a grain of truth. And now, as Baxter had laid out his ideas, Matt started to think that certain pieces didn't fit.

'Ella told me Bryan had been intimidating her, is that possible?'

'I'd say so. Bryan liked to think he had a way with women. He was a good talker if he wanted to be, and I suppose he was the sort of guy some women seem to like. But he had another side. A pretty nasty side.'

'How nasty?' Matt asked, thinking about Ella's story of phone calls and footsteps following her at night.

'Bryan and Jake, they've never minded taking food from somebody's mouth if it got them what they wanted,' Baxter said. 'The pair of them ran foul of a few people over the years, and got in some pretty ugly fights now and then. That's how Ella started having run-ins with them, when they fished her spots, or fouled her gear. But I guess this election made things a lot worse. If Ella went into the cove that night I could see Bryan doing something stupid like pulling a rifle on her. Maybe to get her back for doing the same thing to him earlier. Howard's marina means there's a lot more at stake than just a few lobsters.'

'Which is what bothers me. It doesn't make sense for Ella to deliberately go into the cove and pick another fight with Bryan. She's not stupid, and she knows what he can be like. I just can't see her doing that,' Matt reasoned, and he could see Baxter was thinking about that. 'But okay, let's suppose she did, and there was some kind of shooting. How did she get his body back to her boat? How much did he weigh do you think?'

139

'Maybe two twenty or so.'

'Big guy. No way could Ella move him alone. But even if somehow she managed that, so what then? She went back and cleaned up the house, got rid of any evidence of a fight, or that she was there? But the only print you found wasn't hers. Doesn't mean anything one way or the other. But it's an inconsistency. Then there's the gun. Ella says she lost her rifle, but Bryan's gun is missing as well. That doesn't add up. I guess she didn't shoot him with both of them. You see what I mean? Too many things that don't make sense. But most of all it comes back to what you said to begin with. You don't believe Ella could kill anybody in a deliberate, premeditated way. And for her to have gone into that cove, I think that's exactly what she would have had to have had in her mind.' Matt shook his head. 'I don't buy it.'

Matt didn't add that despite all that he'd just said, he felt that Ella knew more than she had admitted.

Baxter tapped his pencil a few more times, then pointed it towards Matt. 'There's still the question of what Ella was doing that night. She says she was fishing, but I don't buy that either. I talked to Tom Spencer about sending a diver down where Carl Johnson saw her that night.'

Tom Spencer, Matt knew, was the harbourmaster. 'And?'

Baxter shrugged. 'There's a channel runs off the island. According to Tom it's way too deep for any diver. Only thing that'd do it would be a submersible, but my budget doesn't run to that kind of thing. But let's say that you're right. If Ella didn't kill Bryan, whether she meant to or not, what the hell happened to him?'

'Maybe I can help you there.'

Baxter's eyes widened. 'How?'

'For the moment let's assume that Bryan was killed, but Ella had nothing to do with it. So somebody else did, right?'

'Okay,' Baxter said cautiously.

'Who else might have had a reason for wanting Bryan dead? Motive, it's always the first place to start looking for a suspect.'

'That doesn't help a lot. Plenty of people might not have

liked Bryan too much, but that doesn't mean they had a reason to kill him.'

'Most murder victims are killed by people who know them well,' Matt said. 'It's a fact. Often it's the result of a domestic dispute between husband and wife. Or a guy and his girlfriend. Who was Bryan seeing lately? You said he liked women.'

'Last I recall he was seeing Jill Peterson. They were going around for three or four months I guess. But that was in the winter.'

'Maybe you should start with her.'

Baxter shook his head. 'She left the island a couple of months back. Got a job in Portland I think. Far as I know she hasn't been back.'

'Anybody else you can think of?'

'Not right now. I could ask around.'

'How about if he was seeing somebody he didn't want people to know about. Somebody who was married?'

'It's possible,' Baxter said. He gazed at Matt, his eyes narrowing a fraction as he thought. He picked up the pencil again and started tapping his chin. 'How come I get the feeling all this is leading somewhere?'

'Okay, I have a possibility,' Matt admitted. 'It isn't based on much right now, except a hunch, but sometimes that's as good a place to start as anywhere.' He outlined what Ben Harper had told him about seeing a woman in the cove early Tuesday morning. 'Does the name Kate Little mean anything to you?'

Baxter stopped tapping with the pencil, and it remained poised in mid-air. After a moment he said cautiously, 'What about her?'

'She could've known Bryan. She lives above the cove. When I asked her she claimed she didn't, but I don't know, I felt she wasn't telling me everything.'

'You talked to her?'

'This afternoon. I get the feeling she and her husband aren't exactly close, and she's a good-looking woman. The kind married women don't like as much as their husbands do. That's the

141

impression I got when I mentioned her name a couple of times around town.'

Belatedly Matt saw that Baxter's attitude had changed. He leaned across his desk and suddenly he sounded a little pissed off. 'You ought to know better than to listen to people talk, and you had no reason to go bothering them. There's no evidence to connect Kate Little to this thing.'

'Well, maybe not. But there was no harm talking to them. They might have remembered something they heard the night Bryan disappeared. I could be on the wrong track with Kate Little, but what I'm saying is if you think somebody killed Bryan you should be looking at other people besides Ella.'

'Yeah, well I'll look into it.' Baxter rose to his feet. 'The thing we ought to get straight here though, is I don't want you going around questioning people that we've already talked to. I had some officers call at all the houses on the point. Nobody heard a thing because they were all asleep. I could have told you that.'

Baxter went around his desk and opened his office door and Matt took the hint.

'I think it would be a good idea if you let me do the investigating around here from now on,' Baxter said, his expression unreadable. 'This really doesn't concern you now anyway, does it?'

Matt started to comment that Baxter apparently hadn't thought so ten minutes ago, but he decided that maybe he should just let it go. As he left he could feel Baxter watching him all the way across the reception office and out through the doors, and it wasn't an entirely comfortable sensation.

CHAPTER SIXTEEN

The *Santorini* rode a slight swell four miles east of St George. Overhead the sun shimmered and burned, and poured heat upon a breathless day. On the horizon a thin line of dark grey cloud that appeared frayed at its edge warned of a front coming in from the Atlantic. The humidity was high, the atmosphere close and thick. Ella shielded her eyes and watched a boat move across their bow a mile away. She wiped away a trickle of perspiration that ran from her forehead to the corner of her eye.

'Any luck?' she said.

Gordon stood in the engine compartment below the wheelhouse, stripped to the waist. 'You were right. I think it's the fuel pump.' He had a smear of grease across his cheek, and his back and chest were pale, mottled with freckles. There were distinct bands around his neck and upper arms that marked the lines of the T-shirt he normally wore.

Ella wiped oil from her hands with a rag. When the engine had spluttered and died on them an hour and a half earlier she'd opened the hatch and climbed down to try and figure out what the problem was. She'd checked the electrical connections and tested the plugs, then turned her attention to the pump, which had given her problems before. After a while Gordon had offered to take a look.

'Bloody hell,' she muttered to herself, more out of frustration than anything else. It seemed like she couldn't get a break right now. 'Can you do anything?'

'I'm not sure.'

With the pump out of action, Ella thought, she would have to try and raise someone on the radio. The best she could hope for was a tow back to harbour, which meant losing a day's work. They were still half a mile from where they had set the trap string.

Gordon examined a part from the dismantled pump. His brow furrowed. 'Maybe I could fix something up.'

'See what you can do,' Ella said. She was no slouch herself when it came to getting her hands dirty. The *Santorini* was an old boat, and she knew every inch of it, but Gordon was a natural when it came to coaxing life from seemingly defunct machinery. She watched him as he worked, his brow furrowed in concentration, his fingers nimble. Between the two of them they had patched and mended just about every piece of equipment on the boat.

He hadn't mentioned his dad, though he was quieter than normal and she guessed he had things on his mind. The more she considered the possibility of losing him, the less Ella liked the idea. During the past year that he'd worked for her he had changed, growing from the boy she'd hired to the young man he was now. She didn't want to be the cause of a rift between him and his dad, but she figured Gordon had to make his own mind up about her.

She left him working and went back along the deck, where it was a little cooler in the breeze. The boat rose and fell on the swell, and as Ella stood at the bow she peered through her glasses across the water, looking for her buoys. They had set a couple of strings out here in deeper water hoping to find some lobsters. Fifty traps to a string, with a marker buoy at each end. She fixed on a seiner that had earlier crossed her bow and was now three quarters of a mile away, and watched for a while as the men on deck hauled in a net. The catch appeared to be small.

She lowered her glasses. The last six months had been tough. After her father had died she'd discovered his finances weren't in good shape. The house, which Ella's mother had believed long since paid off, had been re-mortgaged, while his insurances had been allowed to lapse. Ella had kept this from her mother, and somehow she'd managed to keep up the mortgage payments as well as meeting the loan on the *Santorini*. Slowly, inexorably it seemed that matters were improving, despite the almost constant niggling problems of fouled gear and lost traps that were pretty much attributable to the Rodericks. However, since she'd decided to run against Howard, things had gotten worse. If she had to ask herself honestly if she could keep on going over the winter, she wouldn't be certain of the answer. Her credit was stretched so tight it kept her awake at night with worry. But then that was the least of her worries now.

She wondered how the island would look in a few years' time if Howard got his way. She guessed the islanders themselves would become oil to the machinery of a new economy. Boutiques selling trinkets and designer labels would take over the shopping area in town, and the traditional stores like the market and the bakery and the clothing stores on Independence, the chandlers and outfitters along the waterfront would be forced out to new strip malls on the shore. The harbour would fill up with excursion ferries and charter boats, McDonald's and video stores would look out over the docks and during the summer more and more people would come to the houses they would build backing onto golf courses or the ocean front, and the fishermen would sell their boats to buy a gardening franchise or sell ice-cream and hot dogs to bored teenagers from wealthy families.

What would her father, an old-fashioned St Georgian, have made of it. She'd grown up with a man she both idolized and resented. Resented because she'd always sensed his lingering sadness over the son he'd lost. A gap she couldn't fill. Subconsciously, from a young age she'd recognized his need and had even tried to become both son and daughter to him, setting herself an impossible aim. He'd loved her, she knew that, and she'd loved him, though her feelings were complex. She'd found him once, stinking of liquor in their ruined front room, with pictures and ornaments swept to the floor where they lay broken. In her room she'd listened to the sound of her mother sobbing.

She blanked out the memory, and the maelstrom of feelings it evoked.

On the horizon the clouds were thin and hazy, but dark in places like factory smoke. The air was oppressive and close. Ella's shirt stuck to her back, and she found herself wishing for rain. The forecast had promised a break in the weather last week, but it hadn't happened, and the warm humid air that flowed into the gulf from the south held off any weak Atlantic front building over the ocean. The last big storm that had hit the coast had been in February, when gales had whipped up the seas and kept the fishing fleets in their harbours. The rain had lashed the windows of the little house she had rented on the southern side of town. The wind had whistled in the eaves, and water had cascaded from a broken pipe outside. When the phone had rung late at night she'd been drifting into a deep sleep, and for several moments she'd been disorientated, scrabbling in the dark for the light switch, knocking over a vase of flowers. But by the time she lifted the receiver she was awake, and even before she heard her mother's voice, she'd felt the clutch of foreboding tighten in her chest.

Her mother sounded worried. There had been an argument, she said, and Ella's father had left the house. Ella could hear the wind and rain down the phone line and her mother's voice suddenly snatched away.

'Mom, where are you?'

'I'm at the dock. His boat is gone. Ella, your dad took his boat out in the storm.'

And then Ella's foreboding hardened into something real. She put on a coat and drove through town, the streets awash with water, the lights dim and wavering as if shining from underneath the sea. At the intersection on Independence the traffic signals were stuck on red and were swinging crazily in the wind. She pulled up by the phone where her mother was waiting, and by the time Ella had wrenched open the door, battling against the wind, and climbed into her mother's car she was wet through. Her mother looked white, her hair stuck to her head. Ella reached out for her, and felt her wince.

'What happened? Are you hurt?'

Her mother shook her head. 'I'm okay. I fell.'

In the dim light coming through the windscreen her mother averted her eyes. For a second neither of them spoke, then gently Ella hugged her. Beyond the dock she saw the empty mooring where her father's boat would normally be. Out in the harbour it was too dark to see anything, but the waves crashing on the docks conjured images of violent seas.

In the morning the wreckage of her father's boat had been washed up at the foot of the cliffs, beyond the reef at the mouth of Stillwater Cove. Her father was missing, presumed drowned, and his body was never recovered. Three days after the wreckage was found Ella and her mother had stood silently side by side in the small cemetery as the crowd of mourners gathered around an empty grave next to Danny's. It was the anniversary of Danny's death. He would have been a little over two years younger than Ella, had he not died in his sleep one night at the age of just three months. The cause of death had been recorded as infant cot death syndrome.

A week later Ella had moved her things back home and given up the cottage she had rented ever since her brief marriage had abruptly ended six years earlier.

If she let her focus turn inwards Ella could see her dad as clearly as if he stood before her. His eyes were the colour of the Atlantic on a day when clouds raced overhead, the sea changing shades of grey. When he smiled the creases around the corners of his eyes were etched deep in his weathered skin as if carved there, and when he was in a sombre mood his eyes looked inward and he became brooding and melancholy. He had been a quiet man, outwardly strong and not given to expressing his feelings. He was a fisherman from a long line of fishermen, and he was well versed in hardship. But in some men the silence that appears as strength masks a deep flaw. Danny's death had sown a bitter seed inside him, which over the years had grown and spread its tangled roots through his being. He had lost the only son he would ever have, and he could never forgive the world for taking him. The loss tortured him, setting loose demons in his mind and sometimes in anger and frustration he hurt those who he loved the most. Ella had grown up in a house with a secret that was kept hidden from the outside world.

The radio crackled from the wheel-house, rousing her from her thoughts, and Ella went back to answer it.

'Is that you Ella?' a voice asked. 'This is Bo Winterman. Everything all right over there?'

She looked through the window at the boat still three quarters of a mile away and recognized the *Rose Marie*. She glanced at Gordon, silently framing a question.

'I think I've just about got it,' he told her.

'We're fine thanks Bo. We had a little trouble with the fuel pump, but I think we have it licked. My sternman here is a genius,' she added for Gordon's benefit, at which he grinned.

'Okay then, if you're sure. Call us if you need any help.'

'I will, thanks. How're the fish biting today?'

'So so.'

'Good luck, and thanks again.'

Ella flipped the transmit switch off. 'How long do you think?' she asked Gordon.

'Maybe half an hour or so.'

On the horizon the strip of grey cloud had grown visibly wider, faint streaks melting towards the sea and merging. It was raining over there, but it was a long way off. Ella stayed in the shade, trying not to think about the heat.

A little over a mile away to Ella's stern the *Seawind* was heading towards her at a steady eight knots when Jake picked up Bo Winterman's message. He focused his glasses on the *Santorini* until he found Ella standing on the deck. His grip on the glasses tightened as a throbbing ache flowered in the back of his neck and flowed upwards through his head like a spreading ink stain. With one hand he massaged a spot at the base of his skull. He was barely aware of doing it. He thought of the ache as a colour. It started off as grey, and settled over his brain like fluid that slowly hardened and became a pliable film. As it continued to harden it shrank, squeezing his brain in its grip, and as it did so the throbbing increased in pitch and the grey darkened towards black. Sometimes it was as if it was leaking down behind his eyes and the light faded in the world outside and he saw everything through a grainy film.

Since Bryan had disappeared Jake's headaches had been growing steadily worse. He knew that his brother was dead. He'd known it since the first day. He'd felt it. And he didn't need Howard-goddamned-Larson to tell him that Ella had killed him. Howard was only interested in the vote, Jake knew that too.

The radio crackled again and Jake heard Bo Winterman's voice.

'We're about done here, Ella. You sure you don't need any help.'

'No everything's fine Bo. Gordon fixed the pump and we're about to leave ourselves. Watch out that you don't snag my string over there.'

'Don't worry. I see your buoys. Good luck.'

'Same to you.'

As Jake listened to the exchange he watched the *Rose Marie* as she changed direction to a heading north-east, steering away from the *Santorini*. Ella's buoys were between the two boats and Jake shoved forward on the throttle and steered a course towards them. The thump of the big diesels rose in pitch as the *Seawind* picked up speed. A moment later Calder Penman came to the door and glanced at the fish finder.

'We got something?'

'Yeah, we got something,' Jake replied.

Penman looked ahead. 'That's the *Santorini* ain't it?'

Jake didn't bother to reply. 'Get a man on the side with a gaff,' he said. He planned to snag the first of Ella's buoys on the blind side of the *Rose Marie*, then drag the float line and the traps attached to it across the seabed. By the time he was finished Ella's string would be a tangle of junk.

Penman hesitated, guessing what Jake was planning, then he voiced his reluctance. 'Jake, maybe this isn't such a good idea with the *Rose Marie* right there.'

Jake grinned. 'Accidents happen, Calder, that's just the way it is.'

Penman tried again. 'Look, we're all with you in this thing. Ella ought to get what's coming to her, but you know how it is. Stripping her traps at night is one thing, dragging off a string right here where everybody can see us clear as day, that's something else.' His words fell on deaf ears.

'This isn't a goddamned debate, Penman. Unless you want to find yourself looking for a new job, quit your damn bitching and do what I say. Now have somebody grab that buoy.'

Penman hesitated for a second longer, then he went out the door and shouted to one of the crew to grab a gaff.

As the boats on the surface converged, the orcas were approaching from the north. Swimming in a series of shallow dives, the bull was listening to the sound of humpback whales hunting at great depths further out to the east. The water above the bank was suffused with light and colour, of hues of blue and aqua, and below were waving forests of seaweed of all shades of green and brown and yellow. Shafts of sunlight pierced the ocean as the sun broke through drifting cloud, and shadows raced eastward. For the bull orca this submarine world was alive with sound. As he swam, his senses were finely tuned to filter the mundane from the significant. He listened to the distant booms of the humpbacks as they hunted squid, and to the south he heard fishing boats working, and others further out to the east. One of them was discharging its bilge pumps, emptying polluted water into the sea. Of the three to the south he could distinguish each from the tone of their engines. One of them had just completed drawing in a net. It made a sound like wind raising a fine spray as it whipped across the surface of the sea, and the motors driving the winches made a low vibrating rumble. The bull sonared ahead, listening to the returning echoes and searching for the fish that the boat must be hunting, but there was nothing there.

One of the vessels ahead picked up speed. The sound of its engines changed from a steady slow thump to a continuous growl. The bull slowed in the water, recognizing the signature of this boat. Suddenly he detected a new sound. It was the distinctive pattern of bluefin tuna, approaching from the west. They were swimming in loose formation, streaking through the sea as they hunted, and they were heading on a course that would coincide with the position of the boats. The swish and hiss they made as they quickly turned and swooped with power- ful thrusts of their tails was unmistakable. The bull was wary of the *Seawind*, but hunger and the needs of the pod outweighed the risk, and the orcas quickly picked up pace.

Bo Winterman wondered what Jake was up to. His mate, Rob Taylor, stood beside him, smoking a cigarette.

'I think that sonofabitch is planning on snagging her string.'

'That's what I was thinking.'

The *Santorini* was moving now, but she was a lot smaller and slower than the *Seawind*.

'I don't like to just stand by and watch,' Taylor said. He turned and spat out the door, as if to emphasize his opinion.

Jake and his brother had never been exactly popular in the harbour, Bo thought, especially among the lobster gang, but fishermen were a tribal bunch, and Sanctuary had its share of rogues like anywhere else, and in the Rodericks they'd quickly found their leaders. But then Ella wasn't about to win any popu- larity contests right now either. There had always been those who resented her. Now with her running for mayor and this business with Bryan, it was hard for anyone to know what to think. Bo had known Ella all her life, and her father too before he'd died, and until a few days ago he hadn't taken much notice of the talk. Mostly it was from people who were too stupid to know any better, or else they just plain didn't like Ella. But since Carl Johnson had told everybody what he'd seen the night Bryan had gone missing, even Bo had to admit he had his doubts.

'We going to do anything about this?' Taylor said, interrupting his reflection.

The *Seawind* was almost upon the first of Ella's buoys. Bo was reluctant to get involved, but if Ella had done something wrong, it ought to be the law that punished her. It wasn't for Jake to take things into his own hands, and besides which, running down somebody else's gear was stepping way over the line, and Jake knew it.

'Damn him,' Bo muttered, and making his decision he swung the wheel to bring the *Rose Marie* around.

Just then one of the crew shouted from the deck. Bo followed where the man was pointing and at first he didn't see anything, then some of the other men started shouting too, and he saw what had got them so excited. A quarter mile west of the *Santorini* the surface of the ocean was broken with the spray of leaping fish. The sun flashed silver on a school of tuna as they hunted smaller fish at the surface.

'Bluefin,' Taylor breathed.

They watched in silence, mesmerized by the spectacle as the giants moved rapidly towards them. Some of them looked to be around eight or nine feet long, maybe nine hundred pounds of prime fish. Bo couldn't remember ever having seen such a thing, not even when he was a boy, and back then bluefin this size had been a relatively common sight when they migrated into the gulf each year.

'Look there.' Taylor pointed.

From the north, heading straight towards the boats, a number of large black dorsal fins rose and fell.

'Orcas,' Bo said quietly. He watched for a moment, figuring that the orcas were planning to intercept the tuna, and it was going to happen right around where the *Rose Marie* was positioned. He hesitated, torn between going to Ella's aid or going after the bluefin. There was no time to set a net, but the *Rose Marie* carried harpoons, though they were rarely used.

He made up his mind and swung his heading away from the *Seawind*. He felt a momentary regret, but just one good giant was worth a lot of money and he had a living to make. He consoled himself with the reminder that no boat owner these days knew what the future held. A chance like this might never occur again, and who was to say what might happen next week, or next month? Who was to say the *Rose Marie* would still be fishing these waters a year from now? You had to take the chances when they came.

'Rig the harpoons,' he said.

Ella's grin quickly faded as Gordon finished re-fitting the pump and the engine sputtered back into life. She saw the *Seawind* making straight for the first of her buoys and she guessed immediately what he planned to do. A string of fifty traps, apart from the loss of her catch, would cost upwards of four thousand dollars to replace. It was a cost she couldn't afford. Ella knew she was witnessing the end of her livelihood.

She and Gordon could only watch helplessly as the *Seawind* overhauled them. When the *Rose Marie* altered course she allowed herself a moment of hope when it seemed that Bo planned to intervene, but almost immediately she veered away again.

'What's he doing?' Gordon said dismayed.

Ella's heart sank. She could see Jake clearly standing in the wheel-house and she pictured his smirk of triumph, the smouldering hate that would be present in the depths of his eyes. As she watched one of the crew leaned over the side to hook the first buoy. She imagined her traps being dragged along the seabed, breaking open and buckling as they bounced off rocks. The lines would become hopelessly fouled, and eventually severed, and there was nothing she could do about it. Her knuckles turned white where she gripped the wheel and she bit down so hard on her lower lip that she tasted the thick saltiness of blood.

'Ella.'

Gordon seized her arm and pointed towards something off their starboard side. She saw the flash of sunlight on silver, the splash of bodies as they re-entered the water and she knew why Bo Winterman had changed direction. With his sabotage complete, Jake too altered course, no doubt having seen the approaching school of bluefin. They were moving rapidly on a course that would take them directly between the two boats and Ella saw with bitter realization that the school would pass wide of the *Santorini* and that she didn't have the speed to catch them. But as the tuna drew nearer it became clear that they were spread over a fairly wide area, and that the occasional fish was hunting way out on the southern flank. There was a slim chance one might come close enough to take a bait if they could get some lines over the side fast enough.

She saw that Gordon was thinking the same thing as she was and she cut the throttle back and they went to work. The *Santorini*, like many other small boats, was equipped for different types of fishing. Though she was primarily a lobster boat, at different times of the year Ella turned her hand to line fishing. If a big fish was hooked the line was transferred to the hauler to bring it alongside, and this was what she had in mind now.

Gordon broke out hooks and lines and they baited up. A hundred yards off their bow a fish leapt clear of the sea, in pursuit of a striper. Ella gasped, calculating that it must have been twelve feet long, maybe a thousand pounds of prime bluefin. Already she was figuring what a fish like that might be worth. Enough to settle her financial worries for a year. They worked frantically, getting lines out as fast as they could.

And then something else caught her attention, the rise of a fin above the swell. 'Look there,' she said to Gordon.

A pod of orcas were approaching from the north, and it was apparent that they too planned to intercept the bluefin, and that both they and the two boats ahead would converge in one area to compete for the same prey. Ella felt a veil of foreboding settle over her.

Jake watched the orcas as the pod cruised between the two boats. They seemed to stay closer to the *Rose Marie*. He cradled his rifle, holding it loosely across his chest, looking for the big bastard with the double notch in his dorsal fin.

'There you go, you sonofabitch,' he said quietly when he spotted the bull, and he raised his rifle, but the orca dipped in the trough of the swell and vanished. The others followed suit and it became clear they were staying beneath the surface, only rising to breathe. Jake watched the area where he thought the bull would reappear, but when it did it was fifty yards north of where he'd expected. He squeezed off a hurried shot, but he was too slow and the bull dipped beneath the waves again.

'Dammit.' He wondered why the orcas remained between the boats, but as he watched the approaching tuna he saw the reason. 'That bastard is using us,' he said to himself as he understood that they were using the boats to conceal their presence from the bluefin. He went into the wheel-house to raise Bo Winterman on his radio.

'What is it Jake?' Bo's voice crackled over the set.

'Those damn killers are using us for cover. Soon as those bluefin figure out what's waiting for 'em they're going to be a hundred miles from here in about a minute flat. Are you gonna just stand there and let them take our fish? Use your damn rifle.'

'There's no need to do that Jake.'

'What the hell is the matter with you Winterman? You know how much one of those giants is worth? I already lost one to those thieving black bastards a couple of days ago. I'm not about to let that happen again.'

'You're wrong, Jake. Take a look for yourself. Behind the bluefin.'

Jake looked and then he saw them too. Trailing the school by a couple of hundred yards or so were three orcas, spread out in a line. They were holding their position, their fins visible as they rose and fell through the waves, the flash of white patches contrasting with their smooth black bodies.

'You just keep an eye on those three Jake. You might learn something,' Bo said.

Just then Jake heard a shouted warning from the bow and he dropped the radio mike with a curse.

'They're turning,' Penman yelled.

Less than a hundred yards away the bluefin school suddenly veered south-west as the front runners became aware of the orcas that were waiting for them hidden between the two boats. Jake snatched up the mike.

'Maybe next time you'll listen to me Winterman, you dumb fuck,' he shouted. He spun the wheel to bring the *Seawind* about as he opened up the throttle. He glimpsed flashes of silver just beneath the surface of the water as thousands of four-pound stripers streamed past the bow as they fled from the tuna. As the *Seawind*'s engines roared and her screws churned up a great mass of froth in her wake, Jake found his course and punched in the autopilot. Hurriedly he pulled open the locker behind him and took out a box of cherry bombs and ran out onto the deck and passed them out to the crew.

On the *Rose Marie* Bo Winterman could only watch with frustrated rage as he saw disaster looming. He shouted himself hoarse into the radio mike, but in the end he gave up and angrily threw it down.

'That idiot is going to mess things up,' he said as the first of the explosions sounded.

Bo had fished these waters for fifty years, and he'd seen the way orcas worked before. He knew that the three in position behind the bluefin were there for a reason, and even now he could see they'd reacted to the tuna's altered course as they swam around to the south flank to head them off, banging their flukes on the surface so the tuna knew they were there. If Jake had let things be they would have driven the panicked fish back between the boats towards the rest of the pod and the bluefin would have been trapped. There would have been enough for man and orca alike to take their share. Bo himself had witnessed orcas in the past herding fish towards a purse seiner's net that had been set ahead of the school. The seiner's skipper and the orcas had cooperated, the orcas allowed into the open net to take their share of the spoils before the purse was drawn closed. But now Bo could only watch with anger as the cherry bombs drove the orcas back, and in the process allowed the bluefin to scatter.

'You bloody fool,' Bo said, half in anger, half in despair.

As the three orcas in position to the rear of the school had closed in, their blood-curdling screams and machine gun-like bursts of clicks had alerted the tuna to their presence, letting them know that from hunter they had suddenly become the hunted. Momentarily the school had found themselves being herded together by orcas on both sides as the orcas between the boats had begun vocalizing too.

Suddenly a shock wave of sound from directly in front of the bull battered his sensitive hearing. It was of such intensity that it pierced his ears with a bright lance of pain. To his flank a young male screamed in agony. Another explosion followed, and then another. Disoriented and dazed the orcas turned back and milled in confused circles as they tried to escape the noise. The bull understood what was happening and swam directly away from the source of the explosions, and when he was clear he repeatedly called the rest of the pod until one by one they locked on to his voice and using it like a beacon swam almost blindly towards him, their ears still ringing painfully. As they reassembled far away from the boats the bull spied across the surface of the sea. From the deck of the *Seawind* men continued to lob objects into the water, and each was followed by the now dull thud of an explosion. The tuna, suddenly finding that they were no longer hemmed in had begun to stream away in the opposite direction. The opportunity was lost.

When the entire pod had reformed, the bull turned and led them north-west, heading for a shelf where experience told him they might find schools of bluefish.

When the pod had fled Jake's elation was short lived. Though the cherry bombs had turned back the orcas they had also turned the bluefin who were now streaming southward at speed where there was nothing to stop their flight. A single fish at the rear of the school streaked through the sea, just below the surface in front of the bow, and Penman who was standing at the ready with his harpoon signalled directions to Jake in the wheel-house. As Jake swung hard to port he registered that the *Rose Marie* was heading on a converging course, apparently chasing the same fish

The radio crackled into life and Bo Winterman shouted a warning.

'Give way Jake!'

He snatched up the mike. 'The hell with you.'

He kept his eye fixed on Penman, who waved his arm again frantically, directing him further to port.

'This is my fish, Winterman,' Jake said into the mike, then he flung it down and swung the wheel again.

On the *Rose Marie* Bo cursed but held his course. He had already targeted the bluefin when the *Seawind* had altered direction and by rights the fish belonged to him.

At the last moment he acknowledged that Jake would not give way. Though Taylor was at the bow getting ready to throw his harpoon, so was Penman on the *Seawind*. Bo hesitated for a moment longer, reluctant to give up, but then calling Jake every name he could think of he frantically spun the wheel, but he already knew it was too late. The two boats came together, both skippers trying desperately to break off at the last second, their bows turning aside with agonizing slowness, the sea churned into a massive white froth in the narrowing channel between them, and then with a sickening elongated grind they collided, sending men on both of them sprawling to the decks. The sound of splintering wood and steel followed in a long wrenching sound that was torture to hear. Bo staggered and hit his head on the metal case of the fish finder, opening a gash along the side of his forehead, and he fell to his knees, momentarily stunned.

When he rose shakily to his feet again, he felt the wound on his head and his fingers came away sticky with blood. The *Seawind* wallowed on his starboard side. Both harpooners had lost their balance, and their weapons, and the bluefin had escaped unharmed.

Ella shook her head sadly when she heard the first of the explosions. She wished there was something that she could do. Like Bo, she too had understood that had Jake appreciated what the orcas were doing, there would have been fish enough for all of them. But Jake had no interest in cooperating or sharing the spoils of the ocean. He would have killed the orcas if he could, and she resented him bitterly for it.

Just then her attention was diverted when one of the lines beside her began to spin frantically off its spool. She stared at it as if mesmerized for a full second or two before she realized what had happened, and suddenly galvanized into action she released the free end of the line and hurriedly ran it through the pulley wheel to the hydraulic hauler. Sixty feet away a nine foot long bluefin leapt full clear of the sea, rising into the air like a missile, before it twisted and arched its body to dive again as it tried to shake off the hook that held it.

As the fish sped away Ella increased the tension on the line so that the drag would slow it up, then she handed over the control to Gordon and dashed for the wheel. As she brought the *Santorini* around she was vaguely aware that the *Seawind* and the *Rose Marie* were on a collision course, but after that her entire focus was given over to the fight to hang on to the bluefin.

She steered after the fish at low speed, so that it was half towing them. Her aim was to tire it before they tried to bring it in, but not too quickly or the struggles of the fish would generate such muscular energy that the flesh would spoil. She knew that the better the condition it was in when landed, the greater the price the bluefin would fetch on the dock. The fish went deep, and Gordon hauled in some line. A few minutes later the tuna rose and burst from the surface, leaping into the air again before it streaked eastward in a flash of speed and power. Gordon released the tension as Ella opened the throttle and gave chase. In this fashion they fought the fish, and pursued it for miles. Ella slowed the engine, and Gordon hauled in more line. They worked in tandem; Ella chasing and controlling their speed, Gordon judging when to let the tuna run and when to bring it in a few more yards. Each time they thought it was beaten the great fish found new reserves of strength and streaked away again. They fought it as the sun sank lower and the day drew out, the sea changing colour from cobalt blue to silver and copper.

Eventually the bluefin's dives became less frequent, and its struggles grew weaker as it tired. It took them three and a half hours to bring it alongside where together they gaffed it and

Gordon leaned over and drove a spike through its skull, piercing its brain and killing it instantly. They looped rope around each end of the fish and used the hauler to bring it aboard, and then Gordon quickly set about gutting it and ripping out the spine. He made incisions to bleed the flesh, and together they packed the body cavity with ice. When they were finished, they stood to admire their catch.

Ella grinned, barely aware of her fatigue, the ache in her arms. Her troubles were momentarily banished from her thoughts and in her exhilaration she hugged Gordon tight, wrapping both arms around him as they lurched like drunkards about the deck. When they parted they were both laughing like fools.

'How much will it fetch do you think?' Gordon asked when they had recovered themselves.

'I don't know. Enough for you to buy that motorcycle you always wanted with your share I guess.'

'What about you? What will you buy?'

Ella thought for a few moments. 'A little time,' she said soberly.

At their feet the tuna lay glistening in the setting sun. It was designed for speed and power, its life always precarious in a savage sea, where it was prey for sharks and orcas and man. Though she was vaguely saddened at its death, Ella still felt the residue of the elated high the hunt had produced. She imagined her own eyes shone as Gordon's did. She looked down at herself, her oilskin pants filthy with blood and fishy gore.

Her life, she thought, seemed marked out in absolutes of life and death. Of struggle and survival as old as the sea itself.

CHAPTER SEVENTEEN

Matt woke early, the sheets and blankets on the bed twisted tightly around his body. He was sweating, breathing hard, and he blinked in the darkness, unsure at first where he was. The dream that just a moment ago had been all too vivid, receded. One puzzling remnant remained, the smell of the sea, but then the curtain fluttered at the open window and Matt remembered that he was no longer in the apartment where he'd lived in the city. Disentangling himself from the bedclothes he rose and crossed to the window. Outside the night sky was deep velvet and studded with bright points of light. The breeze was warm and the air thick with humidity.

It had been a long time since Matt had dreamed about his brother. Paulie was older by two years. He was stockier, and had their father's build, who'd wrestled at college, whereas Matt took after their mother's side of the family.

Paulie was thirteen the day he and Matt went out in the little dinghy they kept in Stillwater Cove. They were both good swimmers, but they'd been taught to respect the sea and they only ever went out when the weather was fine, and never ventured as far as the reef. As Paulie grew older, though, bravado took the place of caution. One day at his urging they went out when the weather was looking messy, the sky clear one minute and blown about with grey cloud the next. Matt remembered standing on the beach, watching the water peaking and chopping up when the wind changed, and Paulie telling him not to be such a chickenshit, that it would be all right. They sailed right out towards the entrance, until they could see the swirlling patterns on the surface of the water where the reef lay. It began to rain, and the wind felt suddenly cold.

'We should go back,' Matt said.

Paulie scanned the sky, which had turned ominously dark. The swell was rising and the water was getting rougher by the minute. 'Yeah, okay,' he agreed, trying to sound as if he was only making a concession for Matt. His brow, however, was furrowed in lines that belied his casual air.

They came about, and started tacking back. The wind was strong offshore, and they had to tack on a narrow angle. Coming about on a turn, the boom swung across as they changed sides, the wind again filled the sail, then a freak gust caught them off guard and tipped them into the water, capsizing the dinghy. Neither of them was wearing a life jacket. They'd been capsized plenty of times before, and this time ought not to have been any different. Normally they could right the boat again, climb back in and carry on as if nothing had happened. The water, however, seemed suddenly cold.

Matt came up spluttering, and when he looked around he couldn't see the boat or Paulie. It was raining hard, sheets slanting down in the wind, and the world was suddenly uniformly grey. Waves were breaking and whipping salt spray into his eyes. He struck out blindly, trying to quell his growing panic and then rising on a wave he glimpsed Paulie clinging to the dinghy. He was shouting, telling Matt to swim over, and maybe it was the note of panic in his brother's voice that really scared Matt. The distance between them was only a few yards, but it was widening. He struck out again, and every now and then when he rose on a wave he caught sight of Paulie still clinging to the dinghy with one arm, the other outstretched, water streaming down his face as he called out. It seemed to Matt that he wasn't getting any closer, and he became tired, and the more weary he felt the more he was afraid and the more frantic and uncoordinated his efforts became. The reef was much too close, and the water was foaming. He felt the eddies and currents clutching at his body like insistent, invisible hands.

Their father had warned them a thousand times, take deep breaths if you get into trouble, don't thrash around, and try not to waste energy. He could hear this tiny distant voice in his head, but somehow he couldn't stop himself as he flailed and struggled against the current. A wave broke in his face and he took a mouthful of water and choked as he tried to spit it out. Another wave swamped him and he went under. There was a moment when he surfaced again and opened his mouth to cry out in terror before he went under for the second time, and then everything slowed down. He felt as if he was two people. As if his mind had separated and part of him was conscious only of his sluggish movements in the water, of feeling like a giant claw had gripped his chest and was squeezing the life from him, while another part of his mind wandered, distracted. He saw his parents and Paulie seated around the big polished oak dining table at home. His father was carving from a joint of beef, and his mother was smiling at something Paulie had said. The room was warm and lit with the glow from the lights on the wall and outside through the window it was dark, but snow flakes drifted against the glass. It was a weekend from the previous winter, after Paulie had broken his arm playing football, and he was making the most of the attention he was getting with his arm in a cast. Matt felt as if he was right there in the room but it was moving away from him and though he tried to call out so that somebody would notice him he couldn't make a sound. The scene faded and he experienced a deep sense of loss and loneliness. Then the images fragmented and his parents and brother became like ghosts and all at once Matt was aware of the water again, the burning sensation in his lungs. He ceased struggling and inertia swept over him and he knew he was dying.

A hand grasped him and hauled him to the surface and suddenly he felt cold air on his face and opened his mouth and breathed.

'Swim Matt, dammit!'

He heard Paulie's voice but the words didn't register and he struggled and kicked, fighting the water and Paulie at once, scared to death.

'Don't struggle so much.'

163

Paulie's grip tightened around his chest and he fought to turn around, to grasp his brother as if he was an island.

'I said don't fight me you little shit.'

This time Paulie's words penetrated, and Matt stopped struggling. Paulie urged him to help, to kick with his legs, so he had, then he started using his arms as well, and the two of them eventually made it back to the dinghy. The sudden squall passed and the sky began to clear.

The water calmed as the wind died down, and once Matt felt the wooden hull beneath his hands he knew that he wasn't going to die that day after all.

There had been a time when he'd had the dream often. Almost nightly. Ever since that day in the cove he'd been afraid of the water, and after Paulie had died he'd suffered from an illogical guilt that he hadn't been there to save him that day in the convenience store where Paulie had been shot. That he hadn't been there when he was needed to repay the debt he somehow believed he owed his brother. The obsession with which he'd later pursued his job as a prosecutor stemmed from that guilt. And even now Matt knew it affected him still, causing him to doubt the woman he loved.

He spent an hour helping Henry with the cider shed after he got out of bed. The framing was up and they began cutting lengths of timber planking to form the walls. As they worked Matt thought about Baxter's reaction when he'd heard Kate Little's name. He finished sawing a plank to length and turned off the machine.

'Something on your mind Matt?' Henry asked.

'I was thinking about Chief Baxter. He's not married is he?'

'Nope. Never has been.'

'You ever hear of him seeing a woman called Kate Little?'

'I never heard the name.'

'She lives up on the point with her husband. Evan Little. They're summer people.'

'Can't say as I know much about anyone who lives up there. Why do you ask?'

'I'm not sure,' Matt said. He'd been playing with the idea that there was something going on between Baxter and Kate Little. But the more he thought about it, the more ridiculous the idea seemed. All the same, Matt had the feeling that Baxter wouldn't be following up on his idea that Kate might have known Bryan Roderick.

He checked his watch and took off his gloves, remembering that he had a law practice he was meant to be running, even though he didn't have any clients yet. The day before there had been a message on the answer machine from a woman who said she suspected her husband was having an affair. She wanted to talk to him about getting a divorce. It seemed the husband worked on the ferry that ran between the islands and the mainland, and his wife said he'd been staying away more often than usual and she didn't trust him. It didn't sound like the kind of case that Matt would gain much satisfaction from, but he figured he was in no position to be choosy.

'I have to go into town for a while,' he told Henry. 'I'll try and get out again this afternoon.'

'I'll be here.'

When Matt drove down into Sanctuary he passed by the harbour and there seemed to be more activity than usual. There were cars and trucks parked all along the waterfront, and there were people climbing all over the pleasure craft moored out in the harbour. In contrast the fishing docks were almost deserted. Normally on any given day there would be a few boats tied up between trips or else refitting, but today the berths were empty. Matt slowed, and when he recognized Ben Harper's launch tied up to a dock he pulled over and got out. Ben had the engine hatch on his stern deck open and there were parts spread out around him. He looked up as Matt approached, the sun flashing on his glasses.

'Problem?' Matt asked.

'Damn thing keeps dying on me.'

'What's all the excitement?' Matt gestured toward the motor-boats and small yachts out on the moorings.

'You haven't heard?'

'Heard what?'

'Somebody brought in a giant bluefin yesterday. Weighed over nine hundred pounds. Apparently there was a whole school of them out there. Practically half the town is out there today.' Ben gestured at the parts on his deck. 'I'd be out there myself if it wasn't for this.' He registered Matt's uncomprehending expression. 'A bluefin is a type of tuna,' he explained. 'They can be worth a lot of money. There aren't too many of the giants around any more. A fish weighing nine hundred pounds, if it was in good condition, could be worth, oh, fifteen, maybe twenty thousand dollars.'

Matt let out a low whistle. 'That's a lot of money for a fish.'

'You bet. You come down here tomorrow, there won't be a single boat in this harbour.'

'Including yours I guess.'

'Well, I hope so. But it's not the fishing I'm interested in. I heard there was a pod of orcas out there as well and I'd like to take a look at them.' Ben sat back on his haunches. 'Actually I thought you'd know all about this.'

'The only tuna I know about is the kind that I get in a can from the market,' Matt said. 'Anyway, why would I know?'

Ben grinned. 'That woman you were interested in the other day. The one that's running for mayor. She has a boat doesn't she?'

'Ella Young?'

'Yeah, that's her. It was her boat that brought in the bluefin. The *Santorini.*'

Matt spent the rest of his day clock watching. Apart from a visit from the woman who wanted to divorce her husband he didn't speak to another prospective client. The woman called around mid-morning and arranged an appointment for just before lunch when she said she would be in town. She arrived on time, and looked around curiously. She turned out to be younger than Matt had expected. He guessed she was in her late twenties. She wore jeans and a T-shirt.

'I've never had to see a lawyer before,' she told him as she took the seat he offered.

He imagined his slightly shabby office didn't fit with those she'd seen on TV shows. He offered her coffee, and while he made it she told him about herself. Her name was Ruth Thorne and she'd been married for five years and had two small children. Her husband Charlie worked for the Island Ferry Company which plied the routes between the mainland coast and the half dozen islands offshore, of which St George was the most distant. The facts were pretty much as she'd already told him. Her husband sometimes had to spend a night on the mainland, depending on the shifts he was working. Lately however he'd been staying away more often than he used to, claiming it was how the rosters fell. She was suspicious of him and several times she'd called the guest house where he was meant to be staying and been told that he wasn't registered.

'You asked him about these occasions?' Matt said.

She nodded. 'He said he stayed with a friend at the last minute. He looked like he was lying though.' She looked saddened as she said this.

'He could be telling the truth,' Matt suggested.

'I'd like to think that, I really would. But the truth is we haven't been getting on so well lately. We seem to fight all the time when he's home. Charlie doesn't make a lot of money, and sometimes it's hard to make ends meet.'

When she asked him about how she would go about getting a divorce, Matt outlined the process. He said he could call somebody if she wanted and see what her husband did on his next layover.

'You mean have him followed?' she said biting her lip, her eyes widening. She thought for a minute. 'How much is all this going to cost Mr Jones? I don't have a lot of money. I mean I have a little put away.'

He gave her his estimate and he counselled her to maybe go away and think about it.

'Okay, I will. But I don't care about the money. If Charlie's cheating on me, that's the finish of us. I don't need a husband like that. I can get by on my own if I have to.'

Matt showed her out and said to call him if she wanted to

take it further and she thanked him and shook his hand. He hoped that she could work things out, that she was wrong about her husband and that he wouldn't see her again. He liked her. The quick defiant light in her eyes reminded him of Ella, and he thought that Charlie Thorne, if he was cheating on his wife, was a fool.

At lunch-time he went over to the coffee shop, which was quieter than usual. Sally Brewster slid into the seat opposite and lit a cigarette. She looked around at the handful of people.

'It's been like this all day. And all anybody's talking about is the fish that Ella caught. I guess you heard about that?'

'I did.'

'Well, I'm glad for her. She could use some good news. Rather her than Jake Roderick.'

'Jake?'

'He was out there too I heard,' Sally said and she filled him in on the gossip that was going around about what had taken place. 'I guess he wasn't too happy about Ella beating him out on a fish like that.'

'I guess not,' Matt agreed. He finished his sandwich and went back to the office. It bothered him that Jake now had another grudge against Ella, to add to the ones he already had. Towards the end of the afternoon he ran out of things to occupy himself with in the office, and so he turned the answer machine on and went down to the waterfront. Many of the pleasure craft that had been on their moorings earlier were now gone. On others people were still working, adapting their boats in various ways for fishing for bluefin. Matt sat on an iron cleat and watched a man row a dinghy out to a motorboat. He threw coils of line up on to the deck and then climbed up himself and started hauling up what looked like a clutch of stakes. Matt looked on puzzled as to their purpose, until he realized they were harpoons. From other boats came the sound of power tools as long put off repairs were made, and the sound of a motor turning over, finally catching, and a cloud of blue white smoke rising and dissipating in the air.

The first of the fishing boats began returning around five. A

168

mob of herring gulls wheeled above a dragger as she came towards the dock, and as she tied up, the crew started unloading their catch. A small crowd gathered around to watch, and Matt wandered over and joined the fringes. There were no bluefin coming off, and the onlookers muttered their disappointment. Someone called out to one of the crew, asking if any had been seen. The man straightened up from his task, cigarette in the corner of his mouth.

'Didn't see a single one,' he said. 'Nor did anyone else far as I know.'

The crowd nevertheless moved on to the next boat as it came in. Matt hung about waiting for the *Santorini*. She chugged across the harbour from the heads, and by the time she docked everybody knew that no bluefin had been seen that day and the crowd had largely disappeared. Matt stood back out of sight watching Ella and her sternman start to unload their catch. Crates of lobsters were lined up on the deck, maybe eight or ten to a crate, their claws bound with bands to stop them fighting and damaging one another. There were three crates.

When they'd finished Ella went to the dealer's office along the dock and Matt waited for her to come back. He wasn't sure what he was doing there, except that the return of his old dream had reminded him of how much he'd already lost in his life because he hadn't laid old ghosts to rest. The distance that had come between himself and Ella was partly of her making, but he knew at least some of it was a response to his reaction when she'd told him outright that she hadn't killed Bryan. He wanted a chance to talk to her. He couldn't deny the doubt he'd felt, but he could try to explain it, and he knew there were things about this whole business that Ella hadn't told him. What he wanted was to bridge the gap. Convince her that they should talk. If they didn't they would both be losing something precious, and he for one didn't want that. He just hoped she felt the same.

The sound of footsteps interrupted his thoughts, and Ella appeared. When she saw him on the dock she stopped. He saw the flash of some emotion in her expression, though exactly what it was he couldn't say.

'I heard about your fish, Ella. I wanted to come down and congratulate you. I'm glad it was you.'

She acknowledged this with the ghost of a smile. 'Thanks.'

Neither spoke and in the awkward moment that followed Matt wasn't sure how to say what he wanted to. Then they both started at once.

'Let me,' Matt said, when they both stopped.

Ella nodded. 'Okay.'

'I came here because I want to apologize. I doubted you the other day, and I shouldn't have.' He held up his hand when she tried to intervene. 'Please, Ella, let me finish. I guess I've spent too long as a prosecutor. You develop a suspicious nature in that job, maybe it makes a person view the world with a slant that makes everything seem tainted. If I'm honest with you I'd have to admit I was kind of taken aback by what happened between you and Bryan, and the fight you had with Jake. I admit that. But I told you once that I came here because I had an idea that I might build a life here, and I'd started to think you might be a part of that. I'd like it if you were. I'd like to wind the clock back to where we were before this started, if you'll give me another chance at it.'

She kept her eyes fixed on his as he spoke, and he could see her thinking about everything he said. When he finished she looked away, across the water towards the heads. The sun lit her features and the ends of her hair were shot through with white light. He waited until she turned back to him.

'Matt, you didn't have to apologize to me. I shouldn't have reacted the way I did. It was just that when I saw how you looked at me, I don't know, I felt like you were condemning me.'

'Maybe I have to adjust to the idea of going out with Annie Oakley,' he said.

She smiled. 'Look, I'm glad you came down here today. And I'm glad about everything else you said too.'

'So, I get another chance?'

'It isn't a case of giving you another chance.' She shook her head. 'It's difficult, Matt. I'm not sure this is a good time. There're are things I can't explain to you right now.'

'Ella, this isn't going to work unless we talk. Can't you try to trust me?'

She appeared to struggle for some way to explain. 'It isn't that I don't want to.'

'Look, whatever's on your mind Ella, you don't have to tell me right away. We can just take it easy, get to know each other again.' He thought he saw something in her eyes, as if she wanted to go along with him, as if she wanted to talk, but he sensed that she needed time, that she needed to trust him first. 'Listen,' he said lightly, hoping to make it easy for her to take the first step. 'You better take me up on this while you have the chance, there's a big demand for someone like me around here you know. Successful lawyer type, thriving practice and all.'

She grinned slowly. 'There is that I suppose. Of course you're talking to the owner of a budding shipping empire here, I'm not easily impressed.'

'That's better. How about dinner tonight? Somewhere quiet, just the two of us?'

As he waited for her to answer a police cruiser pulled over at the end of the dock and Baxter got out. Something about his expression sent warning signals flashing in Matt's mind and as Baxter started over towards them Ella looked around to see what was wrong.

'I wonder what he wants?' Matt said, but Ella didn't reply.

When Baxter reached them he offered a kind of apologetic half smile, and wiped a sheen of perspiration from his forehead. He looked at Matt and then at Ella.

'I'm sorry Ella. I have to arrest you on suspicion of having committed the murder of Bryan Roderick.' He reached around his back where his cuffs hung on his belt, and then as if he remembered where he was and who he was talking to he stopped himself. He made an awkward gesture towards his car.

'I'm going to have to ask you to come with me, Ella.'

CHAPTER EIGHTEEN

Once a week Judge Walker presided over hearings in the St George courthouse, and for the rest of his working time dedicated himself to the chandler's store he owned and ran on the waterfront. The court dealt with minor cases and covered such misdemeanours as the occasional damage caused by bar room fights among the fishermen, or else domestic disputes that arose from time to time. More serious cases, which occurred very rarely on St George were referred to the state attorney's office on the mainland, and if they went to trial they went before a court in Brunswick.

When he arrived at the police department Matt discovered that Baxter had already arranged for a hearing to take place before Judge Walker the next morning, to determine whether there was sufficient evidence for Ella to be handed over to the jurisdiction of the state police so that her case could be dealt with on the mainland. Until then Ella had been housed in the cells which were located in the rear of the building, where she was locked up by a regretful-looking Officer Williams. Matt asked to speak to Baxter in his office.

'So what's this all about?' he asked as soon as they were alone.

'I didn't have any choice in this,' Baxter said. 'New evidence came to light this afternoon.'

'You found a body?'

'No, we didn't do that. But we have an eye-witness. Says he saw Ella on Monday night at Bryan's house. He gave a sworn statement saying he looked through the window and saw Bryan lying on the floor with blood all over him, and Ella standing over him with a gun in her hand.'

Matt was stunned into momentary silence. He felt like his world had been knocked off kilter, and that his hopes for himself and Ella had just been dashed to the ground and stamped into the dirt. When he managed to rearrange his thoughts Baxter was watching him with a sympathetic expression.

'I'm sorry Matt. I called by your office, but you weren't there.'

Matt looked around for a chair, and Baxter sat on the corner of his desk. 'Who is this witness?' Matt asked at length.

'Name's Jerrod Gant. Lives out on the north road.'

The name meant nothing to him. The shock of Baxter's news had temporarily numbed Matt's ability to think. The image that remained uppermost in his mind was that of Ella as she turned to him on the dock when Baxter had arrested her, some kind of silent appeal in her expression. But whether for help or understanding he couldn't say. He'd told her to go with Baxter, and reassured her that it would be okay, that there had to be some kind of mistake, though the look Baxter had worn had put the lie to this.

Now his brain started to function again, and above all he was angry at himself. In all his years in court one thing he'd learned early on was that the most unreliable evidence of all in the investigation of any crime was often that provided by a witness. Witnesses were prone to human weakness. Unlike, say, hard forensic evidence, witnesses made mistakes, told lies, and sometimes brought their own set of motives to a case. The settlement of a grudge perhaps, or a basic character flaw like racism which had caused many a witness to lie under oath before now. The lesson Matt had learned early on was never accept anything a witness says at face value. Look hard at their testimony and examine it for inconsistencies, or self-serving motives. The fact that he had temporarily forgotten that lesson brought home to him how ready he still was to doubt Ella's word, despite everything he'd said to her less than an hour ago. It was that more than anything else that made him angry. Now, as he thought about it one glaring question presented itself.

'How come it took this Jerrod Gant so long to come forward?' he asked Baxter. 'It's been nine days since anyone saw Bryan.'

'Gant said he didn't want to get involved.'

'Didn't want to get involved? Are you serious?' Matt said incredulously. 'We're talking about an eye-witness to a murder here, not somebody who ran a red light. So what changed his mind? Did he suddenly have an attack of conscience?'

Baxter looked uncomfortable and all at once Matt suspected that in fact Baxter had his own doubts about this Gant character. 'You don't believe this guy do you? This is some kind of smoke-screen isn't it? Come on Chief, what the hell is going on here?'

Baxter rounded on him angrily. 'You think I'd arrest Ella for no reason? I got a sworn statement here from a man who says he saw Ella in Bryan's house that night. I've had Gant in here half the afternoon going over his story but he won't budge a goddamned inch. Right now I don't have any choice but to take him for his word. If he's lying about this, then let the troopers figure it out.' He stared angrily at Matt, and then he ran a hand back through his short hair. When he spoke again his tone was more conciliatory. 'Listen Matt, the way I figure it maybe this is the best thing. This way this whole damn mess gets sorted out before anyone else gets hurt.'

'Anyone else?'

'You heard about Ella catching that bluefin yesterday? Well, Jake was out there too and he was running down Ella's lines. Bo Waterman saw the whole thing. He already thinks Ella killed his brother, how do you think he feels about Ella being the one that caught that fish? And how long do you think it'll be before he does something really stupid? This is for Ella's own protection as much as anything else.'

Matt thought that Baxter believed what he was saying, at least to some extent but that didn't make him right. 'Come on Chief, you can't lock Ella up and claim it's for her protection,' he protested.

'That isn't what I said. Ella's been arrested because a witness claims he saw her standing over Bryan's body.'

'A witness you don't even pretend to believe.'

174

'Maybe there's some things that don't add up, but that doesn't mean Gant made all of this up.'

Matt wondered if Baxter had some other reason for wanting Ella handed over to the state authorities. He thought about the way Baxter had reacted when he'd raised the possibility of Kate Little being involved in Bryan's disappearance, and though he didn't like to think that Baxter would allow his personal feelings to interfere in an investigation, he couldn't entirely shake off the idea.

But Baxter appeared intractable, and in the meantime Matt could see that it was pointless arguing and he would be better off preparing for Ella's hearing in front of Judge Walker in the morning. 'I want to see Ella, and I want to see a copy of Jerrod Gant's statement,' he said.

Baxter nodded. 'You can have whatever I can give you. And you can see Ella for as long as you like. I already sent Minelli up to her house to get her some things she might need. I don't want to make this hard on Ella, believe me, Matt.'

Unable to resist seeing how Baxter reacted Matt said, 'Did you get a chance to ask around about Kate Little, to see if she might have known Bryan?'

Baxter stared at him. 'I don't know why you keep bringing her into this. She doesn't have anything to do with it.'

Something in his manner however, struck a discordant note with Matt.

Ella looked up from her bunk when Matt was shown to the cells. He waited for Minelli to unlock the door and discreetly leave them alone, then he sat down next to her. For once she didn't look quite so tough. She searched his face.

'Chief Baxter told me what Jerrod Gant said. It isn't true Matt. I swear it isn't.'

Even if he'd had any doubt about that before, just looking at her would have convinced him she wasn't lying. 'I know it isn't,' he said, and her relief was visible. 'What's more I think Baxter knows it too.' She looked puzzled at that. 'He claims he's worried about you getting hurt. Is it true that Jake ran down your trap line?' She nodded. 'Well, maybe Baxter's right about that at least. Whatever happens, you have to look out for Jake, Ella.'

'I know.'

He smiled. 'I guess we have to postpone dinner. First thing here is, you need to officially retain me as your lawyer, okay?'

Ella hesitated, then she nodded. 'Okay, you're hired.'

'Next thing is we have to get you out of here. The bad news is I can't get you out until the hearing tomorrow. By then I'll find a way to convince the judge that this is a crock and we'll get you released.'

'You can do that?'

'Sure I can. I'm a hotshot lawyer aren't I? I need to go over this statement Gant made. Any reason you can think of why he should come forward now with this story? Does he have any reason to hold a grudge against you?'

Ella shook her head. 'I hardly even know him.'

Matt chose his next words carefully. 'Ella, Gant says he saw you in Bryan's house that night.' He held up his hand quickly when she started to protest. 'Hear me out, okay?'

'Okay.'

'If I'm going to help you, then you have to help me too. You have to tell me everything. Everything Ella. What happened that night?'

Her gaze never wavered from his, but he could almost hear the machinery of her mind as it worked at a frantic pace. The whirring and clattering of wheels within wheels.

'I didn't kill Bryan, Matt, I swear it. And I wasn't in his house that night or any other night.'

He was aware that she hadn't actually answered his question, but for now he sensed that if he pushed her she would clam up and he didn't want to lose the little ground he felt they had made up. For now it came down to the simple question of whether or not he believed her. He gave her hand a reassuring squeeze.

'Thank you,' she said, though he wasn't sure if it was his help she was thanking him for, or the fact he hadn't pressed her. He asked if there was anything she needed, if he should call and see her mother, but she shook her head.

'I called a neighbour to stay with her, and I spoke to Mom and told her I was okay. I'll call her again and let her know what's happening.'

'Tell her you'll be home in the morning.'

Matt hoped he wasn't making promises he couldn't keep.

Jerrod Gant's statement read pretty much as Baxter had outlined, and on the face of it was about as damning as the proverbial smoking gun. Matt read it through sitting at the table on his porch with a cup of coffee in front of him. He looked for inconsistencies in what Gant claimed to have seen, either in terms of timing or visual detail, and when he found none he read it through again searching for some ambiguity he could exploit. Years of experience told him that when an incident was witnessed at night and there were other complicating factors such as it being seen through a window, as in this case, and maybe from a distance, identifications could be cast into doubt. But Gant claimed he'd been standing right at the living room window, that a light had been on inside the room, and Ella had been turned towards him. No room had been left for ambiguity. Matt put the statement down. Gant was the perfect witness. Unless he turned out to be clinically blind, his testimony seemed to be incontrovertible. It was this fact more than anything else that convinced Matt that Gant was lying. His testimony was simply too perfect. It just didn't ring true. Add to that the fact that Gant had taken so long to come forward, and the reason given for his delay was so patently weak, the whole thing had the stink of a set-up. The question was, why would Gant lie, and more immediately how was Matt to convince Judge Walker that he had.

Later on Henry came over, and he brought with him a plate of tomatoes from his garden, beaded with drops of moisture after he'd washed them.

'Do you know this Jerrod Gant?' Matt asked.

'Sure,' Henry said. 'He runs the marine repair shop along the south shore.'

'What kind of guy would you say he is?'

Henry finished eating and began to roll a cigarette, filling the paper with shreds of tobacco and deftly twirling it between his fingers to form a tube. 'To tell the truth I never had a lot of time for Jerrod. He's lived here all his life, but somehow he never seems to make much of anything he does. Married some girl from one of the other islands, though I never understood what she saw in him.'

'You think he could invent something like this?'

'Some people will do just about anything when their back is up against the wall in my experience. I doubt that marine shop of Jerrod's has paid its way in the last little while. I don't know why that would make him invent a story like that if it wasn't true though.'

'Maybe I should ask him,' Matt said.

'Maybe you should,' Henry agreed.

The house where Gant lived was on the north road, several miles past Stillwater Cove. In his statement Gant claimed he'd been setting snares in the woods behind the cove when he'd heard a shot. Matt thought about that as he drove. A man hears a rifle shot, then makes his way to the closest house where he looks through a window and sees a woman he recognizes holding a rifle over the body of a man he also recognizes, whose house this is. Then he simply turns away and says nothing for more than a week. It didn't only not make sense, it was almost laughable.

Matt slowed as he drew close to where he figured the turning to Gant's house must be, and in the gathering gloom he picked out the wooden sign and mailbox in the headlights beside the trees at the side of the road. He made the turn and followed a rutted track for about a quarter of a mile until he came on a small house with a wrap-around porch at the front that had partially collapsed and was propped up at one end by wooden crates. In the yard out front, which consisted of an irregular patch of brown grass and a tangle of weeds growing through the rusted remains of an old truck, was a small Ford sedan that had seen better days. There were lights on in the ground floor windows, and as Matt climbed out of his car the front door opened and a splash of yellow light fell on to the porch and slanted across the steps to the yard. The silhouette of a figure was framed in the doorway.

'Hey,' called a woman's voice. 'Is that you Chuck?'

'Mrs Gant? My name's Matt Jones, I'm a lawyer.' He stepped into the light at the bottom of the steps so that the woman in the doorway could see him.

'Oh,' she said.

'Hi, are you Mrs Gant?'

'Yes,' she answered uncertainly after a pause.

'Mrs Gant, I'm looking for your husband.' She looked at him blankly without responding. 'Jerrod? Is he home?'

'He's gone away.'

'Away? Do you know how long for?' Matt stepped up on to the porch as he spoke and he got a better look at her. She was quite young, maybe in her mid-twenties, which surprised him because from what Henry had told him he'd figured Gant to be middle-aged. She had dark blonde hair that was cut badly and hung about her face in straggly lengths, and she was wearing an old pair of jeans and a shirt that wasn't tucked in. Her eyes were small and pale in colour, and she stared at Matt warily, like an animal that's getting ready to jump any second. Matt smiled at her, thinking if she didn't have the look of somebody who was so inherently suspicious of strangers she might even be pretty in a way.

'He didn't say when he'd be back.' She made no move to invite him in, and in fact the way she stood squarely in the doorway she gave the impression of wanting to keep him out.

'Well, do you know where I might find him?'

Beyond her he could see into a kitchen-cum-living room. A big scarred wooden table dominated the space, around which were half a dozen chairs, none of them matching. The rest of the furniture that was visible appeared old and worn.

She shook her head. 'He didn't say where he was going. Sometimes he goes off looking for work on the other islands. Usually he's gone a day or two. Three maybe.'

179

'And you don't know anyplace I might reach him?'

'I didn't even know he was going until this afternoon.'

'Mrs Gant, your husband made a statement today to the police about an incident he claims he witnessed about a week ago. It seems kind of strange that he would have just up and left.' The woman stared at him, but didn't respond. 'Do you know anything about what your husband saw Mrs Gant?'

'He doesn't tell me anything.'

Matt wondered if it was really possible that she didn't know what he was talking about, which is the impression she gave. 'We're talking about a murder Mrs Gant. Your husband claims he witnessed a murder. He didn't mention that to you? That's a little strange don't you think?'

'I don't know anything about it,' she insisted doggedly.

Matt was perplexed at her attitude. It was clear she didn't want to talk to him.

'Mrs Gant, this is a serious matter. I'd like to come in and talk to you about it. Can I do that?' She hesitated and he could see her thinking about the fact that he was a lawyer, weighing up whether he was just asking or whether he had the power to insist.

'You might want to do it now, rather than come down to the court in the morning,' he prompted.

Reluctantly, she stood aside. 'Place is kind of a mess.' She waved him vaguely towards a chair. As she closed the door, she peered into the darkness outside, as if she was looking for somebody there.

Matt didn't get much out of Lucy Gant that was directly useful. It turned out that she'd been telling the truth when she said that her husband didn't tell her much. Matt formed an impression of a young woman, even younger than her years, married to a man fifteen years older than her, stuck out in the woods in a run down house, without much money on an island where she had few friends. She came from another island in the north, where her circumstances had probably been even worse. When Jerrod Gant had offered to marry her, she saw it as a chance to escape. She now seemed inhabited with a mixture of disillusionment and resignation. She chain smoked as Matt asked her questions, stubbing out one cigarette after another. She seemed nervous about something, but she answered without guile, and he didn't think she was holding anything back. She simply didn't know, and she seemed uninterested and completely lacking in surprise that her husband might come home one night and fail to mention that he'd just witnessed a murder.

'Do you remember that Monday night?' Matt questioned. 'Can you remember what time your husband came in?'

She thought for a moment, and then lit another cigarette. 'Sorry. The days seem all the same I guess.'

He asked her a couple more questions, and then figuring she couldn't tell him anything else he gave up on her. As he rose to leave she smiled for the first time, as if she had passed a test of some kind and was glad it was at an end. She kept glancing at the door and went over to open it as if she was in a hurry to get rid of him.

'Well thanks for your time.' Matt gave her a card. 'If your husband should show up, tell him to call me. Or if you think of anything.' She took the card but didn't look at it.

'Okay.'

Matt went back to his car and as he left he looked back as the door closed, and he imagined her going inside and throwing his card in the trash.

CHAPTER NINETEEN

The hearing before Judge Walker was at ten, and Matt spent the hours from six in the morning until then trying to substantiate his conviction that Gant's testimony was at best unreliable, at worst a complete fabrication. He called at Jerrod Gant's workshop, which was, as Henry had told him, situated on the south shore a little way past the town boundary. It was the first time Matt had been in that direction. The Ash river flowed into the sea here, and the inlet was protected by a natural harbour. This was where Howard Larson planned to build his marina and then later on the services and business that would support the people and craft who would use it. Extending further south the shore was rocky, and the broad meadow-lands that rose gently inland towards the low wooded foothills beyond made perfect housing sites. Along the shoreline the views out over the gulf were spectacular. Wooden stakes marked out lots and Matt tried to envisage all this buried under concrete, the grass and wildflowers ripped up and replaced with roads and gas stations and pizza restaurants.

Gant's Marine was announced by a peeled and blistering sign over a dilapidated shed on the banks of the river inlet. It was part of a small light industrial area. A slipway led down to the water, and some rusting pieces of machinery lay half buried in the mud at the water's edge. Matt tried the wooden door but it was locked and the place had about it a forlorn air. He went to the building next door where a red truck was parked outside. A sign read 'Decoy Auto Repairs'. A man was bent over the front of a jeep inside, with the hood up and a light hanging overhead. He straightened up when he saw Matt, and when Matt asked if he'd seen Jerrod Gant around he shook his head, then came outside and looked back along the inlet.

'His boat's gone. He keeps it here so he must've gone off somewhere. Try tomorrow, or mebbe the next day.'

'Thanks.' As Matt started to leave, he looked back towards the meadow where all the stakes marked out the lots. 'I guess if this all goes ahead, things will pick up for you,' he said.

'Could be. That's what some say anyway.' The man lit a cigarette. 'These places'll be gone though.' He gestured towards the building where he worked, and the others on either side.

'Gone?'

'There's plans for berths on the river here. Over yonder's going to be some new buildings for the likes of us here.' He pointed to a piece of land further up river, beyond a belt of beech trees.

The man sounded less than happy at the prospect of moving to a new building, which Matt didn't understand since it occurred to him that anyone currently working here would get a good price for the land they were occupying. Including Jerrod Gant. But when he said as much the man shook his head.

'These places are all leased. Howard Larson owns most of this land around here. I guess in the end it won't make much difference what happens. If the marina gets built we'll get more business, but then Larson will make us move and you can bet we'll be paying more rent in the new places, so we'll likely be no better off anyway.' He shrugged. 'What can you do?'

The man wandered back to his work, and Matt looked thoughtfully back at the building that housed Gant's Marine.

They were waiting for him by the time he arrived at the courthouse. The hearing was being held in Judge Walker's office, and as Matt came down the corridor Baxter was at the other end talking to Howard Larson. When they saw him they broke off their conversation and Baxter came to meet him at the door.

'Ella's inside.'

'Was that Howard I saw just then?'

Baxter looked around, as if he wasn't sure and needed to check. 'Yeah,' he said and didn't volunteer anything else.

'Something to do with Ella?'

Baxter stared at him. 'Why should it have anything to do with Ella?'

'You tell me.'

Baxter ignored the question and opened the door. 'We better go inside.'

Ella looked both relieved and a little anxious when she saw him. He gave her a smile of encouragement, and after he'd shaken hands with the judge he went over to where she was sitting on a big leather couch.

'I was getting worried,' she said.

'Sorry I'm late. Just sit tight and don't worry. Answer whatever questions you're asked truthfully, okay?'

Ella bit her bottom lip, then nodded.

'You'll be out of here soon,' he promised.

Judge Walker was thin and stooped, and he was mostly bald. He looked to be in his sixties, and for the hearing he'd come dressed in a grey suit which he wore with a blue shirt and a badly knotted maroon tie. The gaze he fastened on Matt, however, was scrutinizing and intelligent and Matt decided he shouldn't be fooled by appearances. The judge sat down behind his desk and put on his glasses. In front of him were the papers concerning the charges against Ella, including the witness statement made by Jerrod Gant.

He began without preamble. 'Let's get on with this thing.' He looked at Ella, and said, 'You okay there Ella? Anything you need?'

'I'm fine thanks Judge.'

'Right, just so you know, we're here to decide whether there's enough evidence to proceed with the charge that Chief Baxter here has brought against you. If we decide there is, all that means is that your case will be handed over to the jurisdiction of the state attorney's office on the mainland.' He peered over his glasses. 'That means we'll have to hand you into the custody of the state police, Ella. Do you understand?'

She glanced at Matt. 'Yes.'

The judge turned his attention to Baxter. 'I guess it's you first Chief.'

The facts of the charge Baxter laid out were straightforward enough. As evidence supporting it he listed the threat Ella had made to Bryan, the testimony of Carl Johnson, but most damning of all, Gant's statement. Matt listened without interruption. Baxter spoke without looking at either Matt or Ella, and when he'd finished he seemed glad about it.

Judge Walker made notes as he listened, but made no comment, then he looked to Matt. 'Your turn Counsellor.'

'First of all Judge,' Matt began, 'I'd like to start with the argument Ella and Bryan had that night. Ella isn't denying it happened, but plenty of people saw Bryan walk away afterwards. It doesn't mean a thing.' He went on to state that the rest of the evidence, such as there was, was entirely circumstantial, and that without corroborating evidence it was worthless.

'What about this statement of Gant's? That's corroborating.'

'Judge, I don't believe that statement is worth the paper it's written on.' He explained how he'd gone to Gant's house and spoken with his wife the night before. 'I mean first off this man claims he witnessed a murder, and at the time he doesn't do anything about it, then he doesn't even mention it to his wife, which you have to admit is pretty strange.'

'I don't know, there's a few things I don't mention to my wife,' the judge cut in and Matt smiled. Judge Walker waved a hand. 'I take your point. Go on.'

'Then there's the fact that Gant waited for ten days before he decided to make a statement. He claims he didn't want to get involved, but he doesn't give any credible explanation as to what changed his mind. None of this makes sense.'

'In my experience people often don't make much sense,' Judge Walker commented. He looked at Baxter. 'You're pretty quiet there, Chief. Don't you have anything to say about this?'

Baxter glanced quickly at Matt. 'I'll admit it's been bothering me too. But I went over this with Jerrod for a couple of hours yesterday. He swears it's the truth Judge. I don't see what option

I had but to bring Ella in.' He turned to Ella. 'The fact is I'm worried about you as much as anything, Ella. This whole thing looks to me like it might blow up and I don't want to see anyone get hurt.' He turned back to Judge Walker. 'There's already been trouble between Jake and Ella, Judge. I hate to think how he's going to react if he hears I let Ella go after this.'

'We're not here to do what Jake wants,' the judge reminded him.

'I know that. But we don't know that Jerrod Gant is lying. I just think we ought to hand this over to the state police. Give things a while to calm down.'

Matt shook his head vigorously. 'Come on. Since when do we start locking people up because it seems like an expedient thing to do? If the chief here really thinks Jake could be a problem, it's him he ought to be locking up, not Ella.'

'Now hold on there,' Judge Walker said to both of them. 'What we ought to be concentrating on here is Jerrod Gant's evidence, since that's what this all swings on. I'd like to talk to him myself.'

'He's gone Judge. His wife doesn't know where he is, and neither does anyone else. I went by the place he works from and his boat is gone.' Matt gathered from Baxter's expression that this was news to him. 'And if nobody can question Gant about what he claims he saw, that has to make his evidence unreliable.' He picked up his copy of the statement. 'Gant says he just happened to be in the vicinity of Bryan's house when he heard a shot, and he even knows exactly what time it was, which is pretty convenient as it ties in with what Carl Johnson already heard. Then he looks right in a lit window and sees Bryan Roderick on the floor with Ella standing over him with a gun? I mean, come on.'

'Judge,' Baxter interrupted. 'If Matt here thinks Gant is lying, he ought to cross examine him in court.'

The judge waved a hand to silence Baxter. 'The state attorney's office aren't going to thank us for handing them this thing without there being some kind of reliable evidence, Chief. I want to hear what Matt has to say. So, you don't believe him. But why would he make up a story like this?'

'I'd like to ask him that myself. But I can't do that because he's conveniently disappeared. This whole thing looks like a set-up to me.'

'A set-up? This is St George you're talking about Counsellor, not Chicago. Why would anyone want to set Ella up?'

'Maybe someone who'd like to see her out of the way. Jerrod Gant's business isn't doing too well, but he works from a building on the inlet on the south shore. If Ella is charged and handed over to the state police she won't have a prayer of winning the election next week. Gant has a lot to gain from seeing that marina go ahead. Everybody here knows that Ella is opposed to the plan.' Matt paused, letting the implication of what he was saying sink in, then, looking at Baxter, he added, 'Maybe other people might have their reasons for wanting to see Ella out of the way too.'

'Other people?'

'The thing is, Judge, this whole thing with Gant's statement feels wrong to me, and without it there's no real evidence against her, in fact the truth is there's no real evidence that Bryan is even dead. Right now, we don't know what happened to him. But even if he is dead, Bryan must have had his fair share of enemies. I don't think enough has been done to look at who else might have had a reason to want to kill him.'

Baxter looked sharply at Matt, suddenly suspicious of what he was getting at. He started to say something, but the judge held up his hand. 'Wait a minute, Chief. I haven't heard from you yet Ella. I'd like to hear what you have to say about all of this.'

'I don't know why Jerrod Gant gave this statement Judge, but I swear that I did not kill Bryan Roderick. If Gant really did see anybody in that house that night, it wasn't me.'

The judge nodded slowly, and looked thoughtful. 'Okay,' he said after a while. 'I have to agree with Matt about what Jerrod Gant says he saw. It all sounds a little fishy to me. Especially since he's up and taken off someplace. So, until he shows up and we can question him I don't think we've enough evidence to warrant turning Ella over to the state authorities. Even if we did, my guess is that Matt would have her out again within the day anyway, based on what we have here. But I can't just ignore Gant's sworn statement either. So here's what I'm going to do. Find Jerrod Gant and bring him here so that I can question him, let's see if this thing holds water or if he really is playing some dirty game to stop Ella being elected. I'll give you a week, until the day after the election. If you haven't found him then or he hasn't turned up by himself we'll pass this over to the state and they can decide what to do.'

He looked at Ella. 'That's the best I can do Ella. The fact is, if Matt is right about Jerrod Gant I'm afraid releasing you isn't going to help a hell of a lot. People are going to hear about this anyway and make up their own minds. Unless Matt can find Gant before the election and prove he was lying, he may just have scuppered your chances anyway. But in the meantime, you're free to go.'

CHAPTER TWENTY

Ella hung up the phone after speaking to her mother. She turned to Matt. 'So what happens now?'

'Like the man said, you're free to go. I don't think the judge believed Gant's statement any more than I did.'

'But it doesn't matter, does it,' Ella said bitterly. 'Maybe I didn't have a lot of chance of winning the election before, but this pretty much seals it. Judge Walker was right. People are going to know what's going on and a lot of them are going to think there's no smoke without fire. I know the way their minds work.'

Matt didn't argue. Even though Ella wasn't under arrest any more some of the mud was going to stick. He didn't say so, but if Gant turned up and he stuck to his testimony, Ella was going to have to worry about a lot more than just losing an election. Ella guessed that he was worried and asked why.

'The fact is I don't know for sure why Gant lied. I'm only guessing that it had anything to do with the election.'

'What other reason could he have?'

'Maybe he didn't lie about everything he saw that night,' Matt said. 'I'm not suggesting that he really saw you in that house, but maybe he saw someone. Could be he even believes it was you.'

Ella worked out what that could mean. 'You're saying I could still be charged.'

'If Gant sticks to his statement.' Matt allowed a moment or two for Ella to absorb what he'd told her. 'Of course there's a

189

way to beat this,' he went on, 'so that Howard doesn't win the election and you don't face a murder charge.'

'And what would that be?'

'All we have to do is prove to everyone that you didn't kill Bryan. Which means I have to find out who did.'

He waited for her to say something, but she just looked at him and he couldn't figure out what she was thinking.

'Ella, you said on the dock that there were things you couldn't explain, and when I asked you what really happened that night you avoided the question by telling me that it wasn't you Gant saw in that house, and that you didn't kill Bryan. I believe you on both counts, but I think you know more than you're telling me.'

She stared at him, and her eyes were the smoky, half grey, half green colour they became sometimes. She appeared torn with indecision.

He took a chance and pressed her. 'What happened that night Ella?'

She reached a decision and gave a small shake of her head. 'I don't know.'

She was lying, and that knowledge weighed heavily on him, but her chin had a stubborn thrust that told him no amount of persuasion from him would change her mind right then.

'I'm sorry. I have to go,' she said.

When Ella got home her mother was pale, her expression pinched with worry. Ella made her sit down. 'Did you take your medicine?'

Helena dismissed her question with a wave of her hand, as if it was of no importance. 'I'm fine, don't fuss. What about you Ella? Are you all right?'

Ella assured her that a night in jail hadn't been so bad. 'The food was fine, and everybody was nice to me.' She made it sound as if she'd spent the night in a motel. In fact she had found the experience terrifying and more disturbing than she could have imagined. To have somebody close a door and turn the key in the lock, and know that person controlled your freedom, controlled everything about your life; when you ate, when you slept, how you filled your day, when you saw the sky and breathed fresh air, was a sobering lesson. It was hard enough being confined to the jail in town, where at least she knew her jailers, she couldn't imagine how it would feel to be locked up in a prison on the mainland. It was something she couldn't contemplate.

'Ella,' her mother took both her daughter's hands in her own. Ella noticed how fragile her mother's were, her skin felt brittle to the touch. Over the course of only six months she had aged beyond her years. The stroke she had suffered after Ella's father's death had drained her strength, abruptly robbed her of her vitality and made her into an old woman before her time. She came from a Greek family who had prospered around Provincetown. In pictures of them the men stood straight with their chests thrust out, their chins forward, the women sat stoically staring at the camera. Helena had run away to marry Ella's father when she was twenty-two, and hadn't spoken to her own father since.

'I think we should tell him. I think we should tell Matt everything,' Helena said.

'No.' Ella shook her head firmly. Her night in jail had reinforced to her that what her mother was suggesting was something she couldn't do. 'It'll be okay, Mom. It'll work out, I promise.'

Helena looked into her eyes, searching to see if Ella was telling the truth. In the end she nodded gently, accepting for now that she was.

Ella couldn't imagine how it would feel to not go out on the *Santorini* each day. She knew the coves and bays and headlands of the island like the back of her hand. She knew the forested slopes where the hills rose in a spine-like ridge, and the meadows in the north where cows grazed, she knew the cranberry bogs on the eastern side. She knew the changing palette of the island and looked forward to the seasons. The deep green of the hemlocks and cedars which held the high ground year round, the flowers that lit the meadows in spring with sparks of indigo and yellow and orange, and the scarlet fires of maple leaves and golden browns of oak in the fall. She saw it all from the sea. In

191

the summer when the heat boiled and the deck planking burned bare skin, and in the winter when the seas rose in grey slabs of fluid movement and the sky pressed down and the water changed from blue to charcoal to pale grey flecked with white. When bitter winds whipped spray into her face which stung like needles, when hands grew so cold they became numb and turned blue and the pain as they thawed later was excruciating. All of this was part of life, of her life, and Ella had never wanted anything different. Even though it was hard to make a living, she survived as did many others. They were the last true hunter gatherers alive, part of the circle of life and death, of decay and renewal, and she didn't ever want the island to change. She didn't want the meadows ploughed under, and the island to be invaded by people wearing designer clothes, didn't want fancy bars and restaurants springing up, or new roads for the summer people to drive their expensive cars and a yacht club where they could sit and watch their gleaming white boats. She wanted things to remain as they were.

The irony was that by keeping silent she risked it all, but she didn't know what else she could do.

When she went down to the docks later Ella was aware of the curious looks people cast her way. She guessed by now everybody knew she'd been arrested and released, that speculation was running at fever pitch. Twice it seemed to her that people deliberately crossed the road when they saw her coming, but she told herself she was being paranoid. All the same she had the uncomfortable sensation of low conversations suddenly dying as she approached, and starting up again after she'd passed by and the back of her neck prickled all the way to her boat.

Gordon was working, mending pots while he sat on the deck of the *Santorini*. He grinned when he saw her. Hers was one of the few boats in the harbour. Most of the others were out again looking for the elusive bluefin.

'I heard some were seen south, in close to the mainland,' Gordon told her. 'And there's a story one was caught this morning near Bear Island.'

Ella went to Art Turner's office, and when he saw her coming he jumped out of his chair and insisted she sit down. Then he pulled open a drawer and handed her a cheque. She read the amount, her eyes wide.

'You took your cut?'

'Fifteen percent. The rest is all yours Ella.'

She read the amount again, double checking the number of zeroes. The fish she and Gordon had caught had taken them a long time to beat, and so it hadn't been in perfect condition. She'd figured to get less than half of what Art had paid her.

'Right about now that sucker will be making sushi in some fancy restaurant in Tokyo,' Art told her. 'Beats the hell out of me how much those Japanese fellas'll pay for one fish, but I ain't complaining.'

'Neither am I.' She stood up and folded the cheque, then leaned over the desk and kissed Art impulsively on his cheek. 'I have to get to the bank.'

She deposited two thirds of her share of the money in her account. Though a lot of it would go to cover the loan payments she was behind on, there would be enough left over to give her some peace of mind, for a while anyway. The rest she carried in a folded wad in her pocket, and when she got back to the *Santorini* she gave it to Gordon, enjoying the way his eyes goggled at the amount.

Before he could even think about arguing with her she clasped both of his hands around the notes. 'You keep it. You earned this Gordon.'

That night, after her mother was asleep, Ella sat by the phone, Kate Little's number written down on the pad beside her, and several times she began to reach for the receiver, but each time she hesitated and let her hand drop. She rehearsed over and over what she would say, and each time she became confused, and forgot her words and finally she knew that she couldn't make the call. In the end, she turned out the light and went to bed.

Part Three

CHAPTER TWENTY-ONE

Howard lay on the bed with his hands behind the back of his head, watching Amy Tucker as she came back from the bathroom. She was naked, her pale breasts jiggled and bounced as she hopped on to the bed. She retrieved the piece of gum she'd stuck to the bed-head earlier and popped it in her mouth. Howard caught a glimpse of her pink tongue, and seeing the way he looked at her she reached over and took hold of his flaccid penis.

'What're you thinking about Howard, as if I didn't know?'

She straddled him, and he caught a glimpse of the dark cleft between her legs and felt himself harden.

'Whoa, Howard, look at this. You are an animal, I swear.'

Amy leaned forward and kissed him, thrusting her hard little tongue between his lips. She tasted of juicy fruit and a lingering remnant of the cigarettes she smoked, which was less pleasant. With one hand she guided him, and settled over him, wiggling her hips like she was making herself comfortable in her favourite chair.

'Jesus Howard, you know how to hit the spot.' Amy closed her eyes, adopting a rapturous expression, her lips a little apart, uttering soft kittenish mewing sounds as she rocked her hips back and forth. 'God, that sure feels good. I get so damn horny when I'm with you.'

Howard knew at least part of it was an act, and he wasn't fooled, but maybe Amy knew that too and so it didn't matter. It was all a game. Life was a game, full of winners and losers, he thought to himself, pleased to consider himself one of the former. One thing about sex with Amy, no matter whether or not it was based on a little mutual deception, it was good, there was no denying that. He took her hands and guided them to her breasts.

She didn't even falter, just carried on mewing and rocking and started massaging herself, caressing her nipples between finger and thumb. Howard started to feel himself build to a climax. Amy opened one eye, sensing him stiffen, and she ground herself down against the bone in his groin lest she miss out herself, and a few seconds later, slick with sweat she collapsed over him, the two of them panting like dogs in the heat.

'Whewee,' she said after a while, and rolled off him. 'You're a pistol Howard, you know that?'

He smiled with pleasure despite himself. 'Plenty more where that came from, honey.'

She got up on one elbow and swept the hair back out of her eyes, one finger started tracing patterns on his chest. 'We could do this every night if we wanted,' she said in what she imagined passed for a coy tone.

Howard sat up on the side of the bed, the mattress sagging underneath his weight. They were in Amy's apartment over the hair and beauty salon she owned. The window was open and the smell of the harbour – fish and salt and mud – lay draped over the town in a limp humid haze. He could feel Amy's sulk.

'Come on,' he said. 'You know if we did this every day it wouldn't be fun any more. We'd get sick of each other.'

'I wouldn't get sick of you,' she pouted.

'You would if I wasn't about to get rich.'

She crawled over to him and wrapped her arms around him, squashing her plump breasts into his back. 'Is that what you think? I don't care about your money. I don't know why you want to stay with that wife of yours anyway. When was the last time she fucked you the way I do?'

Amy had a point, Howard had to concede. But what Amy didn't understand and he could never explain to her was that his wife had more class and more allure in one shapely calf than

Amy ever would in all her fleshy, gaudy curves. Some women were built for fun, and some were built to marry. Amy was definitely the former. He knew she wouldn't press her case. She brought it up now and again to see if he was weakening, but he didn't really think she minded being his mistress instead of his wife. The truth was he suspected she liked it that way. She still got the benefits of his money without having to put up with the dull routines of domestic togetherness.

She let go and flopped back on the bed and reached over for her cigarettes. Howard pulled on his socks and stood up looking for his shorts. He caught sight of his pale bloated belly and his thin legs and was vaguely repulsed. Like most people he nurtured an image like an air-brushed picture of himself in his mind and he resented being confronted with the truth.

'You're not exactly Rockefeller you know, Howard,' Amy said.

'You won't be saying that a year from now. Once I win the election and get the go ahead on that marina the money is gonna pour in. I've got investors dying to get in on this thing.'

'*If* you win the election.' Amy blew smoke into the air.

'Don't you worry about that. Didn't you hear about Ella being arrested? Who the hell is going to vote for her now?'

'But she was released Howard. And nobody knows where the hell Jerrod Gant is.'

Howard started to say something, then stopped himself and grinned.

'What are you looking so pleased with yourself about?'

He shook his head. 'Nothing. Anyway, doesn't matter that she's been released. Ella doesn't have a chance of winning next week.'

Amy took a drag on her cigarette and eyed him speculatively. 'Is this thing really gonna make you rich Howard?'

'Oh yeah. You can bet on it.'

'How rich? Does this mean we could go on a vacation together like we used to talk about. You know, on a cruise to the Bahamas or something?'

'Why the hell not? Soon as things have settled down that is. I'm going to be pretty busy for a while, Amy.' He found his shorts and pulled them on. As a matter of fact he'd been thinking he might have to get rid of Amy. If things turned out the way he hoped he couldn't take the risk of someone finding out about them. He was going to have wealthy friends, contacts, important people. They would be friends with his wife, he couldn't take the chance of embarrassing her. It was too bad. Amy was without doubt good in the sack.

She sidled over the bed. 'When will I see you again?'

'Couple of days,' he said. No point in letting her go yet.

He let himself out the back door, cautiously checking the street before he left. His car was parked near his office on the waterfront. It was dusk and the harbour was full. The bars and restaurants in town were doing a roaring trade from the swarm of people who'd descended on the island from nowhere. They hadn't wasted any time getting here. Once the news had leaked out about the bluefin Ella had caught people had begun arriving the very next day. Boats of all kinds were turning up by midmorning. Some of them were carrying charter groups, others were professional fishermen; draggers and lobster boats from the mainland, and many more were just opportunists; vacationers with their launches and yachts of all sizes. Even the ferry had been fully booked, people coming over on the off-chance that they could buy their way on to a boat. Everyone hoping they might get lucky and catch themselves a ten-thousand-dollar fish. It was incredible. Like a goddamned gold rush.

Howard paused to watch a man painting a crude sign on a piece of wood offering charter fishing for two hundred dollars a day per person. The man wore a faded T-shirt and old jeans, and as he worked his brow was creased in a concentrated frown. Howard recognized him. He'd worked at the plant for a few months last year, but he'd been fired because he was often drunk when he turned up. Lucky, people called him, which Howard guessed was an ironic nickname.

'You spelt that word wrong,' Howard said. Lucky looked back at him, half vacantly, dripping black paint on his jeans.

'Huh?'

'Charter. It's "e r" not "u h".' He had spelt 'Charter', as 'Chartuh'. Lucky gazed at his handiwork, and made the correction.

'Thanks.'

Howard looked at the crabber that was tied to the dock. The paint was blistered and all but gone, and the engine on the back was rusted. He figured Lucky would need to pay him to go out in that thing, and he hoped the man's fortune lived up to his name for once when he went out in it. 'You had any takers yet?'

Lucky looked back at him. 'Sure. Couple of guys from Connecticut who were on vacation over on the mainland.'

Howard shook his head in wonder. The things people would do for the chance to make a little money.

CHAPTER TWENTY-TWO

Matt had spent a frustrating afternoon trying to track down Jerrod Gant, but without much success. He called in at the harbourmaster's office and got a list of Tom Spencer's opposite numbers on nearby islands, but after eventually speaking to them all and following up on the leads they gave him, he drew a blank. Gant was well known, and several of the people Matt spoke to had hired him in the past, but none had seen him during the last few days.

The only other thing he'd done that afternoon was to speak to Ruth Thorne when she called.

'I thought about what you said Mr Jones, and I want you to find out if Charlie is cheating on me. If he is then I'm too good for him, and I don't want to stay with someone like that a second longer than I have to.'

There was no trace of indecision in her tone, and though Matt didn't much like the role he was taking on he thought, good for you. He liked Ruth Thorne, and he hoped whichever way it turned out that he could help her.

'Call me Matt, by the way,' he told her. He asked her to check out when her husband would next be staying away the night, and to give him a call and he'd find out where he went. 'Then we'll get together and you can hear what I have to say before you decide what you want to do, okay? I want you to take this a step at a time. I'll just charge you for the time each step takes. And as you're my first client this week, you get a special forty percent discount as well.' He wondered why he'd added that last piece, not having planned to, but when he heard how grateful she sounded, he was pleased that he had.

'I really appreciate that Mr Jones. I mean Matt. To tell the truth I was kind of worried about how much this would cost.'

'Don't worry,' Matt found himself saying. 'We'll work something out.' As he hung up, he hoped that there was going to be a steady demand for Henry's cider, because he doubted he was going to make much money as a lawyer.

He went home and changed, and thought about calling Ella, but he guessed she'd want some time alone with her mother after spending a night in jail. After dark he headed into town in need of a change of scenery. He wondered briefly whether Baxter had fared better in his search for Gant, assuming he'd even been looking. The fact was he no longer knew what to make of Baxter. He kept thinking about the chief and Howard Larson standing together at the end of the corridor when he'd arrived at the court house. He wondered what they'd been talking about.

Matt parked his car near a bar called *The Lobster Pot* opposite the docks where the pleasure craft were moored, and as he crossed the street he saw Kate Little's Mercedes parked outside.

The door to *The Lobster Pot* was at street level, and opened to a narrow flight of stairs that led to a bar and restaurant where the tables looked over the harbour. It was gloomy inside, the red lampshades on the tables contributing to a slightly dated atmosphere. The place had the feel of somewhere that might have been popular elsewhere back in the early eighties.

The restaurant was busy, many of the tables taken by people eating dinner. Talk drifted loudly about fishing, rumours exchanged about bluefin that had been seen that day. The customers were mostly visitors, and if they were bothered by the decor they didn't show it. The menu on the wall featured lobster and crab heavily, along with other sea food. Plastic lobsters and old pots had been hung around the walls, and above the bar a dusty net hung down, studded with fake fish and molluscs.

Matt went to the bar and ordered a beer and found himself charged an extra buck. When he expressed surprise the bartender apologized.

'Sorry, thought you were one of them.' He nodded towards a table of guys who talked and looked as if they were from the city. 'Locals get a discount.' He indicated a new price list had been posted behind the bar. It appeared that inflation had inexplicably run out of control on St George. The bartender gave Matt his dollar back, winked at him then went to serve somebody else.

Matt looked around for Kate Little, and spotted her sitting alone at a table in the corner where she was gazing out of the window. She was dressed in light coloured pants and a dark navy jacket, and in the red glow from the lamp her hair shone like hot coals on a fire. He watched her for a few moments unobserved, trying to form an impression of her. She had an almost empty glass in front of her, and an ashtray full of stubbed out cigarettes. She appeared lost in some private contemplation, her gaze distant and unfocused through the window. Outside the lights in the harbour were blinking, and Kate's reflection stared back at her.

He spoke to a waitress, then went over to Kate. 'Would you mind if I join you?'

She looked up, startled by the sound of his voice, then when she recognized him she indicated a chair. 'Help yourself.'

He sat down, and a waitress brought over a screwdriver. 'I saw your glass was about empty,' Matt explained.

She stared at him for a full five seconds as if trying to decide whether to accept the drink, then she made a small movement of her head. 'Thank you.'

'You folks eating this evening?' the waitress asked.

'Would you like to join me?' Matt said.

'Thanks but I have to go back and fix dinner for Evan.' She lit a cigarette from the pack on the table. She wore several rings on her long elegant fingers. The diamonds glittered in the light.

'Let me know if you change your mind,' the waitress said.

When they were alone Matt raised his drink, and after a second Kate responded and they touched glasses. 'I understand you've been coming to the island for a while. Do you spend the whole summer here?'

'About three months normally.'

'It must seem pretty quiet after New York.'

'Evan likes it that way. He doesn't like to have a lot of people around. Did you have any luck with your missing person?' Kate said after a while.

'Bryan Roderick? Not yet.'

'The police didn't find anything when they searched the cove did they?'

'No.'

'Do you think he's dead?'

The query was almost casual. Almost but not quite. 'I don't know,' Matt said.

She lit another cigarette and blew smoke across the table. 'I heard that somebody was arrested yesterday.'

'Ella Young. The woman I mentioned to you. She was released again this morning. Ella's my client.'

Kate stared at him and her surprise was obvious.

'How is your husband today Mrs Little?' he asked her.

'He's a little better. He has good days and bad.'

'Do you mind if I ask how he was injured?'

'It happened on a skiing trip. Evan hit a tree. He was lucky he wasn't killed.'

'I'm sorry.'

She emptied her glass and put it down on the table, then signalled for the waitress to bring her another. Matt wondered how many she'd had. She didn't seem drunk, but then a lot of people who drank all the time could appear sober when others would have passed out under the table.

'It was a long time ago now. He was a very active man before his accident.' Kate looked out the window again, and Matt had the feeling she didn't see her own reflection or the lights in the harbour, but was looking inward at her own memories. When the waitress brought her drink Kate seemed to remember that Matt was there.

'We'd only been married for eighteen months when it happened. I was a model when we met,' she told him.

He could believe it. She was an attractive woman. 'This was in New York?'

'Yes.' She smiled for the first time since he'd sat down. 'I didn't even like him at first. Evan was already wealthy then, he'd started his own software company before that kind of thing really took off. Have you ever been married Mr Jones?'

'Matt. And yes I was once.'

'Did you fall in love with your wife the day you met her?'

'I don't think so. I think it took a while.'

'I think it can sometimes. Funny isn't it? Evan used his money to impress people, but when that didn't work with me he was intrigued. I guess he saw me as some kind of challenge. He had to revert to the old-fashioned methods, the tried and true.' She picked up her drink and took a long sip. 'He was quite different then. Charming, funny. I hardly even knew I was falling in love with him. The accident changed him.'

'You mentioned that the medication he takes affects his moods?'

'It exaggerates them. Evan was always a little obsessive. The drugs just made him worse.'

'That must have been difficult for you.'

'You could say that.'

There was a trace of bitterness in her tone, but more than that she sounded sad. Matt sipped at his beer. He could only guess at the exact nature of Kate's relationship with her husband, but he imagined their marriage was not a happy one, and probably hadn't been for a long time. 'A lot of people would have found your situation difficult to handle,' he ventured.

She regarded him levelly. 'Are you wondering why I didn't leave my husband Mr Jones?'

'No, I didn't mean that,' Matt said, but he knew she wasn't fooled.

'Most people assume I stayed because of his money. They're wrong.' She jabbed out her cigarette in the ashtray with short stabs and Matt wondered how often she'd been accused of being a gold digger. 'People always assume the worst don't they? Love and hate are intense emotions. Maybe it's true what they say, that they're only divided by a thin line.'

He wasn't sure what she meant by that, except that he recalled that for a time shortly after Kirstin had left him to live with another man, he had hated her too. He'd felt betrayed and humiliated, and later he'd been consumed with self-pity. He'd begun drinking heavily, and through that period he'd mourned the breakdown of his marriage, and he'd both loved and hated Kirstin at the same time, his feelings sometimes fluctuating a dozen times within an hour.

Kate Little put her cigarettes away in her purse, and looked at her watch. 'I should be getting back.'

'There was something I wanted to ask you,' Matt said. 'Your husband seemed very certain that he didn't sleep in his office on the night Bryan Roderick disappeared. I mean with all the medication he takes, he could be wrong couldn't he?'

'It's possible.'

'You don't remember yourself where he slept?'

'No. Evan and I have separate rooms, even when he's upstairs. He gets very restless at night and he needs a special bed.'

Matt thought about that. 'So, when your husband said you were both sleeping around two fifteen that night, when shots were heard in the cove, he was actually only speaking for himself. In the sense that he couldn't have known whether you were in your room or not.'

'I suppose so,' she admitted.

'Did you hear anything that night Mrs Little?'

'No.'

'Were you home the entire night?'

She regarded him levelly for several seconds. 'Yes, I was.'

Matt was struck with a conviction based on nothing more than instinct, gut feeling, that she was lying.

She drained the remnants of her glass. 'And now, unless you have any other questions, I have to go.'

'No, I don't have any more questions,' Matt said, rising with her. 'Goodnight Mrs Little.'

'Goodnight.'

Through the window he saw her emerge on to the street and cross to her car. It occurred to him that she shouldn't be driving with the amount she'd had to drink, but it was too late for him to stop her now. As she got in her car she glanced up, and just for a moment their eyes met, but her expression was enigmatic.

Matt stayed to finish his beer, thinking about Kate Little, ideas going around in his mind. The waitress came over to clear the table, and on impulse he asked if Kate came in very often.

'She's pretty regular.'

'You ever see her talk to anyone in particular?'

The waitress looked at him shrewdly, figuring he was interested in Kate himself. 'You mean a guy? She's married you know.'

'That's not what I had in mind.' He found a five dollar bill to tip her.

'Well, she talks to a lot of people. There was one guy she used to be in here with for a while, Jordan Osborne, but that was last year.'

Matt made a mental note of the name. 'Nobody recently. How about Bryan Roderick? You ever see her with him?'

The waitress shook her head. 'No, Bryan didn't come in here much, but I guess she would have been his type. He would have thought she was classy.' She pulled a face, as if it was an opinion she didn't agree with.

Matt thanked her, and finished his beer before he left. He thought about going somewhere to get something to eat, but everywhere appeared to be busy catering for the sudden influx of people to the island. He knew that all he had at home was half a loaf of stale bread and some of Henry's smoked fish. He hadn't been able to muster the will to buy any groceries lately, much less actually turn his mind to fixing himself dinner. He'd survived on what Henry gave him, and what he could heat in the microwave, but neither option appealed to him right now. In the end he decided he wasn't hungry.

Outside as he crossed the street to his car, he met Ben Harper coming from the direction of the dock, and they stopped to exchange a few words. Matt asked if he'd fixed his boat yet, and Ben said he thought he needed a new part. Since Matt was heading that way, he offered Ben a ride to the inn where he was staying.

'How's your research going with that whale?' he asked as they drove along the waterfront.

'Orca,' Ben said, correcting him. 'I've taken some samples which I'll take back to Woods Hole. That's about all I can do. The rest I'll leave to nature.'

'How much longer are you staying?'

'Couple of days maybe. Depends when I can get a part for my boat. I wouldn't mind a look at those bluefin everyone's talking about while I'm here.'

They pulled up outside the inn. 'You figure out who that woman was I saw in the cove yet?'

'I know who she is. Don't know if it helps me much yet,' Matt said.

'I heard about Ella Young getting arrested. She your client?'

'Yes.'

'The whole town's talking about it. That and the bluefin of course.'

'What are they saying?'

'That she was charged with murder. And there was a witness.'

'Well she was, but she's been released. For now anyway. And nobody knows where the witness is. What do people think? They think she did it?'

'From what I've heard it sounds as if opinion's divided, but probably more think she did than think she didn't.' Ben sounded apologetic about being the bearer of bad news. 'It's just what I've overheard. An impression. I could be wrong.'

'No, you're not wrong,' Matt said wearily. He hadn't expected any different.

'I guess you think she's innocent? Sorry, this is none of my business is it?'

'It's okay. And yes, I think Ella's innocent.' Partly out of a need to talk, to try and get matters straight in his own mind, partly because Ben was a good listener, he related the facts that were common knowledge, about the election, what Johnson claimed to have seen, and Gant's testimony.

'And you don't know where this guy Gant has gone?' Ben said when Matt had finished.

'No, but I need to find him and figure out exactly what he actually saw that night. Or else I need to find who really killed Bryan.' He looked across at Ben who appeared to be deep in thought. 'What is it?'

'I was just thinking, if somebody said they saw Ella dump something over the side of her boat that night, and I'm assuming the suspicion is that was a body, why don't you send a diver down to take a look? That'd help clear things up wouldn't it?'

'It's been considered, but there's a channel runs off the island there. It's too deep for a diver. But thanks for the suggestion.'

'Wish I could be of more help,'

'If you think of anything else, let me know.'

'I will.' Ben climbed out. 'Well, thanks for the ride.' He saw Matt looking at the sign out front which declared the inn was full. 'They offered me my money back, plus fifty dollars a day if I moved out. I talked to one guy sharing a room with two of his buddies. They're paying three hundred a night.' He shook his head, and raised a hand. 'Goodnight.'

CHAPTER TWENTY-THREE

The yard that Jordan Osborne owned consisted of two large
sheds and a large paved space out front surrounded by a chain
link fence. It was situated on the shore on the southern side of
the harbour. The yard had a slipway to the water for launching
boats, and directly across the harbour was the processing plant
owned by Howard Larson. Smoke from the plant was drifting
in an almost straight line south.

Matt spoke to a man who was working outside on the frame
of a boat, who went to fetch Osborne. Beyond the harbour there
were boats of all sizes dotted on the ocean towards the horizon,
some of them clustered together like roving packs of predators.
The air was tainted with the smell of fish from the processing
plant. The smell hung over the whole town, but here it seemed
stronger.

'It's the breeze. When it's blowing dead south like today, it
smells like we're right next door to the place.'

Matt turned and Jordan Osborne held out his hand.

'Even we notice it some days. You'd think we'd be used to it.'

The man who Matt had spoken to earlier had gone back to
his work. He was standing a little way off, stirring a glue pot
ready to put in some struts.

Matt introduced himself. 'Is there someplace private where
we can talk?'

Osborne nodded towards one of the sheds. 'We can use my
office.'

As Matt followed he glanced through the open doors of a

shed where, inside, a fishing boat was taking shape. The deck-housing was at the stern, and overall the vessel was around forty feet long. One man was using an electric sander, wearing a face mask, and there was a powerful smell of solvent in the air. The second shed was largely empty. At the back was a partitioned area with a roof. It resembled a large packing crate to which a window and door had been added. Inside was a small desk, a couple of chairs and some filing cabinets. Osborne leaned back in his chair, balancing on two legs so that it tipped dangerously.

'We use this shed for second stage construction when we need the space. Which right now we don't,' Osborne added ruefully. 'That boat you saw next door? That's an order from a guy on the mainland. He's bought from us before and he knows our work, but even so I'm covering costs and that's about it. I'm down to two guys. Lyle, the guy in the yard, that's a spec boat he's working on. We don't have an order for it, which means when it's finished I have to sit on it until somebody buys it. Ties up a lot of working money.'

'Could be things are picking up,' Matt said. 'There isn't a boat in the harbour today.'

'Yeah, maybe.'

'You don't think so?'

'I'd like to, believe me.' He gestured around at the empty shed as evidence of his sincerity. 'But those bluefin everyone is out there trying to catch are just a freak. Truth is there are too many boats already. And not enough fish anymore.' He shrugged philosophically. 'But you didn't come here to listen to my problems. What can I do for you?'

'I wanted to ask you about Kate Little.'

Jordan Osborne wouldn't have made a good poker player. His smile wavered. 'What about her?'

'I'm representing Ella Young. I'm looking into the disappearance of Bryan Roderick, and Kate Little's name came up.'

'What makes you think I can help?'

'I heard that you and she used to spend a little time together. Whatever you say goes no further than this room,' Matt added. Before he'd come down here he'd taken the time to find out about Osborne. One of the things he'd discovered was that he had a wife.

Osborne got up and shoved his hands in his pockets. He walked across the room, and at the wall he turned. 'You know I'm married?' he asked, and Matt nodded. 'I've always been afraid Mary would find out about this.'

'She's not going to hear about it from me,' Matt assured him.

Osborne considered this, as if he was trying to decide whether or not he could trust Matt. 'What is it you want to know?' he said at length, sitting down again.

'You were seeing Kate?'

'Last year. It went on for about two months. We used to meet once, sometimes twice a week if I could make it without my wife getting suspicious.'

'How did you first meet each other?'

'I'd seen Kate around, but that was all. Then one night she was in *The Lobster Pot* and we got talking. We had a few drinks.'

'And you started seeing each other after that?'

'Yeah. I don't know, I was having problems with the business, it was putting a little strain on things at home. I'm not making excuses, but I guess Kate was having a hard time with her husband. Things sort of happened.'

'So where did you go, the two of you?'

'Here sometimes. Different places.' Osborne shook his head. 'I know what you're thinking. With her husband being in a wheelchair and all. If it had been anyone else I wouldn't have felt right about it, but that guy she's married to is a real asshole.'

'She talked about him?'

'Not really. But I picked up enough to get the picture. He put her down, made her feel like she wasn't worth a damn. I guess that's why she drinks more than she should.' He paused for a moment. 'You know, I think she just wanted some company. I don't think she was even interested in the sex part, she always seemed glad when it was over if you want to know the truth.'

'Why did you stop seeing her?'

'She ended it. It was a couple of weeks before the end of

213

summer, before she went back to New York. I was expecting it. I mean, it wasn't like either of us had ever kidded ourselves it could go on forever.'

'Because you were married?'

'I guess. I never thought I was the first guy Kate had done this with. You hear talk abut her, you know. But like I said, I think Kate just wanted company, somebody to be nice to her. She's lonely. She wasn't interested in busting up anybody's marriage. She used to ask me about my wife, and then she'd go quiet for a while and I could tell she felt guilty about what we were doing. I never understood why she stayed with her husband. At first I thought it was his money.'

'But you don't now?'

'No.' He thought for a little while. 'I think it's because she cares about him.' He shrugged.

'So, after she ended your relationship, nothing happened after that? Not even when she came back this year?'

Osborne hesitated. 'To be honest, I thought about it, but Kate let me know she wasn't interested. She didn't say anything directly, she didn't have to. I just knew. When we met she was polite, you know. Friendly, but that was it. I didn't push it. In a way I was relieved. Because of my family. I know how that sounds.'

'Was Kate seeing somebody else?'

'How would I know that?'

'She might have told you. Perhaps you saw her with someone.'

Osborne picked up a pencil and twirled it between his fingers. 'You mean Bryan Roderick?'

'Why do you mention him?'

'Why else would you be here asking about Kate?'

'Was she seeing Bryan?'

'Not that I know of.'

Matt didn't believe him. Osborne avoided his eye and stood up.

'Look I can't tell you anything else. If that's all, I have work to do.'

Matt walked with him to the shed door. 'One more thing. Where were you a week last Monday night?'

214

It occurred to him that if Osborne was lying, if Kate had been sleeping with Bryan and he knew about it, then maybe Osborne might have had his own axe to grind with Bryan.

'I was home all night. With my wife.'

'Would she back you up on that?' The threat wasn't very subtle. If he questioned her, Osborne's wife might also find out about her husband's affair with Kate. Osborne got the message and his expression hardened.

'What was that you said earlier? About my wife not hearing about any of this from you?'

'There are other people's lives at stake here,' Matt told him.

'You think I had anything to with whatever happened to Bryan, you're wrong. If you want to ask my wife where I was that night, go ahead. She'll tell you the same thing I did.'

Now Matt believed that Osborne was telling the truth, about that much anyway. 'But you do know something about Kate and Bryan don't you? Was she seeing him?'

But he'd lost his chance. His threat had turned Osborne against him, and made him stubborn. Whatever reasons he had for lying, he wasn't going to change his story now.

'There's nothing else I can tell you,' he said flatly.

When he got back to town Matt drove to the police department and asked to speak to the chief. He waited while Officer Williams went to fetch him. When Baxter appeared his expression was guarded.

'What can I do for you?'

'I'd like to talk if you've got a couple of minutes.' Matt was aware that Williams was trying not to make it obvious that he was listening to every word. They went through to Baxter's office, and Baxter sat down behind his desk. He took a stick of gum from its wrapper and popped it in his mouth.

'What's on your mind?'

Baxter was a little pissed off, Matt figured. He hadn't missed the implication Matt had made that maybe Baxter had his own reasons for wanting Ella to remain under arrest. That way he didn't have to investigate the possibility of somebody else being involved in Bryan's disappearance, like Kate Little for instance. Other scenarios had occurred to Matt. He thought about Howard and Baxter talking in the corridor outside Judge Walker's rooms. Howard hadn't been subtle about offering inducements for Matt's support, perhaps he'd done the same to Baxter. He hoped that he was letting his imagination run away with him. Baxter hadn't struck him as some small town cop who would be easily corrupted, but then you never could tell. But Matt had decided he had to give Baxter the benefit of the doubt because, if he was going to help Ella, he needed Baxter's help.

'I'm here to make peace. I figure you and I ought to put what's happened behind us and start again. Seems to me we're going to get more accomplished if we're working together. We both want the same thing here, Chief.'

'Last time I looked, you and I were on opposite sides of the fence,' Baxter said.

'Come on, if I thought Ella had really killed Bryan Roderick I wouldn't be sitting here now. And I don't think you really believe she did either. I think we both want to get at the truth don't we?'

Baxter sat back in his chair, contemplating what Matt had said. When he spoke again, he sounded less defensive. 'Okay, I'll admit I don't see Ella as some kind of cold-blooded killer. But I have to keep an open mind here.'

'That's all anybody can ask.'

'I always had my doubts about Jerrod Gant, same as you. But like I told you before, I couldn't shake him on his story, and I still figure that getting Ella safely out of the way might be a good thing until this is all cleared up.'

'You think she's in danger?'

'I think Jake is pretty wound up about all of this, and right now I can't do much about keeping an eye on him. We're pretty stretched. Somebody threw a brick right through the window of the *Striper Grill* last night. Then whoever did it went inside and took a goddamned axe to the tables. Turned half a dozen of 'em into kindling.' Baxter shook his head in bewilderment at such destruction.

'Who'd do a thing like that?'

Baxter's expression became pained. 'Well, Kurt claims it was Dave Lamont. He owns the *Surfside*. You know it?'

Matt had been past. It was a small bar and restaurant near the docks.

'According to Lamont, Kurt told some guys off a charter boat not to go near the *Surfside*. Lamont claims Kurt said if they did they'd be likely to get food poisoning.' Baxter shook his head. 'We've got our hands full with that kind of thing. Did you see how many boats there were in the harbour this morning? The whole state knows about that fish Ella caught. We've got people coming from all over. You know how many fights we had to break up last night? I'm talking about islanders fighting each other, everybody scrambling to make a buck one way or another from all these people coming here. What's funny about Kurt and Lamont is if every restaurant filled their tables three times over people would still go hungry.' Baxter appeared weary. 'Anyway, like I said, I can't keep an eye on Jake Roderick night and day.'

Matt hadn't taken Baxter's concerns about Ella's safety all that seriously before, thinking it was just a smoke-screen, but now he wondered if Jake really might be a threat. Perhaps Baxter was right. Who was to say what Jake was capable of. Which made it all the more important to prove her innocent.

'You have any luck tracking down Gant yet?' Matt asked. Baxter frowned, and related that so far they'd drawn a blank. He'd tried all the avenues Matt had, plus a few others, but without luck.

'Jerrod's been picking up some work lately around the other islands. We're still checking with the people he worked for to see if any of them have seen him.'

'I have another lead,' Matt said cautiously. 'I think this is worth looking into.' He watched Baxter carefully. 'I think Bryan might have been seeing somebody, a married woman, and I think you ought to question her to see if she might have had a motive to kill him.'

'Who is it?' Baxter sounded immediately suspicious.

He related his talk with Jordan Osborne. Baxter began to look unhappy at the first mention of Kate Little's name. When he'd finished, Matt waited for Baxter to comment, but he didn't.

'How come every time I mention Kate Little's name I feel like you want to throw me out of your office, Chief?'

Baxter picked up a pencil and started tapping it against the edge of the desk. 'I just don't see why you have to keep bringing her into this, that's all. There's nothing to link her with any of this. You don't even know that she knew Bryan.'

'She's in an unhappy marriage, and she had an affair with Osborne, so why not Bryan Roderick? He had a reputation when it came to women didn't he? Plus I got the feeling Osborne was holding something back when I mentioned Bryan's name. What if Kate was seeing him? The night Bryan disappeared she can't prove that she was at home. She and her husband have separate rooms. Maybe Kate and Bryan had a fight and there was some kind of accident. Remember Ben Harper saw her in the cove that morning. What was she doing out there so early?'

'This is all pure guesswork. You don't have a shred of evidence.'

'You're right,' Matt agreed. 'But don't you think it's worth looking into? I mean if Bryan was murdered, and Ella didn't do it then somebody else did.'

He didn't mention to Baxter the scene he'd witnessed outside the post office, the looks Ella and Kate had exchanged, which continued to sit uncomfortably at the back of his mind.

'Call it instinct,' he went on, 'but when I talked to Kate I had the feeling she was lying. And now today with Osborne, I had the same feeling.'

Baxter stared at him. 'I'll look into it,' he said at length, but from the way he said it Matt doubted that Baxter would do a thing.

CHAPTER TWENTY-FOUR

Howard paused as he fastened the buttons on his shirt. He looked out of the window of his and Angela's bedroom, and caught a glimpse of the sea. There were boats all over the place, like handfuls of toys thrown down in the gulf.

'Dammit,' he muttered sourly.

'What is it?' Angela asked absently as she went by. Her night-gown made a silky rustling sound, and a waft of scent lingered in her wake.

'Look at that. Those damn fish are all anybody seems to be thinking about.'

Angela gave him a puzzled look. 'That's because they're worth a lot of money, Howard.'

He knew that, for chrissakes! The point was it seemed as if everybody had forgotten about Ella all of a sudden. And Howard didn't want them to forget. Not yet. It was as if the whole damn town had gone crazy. A couple of fish had been caught the day before. Not as big as the one Ella had landed, but still worth a lot of money, and enough to fuel the fever that had gripped the island. Several large schools had been spotted, and there were reports coming in of more sightings up and down the coast of Maine and into Massachusetts as far as the Cape.

Angela asked Howard if he wanted breakfast. He stared at her, and saw that she didn't have any idea what he was going through. His whole life, and hers too, rested on him winning this election. He hadn't told her the extent of their commitment to his development plans. He'd already sunk a lot of money into studies and investment portfolios and buying up land and property that if this all worked out would quadruple in value. He was stretched. It was true that right now Ella didn't have a hope of winning the election, but this was no time for taking chances. He couldn't let people forget.

'I'm not hungry,' he said, and he grabbed his jacket and went downstairs.

It was almost noon when Baxter saw Howard coming straight at him along the sidewalk, and looked for a place to duck for cover, but it was too late, Howard had already seen him and called out.

'Chief. How're things?' Howard beamed. He was sweating heavily, and he looked pale. 'How about this heat? I was just going to get a coke. You got a minute? Come on, we can sit there in the shade.'

Baxter found himself propelled against his will to the soda stand at the front of Keiler's store, and Howard pressed a coke into his hand and led him to sit on the low wall in the shade of a maple across from the muddy beach at the far north end of the dock.

Howard mopped his brow with a handkerchief he took out of his jacket pocket. He was wearing a light fawn suit that was rumpled and a little grimy. He looked like a man fighting to keep up appearances and losing the battle. Baxter thought of him as somebody who was always trying to get somewhere other than the place he was, and wherever he was aiming for it was an uphill slog under a hot midday sun. One of these days the strain was going to kill him, Baxter thought.

'So what's happening, Chief?' Howard said. 'I guess you must be pretty busy right now.'

The harbour was empty, not a boat in sight. They had all left before dawn. Baxter and his men had been kept busy the night before. A lot of the visitors had been up most of the night drinking and having a good time. There was a kind of festive air among some of them who were here for the sport and the thrill as much as anything else. But for the local fishermen the bluefin were a serious business, a chance to alleviate their financial problems for a while at least, and they resented the influx of a bunch of amateurs fishing in waters they regarded as their own. They liked even less the arrival of fishermen from other harbours, who were a greater threat as they stood a greater chance of actually catching a fish. Tensions were running high.

All along the waterfront and through the town the stores and bars and restaurants were waking up. Doors and windows were opened, rubbish collected into piles, boxes of supplies opened up. The town moved with a kind of sluggish torpor, as if suffering from a collective hangover. Rooms were being rented for astronomical rates, prices everywhere were hiked. There were accusations of dirty tricks between people who ran businesses who suddenly considered themselves rivals. The police department was being run ragged trying to keep the peace. Howard was right, Baxter reflected. He was pretty busy right now.

'I guess you don't need any more problems, like with this business about Bryan. How about you having to let Ella go?' Howard shook his head as if in amazement. 'Lawyers, huh? That Matt Jones, how about him? Comes over here and runs rings around us country folk.'

Baxter sipped at his coke. Though he didn't have a hell of a lot of time for Howard, the cold drink was welcome. Later on the bars would be full. Fights would break out. Inwardly he sighed. Howard was right again, he really could have done without having to deal with a murder as well.

'Didn't I see Matt Jones coming out of your office yesterday?' Howard said. 'What was he doing? Poking his nose in again I bet.'

Baxter allowed his mind to wander a little. He didn't mind keeping Howard waiting a while. The thing was, Baxter couldn't remember a time when Howard had ever given him much more than a cursory hello if they met in the street. He sure as hell hadn't ever wanted to buy him a coke before. Baxter guessed he ought to feel offended that Howard obviously thought he was stupid, that he couldn't see what he was trying to do, but Baxter wasn't an easy person to offend. His passions were generally slow to be aroused. That was probably why he'd never really gotten anywhere in his life, and why he probably never would. He simply lacked ambition. He didn't want to be better than anyone else, and he didn't need much more than he already had, which was a pretty nice house and a boat for fishing at weekends and a truck that was all paid for.

He loved the sea, and he liked to get out on the water when he could. From where he lived he could look out on a stretch of the gulf south of the island, and on a clear day he could see the coast of Maine. It gave him a good feeling. There was nothing much more he'd ever wanted. Except that sometimes he felt a little lonely, living by himself.

'Nothing else happened has it?' Howard said, sounding as if he was becoming impatient.

'Not that I know about.'

'You haven't found Jerrod Gant then I guess.'

Baxter looked at him, wondering just how much Howard knew about that. When he'd turned up at the courthouse yesterday Howard had seemed to know a lot about what Gant had seen.

'You know what,' Howard said. 'Matt Jones could end up making us all look like idiots out here. A man sees Ella Young commit a murder, and what do we do? We let her just walk free. I mean I'm not blaming you Chief, there wasn't anything you could do about it. That Jones fella, he's been doing this kind of thing all his life. Getting criminals off. City lawyers. You didn't stand a chance against someone like that.'

'He used to be a prosecutor,' Baxter pointed out.

'Well, whatever, it's the same thing when you get down to it.'

Baxter finished his coke and put the can down on the wall. 'I guess I should get on.'

Howard got up as well. 'I'll walk with you. You know, I was thinking, maybe you ought to call in the state police anyway.'

Baxter stopped. 'Judge Walker gave it a week. Until after the election,' he said pointedly. 'Maybe Gant will show up by then.'

'Judge Walker doesn't have any more experience of this kind of thing than the rest of us. Hell, when was the last time we had a murder on the island?'

'Suspected murder. We still don't know for sure what happened to Bryan.'

'Jesus, Chief, you're starting to sound like Matt Jones yourself. We all know Bryan's dead. All I'm saying is let the state boys take over. Who the hell said we ought to let some Boston lawyer call the shots around here? You don't want him to make you look like some hick hayseed do you? Get the state boys in now, that's my advice, let them figure this out.'

'How come you're so interested in this anyway?' Baxter asked.

'Listen, I'm just trying to do you a favour.'

Right, Baxter thought, and the Pope isn't a Catholic.

'You have a boat don't you, Dave?' Howard said suddenly.

'Yep.'

'I thought you did. I've seen you rowing out to it in the harbour. Me, if I had a boat, I'd want to keep it in a marina if there was one around here. Imagine that? A dock of your own, maybe close to a nice little place with tables right by the water where you could sit and have a beer. Some pretty girl serving you. That'd be something wouldn't it?' Howard let his question hang, then clamped a hand on Baxter's shoulder. 'Anyhow, you think about what I said, okay?'

'I'll do that,' Baxter replied enigmatically.

Howard frowned a little, then decided to interpret Baxter's answer favourably and smiled. 'You have a good day.'

Baxter watch him walk away. He would have liked to think that there was no way in this wide world he was going to think about anything that Howard said, but the fact was he wasn't a hundred percent sure that was true. It bothered him that Matt kept trying to drag Kate Little into this Bryan thing. Baxter thought about Kate for a while. The kind of sad look she sometimes wore when she appeared to be gazing into some distance only she could see. Howard was just a small figure along the dock now.

Baxter looked up at the sky, and wiped his brow. It sure as hell was hot. Along the street the blacktop was melting. Sticky pools shimmered wetly and the signs above the stores wavered like images from a mirage.

CHAPTER TWENTY-FIVE

The final meeting before the election had been scheduled for seven p.m. on Saturday. Outside the council building Matt passed Howard Larson who was engrossed in furtive conversation with a grizzled old guy wearing a faded Hawaiian shirt. Howard saw him, and stopped talking, then guided the old guy by the arm into a recess by the steps where they resumed their conversation.

Matt was there fifteen minutes early, but it was already apparent that the turn-out was going to be low. The chamber was barely a third full, and the square outside was deserted. He joined Ella and George Gould, both of whom were trying unsuccessfully to remain optimistic.

'Hi, I'm glad you came,' Ella said. She smiled and her hand rested briefly on his arm and even after she withdrew it Matt could feel the place where it had been. Despite the evidence of strain around her eyes, the not-quite-so-bright smile, Matt thought she looked pretty good considering what she had been through lately. She wore jeans and a faded blue shirt and her hair was tied back away from her face. He couldn't take his eye off the small hollow in her neck beneath her ear lobe. He wondered what it would be like to place his lips there and inhale her scent as he kissed her. She caught his eye and gave him a quizzical look.

'What?'

'Nothing. I was just thinking about something.'

A faint flush of colour rose above the collar of her shirt, as if she had discerned from his gaze something of the nature of his thoughts.

'Any sign of Jerrod Gant yet?' she asked.

'Nothing yet.'

'Better get up there Ella,' George said, indicating the small stage where half a dozen chairs had been placed alongside the podium. Howard Larson was already taking his place. He looked relaxed in dark coloured pants and a pale jacket even though the jacket looked to be tight around the arms and it had probably been a long time since the buttons had ever joined in the middle. He smiled and chatted to his supporters.

'Wish me luck,' Ella said.

Matt took her hand and squeezed it. 'Knock 'em dead.'

She returned the pressure of his hand, then the chamber gradually fell quiet, and as the last murmurs faded, Joanna Thompson addressed those gathered. She talked about how this was the last opportunity for an open debate before the vote, and she made a joke about the poor turnout.

'I can't imagine where everybody is,' she said with deliberately false ingenuousness.

There were polite chuckles among those gathered. Matt cast his eye over them. There wasn't a fisherman among them. In fact the audience was made up mostly of people who were too old to either go chasing bluefin themselves or to cash in on their sudden appearance in other ways. The majority of the townsfolk were either running restaurants and bars, overcharging visitors outrageously, or else they were working extra shifts as waitresses and bartenders. The stores were all open late, their windows full of signs announcing 'specials'. Someone had printed up T-shirts with a picture of a leaping bluefin on the front, bearing the legend 'St George. I Was There'. They were selling from a stall on the sidewalk for fifteen dollars apiece which had provoked a heated exchange with a nearby store owner who had his own stock of T-shirts to sell. The two men had come to blows and one of them had suffered a broken finger, the other had smashed the front door to his own store when he had fallen through it.

Around two thirds of the people in the chamber had taken seats on the left, aligning themselves with Howard's camp. Matt recognized some of them from the last meeting, only that time they had been supporters of Ella.

Howard got up to speak first. He put up his charts and graphs and pictures that showed what the marina and surrounding development might look like. There was a picture of white hulled boats on blue water, beneath clear skies, people walking with children and dogs and lots of green space. The audience listened politely, but it was clear their minds were already made up. Many of them kept looking at Ella, and Matt had the feeling it was her they'd really come to see.

When she took her place at the lectern she'd barely started talking when a man in a Hawaiian shirt sitting towards the back stood up. Matt recognized him as the one he'd seen talking to Howard earlier.

'I've lived all my life on this island,' the old man said loudly, his voice rattling as if he had something stuck permanently in his throat, interrupting Ella in mid-sentence. 'At the start I wasn't sure if I was for or against Mr Larson's development. I listened to what he had to say, and I listened to your side of it.' He fixed a baleful gaze on Ella. His whole manner exuded a kind of quivering indignation, like a TV evangelist. 'I thought you put a pretty good case. A lot of us here did. You talked about the things we were concerned about. Lot of us didn't like the idea of a whole bunch of outsiders coming here, sending real estate sky high so people who were born here wouldn't be able to afford to buy their own house anymore, changin' our way of life. I didn't want to see my grandson end up washing dishes or delivering pizza instead of catching fish the way his dad does, the way I did before I got too old for it, and the way my dad did before me. We never made a lot of money, but we did okay, and we didn't answer to anyone and we could hold our heads high every day knowing we had to work for what we had.' The old man's anger grew as he went on, his eyes fierce and perhaps a little mad.

'You made a lot of sense when you said we'd need a bigger

police department to deal with all the drugs and robberies and all. You asked us if that's what we wanted. Well I guess we didn't. We listened to you, Ella Young.' He paused for a moment. 'I never did agree that a woman should be running a damn boat. I know it ain't fashionable to say so these days but I guess I still think a woman ought to stay home and look after kids and such. Men and women, they oughta stick to the things they're naturally made for in my opinion. But I knew your dad, Ella, and though I don't always agree with you about everything, I was prepared to believe you on this. But now I think I was wrong. Mr Larson here says the kind of people that'll come here aren't the sort who take drugs and such. He says all this talk of crime is just to scare us folks, and he's guaranteeing that island people will get first take on the new stores and restaurants. There's even gonna be someone to help people set up the kind of places these new people are gonna want.' At this he looked to Howard for confirmation, and Howard nodded gravely. 'Seems to me this whole thing comes down to a question of whose word do we trust. Well, I ain't afraid to admit my mistakes. I guess you can't keep things the same for ever, and the young people need some kind of opportunities. So what this boils down to is this; everybody in this room knows what Jerrod Gant saw, and on top of everything else that's been going on that's good enough for me. Maybe your fancy Boston lawyer friend sitting there can keep you out of jail for a while, but it don't make no difference. I know who I'm going to be voting for come Tuesday.'

At that the old man abruptly walked from the room. In the ensuing moments only the clump of his feet going down the corridor outside broke the silence. At the podium Ella stood white faced, unable to speak. Her gaze roamed the room and wherever she looked eyes were either averted or she was met with a hostile look. Even among her supporters there was some uncomfortable shifting of position. Then the scrape of a chair broke the silence. Wordlessly a man rose. He paused as if he might speak, but then he simply turned and left the chamber. It was as if a single rock had skittered down a slope, dislodging others along the way. One by one people rose to leave, and

227

soon the scrape of chairs became a continuous grating sound that went on and on, until at last when the chamber had all but emptied, Ella left the podium and without a word, grim faced, she swept out through the doors. Matt rose and went after her.

He caught up with her as she fled along the side of the square where the fading light already cast the street in deep shadows.

'Ella.' He caught hold of her arm, and she turned to face him, her eyes blazing with hurt and anger. 'He's just one person. Don't let it get to you. I saw him talking to Howard earlier, I think maybe Howard put him up to this.'

'He wasn't alone. You saw how everybody left. They all think I killed Bryan.'

'Not everybody thinks that. Come on, the place was two thirds empty.'

'Yes,' she said bitterly. 'Nobody else even bothered to come and listen. They've already made up their minds about me, and anyway they're all too busy making a buck.'

She sounded dispirited, beaten almost, and Matt didn't know what he could say to make her feel any better. She was right and they both knew it.

'Maybe I never had a chance anyway, not really. Even without having a murder charge hanging over my head. People don't care enough about the island when it comes down to it. What they care about is money, and how they can make more of it. What some people are doing is no better than Jake shooting at orcas because they eat the fish he believes are his by right.'

'You're just feeling low. Before Bryan disappeared you didn't believe that. You thought the people here would vote for you, and a lot of them would have. You're a fighter, you can't give up now, you have to roll with the punches,' Matt told her. 'This isn't over yet.'

'Matt, the vote is four days away. And you're no closer to finding Jerrod Gant. These people don't believe there's smoke without fire.'

'Gant isn't our only chance. I have an idea I'm following up. Somebody who may know what happened to Bryan.'

Ella looked surprised. 'Who?'

'Kate Little.'

Her reaction was immediate. Her eyes widened in shock, or surprise, mingled with what? Alarm? He couldn't interpret it. She pulled back from him, a subtle movement but he noticed it. He dropped his hand from her arm.

'What is it?'

She shook her head. 'Nothing.'

'Ella, do you know Kate Little? Do you know if she's involved in all this?'

'No. I don't know her.'

He remembered the day he'd seen her outside the post office when she'd almost run into Kate, the look they'd exchanged.

'Look, Matt, I have to go.'

'I'll walk with you.'

She hesitated. 'I need to think. Tonight, everything, I guess it's getting to me. Do you mind if I walk alone? I just need some time. Please.'

Reluctantly he agreed. 'I'll call you.'

She attempted a smile, but it failed. She appeared tired and drawn. 'Thanks,' she said. He watched her go, listening to the sound of her footsteps on the sidewalk, echoing off the buildings. Then he was alone in the square, light spilling from the open door of the council building.

CHAPTER TWENTY-SIX

The orcas were moving south-west, travelling in from the deep slope water beyond the shelf where they had been patrolling in search of food. It was early, before sunrise, and the old bull was dozing. The sea was calm, almost flat, and on the surface the orcas' streamlined bodies made a gentle suck and splash as they swam in a series of shallow dives. As the sky began to lighten it was clear the day would be hot. The high pressure system which had stayed over the gulf for two weeks now showed no sign of moving. Often at night the western horizon was lit with flashes of sheet lightning, and thunder rumbled like a continuous drum roll, sometimes appearing to draw closer, but then fading again, and each morning the sun burned off high cloud and beat down once more on the sea.

Ben Harper had hitched a ride on the *Santorini*. His own launch was still giving him engine problems, but not wanting to miss out on witnessing the bluefin hunt, he'd approached Ella and offered to pay her if he could go along as a passenger. She'd told him to keep his money, but that he was welcome to go along.

They were drifting about eight miles from St George. A flotilla of boats of all sizes dotted the ocean. They came from Sanctuary, as well as from harbours on other islands and the coast. Giant bluefin had been sighted throughout the gulf, from Stellwagen off the Cape, to Canadian waters in the north, and there had been reports of smaller skipjack and yellowfin appearing in greater numbers than had been seen for many years. The big sixty-foot-long liners and draggers working far out on the banks were hauling in good catches of the fish, and even the occasional four or five hundred pound bluefin. Sword boats that normally fished further north were joining the hunt for giants. Among the fishing communities up and down the coast of Maine and Massachusetts there was a palpable buzz of excitement. Sports boats carrying the maximum number of fee-paying fishermen were out in force, every man and also the few women among them, hoping to land a prize fish. As well as all these vessels, there were all kinds of pleasure craft out to join in the fun. The commercial fishermen who relied on the sea for their living regarded these amateurs with varying degrees of disapproval, which ranged from outright hostility to bemused tolerance.

Ella was thinking about the meeting, and how Matt had surprised her when he'd sprung Kate's name on her. She wondered if he'd noticed her reaction. It was all such a bloody mess. When she'd reached her truck she'd almost decided to go back and tell him everything. The idea had suddenly seemed alluring. Unburden herself, trust in him. The memory of what it had been like to be locked up for a night had stopped her. She was torn between the knowledge that she was being unfair to Matt, and the knowledge that there were other lives at stake besides her own. Her thoughts collided and reeled, and in the end she thrust them from her consciousness, concentrating instead on the sea.

Outside the wheel-house Ben Harper stood by the rail. So far they'd been fishing for four hours, with nothing more than a few stripers and some bluefish to show for it. He swept the surrounding sea with his binoculars, and focused on a sports boat close by. The skipper was standing up top under a shade, himself scanning the sea. In the back of the boat four men were sitting around with their lines trailing over the stern. One of them took four beers from a cooler, and passed them around to his buddies. Another emptied the can he already had and tossed it onto the deck. The men looked like salesmen on vacation. They were overweight, dressed in shorts and polo shirts which stretched over their bellies, with baseball caps jammed down on their heads and fluorescent blocker smeared across their noses. They were probably staying in one of the private houses in Sanctuary which had been hastily transformed to offer bed and breakfast. Children and grandparents suddenly found themselves sharing a room while any spare space with a bed was rented for a hundred dollars a night.

Ben thought he'd seen these guys in the coffee shop earlier, kidding around as they ate the 'Big Fisherman's Breakfast Special' of bacon, egg, sausage links and pancakes that was being offered for eleven bucks. He seemed to recall that a couple of days ago the same breakfast would have cost four ninety-five. The men were making bets as to who would catch the biggest fish. Now they just looked bored and were getting slowly drunk.

'If those guys hook anything they're going to be in trouble,' he murmured to himself.

Ella heard him. 'It's the worse thing that can happen to a charter skipper. Paying customers sitting around on their behinds without even seeing a fish. Especially in a flat sea.'

'What difference does a flat sea make?'

'If there's a swell at least you can count on some of them being kept busy losing their breakfast over the side,' Ella said grinning.

The faint drone of an engine high above reached them and Ben shielded his eyes to search for the plane. He found it a long way off to the east and guessed it was a spotter looking for schools of tuna for the big operators to go after. Apparently it was having no luck either and it grew smaller as it faded into the distance. For something to do, he picked up his camera and focused on a boat that was approaching from the west. It was almost a mile away. A man stood outside the wheel-house, something cradled in his arms, which as it drew nearer Ben realized was a rifle. He read the name of the boat, the *Seawind*, and clicked off a few shots. Then he saw the damaged bow and remembered where he'd heard the name before.

'Isn't that the guy you had a run in with?' he asked.

Ella turned to look. 'Yes,' she said, frowning.

He turned his attention back to the beer drinkers on the launch. They were on their feet now, apparently looking at something to the east, then the skipper up top on the flying bridge got to his feet and took the wheel. Suddenly the men below began reeling in their lines.

'Something's going on.'

Other boats began moving in the same direction as the launch and both Ben and Ella swept the ocean with their glasses. At first Ben couldn't see anything, and then a movement caught his attention. He went back, and there it was again. A flash of silver in the sunlight, and then another. He turned to Ella, but she was already going back into the wheel-house.

'I see them.'

'Tuna,' Ben said. 'Looks like a big school. Maybe fifty, sixty pounders.'

All around them now boats were changing course. The sports fishers were big and fast, and with their throttles opened up they could travel at up to thirty-five knots, a lot faster than the *Santorini*. Off to their port side two boats a couple of hundred yards apart begin to overhaul them, churning deep troughs of foaming water in their wakes, their bows lifting and planing over the swell. Ben counted thirteen or more, all converging on the school, with many more slower vessels like the *Santorini* making up the rear.

'This could be a hell of a mess,' he said to himself.

A couple of launches trailing lines off their sterns were the first to reach the area where the tuna appeared to be scattering far and wide. Ben watched but it seemed as if the fish weren't biting.

'This is weird,' he said. The *Seawind* was heading in a northerly direction, and didn't seem to be going after the tuna at all, while as more of the other boats converged on the school, they were cutting dangerously close to one another. Some smaller craft were in danger of being capsized by the wakes of bigger, faster boats which were intent on pursuing the occasional big fish. It seemed that the tuna comprised several schools mixed together, with the odd giant among them, and it was these that the faster boats were chasing. A forty-foot launch and a smaller lobster boat almost collided as the launch recklessly cut across the bow of the other boat. Seeing the mayhem ahead of them, Ella slowed the *Santorini* down.

'Something's wrong here,' Ben said, watching not just the crazy spectacle of the boats, but the behaviour of the fish. 'They're not taking bait.'

He swung his glasses north, back in the direction from which the tuna were fleeing, and three quarters of a mile away he saw what had spooked them. A pod of orcas were breaching, probably mopping up the fish that hadn't got away, and the *Seawind* was heading right for them. Beyond them the horizon was hazy, as if cloud had descended on the ocean, though the sky was clear.

'What do you think he's doing?'

'I don't know.' Ella frowned, but then abruptly she altered course, and opened up the throttle.

As Jake watched the orcas he saw out of the corner of his eye how the *Santorini* changed course. A familiar dull ache began to throb in the back of his skull, gradually spreading outwards as he raised his glasses and focused on Ella. He couldn't understand why the hell Baxter and Judge Walker had decided to let her go after what Jerrod Gant had seen. What was wrong with them? He guessed that lawyer buddy of hers had gotten her off. Twisting things around the way those slippery bastards did. As he watched she seemed close enough to touch. His grip tightened, and the pain in his head reached around to his temples. Little grainy black dots seeped into his vision. Without being aware of it he began to grind his teeth.

Penman appeared at the door of the wheel-house looking anxious. Jake barely glanced at him. 'Rig a harpoon.'

Dead ahead of them an orca rocketed from the surface of the sea until it was almost entirely clear of the water, massive flukes churning the surface. The animal turned in mid-air, glistening black and snow white, its dorsal fin, with the wavy pattern at the tip that was common to this pod, resembling a huge sail.

It crashed down on its side again, creating a tremendous splash. It appeared that the orcas had some fish herded between them. Silver flashed in the sunlight as a giant leapt clear of the sea as it escaped to the south.

'We're gonna be too late,' Penman said. It seemed to him that almost all of the tuna that hadn't already been killed had already fled.

'It's that bull I want,' Jake answered, never taking his eye from the window. 'That bastard has stolen his last fish.'

Penman hesitated. He didn't have anything against killing an orca if the chance arose. Far as he was concerned one less orca meant more fish for them. But there was a look in Jake's eye that bothered him. Some of the men had been talking lately about how Jake was acting a little strangely. Okay, they all knew how he must feel about Bryan, but his preoccupation with Ella, and now the orcas, was getting out of hand. If he hadn't been so intent on running Ella's line down the other day maybe they would have seen those bluefin earlier and caught one themselves, instead of ramming the *Rose Marie*.

Jake turned on him. 'What the hell are you waiting for?'

Penman didn't hesitate any longer and headed down to the bow to rig a harpoon. He knew better than to argue when Jake had something fixed in his mind.

'I want him this time,' Jake shouted after him. Beyond the orcas a bank of mist was sweeping in from the west, like a long low cloud creating a false horizon.

Penman worked fast, and as the *Seawind* drew closer to the orcas he spotted the big double notched fin of the bull. The orcas had given up their hunt. The surface of the water was covered in a shiny slick of oil and blood, but the last of the surviving tuna had escaped. Jake had seen the bull too, and he brought the *Seawind* around. The orca went under, and then its head broke the surface, and as they bore down Penman swore it was watching him. He steadied himself, getting ready to throw when they were close enough. Then suddenly the orca dived, and the entire pod headed east with the bull swimming way out on the right flank.

The *Seawind* shuddered and the note of her engines rose as Jake pushed her to the limit. In calm waters she was a fast boat. From the wheel-house Jake could clearly see the bull as it swam twenty feet below the surface. He knew it would have to come up for air every few minutes, and if he could get a little closer, Penman would have a clear shot.

'I've got you now, damn you,' he said quietly. 'There's nowhere for you to go.' He looked ahead, expecting to see nothing but clear ocean, but instead found that they were approaching a grey-white wall as it rolled to meet them. It was a bank of dense fog, caused by the upwelling of cold currents from the depths meeting warm humid air above the surface, which condensed into thick mist. He realized the bull meant to hide in the mist, but it was too late. There was no way it could outrun the *Seawind.*

Just then Jake saw that the *Santorini* was heading on a course that would take her right across his bow.

Ben watched the *Seawind* edge closer to the orca. 'He's gaining,' he shouted.

'I'm going as fast as I can,' Ella shouted back above the noise of the engine and the sound of the *Santorini* ploughing through the sea. But even as the gap between the boats narrowed she had no idea how she could prevent Jake from killing the orca.

Ben pounded his fist on the rail in frustration. 'Dammit. We have to do something,' he said.

Ella didn't know what she *could* do. The *Santorini* was at full throttle, and sounded like she was going to shake to pieces. The vibrations rattled the deck and rose through her feet and Ella was tempted to ease back on the throttle, afraid that the motor would blow, but she knew that if she did, the orca would be killed, and she couldn't allow that to happen. Gordon glanced back at her worriedly from where he stood out on the deck, grimly hanging on to the rail.

Ahead of them the *Seawind* was closing the distance, but the orca appeared to be aware of the danger and was making for the cover of the fog bank that was rolling in to meet them. Ella thought that maybe if she could do something to slow Jake down, the orca would have a chance. The gap between the two boats was now just a hundred yards and closing fast. If she held her current course Ella felt sure they would collide. The *Santorini* was shuddering with the strain, the engine thumping like a gigantic hammer beneath her feet, threatening to pop the nails from the planks of her decking. A fine mist of spray was flung back over the bow as the little boat cleaved a passage through the sea, a wake unfurling against her sides with a protesting rush and roar. Ella wondered if she could make it across the *Seawind*'s bow, and force Jake to break off, or would he ram her amidships? If he did the *Santorini* would crack apart like an egg, and would be driven down. They would all drown, sucked under by the currents if they survived the initial impact. She could see Penman on the bowsprit, a harpoon in one hand as he readied himself to take aim. Maybe if she held her course she could block his throw. She measured the distance, uncertain if she could make it. It was too close, she decided, she had to turn away.

'What are you doing?' Ben yelled at her sensing what she planned to do.

'He'll run us down.'

Ben shook his head. 'You can make it.'

'It's too close,' Ella said. But he wasn't listening. She glanced at Gordon. His face was white but he remained unflinching and Ella knew she had seconds to make a decision. The *Seawind* bore down on them, the bigger boat looming frighteningly, and the sound of her bow cleaving a path through the ocean mingled with the roar of the *Santorini*'s own passage.

The orca rose to take air, and Penamn steadied himself to throw. Ben looked back at her in a final silent appeal.

'You're crazy,' she said. 'I can't do it.'

But even as she spoke she knew it was already too late to turn away and in that split second Ella made her decision and held true to her course. At the last moment, with the sound of engines and machinery all but drowned out by the roar of the sea, she screwed her eyes tightly closed and prayed for the grace of any god looking down that she might live to remember her own folly. Her heart was in her mouth, her body tensed for the impact.

The last thing she saw was the fog rolling towards them like a great enveloping ghostly curtain.

The *Seawind* loomed over them and Penman hesitated as the *Santorini* spoiled his target and Jake leapt from the ladder by the wheel-house.

Jake guessed at the last moment what Ella was going to do and even as he rushed outside he was cursing her and shouting at Penman to take his shot. There was a moment when the orca was visible and Penman had a clear target before the *Santorini* began to cross their path.

'Throw it, damn you,' Jake yelled as he leapt down the ladder but Penman faltered and Jake swept him aside with one blow, then grabbed the harpoon and with one continuous fluid motion he raised it and glimpsed Ella looking right at him as he threw.

Ella opened her eyes and instinctively ducked even as she was surrounded by an explosion of showering glass. The harpoon shattered the side window and passed right above her head before hitting the wall where half of it passed clean through the wood. She screwed her eyes tightly shut again and waited for the impact as the *Santorini* rose on the wash and she was flung first to the roof and then to the floor, smashing her forehead on the wheel as she went down. She lay stunned and unable to move, expecting to hear splintering wood and the sea rushing in to bear her to a watery grave and for a second she glimpsed a beckoning figure who she thought was her father, then the rushing sea abated and all sound was deadened and her vision misted over.

Ben Harper helped her to her feet, and she rose a little shakily. It wasn't her father after all. She was puzzled by the sudden quiet, until she saw that she must have hit the throttle as she'd fallen, shutting the engine down. The *Santorini* drifted in the eerie quiet of the fog.

'I didn't think you'd do it,' Ben said hoarsely.

He looked pale and shocked. His hand shook when he let her go. Suddenly she felt ill.

'You're hurt.'

He gave her a handkerchief, and held her hand to her forehead, which she now realized ached badly. There was a little blood. Suddenly she froze.

'Gordon. Oh my God, where's Gordon?'

She ran onto the deck, and found she couldn't see the end of the boat. Then he was there, stumbling towards her and she hugged him tightly.

'Are you all right?' he asked worriedly when she let him go.

'I'm fine.'

The rapid thump of her heartbeat subsided. In the distance the dying sound of the *Seawind*'s engine faded.

They drifted for twenty minutes surrounded by thick white mist. Now and then they heard a faint fog horn, but otherwise it seemed as if they'd crossed to another, ethereal world. The only constant was the gentle lap of water against the hull. What had happened seemed like a dream. Eventually, unexpectedly, the fog thinned, and became wisps of trailing vapour. There was a splash close by, and when they looked a dorsal fin sank not more than twenty feet away. A great black and white body glided silently beneath them, and astounded they rushed to the other side of the boat. The orca rose, his snout breaking the surface. For a second he seemed to look at them, then he dipped beneath the surface and was gone.

CHAPTER TWENTY-SEVEN

It was late when Baxter turned up at Matt's office. Matt had been making calls to Boston, calling in favours from people who'd been checking into Kate and Evan Little for him. He hadn't turned anything up. They were exactly what they appeared to be, and neither of them had any prior record. He was about to call it a day when Baxter rapped on the door.

'I saw the light. You're working kinda late aren't you?' Baxter said.

'I was just finishing up.' He switched off the light on his desk and stood up, stretching his arms above his head. He didn't say anything about what he'd been doing.

'I came to tell you something.' Baxter told Matt about the incident that had taken place that day between Jake and Ella. 'It was only luck that nobody was killed. This is just the kind of thing I was worried about,' he added with a faintly accusatory note.

'You think Jake meant that harpoon for Ella?' He conjured a picture of the scene in his mind. The two boats converging and then the long lethal spear whistling towards her.

'Jake's kind of unpredictable.'

'What are you going to do about it?'

'Nothing much I can do. I already talked to him. He claims the whole thing was an accident.'

'Do you believe him?'

Baxter thought for a moment. 'Nope. I warned him off, but that doesn't mean he's going to listen to me.'

Baxter had a 'you see, I wasn't just making this up' kind of look. He took out a piece of gum and unwrapped it, and as he did his gaze roamed around the room. He wore a look of vague curiosity. Matt glanced at the pad of notes on his desk, with Kate Little's name written at the top, underlined a dozen times in heavy black ink.

'Is there something else you wanted, Chief?'

'I've been thinking about what you said in Judge Walker's office. About Jerrod Gant having a lot to gain from the marina going ahead?'

Matt thought he detected a conciliatory note in Baxter's voice. 'What about it?'

'I don't know. I guess I don't see Jerrod Gant dreaming up something like this by himself.'

'You mean he might have had some help. Like from Howard Larson?'

'Yeah, maybe from Howard.'

'You know the man better than I do Chief. Is he capable of something like this?'

'Maybe.'

'But we're not going to know what Gant really saw unless we find him,' Matt pointed out. 'I don't suppose you've had any luck on that score?'

'Not yet. You?'

'No.'

He had the feeling that Baxter was coming around. That part of the reason he'd stopped by was to open the lines of communication between them again, and if that was true he was pleased. Baxter's glance fell to the pad on the desk, and his eyes narrowed a little when he read what was on it. He looked up again, and seemed about to say something, then changed his mind. He looked out of the window, and appeared consumed with his own thoughts.

'I have to go,' Baxter said at length, sounding weary and drained. 'I think it's going to be a busy night.' Amidst all the mayhem on the water that day there had been accusations of lines being fouled, and boats deliberately getting in the way of

241

each other. At the door he paused. 'You know, you might want to look out for Ella if you can.'

'Chief,' Matt called. 'Thanks for stopping by.'

Baxter stared at him, and then it seemed with an almost imperceptible movement of his head he nodded an acknowledgment.

After Baxter had left, Matt tried Ella's number, and when she answered he told her he'd heard what happened. 'Are you okay?'

'I'm fine.' Her tone was leaden. 'I just need to get a good night's sleep.'

There was an awkward pause. Matt had been thinking all day about the way she'd reacted at the mention of Kate Little's name outside the meeting the night before.

'Matt, I'm really tired,' she said, as if in the silence she'd guessed what he was thinking. 'I think I'm going to go to bed.'

'Ella, I need to talk to you.'

There was a long pause, then she sighed. 'I know, but not tonight. Please.'

'All right. But it has to be soon.'

'Yes, soon, I promise.'

In the end, because Ella sounded beat, and because he didn't want to talk on the phone he let it go, and they hung up. Afterwards he sat in the gloom for a while, a nagging worry growing in him as he considered Baxter's warning about Jake.

It was dark when he locked up the office and went down to the waterfront. He found Ben Harper, still working on his boat in the light of a bulb he'd rigged up. When he questioned him Ben related in detail what had happened that day.

'I'm telling you. It was deliberate. That guy meant that harpoon for Ella,' Ben concluded, without a grain of doubt. 'She's quite a woman, you know. Has anything else turned up about the guy who's missing?'

'Not yet.'

'Everyone still thinks he's resting at the bottom of the channel, huh?'

242

'Something like that. What's on your mind?'

'What? Oh, I don't know for sure. I sort of had an idea, but I'd like to check it out first. I'll let you know.'

'Something to do with Ella?'

Ben shrugged.'What she did out there today took guts. I like her. I'd like to help if I could, but like I said, I need to check this out first.' Matt was intrigued, but when pressed Ben wouldn't tell him anything else. 'It might be nothing.'

He promised to speak to Matt first if anything came of it, and then they said goodnight, and Matt walked on along the docks to clear his head. It was dark and the harbour was full of boats. Across the street the *Schooner* was busy. Every time the door opened the swell of voices spilled out, and the press of bodies inside could be seen through a haze of cigarette smoke. It was the same in all the other bars and the restaurants in town. He guessed Baxter and his men would have their work cut out that night.

He looked down at the dark water. It was as black as oil, and further out from the dock the lights cast from buildings along the harbour front made patterns that wavered and undulated with the movement of the water. When he reached the *Santorini* Matt stood for a while looking at the shattered window of the wheel-house. He put his hands on the rail and looked down at the water and a vague disorienting sense of light-headedness washed over him. The boat moved gently, and scraped the dock-side. He took a deep breath, sweat popping on his brow, and then he put one leg over the rail and climbed on board. He planted both feet firmly on the deck, fighting a brief wave of nausea, feeling prickles of cold sweat beneath his collar at the motion beneath his feet. After a moment he went forward to the wheel-house and ran his finger over the jagged hole where the harpoon had splintered the wood as it passed through. When Ella had made her decision to run across the bow of the *Seawind* it could easily have ended differently, the *Santorini* run down, the harpoon skewering Ella.

He climbed back to the dock. The *Seawind* was tied up further along. At first Matt thought she was deserted, but as he drew

243

closer he saw a movement on deck. Jake stood by the rail watching him. His expression was blank, impossible to read.

'I heard there was some trouble out there today,' Matt said, but Jake made no response or gave any indication at all he'd even heard him. 'Somebody could've been killed.'

Jake's gaze shifted. 'Lawyers,' he said with contempt. 'You and Baxter and that Judge Walker. You ain't worth a damn the three of you. Somebody's already been killed in case you forgot. You think I'm gonna stand by and let her get away with that?'

'Ella had nothing to with whatever happened to Bryan, Jake.'

'The hell she didn't! What is it with you people? It isn't enough she threatened him, that Carl Johnson saw her drop him in the sea all trussed up like he was a fucking piece of meat? All this lawyer's talk about evidence, but even when you get a witness who saw the whole thing, you just talk some more and Ella carries on free as a bird. Talk, that's all you people do.'

'Jerrod Gant has disappeared,' Matt pointed out. 'We don't know what he saw exactly until we speak to him.'

'More talk! But then I guess you'd take her side. You like her don't you? What I hear, you two are pretty close.'

'That has nothing to do with this, Jake.'

'Who the hell do you think you're kidding. You telling me if you and her didn't have something going she'd still be walking around after what Gant saw? You think she's such a sweet thing?' Jake grinned mirthlessly, his lips twisted back. 'She's got you twisted round her little finger ain't she? What's she paying you with, huh? You think you're the only one? Hey, I got news for you Mr Lawyer. Ella's been around the block a couple of times.'

Matt clenched his hands at his sides, and told himself not to let Jake get to him. 'Just stay away from her, Jake. I'm warning you.'

Jake laughed. 'What's wrong? Little too close to the truth? Well, let me tell you something, she ain't worth it Mr Lawyer. Hell, she even offered to drop her pants for me if I promised to lay off her. What do you think of that?'

Matt reacted without thinking. Something snapped and he reached out for the rail and vaulted onto the deck. Jake was a little slow to react, but then he suddenly rushed forward, bellowing like a bull. Matt sidestepped and punched him quickly with a short hard jab behind the ear and Jake dropped to his knees with a soft grunt of surprise. His head made a hollow thump when it hit the deck as he pitched forward.

All at once Matt's anger drained out of him. He was breathing heavily, and his knuckle ached from the blow to Jake's skull. He stepped closer, wondering if Jake was badly hurt. He reached out.

'You okay?'

Jake seized his arm and rolled over, then pulled Matt close and smashed his forehead viciously against the bridge of Matt's nose. There was an audible crack, and Matt tasted blood in his throat. He staggered backwards which gave Jake time to get to his feet and throw a punch that caught Matt in the ribs and knocked him off balance. As he crumpled to the deck Jake aimed a kick at the side of his head, which if it had connected would have cracked his skull like an egg. He caught hold of Jake's leg and leaned his weight in to bring him down. They rolled, both fighting for purchase, and then Jake got up on all fours and scrabbled towards him. Matt rolled out of the way, still a little disoriented. Blood was spraying from his nose in an alarming fashion. Jake was heavier, and Matt knew if Jake got on top of him he'd never shift his weight and he'd probably get his skull smashed against the deck. He kicked out and felt his heel connect with Jake's cheek. Jake grunted with pained surprise and fell back.

The two of them got up at the same time, both panting heavily. Matt's shirt was splattered with his own blood.

Jake's eyes shone malevolently. 'What's the matter Mr Lawyer, you don't like hearing the truth about Ella? You know Bryan had her too?' He wiped blood from his mouth. 'She didn't tell you that, huh? He told me all about it. Said she begged him for it.'

'You're lying Jake.'

'Am I? You sure about that Mr Lawyer? Why don't you ask her.'

Matt went to the rail and jumped back down to the dock. He was still leaking blood from his nose, and when he hit the ground a shooting pain flashed through his head. Jake stood looking down on him.

'Stay away from her,' Matt warned.

As he walked away, he heard Jake call after him. 'Ask her yourself Mr Lawyer. You just ask her.'

Matt tried to ignore him, but Jake's taunt echoed in his mind long after he'd left him behind. He wondered if Jake had been right at least about one thing, that if he didn't feel the way he did about Ella, would he still have believed her when she'd claimed she didn't know anything about what had happened to Bryan?

CHAPTER TWENTY-EIGHT

Kate knocked softly on the door to Evan's office. She couldn't hear any sound from inside, so she tried the handle and went in. The room was gloomy in the dusk light, and Evan was sprawled on his bed. Quietly she went over. He was lying at an angle, having hauled himself out of his chair then on to the bed where he'd simply collapsed. His thin and useless legs were draped at an unnatural angle like those of a soft toy. She started to move him, then stopped herself, not wanting to wake him. For a while she stood looking down at his sleeping face.

He seemed peaceful, his features smooth and pale. There was none of the restlessness, the pinched creases at the corner of his eyes that were evident when he was awake. His breathing was regular and shallow. The remains of his meal were on the table. He'd chosen to eat in his office. Some soup and bread. He'd had a good day, he'd said earlier, and didn't want to be interrupted. After he'd eaten she imagined that he'd been overcome with weariness and had simply collapsed and immediately fallen asleep. Beside his empty bowl was a glass and an open bottle of whisky.

As the light faded, Kate allowed her mind to drift. She couldn't have said when exactly she'd fallen in love with him. She supposed it had been a gradual process. At first it had been fun, having him take her out on dates, three, sometimes four times a week. Eating in the best restaurants, seats at sold out shows, the whole razzmatazz, and afterwards she'd allow him a peck on the cheek at her apartment door. Then one night he'd picked her up and called a cab in the street. No limousine, and maybe for the first time he hadn't been wearing a suit.

'Surprised?' he'd said. 'I figured I wasn't getting anywhere, so I'd try a new approach.'

She'd been intrigued. This was a whole new side to him. Up until then he'd been polite, gracious, not ostentatious exactly, but never afraid to spend money, of which he made it clear he had plenty. They went to a little Spanish place he knew in the Village. The most expensive item on the menu cost about twelve dollars and Kate had felt way overdressed. But that evening had been a turning point. Evan had loosened up, stopped trying to impress her, and he'd talked about himself a little. They'd drunk two bottles of wine between them.

'That was fun,' she said when he took her home. Then she'd asked him if he wanted to come in for a nightcap. She'd been feeling a little drunk.

He'd kissed her, just briefly. 'Ask me again some time,' he'd said and grinned at her.

It was that moment, she thought, that marked a change in the way she felt about him. Funny how such things stuck in her mind. How love had sneaked up on her, insinuated itself into her life and took up residence without her being fully aware of what was happening.

She cast her mind forward, wondering when that had all changed, when she had fallen out of love. That too had been a slow process. Long denied, and much, much more painful. The past few years it seemed as if her life had plunged into a black hole. She'd looked for illusory comfort elsewhere, always in the paradoxical and foolish belief that she and Evan might one day recapture what they had once had. Foolish. Self-deluding dreams.

'What are you thinking?'

Evan's voice startled her. The room had grown even more gloomy, and she could barely make out his expression. Tears had made wet streaks across her cheeks which she hoped he couldn't see. She wiped them away. 'I came to see if you need anything.'

There was a pause, while he absorbed the way she was dressed. 'You're going out I see.'

'I need to get out of the house for a while.'

'Of course you do.'

Though Kate couldn't see it, she knew well enough the sneer of his lip when he used that tone. She went to the door and snapped on the light. He blinked, and for a second he looked as vulnerable as he had while he slept. These days that was the only glimpse of the man she'd married she ever saw. She wondered how things had come to this, and why she hadn't stopped it earlier.

'Who are you meeting?' he demanded.

'I'm not meeting anybody.'

Evan struggled to raise himself, reaching for his wheelchair. Kate didn't attempt to help, knowing he would only hate her for it. Instead she turned to look out of the window at the gathering darkness. She heard him manoeuvre himself into his chair at last, then the whirr of the motor as he came towards her.

He took a drink from the whisky he'd retrieved from the table and watched her light a cigarette. 'Don't tell me you're turning over a new leaf.' He smiled mirthlessly.

'Why do you do this, Evan?'

'Do what?'

'Provoke me. Accuse me.'

'I'm sorry,' he said with exaggerated effect. 'Does it offend your honour?'

'You can be such a bastard.'

'Come on Kate. Remember who you're talking to. It was my so called friend that you jumped into bed with remember? When I was lying all smashed up in my hospital bed. I expect you both thought I was going to die. It must have disappointed the hell out of you. You don't expect me to believe he was the only one do you?'

Kate shook her head, from weariness more than anything. How many times had she heard this same old grinding theme? She'd made a mistake, a human error because she had been half out of her mind at the time and she'd needed someone to turn to, and Evan had never let her forget it. And he'd accused her often enough that one day her resistance had collapsed. Why not be guilty of what he accused her?

But now? She didn't know if she could carry on any more. Not now. Her eyes had been opened. She made for the door and he shouted after her.

'Where the hell do you think you're going?'

'Away from here. Out of this place,' she snapped.

He came after her, his features twisted. 'Away from me?'

'Yes. To get away from you!'

It was out before she could stop herself. She saw the way he looked at her, the mixture of fear and loathing and maybe even his love that had been long twisted into need. A heady cocktail, smouldering behind his eyes.

'I know you were out that night, Kate,' he said as she put her hand on the door. She froze, her heart beating wildly. In the silence she could feel him grinning as he saw her reaction. 'You know the night I'm talking about, don't you Kate? The night that fisherman vanished. Maybe I should call the police. Or should I tell that lawyer that was here?'

She turned, and he smiled with gloating triumph.

'You didn't think I heard you did you? I saw you from the window when you came back. You want to know what woke me? It was the shots. I heard rifle shots. What do you think about that, Kate?'

She stared at him, then went out and slammed the door behind her. She heard him as she left the house, yelling for her to come back, but she ignored him. As she drove away the wheels of the Mercedes spun for traction, throwing gravel back in the air.

Dave Baxter was taking a break when Kate Little pulled over in her Mercedes. He was parked near the docks, listening to the sound of loud voices spilling from a bar along the street. She jerked to a sudden stop, the tyres screeching, then she got out and crossed the street, slamming the door closed behind her.

He felt the way he always did when he saw her, which was mostly a deep longing ache that started in his chest and seemed to extend all the way down to the pit of his stomach. The other thing he felt was pretty stupid.

He hadn't meant to end up feeling the way he did about Kate Little. In fact, to begin with he hadn't really been aware that it was happening. It wasn't like some blinding flash, some teenage love at first sight crap like in some of those romance stories they sold at the grocery store. It had been a slow process that had started off as him feeling a little sorry for her. He couldn't even say when his feelings had begun to change, if it had happened over one summer or several. He just knew that when Kate had first started coming to the island, what had struck him most of all about her was not the way she looked, which was pretty hard not to notice, but the way she hardly ever smiled. Not that she was unapproachable, or that she acted as if simply because she had money she was different from anyone else, it was more like she was preoccupied all the time. Like she had something on her mind and whatever it was it made her sad.

That first year Kate hadn't come into town much, except to do some shopping or whatever. There were stories about the guy she was married to, that he seemed to drink a lot and was pretty unfriendly. Frank Hunter who did maintenance at the house saw him more than anyone, and his view was that Evan Little was an asshole. It was the second summer the Littles came to the island that Kate started being seen around town more often, and she was beginning to drink enough that she was being talked about. Baxter didn't know which had come first, the stories about her drinking, or the rumours about her seeing men. Either way, some people started acting like she had some kind of social disease when they were around her. Baxter knew how people liked to talk in places like Sanctuary Harbor. Especially about summer people. Kate was an easy target. She was rich, she drank and she was good looking. Put all that together with the fact that she didn't seem to give a damn and she was bound to get talked about. A lot of what was said about her wasn't true, Baxter knew, but he'd seen her once with a guy called Keller

251

who'd lived on the island for a while, and it was pretty obvious there was something between them. He guessed there might have been others too, like Jordan Osborne.

But underneath it all, Baxter had always felt there was more to Kate than people thought. Whenever he saw her it was the sadness in her eyes that struck him. She was unhappy. When he was alone at his house, or when he was out on his boat, he'd find himself thinking about her. Even over the long winter months when the house on the point was closed down and empty, he'd wonder where she was and what she was doing. He'd never put a name to what he felt, but he came to accept it, as he accepted he would never do anything about it. It was pretty ridiculous, some middle-aged, small town cop who was carrying a little too much weight, feeling the way he did about a woman who had probably never even noticed his existence. A woman who was married anyway.

Across the street, Kate went into a convenience store and on impulse Baxter followed her. She was at the counter, waiting her turn when he went in and he picked up a magazine from the rack which he pretended to look at.

Meg Thorn was behind the counter. She said goodnight to the customer she was serving, then when she saw Kate her expression hardened.

'I'd like a pack of Pall Mall,' Kate said.

Meg hesitated, then it seemed with deliberate slowness she turned around and took a pack from the display which she slapped on the counter. Her expression didn't alter a fraction. Kate handed over a bill and Meg accepted it as if it was tainted then put it down by the register while she rang up the sale. Baxter had seen the way people could show their meanness in lots of small and hurtful ways, but this was blatant.

'Wait a minute,' Kate said. There was a different tone in her voice.

Meg stopped what she was doing and looked surprised.

'I changed my mind.' Kate pushed the Pall Malls back over the counter. 'I want something else.' She looked at the display of brands all plainly there for her to see. 'What else do you have?'

Confused, Meg indicated the display, then resentfully she said, 'This is everything.'

'My eyesight isn't so good. Tell me what's there.'

The two women stared at each other. It seemed like Meg was going to refuse to answer. It was a standoff. Baxter took the magazine he was looking at over to the counter and put it down.

'The lady asked what brands you have, Meg.'

She turned her angry stare on him, then under the weight of so much opposition she gave in, and though she didn't sound too happy about it, she began reciting off all the different brands. Kate waited until she'd been through them all.

'I guess I'll take these after all.' Kate picked up the Pall Malls again. 'Keep the change,' she said and with a brief nod to Baxter she walked out of the store.

He caught up with her outside as she started along the street. She glanced at him as he fell in beside her.

'I've been wanting to do that for a long time,' she said.

'Meg's not so bad.'

'If you say so.' She paused. 'Anyway, thanks . . . I'm sorry I don't know your name.'

'It's Baxter.'

'Well, thanks Officer Baxter. Goodnight.'

She started to walk away, and Baxter watched her go, then at last he called after her. 'Mrs Little?'

She stopped and waited.

He caught up, unsure now what he had in mind. 'Were you going someplace in particular?'

'Yes. No. I was going to have a drink.'

'I was thinking I might have a beer myself . . . I mean, if you wanted some company. I'm not busy right now.'

Kate looked at him for several seconds, and Baxter was glad that it was dark enough that maybe she wouldn't see the way his colour had risen. He could feel the heat in his face, and his palms felt suddenly sweaty. He thought she would turn him down, but then after what seemed like forever she nodded.

'Okay Officer Baxter. Why not?'

He smiled. 'It's Dave by the way.'

'Dave,' she said.

They went to *The Lobster Pot*, and ordered drinks and sat at a table in the corner. Kate lit a cigarette. Rita brought their drinks over and gave Baxter a funny kind of puzzled look which he ignored. They talked for a little while, about nothing much. Kate asked him questions about himself, how long he'd been a cop, had he always lived on the island, things that Baxter felt she really had little interest in. She was just being polite. Every now and then she'd gaze off into space and he had the feeling she hadn't heard what he'd been saying.

'Do you have children?' she asked him after one short silence, during which he'd been trying to think of something to talk about that wouldn't make him seem so dull. As he'd told her about himself it had struck him how ordinary and uneventful his life had been.

'I was never married.'

She looked surprised at that. 'I can't imagine why some woman around here didn't snap you up a long time ago.'

'Well, I don't know myself,' Baxter said, laughing a little. He thought he heard a slight wistful note that made him think that maybe she wasn't being entirely flippant. Inwardly he told himself he was dreaming. 'I keep waiting, you know? But they don't exactly come hammering down my door.'

Kate smiled, and he thought her mood was better than when they had first sat down. She seemed to have forgotten her troubles, or at least put them aside for a little while.

'It's a pity, I bet you would have made a good dad. Didn't you ever want children?'

'I did once.' He shrugged. 'I stopped thinking about it I guess.'

'Perhaps you will someday.'

'Maybe,' he said, though he doubted it. 'What about you Mrs Little. You don't have children?'

Kate looked away, and her expression clouded with regret. 'No. After my husband's accident . . .' She picked up her drink and then shrugged. 'Just one of those things.'

Baxter didn't know what to say. He wished he'd kept his

mouth shut. He changed the subject and started to tell her about how he'd been to New York a couple of times when he was younger, but she only nodded vaguely and he knew she wasn't really listening. He tried to make her smile again, telling her a couple of things that had happened over the years that were kind of funny, but either he was a bad story teller or she just wasn't in the mood. After a while she finished her drink and said she ought to be going.

'It was nice talking to you.' Baxter stood up with her.

'You too,' she told him. 'I'm sorry if I was a little distant.' She seemed about to leave, but then she hesitated. 'That man, Bryan Roderick? Has there been any news about him?'

There was an off-key note in her tone. She tried to make her question sound casual, but it didn't quite come off. 'No,' he told her.

'But you think he was murdered? I mean that's what I hear.'

'It looks that way,' Baxter admitted.

She looked as if she might ask something more, but then changed her mind. 'I was just curious. Well, thank you again.'

'Anytime.'

After Kate had left he sat quietly and finished his drink. He thought about their conversation, musing for a while on a foolish dream he'd long had where she came to his house and they ate barbecue on the patio and sat and talked into the night. For the first time his fantasy seemed a little more real. As if it was something that could actually happen. Then he thought about the way she'd asked about Bryan Roderick, and his good mood dissipated. He remembered what Matt Jones had said, the suggestion that Kate was mixed up in this somehow, and much as he'd fought the idea, it kept popping back up in his mind, refusing to go away.

As he put down his glass Rita came over and asked if he wanted another.

'No thanks, I'm all set.'

She picked up his empty glass and reached for Kate's. Baxter stopped her.

'Leave that would you Rita?'

255

She looked puzzled, then shrugged. 'Sure, whatever.'

After she'd gone Baxter stared at the empty glass, then he carefully wrapped it in a handkerchief he took from his pocket and when he left he took it with him.

CHAPTER TWENTY-NINE

Anne Laine finished examining Matt's nose. 'It isn't bad. Only a fracture.' She went around her desk and sat down. 'I can bandage it for you if you like, but you'll heal just as well without it.'

'I'll go without then,' Matt said, gingerly touching his nose.

'I'll give you something for the pain. Try not to get in any more fights for a while. What happened anyway? I didn't figure you for the type to get caught up in bar room brawls.'

'Well, I'm a dark horse.'

She smiled. 'I had a whole bunch of them in here this morning. One with a broken finger, half a dozen with bruising and a couple with cracked ribs. Russ Williams took a fair crack on the head himself. He told me some vacationers from a charter boat got in an argument with some of our local guys in the *Schooner*. Somebody threw a punch and next thing the whole place blew up.' She shook her head with resignation. 'Then they come in here and expect me to patch them up so they can all go and do the same thing again tonight.' She tore off a sheet from her pad and passed it across. 'Okay, you're all set.'

Matt folded the prescription and put it in his pocket. Anne regarded him frankly. She hailed originally from New Hampshire, from a small town up around the lakes. She wore red rimmed glasses and a red shirt with blue jeans, and other than the stethoscope lying coiled on her desk she didn't look much like a doctor.

'You want to tell me what really happened to you? I had Jake Roderick in here earlier with a cracked jaw, you know.'

Matt grinned, which made his eyes water. 'I guess you could say we had a slight disagreement.'

'Wouldn't have anything to do with Ella would it? You don't need to answer that by the way.'

'It was related,' he said. She started putting her things away, getting ready for the next patient. 'There's something I'd like to ask you. It's about Bryan Roderick. Was he ever a patient of yours?'

'I saw him once or twice.' She thought back. 'I think the last time would have been a year or so ago. He cut his hand I think.'

'What did you think of him?'

'You mean personally? I suppose it isn't a breach of patient confidentiality to say that I didn't particularly like him.'

'Any particular reason for that?'

Anne regarded him with a studied expression, as if weighing up what she felt she could tell him. 'Bryan liked to think of himself as something of a ladies' man. Let's just say that he made a pass at me once that I didn't much like.'

'I thought he had a pretty good track record with women.'

She smiled a little bitterly. 'With some women maybe. I've seen enough of his kind to know the type. And I've seen what happens to women in relationships with men like that. I get the results in here too often.'

'You're saying he was violent?'

'Let's just say that Bryan's girlfriends all seemed to suffer from the same clumsy tendency to bump into hard objects.'

Matt recalled Jake's taunt from the night before. 'Can I ask you something else? Was Ella ever one of those women?' He wasn't sure what reaction he'd expected. He thought the idea of Ella and Bryan was unlikely given everything he'd heard, but he had to admit it was possible that their enmity might have stemmed from some brief affair that had ended badly, perhaps long ago. Anne's astonishment however made the idea even more unlikely.

'Ella? Why on earth would you think that? Ella of all people is exactly the type who wouldn't go within a hundred miles of somebody like Bryan.'

He was both relieved and slightly shamed to think he'd given any credence at all to the possibility, but he was struck by Anne's choice of words and her incredulity. 'Why Ella, "of all people"?'

She pursed her lips. 'Perhaps I shouldn't have said anything. I can't discuss the private lives of my patients,' she said at last.

'You know I'm representing Ella? If there's anything you're aware of that might help me, I could use it right now.'

'I don't think this has anything to do with that.' She frowned, wrestling with her conscience. 'Have you met Ella's mother?' Matt nodded. 'After Ella's father died, Helena had a stroke. She and Ella are very close.' As she spoke she chose her words with care. 'Ella's father was a difficult man. I don't know if you're aware of this but Ella had a brother who died as an infant. It was long before I came here, but I think Ella's father was deeply affected by the loss of his son. I treated him once or twice for minor physical things, and I got the impression he could be melancholy. Perhaps he was clinically depressed, I'm not really qualified to say. I think Ella's mother is a very strong woman, her character I mean. I think she had a lot to cope with over the years.'

Matt read between the lines. 'You're saying Ella's father was abusive? I got the impression that Ella was close to him.'

'She was. I'm sure both Ella and her mother loved him a great deal. But loving somebody isn't always straightforward. We're all of us made up of good and not so good qualities.' She hesitated. 'Look, I'm not really comfortable about discussing this.'

Matt wasn't entirely sure why, but he felt this was important. 'You're saying Bryan was somehow like Ella's father? That's why you sounded so surprised when I asked if there could have been anything between him and Ella?'

'Not really, or at least perhaps in only one sense. I'm not saying Ella's father was the stereotypical wife beater. He wasn't. But I think he was definitely unbalanced at times, and I think Ella probably witnessed some traumatic scenes as she grew up.

259

Ella's intelligent, she would have recognized the type of man Bryan was and she would never get involved with anyone like that. I'm certain of that.'

Matt was sure that she was right. Deep down he hadn't believed Jake's suggestion, but it did occur to him that if Ella considered Bryan was the kind of man who beat women, she may well have hated him for it.

'I have to get on,' Anne said, signalling that she could tell him no more. He had the feeling she thought she had said too much already. He thanked her, but at the door he paused.

'One other thing, Doctor. Is Kate Little a patient of yours when she's on the island?'

'Yes, she is.'

'Did she ever have a tendency to bump into hard objects?'

Anne opened the door for him. 'Patient confidentiality, Mr Jones. I'm afraid there's nothing more I can tell you.'

'Forget I asked. And thanks.' As he left, he thought she hadn't needed to answer him directly. He'd seen all he wanted to know in her eyes.

The drive from Doctor Laine's clinic to the south side of town gave Matt some time to think. Though he still had nothing to back up his hunch he was almost sure now that Kate Little had been involved with Bryan Roderick. He also now knew that Bryan had a history of violence towards women, and with that knowledge his conviction that Kate had something to do with Bryan's disappearance had grown. He saw the beginnings of a motive, and since she lived close to the cove, and the night he vanished she and her husband had slept in separate rooms, she had the opportunity. Then there was the fact that Ben Harper had seen her early the following morning when she might have been returning from Bryan's house, perhaps after removing evidence of a struggle.

The problem was that so far he couldn't prove any of it. Also, he admitted to himself, he felt there was a lot he didn't know. And he feared that it involved Ella.

Jordan Osborne was standing in the doorway drinking a cup

of coffee when Matt pulled up outside the boatyard and climbed out of his car. He said something to the two men beside him, and they threw curious glances towards Matt before going back inside the shed.

'We can talk in there.' Without waiting to see what Matt wanted Osborne led the way to the office where they had talked before. 'I figured you'd be back sooner or later.'

'Jordan, I'm going to get right to the point,' Matt said. 'I think that Kate and Bryan were seeing each other, and I think you already knew that, but you chose not to tell me. Question is why? The way I see it is there are two possible explanations. One is that by admitting that you knew about their relationship, it gave you a motive for maybe wanting Bryan out the way. Could be you thought that way you might have a shot at getting Kate back.'

Osborne started to protest angrily. 'I already told you that I was home all night that Monday.'

'I know. And I believe you. Which means you must have had another reason for not telling me what you know. My guess is that you were protecting Kate.'

Osborne tried to hide his reaction, but Matt felt that he had struck a chord, and he took the opportunity to press his advantage. 'I also think Bryan may have been violent towards Kate, and I think you knew about that too. That sort of makes Kate a suspect. Is that why you were protecting her?'

Osborne stared at him. 'I told you, I don't know anything about this. Anyway, after what Jerrod Gant saw it doesn't matter does it?'

'It does if he was lying.'

Osborne thought about that. 'You'd say that anyway, Ella's your client. Look, I like Ella if you want to know the truth. But I can't help you. I'm telling you I don't know anything.'

'Jordan, I get the impression you're a decent person,' Matt said. 'I can understand you wanting to protect Kate. You have feelings for her. But that doesn't mean you ought to stand by and let an innocent person take the blame for whatever happened to Bryan. Ella didn't kill him. Gant's statement is a lie.'

Jordan Osborne turned away. He stood by the door with his hands thrust in his pockets looking out through the shed, to the water beyond. Matt didn't say anything, letting him wrestle with his conscience. Eventually Osborne went back to his desk, where he stopped and picked up a pen which he fiddled with before putting it down again. Matt decided to try again.

'Were you born here on the island Jordan?'

'I've lived here all my life.'

'So, forget that it's me you're talking to. Think about Ella. You must have known her all your life. How would you feel if she went to jail for something she didn't do? Could you sleep at night?'

He thought about that, and Matt let him, allowing the silence to stretch out. 'Okay. I did know that Kate was seeing Bryan.' He pulled out a chair and sat down. He had the look of a man unable to hold out against an issue that had been bothering him for a while. Maybe he was even relieved, though it was clear he remained reluctant to incriminate Kate. 'But that doesn't mean she had anything to do with this.'

'Maybe not. So, how did you know about Kate and Bryan?' Matt asked.

'I guessed there was somebody else. Kate avoided me whenever she could. Then I saw her one night in town. She'd just parked her car near the docks. I thought she was going to *The Lobster Pot,* and I was planning to go after her. I thought we could talk.'

'When was this?'

'About three weeks ago. I'd seen her around this summer, but she made it clear it was over between us. Anyway she was walking along the docks near the fishing boats. It gets pretty dark around there.'

'And you followed her?'

Osborne nodded. 'Anyhow, before I caught her up, Bryan pulled over in his truck and he got out. He looked pretty mad about something. I hung back for a minute because I wasn't sure what was going on. There was nobody else around. I could tell they were arguing about something, but I couldn't hear what they were saying. Then Bryan grabbed Kate by the arm.'

'Go on.'

'Well, it was pretty clear he was hurting her. I was about to yell at him to leave her alone, but before I could someone came from the other direction. I guess she must have been on her boat and she saw what was going on.'

'She?'

'It was Ella.'

Matt listened in silence, but Ella's name reverberated through him. He was trying to concentrate on what Osborne was saying, but he was also thinking about the look he'd seen pass between Kate and Ella outside the post office that day, and now he thought he knew what that look had signified. It was complicity. A shared secret. He wasn't even surprised, and he supposed he'd guessed the moment he'd mentioned Kate's name to Ella and seen the way she reacted.

Osborne continued recounting what he'd seen. 'Bryan had been drinking. When Ella showed up he started in on her as well. Called her a lot of names. He was cursing her out, telling her she was a frigid bitch and a lot worse. He had hold of Kate by the arm and she was trying to get away from him. She looked mad as hell, and I guess he was hurting her. She called Bryan a whole bunch of things, said she didn't want to ever see him again. Ella was yelling at him to let Kate go. I remember she called him a coward. He looked kind of dumbstruck when she said that.'

'What happened then?'

'He hit Kate. It happened so fast there was nothing I could've done. He bunched his fist and hit her. About here.' Osborne touched his own chest. 'Then he started laying in to her. Like he'd gone crazy. He was cursing her, and hitting her and she was trying to get away from him, and Ella was trying to pull him off. I think he hit Ella too. By then I was running along the dock towards them, but Kate and Ella got free before I reached them, and I grabbed Bryan and wrestled him to the ground and after a little while he quietened down. I felt like I wanted to smash his skull if you want to know the truth, but he was

263

struggling so much by the time I had the better of him I didn't have the strength.' He shrugged. 'That was about it.'

'What happened to Kate and Ella?'

'I didn't see. I guess they were already running when I got there. I don't even know if they saw me. By the time I looked for them they were gone.'

Neither of them spoke. Matt was picturing the scene, wondering why both Ella and Kate had denied knowing each other. Why Kate had denied knowing Bryan. Ideas formed and dissolved and formed again in his mind. After a while he realized that Osborne had spoken.

'What?' Matt said.

'I said I didn't kill him. I know that's what you're thinking. Sure I admit I could've killed him that night. I was angry. I never liked that sonofabitch or his brother anyway. You know, to be honest, if he's dead I'm not sorry. But I was home that night and if I had to prove it my wife would back me up.'

CHAPTER THIRTY

Ella sat beside her mother's bed. Helena was sleeping, her hand clutching the photograph of Ella's father that her mother kept on the night stand. He was smiling at the camera. Tall and fair haired, the image a little out of focus. She felt pressure on her hand and saw that her mother was awake.

'He was a good father to you Ella.'

'I know.'

'And a good husband.'

'Yes,' Ella said. And it was true, most of the time he had been both those things. She sighed, and put the picture back on the night stand.

'Have you talked to Matt?'

'Not since the meeting,' Ella said.

'You know you can't avoid him forever Ella.' Helena smiled. 'I like him. I think he's a good person.'

'I think so too, Mom.'

Helena was quiet for a little while. She closed her eyes, and her breathing became regular and even and Ella thought she had fallen asleep again. She put her mother's hand on the bed and rose to go, but before she got to the door Helena called her name and Ella stopped and saw that she was awake. In the dim light from the passage her eyes appeared moist.

'I think you should tell him Ella. I think you ought to trust him,' Helena said.

Ella nodded, knowing that she was right. 'I know. I'll go and see him in the morning.'

Helena closed her eyes again. 'It will be all right. He's a good man.'

CHAPTER THIRTY-ONE

A shadow fell across the table where Matt was sitting.

'You look as if you could use some company.'

Sally Brewster slid into the other side of the booth. She had on the pale chocolate uniform she wore at the coffee shop where she worked, and as she sat she leaned over and slipped her heels out of her shoes.

'God, my feet are killing me. My mother had varicose veins by the time she was forty. I have to get another job. It's being on your feet all day that causes them, did you know that? I guess you didn't. Guys don't have to worry about getting varicose veins, huh?'

She smiled lopsidedly and gestured to Matt's empty glass. 'I think I might join you if you're offering.' Without waiting for him to reply she signalled to the waitress who came over and took her order for a Bloody Mary.

'And get my friend here another of whatever he's having, Rita, would you?'

'Sure. Another bourbon on the rocks.'

Sally lit a cigarette. She sighed as she blew smoke. 'So how long have you been here?'

Matt glanced at his watch, and was surprised to see that it was after ten. Music was playing in the background and a press of people were at the bar swapping exaggerated fishing stories. 'A couple of hours,' he said.

'Try three.'

'It could be three,' he admitted.

'How many of those have you had?' Sally indicated his glass.

'A couple.' He saw her sceptical look. 'Maybe a couple more. How'd you know I was here?'

'What makes you think I knew you were here? I just stopped in for a drink after a hard day's work.'

It was Matt's turn to look sceptical.

'Okay. It was Rita. She called me. She knows I have a soft spot for guys like you, the sad cases. She said you'd been here a while and you looked like you were settling in for a long night. She thought I might want to come by.'

Rita brought their drinks over, and Sally thanked her and tasted her cocktail. She made a face. 'They never put enough vodka in these things. I should just forget about the tomato juice next time.' She set her glass down, and her expression became serious. 'By the way, what happened to your face? You look as if somebody mistook your head for a punch-bag.'

He managed a smile. 'You should see the other guy.'

'That's better.' She grinned at him.

Matt raised his glass and half emptied it. He was feeling a little drunk, but it was a good feeling he decided. He felt a little numbed. 'I think I lost my faith in people, Sally.'

'Yeah? Well join the club.'

He looked at her askance. 'Don't tell me you're a cynic.'

She shrugged. 'Me? I'm not a cynic, I'm just a realist. I don't expect too much from myself or from anyone else. That way I don't get too many disappointments, and every now and then I get a nice surprise when something good happens, and that makes me think we're not so bad.'

Matt wondered if that was perhaps a cynical view after all. 'That's a little sad isn't it, if that's the best we can expect?'

'Seems to me it's better than expecting too much. That way you'd be disappointed all the time.'

'Are you trying to tell me something?'

Sally finished her drink. 'Nope. Just trying to make you stop sitting there looking so godawful sorry for yourself, that's all.'

'Ouch.'

'Sometimes people need a little kick in the pants,' Sally told him. 'Right now what I need is to get home and get out of this thing.' She plucked at her uniform. 'Listen, why don't you come with me? I can fix us something to eat. I bet you haven't eaten all day and you're sitting here drinking on an empty stomach.'

Matt started to say he wasn't hungry, but she stopped him.

'I'm offering to fix you a meal, Matt. Nothing else. You shouldn't drive yourself anyway, and I live just across the street.'

She was right, and now that food had been mentioned Matt decided that he was hungry. He looked about the restaurant, and thought dinner with Sally was actually appealing. He didn't want to be among a lot of people, but he didn't want to be alone either. He didn't want to go home and think about Kate Little or Ella right now, and what all that he'd learned that day meant.

'Thanks, Sally, I'd like that,' he said.

As they left, Rita caught Sally's eye. 'Have a good night,' she said.

When they reached her apartment, he asked her a question as she slipped off her shoes with a sigh of pleasure.

'You said something one day in the coffee shop, about people lining up to kill Bryan if that's what happened. What did you mean?'

'I did? I don't remember.'

'Sally.' She turned to look at him. 'This could be important. Did you ever go out with Bryan?'

'What? You think I killed him now? That's all the thanks I get for taking pity on you?' He didn't say anything and she saw he wasn't buying her affronted act, and she sighed and sat down. 'Okay. I went out with him a few times. And I'll tell you now what I told you then. Bryan was a gold plated bastard.'

'Did he ever hit you?'

She gave a wan smile. 'Yes, a couple of times. At first he said he hadn't meant to. You know it was an accident blah blah. I guess it took me a while to get it through my thick head that was a crock. He meant it all right. Anyway I told him to take a hike.'

'How'd that make you feel?' Matt asked. 'When he beat up on you?'

269

She studied him, and smoked for a minute in silence, weighing up her answer. In the end she shrugged. 'I'll tell you this. When I heard he might be dead, I poured myself a glass of wine and hoped the sonofabitch got a little of what he gave out before he said goodnight. And that's the truth.'

Once during the night he woke. He'd been dreaming about Paulie, and about that day in the cove, the sensation of water flowing over his head before Paulie had plucked him into the air again. Then he saw Ella, and it was she who dragged him on to the beach where he lay gasping and wet through. She looked down on him, her eyes grey and green like the sea in winter and he reached up and pulled her towards him. He felt her body against his then his hands closed on thin air and she was gone and he was left with a feeling of emptiness, of being alone. When he opened his eyes the room was dark and still. Vaguely he was aware of a feeling of unfamiliarity, of scents he didn't recognize, the scrape of the branch of a tree against the window where there should have been no tree, no window even, but the dislocation was hazy and he let it fall away and drifted back into sleep.

When he woke again it was early in the morning. Soft light filtered through a curtain that ruffled in the breeze and the smell of the harbour was tangy with salt. Matt sat up and remembered where he was. Sally lived in a four-room apartment on the top floor of an old three-storey house one street back from the harbour. He'd slept on the couch, though he couldn't remember how he'd got there. On the bench that divided the room from the kitchen were two empty wine bottles. He got up, and padded with bare feet to the sink where he poured a glass of water. His pants and shirt were folded neatly over a chair, though once again he couldn't remember taking them off. The door that led through to the passage and the bedroom was partly ajar. Matt dressed and went through and pushed open the bedroom door. The light was dim, the curtains drawn, and Sally was asleep. He started to leave, then hesitated and changed his mind. He couldn't just go without saying anything. Though

270

he was encouraged by the fact that they'd obviously slept in separate rooms he wished he could remember going to sleep. They'd eaten spaghetti, and drank a lot of wine, and he thought maybe after that Sally had found some brandy. He had a vague unsettling memory of a fumbled embrace at the end of the night. The dream he'd had during the night came back to him, and he wondered if it really had all been a dream.

Sally opened her eyes, and saw him standing beside her bed.

'Hi,' she said.

'Hi.'

'What time is it?' Her voice sounded hoarse.

'It's early, don't get up.'

Sally groaned. 'My head feels like somebody hit me with a hammer.'

'I know the feeling.'

She got up on one elbow, and the strap of her nightdress fell off her shoulder. Unself-consciously she pulled it up again and swept her hair back from her face. 'You leaving?'

'Yeah. I should get going.' Matt hesitated, wondering how he could broach the question he wanted to ask.

'Well, you want me to fix you some breakfast?'

'No, that's okay.'

Sally watched him, waiting for him to make a move, then a sly smile crossed her face. 'In case you're wondering whether you ought to kiss me, nothing happened.'

'I wasn't wondering whether to kiss you,' Matt said. He bent and brushed her lips.

'Hmm. I think you oughta get out of here before I forget myself.'

Matt grinned. 'Thanks, Sally.'

'For what? We just talked.'

'That's what I mean.'

She waved a hand, dismissing him. 'This is too early for me.' She flopped back on her pillow.

As he left Matt heard her call out to him.

'You better do something about her Matt.'

'Who?' He paused at the front door, but there was no answer.

He stepped out into the half light of dawn. Through the intersection opposite the house he had a clear view of the dock which was already busy as boats put out to sea. He stood on the top step and watched for a while. Out towards the heads half a dozen boats were making their way out of the harbour. The *Santorini* was still at the dock, but even as he watched, Ella's truck pulled up and as she climbed out she looked over and their eyes met. It lasted for a couple of moments. He realized how he must look, coming out of somebody's house where he'd obviously spent the night, and he started to call out to her, but somehow he couldn't. He realized he wouldn't know what to say to her. She had lied to him about Kate, and probably a lot more besides. He felt the gulf between them open up again, and yawn like a chasm.

Abruptly Ella turned away.

CHAPTER THIRTY-TWO

Kate came out of the market clutching a bag under her arm. She wore sunglasses pushed up on her head, and khaki pants. As she loaded groceries into her car, Baxter looked at the fax in his hand. It was confirmation from the lab that the print taken from the faucet in Bryan's house matched the one lifted off a cocktail glass that came from *The Lobster Pot*. It was a right thumb print, and it belonged to Kate Little.

Baxter told himself again that the print only proved that at some recent time Kate had been in Bryan's house. There could be any number of explanations for that.

Yeah, right, Dave, pull the other one, it plays a tune.

He read the fax over again. There were no names. Just sample A matches sample B. The fax paper was the thermal type, it felt insubstantial, like rice paper. He could crumple it into a ball and toss it in the trash and nobody would ever know.

Across the street Kate got in her car and pulled out. At the stop sign she made a right and headed out of town, and after a moment Baxter started his car and followed her. He caught her up on the point road and flashed his lights until she saw him and indicated to pull over. He stopped behind her, and as he approached she wound down the window.

'Hello again. Was I speeding?'

'Nothing like that,' Baxter said. 'I was just heading this way, thought you had a faulty brake light.'

Kate frowned. 'I do?'

'Let me check it.' Baxter went around the back and he called out for her to turn the key and put her foot on the brake. Both lights went on. Baxter wondered what the hell he thought he was doing. He went back around. 'I guess I must have been mistaken. You might want to get them checked out next time you put her in for a service though.'

'I'll do that.' Kate smiled, looking vaguely puzzled. 'Looks like it's going to be hot again.'

'Yes, it does,' Baxter replied. For a moment they both looked through the trees to the glimpse of ocean beyond.

Baxter snapped his fingers, as if something had just occurred to him. 'Hell, I knew there was something I needed to ask you.'

'There is?'

'Yeah. You know what, the guy that's missing, Bryan Roderick? His house is down in the cove. I wondered if you might have been there anytime. Could be you passed it out walking and you needed to use the phone or something? Maybe asked for a glass of water.'

Kate looked at him for about a second and a half, and Baxter knew she wasn't taken in. He guessed that apart from the fact he was a lousy actor, it was just about the lamest thing he'd ever heard himself.

'Why would you think I'd been to his house?' she asked.

'I don't. I mean I just wondered.'

'You just wondered if I might have been in somebody's house? For no reason?'

'Well, it's possible. Maybe you talked to Bryan and you didn't even know who he was.' Baxter could feel the sun beating down on his head and neck, and he felt sweat break out on his back. She didn't believe a word of it and he didn't blame her.

'Well, the answer's no.'

Baxter shrugged uncomfortably. 'That's what I figured. It was just a thought.' He stepped back from her car. 'You have a good day.'

'Thanks. Same to you.'

'Sure.'

He watched as she drove away, and as he went back to his car he told himself he was an idiot. For several long minutes he

274

stared thoughtfully along the now empty road. He took out the fax and read it again. He'd told Matt that handing Ella over to the state authorities, even though he had serious doubts himself about Jerrod Gant's statement, was partly because he wanted to protect her. Was that true? Deep down, he admitted that it probably wasn't. He stared at the fax for a long time, then finally he folded it again and then picked up his car radio.

'What's up, Chief?' Martha asked when he called in.

'See if you can find Matt Jones will you, Martha? Ask him to meet me at my office.'

He put up his radio, and looked ahead through the windscreen, then after a moment he swung his car around and started back towards town.

That afternoon they drove through the gates and up to the Littles' house, along a drive shaded by tall oaks. Kate herself answered the door, and she looked first at Matt, then rested her gaze on Baxter, and didn't seem surprised to see them. She led them through to the living room.

'My husband is working,' she said.

'That's okay,' Baxter told her. 'We just need to talk to you, Mrs Little.'

She gestured for them to sit down, and sat on the edge of an armchair herself and lit a cigarette. Baxter appeared unhappy, and Matt thought they both had reason to feel that way. After the call had come to meet Baxter at his office he hadn't known what to expect. He'd thought maybe there was new evidence, which there had been, just not the kind he'd expected. Baxter had told him about Kate's print matching the one found at Bryan's house. Once he'd gotten over his surprise when Baxter told him how he'd got it, Matt had related what he'd learned from Jordan Osborne.

'There has to be a reason Kate and Ella denied knowing each other,' Matt had concluded. 'And why Kate denied knowing Bryan.'

'You think they're mixed up in this together?'

It seemed that way Matt had thought, though quite how he

275

wasn't sure. A call to the harbourmaster had determined that Ella was out fishing, so they'd decided to confront Kate Little with what they knew first. On the way over Baxter had said Matt should be the one to question her about what he'd learned from Osborne, since he had heard it all first hand.

'Mrs Little we want to ask you some questions about Bryan Roderick,' Matt began. He paused, allowing her a moment to absorb this. 'I talked to a friend of yours yesterday, Jordan Osborne. He told me that three weeks ago he saw you and Bryan Roderick arguing on the dock.' He watched for her reaction, but other than a slight widening of her eyes she gave nothing away. 'Mrs Little, last time we spoke you told me you didn't know Bryan,' he reminded her.

She hesitated for a long moment, but when she spoke her voice was calm. 'There doesn't seem to be any point in denying what you already know, does there? Bryan Roderick and I were having an affair.'

Baxter was looking at a point on the wall. He seemed not to have heard what she said.

'How come you didn't tell anybody this before?' Matt asked. 'We're talking about a man who's missing. Possibly dead.'

She didn't flinch from his gaze. Her eyes seemed almost violet, and though Matt had come here believing there was a strong likelihood that Kate Little was involved in a man's death, he admitted to himself that she didn't strike him as capable of murder. If anything she appeared a little sad. But then he'd thought the same thing about Ella.

'I didn't tell you because it isn't something I'm proud of. And also because I'd stopped seeing Bryan before he disappeared. There's nothing I can tell you about that.'

'When was the last time you saw him?'

'The night you mentioned, at the dock.'

'Ella Young was there too. You told me you didn't know her either.'

Kate dropped her gaze for a moment. She tapped ash into an ashtray at her side and looked up again.

'I wouldn't say that I know her. That night was the only time we've met. Even then we barely spoke more than a word or two.'

'Tell me about that night. What happened?'

'A few days earlier I'd told Bryan that I didn't want to see him anymore. That night he surprised me. He'd been drinking. I told him again that I didn't want to see him, and he became violent. When Ella appeared it made him worse.'

'He hit you?'

'Yes.'

'Had he ever done something like that before, Mrs Little?'

'Yes,' she said quietly. 'That's why I told him it was over.' Kate put out her cigarette. 'I'm not proud of myself, Mr Jones.' She glanced towards Baxter. 'I can imagine what you're thinking. A married woman who has affairs, and her husband stuck in a wheelchair. The truth is my marriage was over a long time ago.'

'We're not here to judge anybody's moral standards Mrs Little,' Baxter said.

'Perhaps. Bryan wasn't the first man I've had an affair with. But of course, if you've talked to Jordan you already know that. You've both met Evan. He's a difficult man.'

Kate paused and smiled with sad reflection. Matt had the feeling she wanted to explain herself, as if she was afraid of what they would think of her. Or at least what one of them would think of her.

'After his accident I think Evan was afraid I would leave him,' she told them. 'We hadn't been married very long. I think rather than have to face that he tried to drive me away. His personality changed after his accident, he could be very cruel. I admit that I did consider leaving him. That sounds terrible, but you have to understand that Evan sometimes acted as if he resented me, hated me even. But I knew that his moods were partly caused by the drugs he was taking, and I kept hoping he would get better, even though the doctors said he might only have a few years to live. But he didn't.' She paused for a moment.

'It began with somebody that Evan knew. A friend that worked for him. He and I spent a lot of time together. He was nice to me, understanding. A shoulder to cry on.'

She stared past them, her unseeing gaze fixed on the window.

'I'm sure I don't need to go into the details of what happened. Evan found out about Chris and me and he's never let me forget it. Perhaps that's why I've stayed so long with him. Guilt. But I'm human and sometimes I needed somebody to show they cared about me. I don't think that's such a terrible thing is it?' She looked at them both, from one to the other, as if expecting an answer.

'Bryan was a bad choice as it turned out,' she said.

All at once the sound of a slow hand-clap filled the silence. They turned to find Evan Little at the open door.

'What a brilliant performance, Kate. What do you think Chief? And you, Mr Jones isn't it? Were you taken in by her? I almost feel sorry for her myself. She's very good at justifying herself. Making it sound as if I'm at fault because my wife turned out to be a goddamned slut.'

His chair made a whirring sound and the tyres hissed across the floor.

'Don't let me stop you. I missed the first part, but I imagine you're here to ask her about that fisherman she was fucking. Has she got to the part where she went out the night he disappeared, or were you saving that for later Kate?' He smiled at her, his eyes glittering.

'Is that true?' Baxter asked.

She looked at her husband, and it was as if she was surprised by what she saw. As if her eyes had been opened. She nodded. 'I was out that night. I couldn't sleep and it was hot. Sometimes I walk a little at night.'

'What time would that have been?' Matt said.

'I'm not sure.'

'It was around three thirty when you came back,' Evan offered helpfully, staring at his wife with open hostility. 'And I know she wasn't in bed when I heard the shots. That would have been around two. I remember looking at my watch. It took a few minutes to get myself out of bed. Not an easy process as you can imagine, but when I went into Kate's room she wasn't there.'

278

'You heard shots?' Matt said.

'They woke me. Two I think, at least.'

'Is what your husband says true?'

'I suppose so, I didn't look at the time.'

'Did you see anybody that night, Mrs Little?'

She shook her head. 'No.'

'You're sure? How about Ella Young?'

'I told you. I didn't see anyone.'

'Did you hear shots?'

'No.'

Evan made a snorting sound of derision.

'How often did you see Bryan Roderick?' Matt asked.

'Maybe twice a week.'

'Always at his house?'

She shook her head. 'Usually. Not always.'

'Did you have keys?'

'Yes.'

'Were you at the house the morning after he vanished?'

'Yes.'

'Why?'

'I wanted to return his keys. I hadn't seen Bryan since the week before. After what happened at the dock I didn't want to go to the house in case I ran into him.'

'So you chose that morning?'

'Yes.'

'What time was this?'

'I don't know. Early.'

'Did you see anybody?'

'No.'

Matt paused. She hadn't flinched at any of his questions. 'Did you see anything in the house that made you think something may have happened to Bryan? Signs of a struggle maybe?'

'No. It looked quite normal.'

'The police believe somebody cleaned up in there, maybe trying to get rid of evidence. Was that you? Were you trying to hide the fact that you'd ever been there?'

She hesitated. 'Why would I do that? I didn't know then that anything had happened to Bryan.'

'Maybe you did know,' Matt said. 'Mrs Little, did you kill Bryan?'

She shook her head. 'No.'

'Maybe you ran into him and there was some kind of fight?'

'No.'

'Did you see anybody else that night?'

'You already asked me that question. The answer is still no. I saw nobody.'

Evan Little wore a sardonic smile as he watched, obviously enjoying himself. Matt wondered briefly whether Evan himself could have had anything to do with Bryan's disappearance. He had motive enough, but it seemed unlikely given his disability. Kate lit another cigarette. She appeared calm, but underneath he sensed her tension. Once again Matt recalled the look she and Ella had exchanged on the post office steps. He searched for some inconsistency in Kate's story. Her husband had heard shots which had woken him around the same time as Carl Johnson had reported hearing something that night. How could Kate not have heard them too?

Matt turned to her husband. 'You said you heard shots that night. You're certain of the time?'

'I looked at my watch.'

'How do you explain the fact you didn't hear anything Mrs Little?'

'Yes, Kate. We'd all love to hear,' Evan said. 'The acoustics on the point are very good. Sound carries a long way in the cove.'

'I can't explain it.'

Something clicked in Matt's mind. Gears slipped into place. 'Acoustics,' he said, half to himself. He was aware that they were all looking at him. 'Mr Little, did you hear anything else that night?'

Evan looked puzzled for a moment, then recollection dawned in his expression. 'Now you come to mention it, I did hear

280

something. It must have been around an hour after I heard the shots. Before Kate came back to the house.'

'What was it?' Matt asked, a vague premonition constricting his throat.

'It was a boat. I heard the sound of a boat leaving the cove.'

CHAPTER THIRTY-THREE

Ella threw the switch on the hauler and waited while the spool wound in the line. She went through the motions as she worked, manoeuvring the *Santorini* between her buoys and hauling traps with the ease born of years of practice. A trap emerged from the sea streaming water and Gordon took out the lobsters it contained, measuring the carapace of each before consigning the keepers to the tank and the others back to the sea. He looped on fresh bait while Ella reattached the buoy, and then she opened the throttle and moved on to the next one while Gordon released the trap so that it slid back over the side and vanished with a soft splash. Ella worked automatically, barely aware of what she was doing.

An image was fixed in her mind of Matt as she had seen him earlier that morning outside Sally Brewster's place. Every detail about him was imprinted indelibly on her memory. The way his clothes were creased, his unshaven features, bleary eyed from drinking. She still felt as she had the moment she'd laid eyes on him, as if somebody had dealt her a physical blow. She had experienced an instant of confusion, but his expression as he'd stared back at her, indecipherable but without remorse or guilt, had tripped a switch in her mind and a cascade of tangled thoughts and emotions had jostled for place. She had felt as she did now, a mixture of fierce anger and humiliation, but more than either of those things, a deep sense of wounded hurt.

When her mother had counselled her the previous night that she believed Matt to be a good man, Ella had agreed. The strain of everything she'd endured these last months and weeks had taken a heavy toll. A deep weariness had sunk into the fibre of her being and had sapped her strength little by little. She had begun to feel she no longer had the will or the stamina to fight the likes of Howard or Jake, or to carry the burden of the responsibility she felt for her mother and for Kate. She couldn't bear any longer the weight of her own sense of guilt. Everywhere she went she felt the accusing stares of people she knew, and heard the whisper of voices in her wake like a constant rustling in the grass of some stealthy predator as it drew closer. But Matt had remained at her side, a presence she could rely on. Her mother had understood how she felt and had said they should put their trust in him, and finally she'd agreed.

Once she had made the decision to tell him everything she'd experienced an immediate sense of release and she'd had the best night's sleep that she could remember having for a long time. She'd hoped that when he learned the truth he would be able to look past the facts and see that sometimes life isn't as straightforward as he wanted it to be. Now she thanked God that she had learned before it was too late that Matt Jones was just like every other man she'd ever encountered in her life who had let her down. She wiped away the tears that stung her eyes and bit her lip until it bled, the sharp pain blotting out the hurt she felt, allowing her to nurture her anger. Her anger renewed her strength. The hell with him. She didn't need him. She didn't need any man.

'Ella?'

Gordon's voice penetrated her thoughts and she snapped to.

'Are you okay?'

'I'm fine. I was just thinking about something. What is it?'

'I need a place to stay for a little while. I was wondering if I could stay on the *Santorini* for a couple of days?'

'But why?' Ella asked, and then guessed the answer. 'Is it your dad?'

'He wants me to stop working for you.'

Ella sighed. 'I don't want to come between you and your dad.'

Gordon shook his head stubbornly. 'He can't tell me what to do.'

Ella looked away, uncertain what she should do. It was hot, sweat trickled uncomfortably down her stomach inside her protective oilskin bib and pants. Sunlight flickered on the water. It wasn't always like this. In winter the seas could be heaving, the wind cold and biting like a blade. It was hard, dangerous work, and if Gordon was man enough for the job, he was man enough to make his own decisions. His faith in her, at least, had never wavered.

She smiled and laid her hand on his arm. 'Stay as long as you need to.'

Baxter parked his cruiser at the side of the road a mile from the Littles' house, and he and Matt got out and walked across the grass to a spot where they could look down on the cove below. It was hot, and the air was close and thick. To the east the horizon was blurred by a dirty haze like the pollution from a thousand factories and the sky bled from blue to an indeterminate dark grey.

'Front coming in,' Baxter observed. 'Forecast is for a storm in the next couple of days.' He took out a piece of gum and removed the wrapper. After a while he said, 'You think Kate was telling the truth?'

'No, I don't,' Matt answered, and Baxter just nodded, his own conclusion confirmed.

'How about her husband? You believe him?'

Before he answered Matt thought over what Evan Little had told them about his wife being out the night Bryan had vanished, and the shots he'd heard. The timing tied in with Carl Johnson's testimony, but Evan Little already knew about that, so he could be lying if he wanted to get back at his wife for cheating on him. But somehow Matt didn't think so. He might not like Evan Little much, but he believed he was telling the truth and he said so to Baxter.

'About hearing a boat as well?'

'Why would he lie about that?' Matt said. He knew what Baxter was going to ask next, and he wasn't wrong.

'You think it was Ella's boat he heard?'

'If it was, there's no way to prove it.' He met Baxter's eye, and from the chief's expression he imagined that they were both experiencing similar feelings.

'This is kind of a strange situation, don't you think?' Baxter voiced what Matt was thinking. 'Ella's your client, so I don't expect you to answer this, but I'll say it anyway. You think she and Kate are somehow involved in this together?'

'You're right, I can't answer that.'

'Aside from her being your client, you like her don't you?'

Matt hesitated, then nodded, though right now, he thought, his feelings weren't quite so simple. 'Let me ask you something, Chief. You and Kate Little . . .' He left the question unfinished.

Baxter stared out across the cove. 'I always felt a little sorry for her. Because of that husband of hers I guess.'

'That's all?'

Baxter didn't answer, but then he didn't have to. Matt sighed wearily, and squatted down in the grass. He picked a piece of grass and shredded it between his fingers, the way he had as a kid.

'How do you think this looks?' Baxter said.

'Like you said, Ella's my client, Chief.'

'Okay, I'll talk, you listen. If we're thinking along the same lines, my guess is you figure that Kate ran into Bryan that night. Maybe deliberately, maybe not. Could be there was some kind of fight, and he got shot. It was probably an accident. Then somehow or other Ella comes into it. Either Kate called her, or she was fishing like she said and she heard a shot and came into the cove to see what it was. She decides to help Kate get rid of the body and she takes it out and dumps it over the channel where Carl saw her. Then later Kate goes back and cleans the house so we wouldn't know about her and Bryan, and she leaves the keys he gave her behind.'

Matt didn't say anything for a moment. He picked another stalk of grass. 'Let's say, hypothetically, that what you just said is broadly true. Why did Ella help Kate? If it was some kind of accident, why didn't she persuade Kate to report it?'

'Maybe they thought no one would believe them. They

285

panicked. Bryan was a sonofabitch, we already know that, and neither Kate nor Ella had any reason to grieve over him.'

'What about Jerrod Gant? What did he see?'

'Maybe he just saw a woman, and he assumed it was Ella. Or he decided it would be better for him if he said that it was.'

Matt stood up. 'There's one problem with all this. Ella is the one that was arrested, she's the one Gant said he saw. So why didn't she tell us the truth, or for that matter, why didn't Kate?'

Baxter frowned, unable to answer. 'You know,' he said eventually. 'Without Gant this is all nothing. Bryan probably deserved what happened to him if we knew the truth of it.'

Far below them the cove looked placid and still, the water shades of green and blue, reflecting back the trees around the shore. It was strange, Matt thought, how life seemed to come around in a circle. He'd nearly drowned in the cove once, and now all that had stemmed from that time and affected his life seemed to be drawing back to him again. He asked himself how he felt about Ella. What was her involvement in Bryan's disappearance, and how did that change her in his eyes? He'd dedicated a big chunk of his life to locking up the bad guys. Was Ella going to turn out to be one of them?

'We should get back,' Baxter said.

Matt let the stalk of grass he was holding fall to the ground, and they went back to the cruiser, each of them absorbed with their own unspoken thoughts.

When Matt arrived back at his office there was a message on his machine from Ruth Thorne. She said that her husband Charlie's roster meant he would be staying on the mainland the following night. Matt had almost forgotten about Ruth, and he'd made no arrangement to have her husband followed to see where he spent the night. He called the ferry company to check what time the island ferry got in, and while he did he thumbed through his diary to see if he could find anyone who might know an investigator in the area. The woman from the ferry company came back on the line and told him what time the ferry arrived on the mainland.

'There's a return ferry to Lucia at eight,' she added helpfully.

Lucia was the next closest island to St George on the run and was only around forty minutes away. It occurred to Matt that maybe Charlie Thorne was spending his nights there and not on the mainland, which he figured he ought to check on before he arranged an investigator. He told the woman he was with the police department on St George and asked her to look at the crew roster.

'Who am I speaking with sir?' she asked.

'Chief Baxter,' he told her.

'Okay, just hold on, Chief.'

She came back in a moment. 'Thorne you said? Charles Thorne? He isn't down to work tomorrow, Chief. You sure you got the right guy?'

'Yeah, look that's okay,' Matt said. 'Thanks for your help.' He hung up, wondering if Ruth Thorne had made a mistake.

On the way home from the dock that evening Ella took a detour and parked at the end of a street at the top of the hill above the town. She followed a path along the ridge which took her beneath the overhanging branches of leafy oaks, where the path was swallowed up in the late afternoon gloom. It led eventually to an iron railing around a promontory on the hill where the sea stretched beyond the island, deep blue and still, glittering with bright shards of copper from the lowering sun. To the west a molten path beat down across the water, and the sky at the horizon was infused with a dusky pink glow that was slowly turning orange and violet.

A railing surrounded Sanctuary's cemetery, where headstones marked the graves of men who had drowned over the years, though their bodies remained buried somewhere deep in the Atlantic. Ella found her father's headstone, next to that of her infant brother, and kneeling down she plucked the weeds from around the edge of the plot. She stood up and gave way to a flood of memories and emotions. She had idolized him, and she had been everything to him. His daughter, his little mermaid, and the son he'd never had all rolled into one. Scenes,

287

small insights from her past flickered against the screen of her mind. She immersed herself in them, lacking the will to resist and for a while she was oblivious to the passage of time.

Dusk had fallen when she was alerted by a sound behind her, and she turned quickly, her mind leaping.

Matt followed Ella after she passed him on her way from the docks. When he saw where she was going he thought about waiting for her by her car, but in the end he went after her. As he emerged from beneath the trees he saw her standing in the cemetery, silhouetted against the sea beyond, and for a while he hung back, watching her, trying to figure out what she was thinking and what he felt.

When she heard him and whirled around they faced each other silently for a moment. Her expression betrayed a torrent of emotions, all too fleeting for him to capture. He went to the gate which creaked when he pushed it open.

'I saw you leaving the dock. I was on my way to see you.' His eye fell to the headstone and he read the inscriptions.

'What do you want?' she said coldly.

He recalled that the last time he'd seen her was as he'd emerged from Sally Brewster's apartment that morning, and as he remembered how she'd turned wordlessly away he wondered what conclusion she'd come to about that. He didn't attempt to correct her. Instead he looked at her father's grave and remembered what Anne Laine had told him, and he thought he understood why Ella had hated Bryan enough to keep quiet about what she knew. If that was all she had done. He'd been thinking that maybe Baxter's theory about what had happened was wrong in one respect. Perhaps it was Ella who'd killed Bryan, not Kate. Whatever had happened, he needed Ella to tell him the truth.

'Why didn't you tell me about Kate and Bryan?' he asked her. She didn't appear surprised that he knew and he guessed she must have figured he'd find out sooner or later. 'I talked to Jordan Osborne and he told me what happened that night on the dock. What did you think when you saw Bryan beating her up? Did it remind you of your father?'

288

She seemed surprised, but it quickly turned to anger. 'Bryan Roderick was nothing like my father! My dad was worth ten of him!'

'But you must have felt something,' Matt insisted. 'Bryan was already a low-life in your eyes, and then you find him beating up on a woman. Osborne told me how you helped her.'

'There's no crime in that is there?'

'Not in that. But I talked to Kate Little today, Ella. She admitted that she was out on the point the night Bryan disappeared.' He waited to see how she would react and he thought she appeared wary.

'What else did she tell you?'

He ignored her question. 'Her husband heard shots about the same time that Carl Johnson did. He also said he heard a boat in the cove.' He wasn't sure what he expected her to say, but she seemed to be waiting for him to go on, as if she was expecting more. Maybe she thought Kate had already told him everything.

'Were you in the cove that night, Ella?'

'You're asking me if I killed Bryan and I already told you that I didn't.'

All along she'd claimed she didn't kill him, and it still held the ring of truth.

'Maybe you didn't kill him, but you saw something didn't you? Did something happen between Kate and Bryan? Did you help her, Ella? Is that what you were doing that night when Carl Johnson saw you? Were you getting rid of the body?'

She stared at him silently. 'What would you say if I told you that I *was* out there, Matt? What if Bryan had attacked Kate that night, and there was an accident? Would you condemn her for that? Would you condemn me?'

'Are you telling me that's what happened?'

'I'm not saying anything. I'm just echoing what you're thinking aren't I? I mean that's why you're here isn't it?' She met his anger with her own. 'Life isn't always the way you want it to be Matt. It isn't always cut and dried, cause and effect. Sometimes people do things that might not be right, but that doesn't make them entirely wrong either.'

289

Matt shook his head. 'Dammit Ella, this isn't some philosophical discussion we're having. A man is dead and don't tell me it was an accident or self-defence. People don't conceal accidents at the bottom of the ocean. We're talking about murder here. Maybe Bryan Roderick wasn't a terrific citizen. Maybe he was the kind of guy who reminds you of something you pick up on your shoe. But he was still a person, and no matter how much of an asshole you or Kate Little thought he was that didn't give either of you the right to kill him.'

He didn't know what he'd hoped for, but Ella stared back at him defiant and unrepentant. He felt as if he didn't know her at all.

'Christ, you must have thought I was an idiot.'

'Is that what you think Matt? Do you think I only wanted to manipulate you?'

'Is there some other way I'm supposed to look at this Ella? You should have trusted me. You should have told me the truth.'

'And should I have trusted you when you said you wanted us to build a life together as well? Is that what you told Sally Brewster too?' Ella retorted scathingly. 'And anyway, let's not forget that I haven't admitted any of this is true.'

'You're saying it isn't? Maybe you've forgotten about Jerrod Gant. Right now the police can't prove anything, but sooner or later he's going to turn up again. And what happens then?'

Ella stared at him and shook her head. The fight went out of her, and she just appeared spent. 'You're so sure aren't you? You're so sure you know all the answers.'

Something about the way she looked at him and the tone of her voice threw him. He had the sudden unsettling notion that somewhere, somehow, he had got all of this completely wrong. Whatever the truth was, it was clear that Ella would tell him nothing more. She started to turn away from him.

'Wait.' He reached out to stop her.

Ella looked at his hand on her arm, then met his eye and held it. 'Are you going to let me go?'

Her question seemed to resonate with the possibility of different meanings. He stared at her, but he couldn't fathom anything of what she was thinking. He no longer knew what to say to reach her. He didn't know if she was guilty, or if she was, of what exactly, and he hardly knew anymore what he felt about her. In the end he released her. She turned away and he watched her vanish along the path beneath the overhanging trees.

CHAPTER THIRTY-FOUR

It was almost dark by the time he got home. He needed to think, but he needed to occupy his body and his conscious mind. He changed into shorts and a T-shirt, pulled on his running shoes and began to jog along the track that led through the woods and down to the road. He started slowly, breathing deeply, stretching the muscles in his shoulders and arms as he ran.

At the blacktop he stopped and leaned against an oak to stretch, pulling out the tightened calf muscles and working the big muscles in his back. When he started running again he took the road that led along the ridge towards the turn-off to the point. It was warm and he was already sweating. He quickly found his pace and allowed his mind to be numbed by the rhythmic slap of rubber soles against the blacktop. His breathing was easy, his limbs working with smooth fluidity. A twinge in his groin caused him to stop briefly to stretch again until there was a slight pop at the top of his inner thigh, and then the pain was gone and he resumed his pace. After fifteen minutes he passed the turn-off to the point.

The air smelt of pine and bayberry with the underlying scent of salt and seaweed and it seemed to wash away the grimy coating on the inside of his skull, the legacy of everything he'd drunk the night before. Eventually he came to the track that led to the clearing outside the house where Bryan had lived. The trees pressed close on either side, a mixture of cedar and scotch pine. The air was heavy with their dark scent and their dense needles partially filtered out the remaining light, then the woods changed to oak and cottonwoods and maples and the darkening sky appeared through the leafy canopy and the air was redolent of the thick loamy woodland floor and the smell of the sea grew stronger.

When he reached the clearing, he slowed to a walk. He was breathing heavily now, and sweating hard. The house was empty and silent and told him nothing. He walked on towards the cove, and emerged from the woods on to the narrow strip of dirty sand against which the water lapped. The wooden jetty pointed out across the bay, a narrow road that led nowhere. He went to the boatshed, and pulled open the door, not knowing what he expected to find. It was as empty as it had been before, the air damp, a scurrying in a dark corner.

Something was wrong. Matt felt it in his bones. He went back to the water's edge and stood looking out, waiting for something that nagged at his mind to come forward and reveal itself, but there was nothing. Nothing at all.

When he got home and pounded up the steps the phone inside was ringing and when he picked it up Ben Harper was on the line.

'You remember I said I might have an idea? Well, I've been doing some checking. I talked to that guy Carl Johnson who saw Ella's boat out by the cove.'

'What about him?'

'Well, it's not him exactly. It's what he said he saw. I guess you'd still like to know if he was right about Ella dumping something from her boat, right? I mean if he was wrong that would put Ella in the clear wouldn't it?'

'How do we do that? It's too deep over that channel for a diver.'

'Maybe not,' Ben said. 'Can you meet me?'

'Where are you?'

'At the harbourmaster's office.'

'I'll be right there.' Matt called Baxter after he hung up, thinking he ought to hear this too, whatever it was, then he went to shower and change.

293

Baxter was already waiting when he arrived. He and Ben and Tom Spencer were standing around a table on which a chart had been spread.

'What's this all about?' Matt asked. Baxter shrugged.

Ben looked as if he was enjoying himself. 'Now that you're here, I'll explain. Carl Johnson said he saw Ella's boat around here.' He stabbed his finger on the chart, and Tom peered over.

'That's it. Right over the channel.'

'Way too deep there for a diver.'

'That much we already know,' Baxter commented.

'But Johnson said that when he hailed her, Ella switched on her lights and motored back towards the harbour. He said he watched her for a while.' Ben traced a line across the chart with his finger. 'Then according to Johnson she stopped again, and it was then he figured that she dropped something over the side.' He looked around at the others, his grin broadening as they saw the light dawning. 'See, if she took roughly this course, which Johnson claims she did, because I checked with him, that put her right about here.' His finger was stuck on a spot closer to the cove. 'There's a shelf here beyond the channel. The water's only fifty or sixty feet deep there. No problem for a diver.'

He went on to explain that if there was anything down there, the currents would hold it roughly in position at least until a storm blew. 'So if you send a diver down, and don't find any-thing, that would go a long way towards proving that Ella was telling the truth wouldn't it?' he finished up. He looked around and appeared perplexed that nobody else seemed as pleased as he was.

Matt looked at Baxter and thought they were thinking the same thing. It hadn't occurred to Ben that sending a diver down, far from proving Ella's innocence, might prove the exact reverse.

Almost reluctantly Baxter asked if Ben would be willing to hire his services to the town to make the dive in the morning, which Ben readily agreed to.

'Okay, that's it then,' Baxter said. 'We go out at first light.'

CHAPTER THIRTY-FIVE

Howard sat in his car outside the *Schooner*. He watched with interest as two men crept stealthily along one of the docks. He'd seen them when they passed by earlier, though neither of them were aware of his presence, and recognized them as local men. He lost sight of them for a few moments, then they appeared again, each carrying a large box which he guessed they'd stolen from the seiner that was tied up at the end of the dock. Howard knew the boat. It belonged to a man from the island who fished for herring which he sold to Howard's own plant. The last few days, however, the seiner had been out looking for bluefin like everybody else. He wondered what was in the boxes. Supplies probably, which they would probably sell to somebody with charter customers. There was a shortage of everything in town, from food and beer to cigarettes. There would be more on the ferry in the morning, but these men obviously weren't planning on waiting.

Howard shook his head, and slipped down in his seat as the two men came back towards his car and crept by. The election was just two days away and though Howard expected to win, the town's sudden preoccupation with those damn fish made everything uncertain. What if half the population simply didn't bother to vote? What if they forgot and somehow that skewed the result in Ella's favour? Not likely maybe, but possible. Howard wasn't about to leave anything to chance. As if to reinforce that view he caught sight of one of Ella's posters on a wall across the street. There weren't many left now but he'd told that Berryman kid to go around and tear down any he found but this one hadn't been touched and it felt almost like a sign to Howard.

Across the street, the door of the *Schooner* opened spilling light and loud voices on to the sidewalk. A bulky figure filled the doorway, then shambled over the road towards a parked truck. Howard hastily got out and reached Jake as he was fumbling for the lock on the door.

'Is that you? Thought I saw you . . .' He stopped abruptly as Jake swung around, his face contorted in surprised anger. Jake grabbed him by the shirt and spun him around and slammed him painfully against the front fender of the truck, knocking the wind out of him. He crumpled to the ground, and scrabbled for his glasses.

'Jesus Christ, what the hell are you doing?' He spoke in a strangled wheeze. Jake looked down at him, tense, his fists bunched at his sides and for a moment Howard thought Jake didn't recognize him.

'It's me Jake, Howard.' To his relief, Jake relaxed a little. 'Help me up will you.' He extended his hand, which Jake ignored.

'What the hell are you sneakin' around here for?' Jake demanded.

Howard struggled alone to his feet. 'I was just out walking and I saw you.' He saw immediately that Jake didn't believe him. He peered closer. 'What happened to you?' Jake's face was swollen and discoloured as if he'd been in a fight that he'd come out of badly. Jake didn't answer, and Howard noticed then that Jake had an odd glazed look in his eyes. It wasn't just that he was drunk, it was something else. Kind of demented. Jake winced suddenly and put both hands against his temples. 'You okay?' Howard asked.

Jake grunted and waved him away. Beads of sweat popped like magic from his skin. He mumbled something like a cross between an animal sound and a lengthy curse. After a few minutes he leaned back against his truck, taking deep breaths, the pain or whatever had afflicted him apparently subsiding.

'What is it? Headache?' Howard ventured. 'I get them too. It's stress.' He didn't know if Jake was listening. He began to think this wasn't such a good idea, but he figured since he was here already he might as well say what he came to. 'I guess you've had a tough time lately.' He paused, Jake was staring at him, some unfathomable process going on his head. 'Doesn't seem right does it? Ella catching that fish, making all that money after what she did? What did I tell you Jake? There's no justice in this world, that's a fact.'

Howard felt a dry constriction in his throat. He licked his lips. It was unnerving the way Jake didn't say anything, but all the same, waves of menace seemed to bleed out of the man. He took an involuntary step back. What was he doing he asked himself?

Across the street the door to the bar opened again and someone staggered out and began throwing up. The sound of laughter rose and fell again as the door swung closed. Howard looked back at Jake, and found him still staring with the same dead eyed look. Howard decided that he was making a mistake here. 'Well, I should go,' he said, and nervously he stepped away. Jake still didn't say anything. Howard went back to his car and got in behind the wheel. Jake remained where he'd left him, immobile, staring off at who knew what. 'Crazy bastard,' Howard muttered to himself, and started his car.

When Gordon woke he wondered what the time was, and still groggy from sleep he felt for the flashlight on the floor beside his bunk. He saw that it was only three in the morning and groaned. He turned off the light and lay in darkness for a while, half awake, lulled by the gentle motion of the boat on the water. Though he tried to will himself back to sleep it was no good, his mind was filled with thoughts that dragged him up through layers of consciousness. He wondered what had woken him, He listened to the creaking of the *Santorini*'s timbers, and the gentle bump of the hull against the old tyres strung along the edge of the dock. Somewhere close by a boat on a mooring had a wind chime which made a pleasant tinkling, though it sounded vaguely muffled. Very faintly a ship's horn carried into the harbour from the sea beyond.

297

The cabin didn't feel so small in the darkness. Gordon lay on his back, with his toes touching the bulwark, one thin blanket covering him for warmth. He knew if he reached out his left arm he could just touch the far wall, and that when he was standing there was barely enough room to turn around in the cabin, but the darkness provided the illusion of space. He didn't mind the cramped quarters anyway. The sense of freedom he experienced in his new home made up for any concessions he'd made to comfort.

Earlier, he'd sat on deck for a while, smoking and sipping a beer, nodding to people who passed by. Some of them stopped to exchange a word or two, others went on by as if he was a stranger, rather than somebody who'd lived all his life on the island. He didn't care about the people who ignored him. They had sided against Ella because they resented her, as much as anything else.

From outside somewhere, maybe on the dock, Gordon heard something. Metal on concrete, or some other hard surface. Earlier, when the bars had emptied out, it had been noisy but now it was quiet. He listened hard. It was never really silent in the harbour. There was always the bump of a hull against the dock, the constant lap and suck of water, the rattle of a loose line in a breeze. A hundred small sounds, each distinct and familiar and comforting in their way. If one of them were to cease without warning, Gordon was certain he would be aware of it immediately, though consciously they barely registered. In the same way, a sound out of place made him curious. He tried to fit an image to what he'd heard, but he couldn't. After a while, when there was nothing else, he dismissed it.

He closed his eyes, willing sleep to come. He heard it again; a metallic scrape. Then in the stillness that followed, as he lay hardly breathing, he heard a muffled thump, and then another, and he knew that somebody was on board the *Santorini*. For several moments he didn't move, unsure what to do. His first thought was that it must be Ella, but when the hatch door remained closed he dismissed the idea. He could hear somebody moving about the boat now, and it seemed to him that the movements had a furtive quality. He swung his legs from the narrow bunk, and groping on the floor he found his flashlight. For the moment he left it off, and dressing by feel he quickly pulled on a pair of jeans before groping his way back through the galley towards the steps that led to the hatch door. At the top he froze, his hand on the latch. His weight on the step caused it to bend and creak. A sound he might barely have noticed another time seemed unnaturally loud. The shuffling on deck ceased. Gordon waited, counting off the passing seconds, his hand slick on the flashlight handle.

He heard a soft thud from the direction of the dock and he lifted the hatch and stepped out onto the space between the wheel-house and the hatch door, and as he did so a flicker of light seemed to move in an arc from the wharf to the deck. The light had a peculiar, ethereal quality, as if seen through a thick haze, and it was a moment before Gordon realized that a thick fog engulfed the harbour. He could feel its clammy dampness against his face. Even as he turned on the flashlight, Gordon knew that what he'd seen was a flame. There was a muffled roar along the deck and he had an impression of a figure already vanishing into the darkness, and then all he could see was blue and yellow flames and he smelt the acrid tang of gasoline. The flames slithered towards him like a living thing, and then there was smoke and heat.

Barely pausing to think, he grabbed the extinguisher from the wheel-house. He fumbled with the nozzle, and lost precious seconds which allowed the flames to envelop him. The heat was intense, and the smoke stung his eyes, but he didn't think about any of that as he directed the spray to the area around his feet and then started working back along the deck. When the extinguisher ran out he ran back for a blanket from below. He leaned over the side to soak it in the harbour before running back again to beat at the flames. He worked furiously to smother them, and because he'd acted so quickly, and the fire hadn't had time to catch properly, he beat them down. From the wharf he would have looked like a madman, working like a devil in the yellow heat that singed the hair from his scalp and eyebrows.

His clothes smouldered and the skin on his hands and feet blistered but he didn't notice any of this.

As the last of the fire died, he was overcome with fatigue. The blanket was singed and burning along one edge. He heard voices shouting, and figures rushed from the darkness, and then hands took him and guided him to the dock and the last thing he saw was somebody peering down at him.

A voice said, 'Jesus, somebody run for the doctor.'

Then he succumbed to the darkness that closed around.

Part Four

CHAPTER THIRTY-SIX

The *Santorini*'s bright blue paintwork was scorched black on the wheel-house where it faced the deck. Earlier a crowd had gathered to stand and stare. They gradually broke into smaller groups and then drifted away, many to their own boats to head out again in pursuit of bluefin, though many were saying the fish had gone, that they had left the gulf as quickly as they had appeared. By an hour after sunrise nearly all the vessels in the harbour had left.

A police cruiser was parked by the harbourmaster's office and an unshaven Baxter, dressed in the jeans and T-shirt he'd pulled on after being dragged from his bed by a phone call at three thirty in the morning, was talking to the man who had first seen the flames. He was a baker who worked in the store across from the dock and he'd been on his way to work when he spotted the fire. He said he hadn't seen how it started.

Ella was alone on the *Santorini*, sorting through the mess of charred and blackened equipment on the deck. Matt watched her from the dock as she crouched to look at something which she held in her hands before she put it aside and stood up. Her expression was blank, numbed by what had happened. She appeared pale and vulnerable and alone and he wondered if this would prove to be the last straw for her. So far she'd remained resilient in the face of everything that had happened, but even somebody as strong as Ella must have a limit to her endurance.

He went over to her, and as he approached she looked up.

'I just talked to Anne Laine at the hospital and she said to let you know that Gordon's going to be okay. He's got some pretty nasty burns on his arms, but apparently they're not as bad as they seemed.'

She closed her eyes as if offering a silent prayer of thanks. When Gordon had been loaded on to the helicopter which had flown him to the mainland he'd been swathed in dressings, the clothes he'd worn had mostly been cut free and lay on the ground, blackened and smelling strongly of smoke and gasoline. Ella had been stricken with grief and perhaps guilt, and Matt didn't doubt that she blamed herself at least to some extent.

'He sent you a message. He said don't worry about him.'

Visible relief washed over her and she took a deep breath and it seemed with an enormous effort of self-control she kept herself together.

'Ella,' Matt said. Though the timing was lousy he wanted to tell her about the dive Ben Harper would make that day. Maybe she would see that it was time now to tell the truth before anyone else got hurt. But she gave no sign of having heard him.

Before he could try again, Baxter came over.

'Any leads on how this started?' Matt asked.

'We found an empty gas can along the dock,' Baxter replied. 'We'll see if we can get any prints off it, but even if we can we can't prove it was used to start the fire.'

All at once Ella snapped from her stunned state. 'It was Jake who did this dammit! Are you just going to let him get away with it? Gordon could've been killed!'

'I talked to Gordon before the chopper took him to hospital,' Baxter said. 'He didn't get a good look at who did this. And I already talked to Jake. He claims he was at home when this happened and his wife backs him up.'

Ella was incredulous. 'And you believe him?'

'I can't prove any different, Ella.'

She looked at Matt and then angrily turned away.

Baxter looked at his watch and spoke in a low voice. 'Harper's ready. We have to beat the tide if we're going to do this. There's nothing much else we can do here now.'

'I'll be right with you,' Matt said. He lingered, trying to think of something he could say that would comfort Ella, but the words that half formed turned to dust in his mouth. In the end he said that he was sorry, but she gave no sign of having heard him. As he walked along the dock towards Ben's launch he could feel her watching him, though he couldn't begin to guess what thoughts plagued her mind.

Ben Harper's boat was a thirty-eight-foot planing launch with a flying bridge up top where Ben could steer from. In the back of the boat a wet suit hung from a rail at the cabin entrance, and scuba tanks, masks and flippers lay on the stern deck.

'We're all set,' Ben said. He started the engines and called out for them to untie her. Baxter took the stern line and climbed aboard with a kind of heavy resignation like a man unable to avoid his fate, compelled by forces beyond his control. It occurred to Matt that if he could have found a half good enough reason to do so, Baxter would have called this whole thing off. He had the air of a man on his way to the reading of a will, the contents of which he feared he wouldn't like. Matt unlooped the bow rope and threw it over. For a second he stood at the edge of the wharf, looking down at the water.

'Everything all right?' Baxter asked.

'Yeah, everything's fine.'

He grabbed the rail and vaulted across. He staggered a little with the slight motion of the boat but hung on to the rail with both hands, aware of the other two men watching him.

'I got a buddy who gets sick every time I take him out,' Baxter said, not unkindly.

'I'm okay.'

Ben called down to them from above. 'Come on up if you like, the breeze might make you feel better once we get going.'

'I'll just stay here for a minute.' Matt let them think he was just seasick. He could feel the blood literally drain from his face as the motors roared into life and the boat turned away from the wharf. This was the first time since the day he'd almost drowned as a child that he'd been on anything smaller than a ferry, and he'd only done that a couple of times in his life. The gut-churning irrational fear that he experienced paralysed him. He'd read about people who had phobias about flying, who couldn't set foot on an aircraft without turning into a quivering mass of neurosis and he imagined they must feel something like he did now. The water beyond the rail slipped by, and to Matt it appeared endlessly deep and threatening. It was placid and calm in the harbour, but once out beyond the heads he knew they would be in the ocean swell. He looked at the blue sky, clear to the horizon where the hazy smudge of the front coming in still lingered. The weather couldn't be better, but he knew how quickly it could change, how fast the sea could become a churning threatening mass ready and willing to seize the unwary and drag them down.

'Jesus,' he muttered to himself. Cold sweat beaded on his brow. He staggered to the ladder and gripped it hard with both hands.

'You okay?' Ben's voice from above was edged with real concern.

'I'm fine.' Matt raised his eyes as they passed the *Santorini* but there was no sign of Ella.

When they were clear of the moorings Ben lined up his course for the mid-channel marker in the harbour, and opened up the throttle. The screws bit deep, and the bow came up as green water rushed past.

Ella watched Ben Harper's launch as it left the harbour, her mouth pressed in a tight line.

She spent the next few hours cleaning up the damage caused by the fire. She went right over the *Santorini* from bow to stern, and though the fire had burnt the paint off the deck, and parts of the wheel-house, the boat remained seaworthy. She worked to keep busy, to occupy her mind, but often she found herself paused in her task, looking out towards the heads, wondering where Ben's boat was. She recalled Matt and Baxter's quiet conversation, something about the tide, and she thought about the scuba gear she had glimpsed in the back of the boat.

A pile of charred wood and other rubbish accumulated on

the dock. The sky was clear, and the sun hot. A series of faces paraded ceaselessly through her mind. Matt, Gordon, her mother and Kate Little. She tried not to think, but again her gaze was drawn towards the ocean beyond the harbour, and the tension in her grew until at last she knew she couldn't just sit here and wait, not knowing what was happening.

The sound of footsteps approaching registered, but she didn't look up until they stopped. A figure stood on the dock and Ella shielded her eyes from the glare of the sun.

'I heard about the fire. I thought you might need some help,' Kate Little said.

CHAPTER THIRTY-SEVEN

During the night the orcas had swum south, passing among the islands towards the coast. There were fewer boats on the gulf at night, and those that remained were the bigger vessels working out of the ports on the mainland coastline from Massachusetts through New Hampshire and Maine. They fished the banks and shelves further out near the slope waters where the gulf met the Atlantic ocean.

A little after midnight, the bull changed course. The pod were spread out in a loose grouping. As their bodies broke the surface tension of the water and their dorsal fins rose into the warm humid night air, small phosphorescent bubbles formed in their wake. A silver moon hung close and heavy in a pregnant night sky. Most of the pod were dozing as they swam. They were in a deeply relaxed state, though their senses remained attuned to their environment so that they were never in danger of running aground by passing too close to the shallow sloping seabed near an island beach, or running into floating debris.

They had eaten their last meal around dusk the evening before. The bull had led them to a shelf, where the water temperature cooled a degree or two as the conflicting currents of the gulf stream and cooler water running offshore from deep trenches collided. The bull had hunted this area many times in the past, when fish that spent the day hiding deep in the trenches during the sunlight hours rose to feed as evening fell. The bull's knowledge of the gulf hadn't let him down, and the pod had fed well.

But now as the orcas moved in a sweeping arc towards the coast before turning back on themselves once more, the bull decided it was time for the pod to move north. During the day there were so many boats out on the gulf that the noise and confusion they caused was creating havoc with the orcas' ability to hunt. Many of the big bluefin that had briefly appeared, had vanished again as quickly as they had arrived. Those that hadn't been caught had headed out again into deeper water, and were moving northward themselves. It was time for the orcas to do the same. To swim out into the Altlantic and go north towards Novia Scotia where they would hunt seals and minke whales.

The bull set a course and for a short time he dozed along with the others. The world through which he moved so effortlessly was an orchestrated, ever fluid and changing environment. A part of his brain was so in synch with fluctuations of temperature, with slight alterations of current, that he was almost a part of the ocean itself.

One of the older females joined him and swam alongside, rubbing close to him as he woke from his dreaming slumber. Soon the whole pod were waking, and they formed into a close group to communicate with one another and reinforce their bonds with close physical contact. For an hour they changed places, swam together, and performed graceful aquatic manoeuvres.

Eventually, the bull tired, and he drifted off a little, while the younger animals continued their contact. He was joined by the female again, and another male who was the next oldest in the pod. These two sensed the bull's weariness, and lately they often swam close to him. Over the years they had absorbed the knowledge of his accumulated experience, and they knew almost as well as he where to hunt, and what prey could be found in a particular place at a given time of year. At some point in the future, the bull would succumb to sickness, or perhaps his heart would simply give out with age, and these two would take over the roles of leading the pod and ensuring their continued survival.

Much had changed, and much was changing still. More and

more the activities of man had the greatest effect on the orcas' environment. Their lives were a constant learning process, understanding where both the dangers and the opportunities lay, and always they were aware of man's unpredictable nature. Some vessels were benign, and their occupants watched with apparent fascination if the orcas passed close by, but others the orcas were far more wary of.

Towards dawn the pod reached a point where they were several miles off the east coast of St George. Already the bull could hear the sound of many boats heading out from the harbour. The bull decided to cruise the waters closer to the island which the boats would largely bypass. He planned to hunt for schools of fish moving east to escape the many fishing vessels, and then at the end of the day he would lead the pod north and during the night they would pass out into the slope waters and head for open sea.

On board the *Seawind* there was an uneasy quiet. The men on the deck said little as they worked but now and then they would cast furtive looks towards the wheel-house where Jake stood with his back to them, scanning the surrounding sea. Occasionally he would come outside and stand against the rail, but he barely glanced at what was happening on deck. He seemed completely preoccupied with his own thoughts, and whatever they were, the expression he wore engendered a vague disquiet among the crew.

Calder Penman worked alongside the other men. He occupied a difficult position now that he was first mate. He was treated with suspicion. The men were wary of his loyalties and were careful about what they said in his presence. He'd been their friend, and equal, but now that Bryan was gone, he directed their work. At times during these last two weeks Penman wished he could have stayed in his old job. He felt that he'd lost the close relationship he'd had with the other men, but had nothing to replace it with. Jake had never been the easiest guy to get along with, and Penman had never exactly felt comfortable around him. He felt he couldn't ever relax, that he had to be wary of what he said in case Jake took offence.

The men took a break after setting a line, and lit cigarettes to smoke with their coffee. Penman joined them, aware of muttered conversations dying away. The men sipped from their mugs and avoided looking at each other, squinting instead as they stared across the sea. There were a lot of boats out, and many of them were trawling, hoping for a sighting of the bluefin.

'Give it a few more days and half of them will be gone,' Penman commented.

'Yeah, back to their goddamn fancy clubs,' one of the men said sullenly. He had a yellowing bruise underneath one eye which he rubbed absently while he watched a forty-foot launch half a mile away.

'Hey, didn't that guy you had a run in with come off that boat?' one of the others said, winking and nudging the man next to him.

'What if he did?'

'From the way that eye looks I guess he wasn't such a lard butt after all. That's what you called him wasn't it?'

Penman cut in before taunts turned into something else. 'Quit it you two.'

The man with the bruise looked away and spat over the side. He glanced up at Jake. 'What's he looking for up there?'

The others all looked at Penman. It was kind of a subtle test, to see which way he would come down.

'What the hell do you think he's looking for? The same as everyone else that's what.'

'We ain't gonna find any more blues out here. Those suckers are gone.'

'Is that right? What makes you such a fuckin' expert all of a sudden.'

The man shrugged. 'It's just what I think.'

'Maybe he ain't lookin' for blues anyway,' another man said.

Penman threw his coffee over the side. 'Are you gonna talk all day or are we here to catch some fish?'

The men finished up, and tossed cigarettes overboard, before starting back to work. They cast Penman sullen glances as he left them and went up to the wheel-house. He guessed he couldn't be their buddy, as well as do his job properly, and at the bottom of the matter, he'd taken the job when it was offered and that was an end to it.

'We're about ready to steam back to the first beacon,' Penman told Jake as he went through the door.

'Well, get on with it.' Jake didn't look at him. He stared through his glasses, sweeping slowly back and forth. In the distance St George rose against a clear sky, looking a pale shade of blue, rather than the lush green it became as you drew nearer.

Jake hadn't shown a shred of emotion when they'd passed the *Santorini* that morning. The men had stood at the rail, looking at her blackened shape. Maybe if Gordon hadn't been on board nobody would have cared too much anyway. But the boy could have been killed, and that had unsettled everybody. Penman was troubled. What was going to happen next? How long before somebody got seriously hurt and then it wouldn't just be Jake who was held to blame.

Penman brought the *Seawind* about and set a course for their beacon and punched in the autopilot. He stayed in the wheelhouse for the next few hours, and during that time, Jake continued to scan the ocean without speaking. Eventually Penman went back down on the deck. The men were huddled in a group by the gantry and when they saw him coming they broke apart. One of them came forward, or the others melted back enough that it appeared he had.

'Calder, we've been talking. We think you ought to talk to Jake.' The man faltered and looked at the others before he went on. 'We're not happy about this thing between him and Ella.'

'Is that right?'

'He's been acting a little weird, you gotta admit. I guess we know how he feels, but none of us want to get dragged into something that's getting out of hand that's all.'

Penman nodded. 'I guess that sounds reasonable.'

The man smiled with relief. 'You see,' he said to the others. 'I told you Calder would understand. He's okay, I told you that.'

Penman stared at him and the man's smile faded.

'So you'll talk to him?'

312

'If you want to talk to him, you go ahead and help yourself. I bet Jake would love to hear what you have to say.'

The man scowled. 'You're the goddamned mate, Calder, not me.'

'That's right, I am. So get the hell back to work, all of you.'

The men turned away, and Penman went back to the steps and lit a cigarette. He watched them muttering amongst themselves.

'Shit,' he said, and tossed his cigarette over the side.

They were approaching the end of their line and the buoy housing the radio beacon. It was late morning, and hot. The sky was smeared with hazy cloud and the sun seemed to shimmer as it beat down. There wasn't a breath of wind, not even a ripple on the surface of the sea, and the air seemed to press in close from all sides. The barometer was rising, and it seemed it wouldn't be long before the front out over the Atlantic moved in and a storm broke. Penman looked at his palms, and even his fingers were sweating, He wiped them on his pants and put his hands back on the wheel.

He altered course a little, preparing to come alongside the buoy which one of the men was standing ready to retrieve.

'Penman.' Jake had his glasses focused on something, and he stood rigid like he'd just taken a shock from a cattle prod. 'Bring her about.'

'What about the line?'

Jake turned on him. 'Didn't you hear what I said? I told you to bring her about. Leave the goddamned line. It isn't going anywhere.'

Penman searched the ocean to the west. They were several miles out from St George, directly parallel to the island which had now changed colour from blue to shades of dark green. A cluster of boats lay south of their position, but none of them was showing any signs of moving. 'What do you see?' Penman asked.

Jake thrust the glasses in his hand and pushed him aside. 'Move over dammit. I'll do it myself.' He started turning the wheel, and the *Seawind* came about ninety degrees. At the same

313

time he pushed forward on the throttle and the big diesel engines gained in tempo.

Down below the crew looked up in surprise. Penman ignored them and raising the glasses he searched for whatever it was that Jake had seen. He swept north and then south as the *Seawind* picked up speed, headed on a straight westerly course. The sea was ten different shades of colour. Here a patch of dazzling aqua, there a green like polished jade and in places swathes of Indian ink. St George lay dead ahead of them but Penman couldn't see anything else. He lowered the angle he was looking at, filling his vision with just the ocean, which temporarily made him lose his bearings, then he found range and distance and he started another slow sweep.

He caught a glimpse of something, and swung back.

He adjusted the focus and found it again. A dorsal fin rising black and clear against the sky, then partially obscured by the background of the swell. And then another. Slightly curled over to one side, bigger than the other and even from this distance it was possible to distinguish the double curved notch.

'Shit,' Penman muttered. He lowered the glasses and turned around to say something but the expression Jake wore took the words from his mouth and a disquieting premonition settled over him.

CHAPTER THIRTY-EIGHT

As they neared the heads Ella steered a course north to take them around the point towards the cove. She was looking for Ben Harper's launch, and when she could see out into the channel and there was no sign of it she was both puzzled and relieved, though the tight knot in the pit of her stomach refused to go away.

So far she and Kate hadn't spoken much. She wasn't even sure what had prompted Kate to appear on the dock when she had, though she guessed they couldn't avoid each other for ever. They had things to talk about, though so far neither of them had shown an inclination to be the one to begin. As Ella steered, Kate stood by the rail outside the wheel-house. They were worlds apart. Kate lived in a big house on the point for a few months each year, and typified summer people in many ways. She drove a Mercedes and wore expensive clothes and probably never had to give money a second thought. Ella wondered how old she was, and thought maybe there wasn't that much between them. Kate had fine high cheekbones, her hair was as black and sleek as the surface of a pool of pure oil. She looked a little as if she might have European blood in her genes. It was her hair, the lustrous colour of it, that made Ella realize that Kate reminded her in some vague way of somebody. It was her mother, as she looked in photographs when she was younger. The same hair and cheekbones. Maybe she and Kate weren't so far apart after all, which she realized she had always known.

Once they were out of the harbour the swell increased, and the *Santorini* rose and fell in the troughs, heading into the wind and the prevailing current. Spray flew back over the bow, and Kate steadied herself, gripping the rail with two hands. She looked at the water, deep and dark just a few feet away and glanced back at the wake behind the boat.

'Don't worry,' Ella shouted over the noise of the engine. 'The *Santorini* was built this way, low in the water. Makes it easier to haul traps over the rail.'

Kate smiled. 'I guess I haven't had a lot of experience with boats.' She widened her stance and began to move with their motion.

'You're getting the hang of it.'

Kate regarded Ella frankly. 'You know, I admire you.'

'Me? Why?'

Kate gestured around. 'You have all this. This is your world.' She struggled to express exactly what she felt. 'You're in control of your life. What you have is from your own hard work.'

'Try saying that in the middle of winter when it's ten below and you feel like you'll never be warm again.'

'I suppose there's that,' Kate agreed. She looked at the sky and the hot sun. 'It's hard to imagine it right now though.'

'I guess you have to live here year round.'

Kate shot her a look, and Ella realized her remark had sounded like a familiar summer people put down. 'I didn't mean that the way it came out.'

'Forget it. I had to develop a thick skin a long time ago. But I don't need to tell you what it's like to have people talk about you behind your back in the street.'

Their eyes met, and Ella wondered which of them would broach the subject that was uppermost in both their minds.

'That night.' Kate hesitated, searching for the right way to say what she wanted to. 'When I saw you on the point. I just want you to know that I didn't tell anybody. The police I mean.'

'I figured you hadn't.'

'Chief Baxter and Matt Jones came to my house yesterday. They know that I was seeing Bryan, and my husband told them that I was out that night, and that he heard shots. There's something else. He told them he heard a boat.'

'I know,' Ella said. 'Matt thinks that I helped you get rid of Bryan's body.'

Kate frowned. 'You helped me?'

Ella tried to interpret Kate's expression. Some note, some emphasis struck a wrong chord and jarred. Just then the *Santorini* rounded the point and the entrance to the cove came into view and what she saw thrust their conversation from her mind. Kate followed her troubled gaze.

'What is it?'

Ella didn't answer. Ben Harper's launch was anchored several hundred yards off the shore. Ella stared at it confusion, and her thoughts were cast back to the night when she'd left the cove in darkness and stopped over the channel. She recalled how she'd been drifting when the *Osprey* had come into view, and Carl Johnson had hailed her. She pictured what had happened. How she'd started the engine and set a course towards the harbour, then waited until the *Osprey* was well under way before stopping again. She tracked the course she must have taken, and suddenly understanding dawned, tightening the knot in her stomach as she saw that she must have ended up in the general area where Ben Harper's launch was now, where she knew the water was relatively shallow.

And then, while she was still trying to deal with this knowledge, Ella saw the *Seawind* approaching from the east.

CHAPTER THIRTY-NINE

The orcas were several miles from St George, when the bull picked up the sound of fish swimming rapidly westward. He stopped in the water and raised his head. A ragged flock of seabirds was circling a hundred feet or so above the sea, diving and wheeling as they fed on a school of small fish near the surface. The school had been herded there as they were pursued by larger predators. From the returning echoes of the brief series of clicks the bull issued he knew the predators were around thirty pounds or so, tuna or some other species that would provide a good meal for the orcas. They were, however, already a long way off, and moving away, and the bull had to weigh the energy cost of pursuit against the likelihood of a successful hunt. The alternative was to continue north-east to a place where he knew they might encounter feeding mackerel at the edge of the shelf.

The bull issued another brief burst of clicks, this time more interested in the pattern of the seabed terrain. The returning echoes formed a map in his complex brain, and far ahead the island registered as a broad mountainous ridge that rose from the seabed, about a third of it being above sea level. The bull recognized the patterns of inlets and bays, and the deep harbour where many boats were based, and the deep water cove on the far side of the point that separated the two. The school was heading towards the cove, which, protected by its curving arm of rocky reef, made it a natural trap and one which both orcas and other, smaller predators, took full advantage of when the situation arose.

The orcas changed course and headed in silence towards the island, already forming the pattern of attack they had used so successfully before, with the smaller animals in the centre of a line whose flanks were made up of the biggest mature adults. For the moment the larger animals maintained a steady pace, they would not increase their speed to draw in the flanks of their trap until they were almost upon the cove. As he swam, the bull monitored the positions of the numerous vessels in their vicinity. Close to the island the very faint but unmistakable steady slap of water against the hull of a launch indicated that it was stationary, while a smaller vessel was heading out from the heads and turning north-east. Behind the pod were many other boats, each distinctive by the sound it made. The bull registered the direction in which each was travelling and when the *Seawind* altered course and her engine pitch suddenly changed, the bull was instantly aware. He recognized her particular sound signature, and aware that this vessel was a threat he signalled to the pod to increase their speed. Before long the bull began to feel the strain of their pace.

Jake's failure to destroy the *Santorini* had produced a bitter anger that was fed by his every thought. He recalled the sudden leap of flame in the darkness, and the deep satisfaction it had briefly given him before he'd realized that somebody was on the boat. He'd watched from a distance as Gordon had put out the flames, and later as he'd steered the *Seawind* from the harbour and he'd seen Ella on deck he had been tempted to pick up his gun and shoot her dead.

His head was hurting, he felt like an iron band had tightened around his skull, and sooty fragments cascaded behind his eyes. He was aware of discontented rumblings from the crew but he ignored them. Let Penman keep them in line since that was what he was paid to do, though sometimes Penman seemed unsure where his loyalties lay. Maybe, Jake thought, when this was over he might go down there and break a couple of heads. When they got back to harbour he'd fire the goddamned lot of them.

The *Seawind* was running at full speed now. The roar of her engines was so loud Jake had to shout to make himself heard. He yelled for Penman to give him the glasses. With one hand on the wheel he focused on the orcas again. The *Seawind* was gaining.

'This time you won't get away,' he muttered.

He rubbed at his eyes. The seascape had taken on a dull grainy texture like an old film, and the pain in his head had spread down his neck. When he moved every nerve ending in his brain seemed to scream in protest.

'Jake? Are you okay?'

He dropped the glasses, ignoring Penman. He could see the orcas without them now. As he looked for the bull he thought about Ella. He should have done something about her a long time ago. He spotted the bull, out on the flank of the pod and he adjusted his course. This was something he could take care of once and for all. Black spots danced in front of his eyes and greasy sweat popped on his brow.

'Get down there and rig a harpoon,' Jake told Penman. He fixed his mate with a withering look. 'I want that bastard. You understand me?'

Penman nodded. The island was getting closer by the minute, A flock of herring gulls wheeled and dived a little way ahead and Jake guessed the orcas were chasing a school of fish headed for Stillwater Cove. The orcas would follow and be trapped, unable to escape without passing the *Seawind*, and Jake thought maybe they would kill more than just the bull. He'd get the whole damn lot of them.

So intent was he on his vision of slaughter that he didn't even see the *Santorini* at first. He saw the anchored launch and registered the fact that another boat was approaching, but only when they were less than half a mile from the cove did he realize it was Ella.

Pain shot in long hot lances that seemed to sear a path from his head to his toes. He lurched and staggered, cradling his skull in both hands. For an instant everything went black, then the pressure eased and he could see again though it was like peering through a fog. He steadied himself as the pain ebbed.

This was more than chance, he thought, it was a portent, it was his time to put right everything that was so fucked up. He was going to make Ella pay for what she'd done, he was going to send her down to the bottom of the fucking ocean just the way she had done to Bryan, he was going to watch her face when he did it, and he was going to stick a harpoon in that bull and chop it up for bait. That sonofabitch had stolen its last fish.

Just then the orcas broke off and changed direction, turning north away from the island.

'What the hell . . . ?' Jake said aloud, but as he watched he saw the bull was holding its course, heading directly for the cove, while the rest of the pod made their escape. They were smart, he'd give them that. But it was the bull he wanted. The others could wait for another day.

At the bow Penman was standing braced and ready. Jake leaned to shout out the door. 'Make sure you don't miss him this time, you understand me?'

Penman stared, then nodded and turned back as they bore down on the lone bull.

As Kate and Ella watched the *Seawind* approach their earlier conversation was for the moment forgotten.

'What's he doing?' Kate said.

'He's after the orca.'

Ella recognized the shape of the fin, and knew this was the same animal that she had saved from Jake a few days ago. She remembered drifting in the mist as the animal had glided quietly past, the way it had seemed to look at them when it came to the surface. The sense she'd had of its intelligence.

She clenched tightly on the wheel. 'He's going to kill it.'

Kate looked horrified. 'Can't we do anything?'

Ella briefly considered cutting across Jake's bow, but she knew it would be suicidal. This time Jake wouldn't hesitate to run her down. The *Santorini* was close to the mouth of the cove. Even on a clear day such as this the water heaved and pounded against the rocks with a muted roar. Ella kept an eye on the reef, using enough power to hold their position. The orca had slowed its pace and the *Seawind* was gaining rapidly.

'Why are they doing this?' Kate said.

Ella didn't know how to answer. She could only watch helplessly as Calder Penman shifted his position and drew back his arm. The orca was an easy target. Penman threw, and the harpoon with its two foot long barbed tip flashed towards the bull with unerring accuracy. It carried behind it an uncoiling line like a dark underscoring of its course. The bull rose to breathe, his fin and a portion of his great broad back clear of the water, his saddle markings of white vividly clear. Ella held her breath but in her heart she knew that Penman had done his job well, and when the harpoon hit home, piercing the orca just behind his dorsal fin, she winced at the impact. She imagined the spear penetrating deep, slicing through blubber and flesh and perhaps beyond to the internal organs where it would anchor deep and fast. The animal went under, and a great stain of blood quickly spread on the surface of the water.

'You bastard,' she whispered, barely aware of the tears that ran down her face.

As the line grew taut the *Seawind* abruptly began to slow and come about so that she was parallel to the entrance to the cove. The gap between boat and orca widened as the wounded animal swam past the reef.

'What are they doing now?' Kate asked.

'They don't want him to get into the cove. They'll take up the line and bring him in closer so that they can kill him.' Ella's voice sounded flat and desolate.

As if in confirmation Jake came out of the wheel-house, a rifle cradled in his arms. He stared over at the *Santorini* and though he was too far away for Ella to make out his features she could feel his enmity pouring out across the distance like poison.

As the *Seawind* all but came to a dead stop Ella saw her chance. She spun the wheel to line up a course across the mouth of the cove and pushed forward on the throttle. Kate staggered and reached out to keep her balance.

'Can you steer us?' Ella said.

Kate looked at her wide-eyed. 'I don't know. I never tried before.'

'All you have to do is keep the bow pointed towards that big rock there.' Ella indicated a point across the other side of the cove's entrance.

Kate took the wheel in both hands.

'Steady her. A little left. That's it.'

Kate nodded, her expression pinched with concentrated effort. 'What are you going to do?'

Ella paused, realizing suddenly that she didn't have any right to put Kate in danger. She reached for the throttle and the *Santorini* slowed. 'I thought maybe I could cut the line.' She shook her head. It was dangerous and stupid.

Kate looked ahead, and understood what Ella had planned. There was perhaps sixty yards between the orca and the *Seawind*. The animal had come to the surface again and was swimming feebly against the drag of the line which stretched from the boat. It was still making progress, but very little. It seemed as if Jake meant to exhaust it before he attempted to bring it along-side. He was watching it struggle, his gun cradled in his arms. He could have shot it anytime, ended its misery, but he seemed content to be a spectator to its suffering.

'Can we do it?' Kate said with sudden resolve.

Ella gauged the distance. 'I don't know. Maybe.' She thought they might make it. The *Seawind* would have to come about from a standing start to close the gap and stop her, but the orca was probably dying anyway. And Jake was dangerous. There was no telling what he might do.

'What are we waiting for?' Kate demanded. 'We can't just stand by and let this happen.' Abruptly she shoved the throttle forward again and the *Santorini* began picking up speed. The motor throbbed and rattled and the deck shook beneath their feet with the vibration. Ella thought she ought to stop this before it went too far, that it was crazy to make futile gestures.

'Shouldn't you do something?' Kate yelled.

Suddenly Ella made up her mind. What the hell, at least this was something she could try to do that felt right. She started to move forward along the deck, but then she hesitated. Their earlier unfinished conversation came back to her. The sense she'd had of something being not quite right, a discordant jarring as if they'd been talking at cross purposes.

'What is it?' Kate shouted.

Ella shook her head. 'Nothing.' There was no time.

As she ran forward the *Santorini* closed the distance to the harpoon line separating the *Seawind* from the orca until it was only fifty yards away. Ella guessed the mid-point of the line was around eight feet above the *Santorini*'s deck.

She grabbed a gaff and a long-bladed knife and then she heard, or maybe thought she heard, a shout, and she looked towards the *Seawind* as Jake raised his rifle. She couldn't hear anything except the sea crashing against the hull and a banging that had developed amid the thump of the engine, but his intention was clear and she flung herself down and yelled a warning to Kate. As she hit the deck a bullet gouged splinters of wood close to her feet. She twisted around and saw Kate duck below the window, the top of her head just visible, her hands still on the wheel to hold their course. A second shot hit the deck three feet away, then a third hit the wheel-house and went clean through the window inches above Kate's head.

Ella crawled to the rail and cautiously peered ahead. The line stretched over her just a few yards ahead and she knew she would have to stand up to cut it. Another shot hit a lobster trap and sent it spinning over the side, the bullet ricocheting off the rail. She calculated the distance remaining and ducked down again while she counted slowly to fifteen. Jake had stopped firing and she guessed he'd figured out what she planned to do. He was going to wait for her to get up, and then pick her off in the second or two that she would be a clear target. Her heart thumped like a hammer. Her throat had the texture of sandpaper, and her hands shook. She was scared to death. Salt spray came over the bow and stung her eyes. She started to rise and then dropped to her belly and crawled rapidly forward. A shot went wild somewhere overhead, and several more smashed into the deck, then she was on her feet, swinging the gaff over her head towards the line.

She caught it and felt a momentary resistance then time seemed to stretch with infinite slowness as she sawed with her knife. She expected a bullet to smash into her body at any moment. Then suddenly the line parted and with the release of tension Ella lost her balance. She fell backwards as the sound of a shot rang in her ears.

Then, abruptly, there was nothing.

CHAPTER FORTY

From the flying bridge of Ben's launch Matt watched helplessly as Ella rose to sever the harpoon line. The debilitating inertia that had overcome him as soon as they'd hit the ocean swell was temporarily forgotten. He seized the radio mike, though he was certain that Jake couldn't even hear him.

'Jake,' he yelled. 'Pick up the radio.'

A shot rang out, and Ella fell even as the line parted. Matt watched the space where she'd fallen, praying silently that she would appear. On the *Seawind* Jake climbed the ladder to the wheel-house. Matt threw the radio down in frustration and pushed the starter button again. The motor turned over, but the engine failed to catch, as it had ever since he'd first realized what Ella intended to do.

'Dammit!' He smashed his fist against the console. He leaned back over the rail and shouted down to Baxter. 'You see anything?'

'Yeah. I think I got it,' came the muffled reply. 'Wait a second.'

Matt peered into the water. The surface was still, barely rippled, and sunlight penetrated into the depths, though there was no sign of Ben. He was on his third dive, completely oblivious to what was taking place on the surface. Matt checked his watch again, noting that Ben had about another ten minutes of air remaining.

'Come on,' he muttered under his breath, willing Ben to appear. He went to the other side of the boat, but there was no sign of him there either. On the *Santorini* Kate shut down the engine and the boat drifted idly. She ran out and crouched down where Ella had fallen. Matt still didn't know what to make of her being there. Back on the *Seawind* Jake had vanished inside the wheel-house, and a frightening thought occurred to Matt and he snatched up the radio mike again.

'Kate, come in. Kate on the *Santorini,* come in.' He clicked off, willing her to hear him but she didn't respond.

The sound of the *Seawind*'s engines increased in pitch, and as she started to come around Kate glanced quickly over her shoulder but then returned to whatever she was doing.

'Kate,' Matt tried again, switching channels. 'This is Matt Jones. Pick up if you can hear me.'

He wiped sweat from his brow as it trickled from his hairline. The sun was merciless, a solid wall of heat beating down that bounced back off the surface of the sea. An image of Ella insinuated itself into his mind and he saw her lying twisted on the deck, her shirt wet with blood.

The *Seawind* had come around and her bow was now lined up with the *Santorini.* The sea foamed white at the stern where her screws churned the water at full throttle.

Down below Baxter called out. 'Try it now.'

Matt hit the starter with a silent prayer, and the motor turned over, sounding sluggish as the batteries drained. 'Come on.' He tried raising Kate, certain now of Jake's intention. He looked again to see if Ben had surfaced, but there was still no sign of him. Just beyond the mouth of the cove Matt glimpsed the placid green waters break as the orca's dorsal fin rose into view, then dipped again. The harpoon still protruded from the animal's back, and an oily slick of blood marked its passage.

He tried the radio again, switching channels constantly. 'Kate. Can you hear me? Kate this is Matt Jones. Move the boat. You hear me, you have to move. The *Seawind* is heading right for you.'

He hit the starter again, and suddenly the engine caught and fired, and the throaty growl of the engine filled the air as a cloud of blue smoke rose from the stern.

Baxter appeared down below. 'He's going to ram her,' he called out.

327

The *Seawind* had picked up speed and was bearing down on the still stationary *Santorini*. Matt pushed hard on the throttle and the stern of the launch settled deep in the water as the screws bit and thrust her forward, the growl of the engine became a roar as the bow rose and planed over the surface and wind and spray were flung back in a fine mist, but Matt knew they wouldn't make it.

Dead ahead Kate at last became aware of the danger and she rose and ran for the wheel-house. The *Santorini* began to move.

'Come on,' Matt urged. His knuckles were white where he gripped the wheel. The *Santorini* gathered speed with agonizing slowness. Kate was clearly visible in the wheel-house as she spun the wheel in a desperate attempt to narrow the angle of impact when it became inevitable that the *Seawind* intended to ram her.

Aboard the *Seawind*, Penman raced for the wheel-house, and it seemed that maybe he was going to try and stop Jake, but he was too late. The two boats collided, the *Santorini* bearing the impact towards the stern as the *Seawind* struck her and began to push her round and plough her under as if she was no more than a toy. Kate ran out on to the deck and was pitched head-long, her arms thrown out to break her fall. The little boat was lifted half out of the water and it seemed as if she would turn turtle and go all the way over. Matt caught a glimpse of Ella's limp form tossed across the deck, then the force and momentum of the collision pushed the *Santorini* around and she crashed against the side of the *Seawind* as it passed by. There was a horrendous screeching and tearing of wood and metal, then the *Seawind* was clear. Matt reached the *Santorini* as she began to go down, and he spun the wheel to bring the launch alongside and pulled back on the throttle. As the roar of the motor abruptly died and the bow settled on to the water he was already leaping for the ladder.

The *Santorini* was little more than splintered wreckage. The initial impact had almost severed her in two, and already the deck was flooded. Kate was up to her knees in water, surrounded by floating debris and splintered shards of planking. She waded, half dazed, throwing things aside as she searched for Ella.

Baxter reached out to her from the stern deck. 'Take my hand,' he yelled.

She had a cut on her forehead and her face was streaked with blood, and when she turned at the sound of his voice her expression registered shock and confusion. He reached over and hauled her aboard and as he did Matt climbed up on to the side of the launch. For just a split second all the old terror welled up in him, and the water appeared suddenly cold and forbidding and his muscles constricted convulsively, then the last of the *Santorini* went under, water flooding across a third of her deck in an instant, welling up over the wheel-house, and as she sank he glimpsed Ella's inert form wedged in a gash in the wrecked side.

Then he hit the water, and it closed over him like a grave.

The sudden change of temperature, and the deadening of sound was like a cold but oddly comforting embrace. It was the realization of a long held fear, and as such it possessed a certain macabre familiarity. At the same time a storm of impulses was unleashed and threatened to engulf Matt in panic. Some small segment of his consciousness remained a detached observer. He heard his father's voice from so long ago telling himself and Paulie that if they ever got in trouble not to panic. 'Conserve your energy. People who panic end up drowned,' he used to say. Images of the time when they had capsized in the cove flashed like star-bursts and he recalled the feeling of inertia that had almost overcome him in the end. He'd given up, and if Paulie hadn't grabbed him he would have drowned that day. The fear only really came afterwards as he lay on the beach gasping for air and choking up sea water. He'd glimpsed his own death and escaped, and forever after he'd felt as if he'd cheated the ocean, but that one day it would claim him back. Now twenty-five years later time melted and faded so that it was like the blink of an eye.

Above him there was light, warmth and air within reach, and this time there was no squall, no storm except the one in his mind, and he knew he could strike out and reach the surface.

329

Below him the *Santorini* was fast settling into the depths where the light grew rapidly dim.

Live! a voice commanded with almost overpowering authority. He almost surrendered, but with a conscious effort he fought against his instinct and instead swam down.

His lungs burned though only seconds had passed. He looked for Ella and found her caught up in the wreckage, her eyes closed and hair floating around her face, gradually falling from him in slow motion. He couldn't tell if she was alive or dead. He grasped one hand that floated free and felt her residual warmth, then he tugged at the splintered wood where she was held fast. It started to come away, but the effort greedily devoured the oxygen in his muscles and he could feel his heart struggle to cope with the dwindling supply. His mind was operating on different levels. With one part he struggled to free Ella, while with another he witnessed a flashing series of images from his life. Kirstin; and then Alex sleeping quietly as an infant, his features placid and untroubled; himself standing at Paulie's graveside on a cold October afternoon as the words of the minister were swept away on the wind; Ella on the dock that night after the meeting when he had first kissed her, knowing suddenly that she was all he wanted or needed in his life to make it whole again.

He couldn't free her. As he struggled his strength began to drain. He was aware of the exchange of oxygen from lungs to the blood; its flow to his brain and muscles, driven by the engine house of his body. His heart was a machine, a powerful industrial monster, thumping its rhythm in a big cavernous basement, but it was growing slower, the machinery straining and groaning, and his blood was becoming sluggish, growing darker as the oxygen was used up. A dark spot formed in his brain and expanded as the cells began to die.

He was hallucinating and he knew it.

In his last few moments he looked at Ella and she appeared to be asleep, at peace, and he was tempted to simply hold her and relinquish life. A protesting inner voice caused him to look up towards the surface and through the shimmering water the light seemed distant but beautiful, and it summoned him. With the final reserves of his strength he gripped the jagged planking that held Ella fast and one more time he pulled. Muscles popped and gave, tendons stretched and howled in protest, and then she was free and he held her and kicked for the surface. His lungs burned and bright lights whizzed and exploded in his brain then faded as a veil of blackness swept over him and he put his mouth to hers and surrendered, thinking they had been so close, and with his thoughts he told her that he loved her.

Then he gasped and instead of filling his lungs with water he breathed air as his face broke the surface of the sea.

CHAPTER FORTY-ONE

A second before the shock of the impact Jake glimpsed Ella lying motionless on the deck of the *Santorini*. He staggered off balance as the two boats collided, and the *Seawind* shuddered in protest and almost stopped in the water, and then her powerful engines drove her forward and the screws churned their wake into a mass of white foaming water.

Penman appeared in the doorway, clutching at the frame, his face pale. He took one look at Jake, and without saying anything lunged for the throttle. For a moment the two men grappled, then Jake bunched his fist and hit Penman hard in the eye. Penman uttered a short grunt and stepped backwards, throwing out his arms for balance, but then he shook his head like a dog that'd been kicked in the mouth, and charged forward again, latching both hands on to the wheel.

'You'll kill them,' he said.

Jake grabbed a handful of Penman's hair and yanked his head back, then shoved it forward as hard as he could against the wheel. There was a dull sound and Penman groaned and slid to the floor, his legs buckling. The *Santorini* scraped by, grating and splintering as she went. Jake could see that she was already sinking, and he put Ella from his mind and turned his attention back to the orca, steering a course past the reef. He could see the bull's fin out towards the middle of the cove, the harpoon protruding a few feet behind, each creating a soft rippling wake, one inside the other. The woods of the point were reflected like a mirror image on the surface of still, green water, and the air was soft and quiet like a balm to the vice-like pain in Jake's head. The dull pounding of the ocean on the reef subsided and Jake cut back the *Seawind*'s speed.

The bull remained on the surface, and Jake figured it was too weak to hold its breath. Without haste now, he bent and grabbed Penman under the shoulder and dragged him to the door. There was a deep red indentation on his forehead that ran back beneath his hair. Jake wondered if he was dead, but Penman's chest rose as he took a shallow unconscious breath. He dragged him to the steps above the deck. Down below the men gaped at him. Without pause he tipped Penman over the edge and let him fall in a heap. He went back to the wheel-house and re-emerged carrying his rifle.

'Any man gets in my way I'll put a bullet in him.'

He waited to see if anyone would challenge him, and when nobody did he went back to the wheel. The orca was just ahead now, and Jake slowed the boat to a crawl. He wondered if the sonofabitch would try to get around him and head back for open sea, and acting on this thought he used the butt of his rifle to smash the window, then aimed through the space and squeezed off a shot. A small plume of water rose twenty feet behind the orca's dorsal fin and Jake adjusted the angle and fired off three rapid shots. The orca responded by picking up its pace and the fin slipped below the surface.

Jake chuckled. 'How's that feel, you big bastard? You're not so goddamned smart now I guess.' He went outside and checked each side of the boat, ready if the bull tried to double back. The water was dark green, and reflected light made it hard to see past the surface. He was certain that at least a couple of his shots had found their mark, and he was pretty sure the orca wouldn't be able to stay down for long. Even if it made for the open sea, he would be able to catch it and finish it off.

He waited, but there was no sign of the orca. Several minutes passed, and Jake checked behind, but all around the cove remained undisturbed. He wondered if he'd underestimated it.

'Come on, dammit, where the hell are you?' he muttered.

As if in answer he heard the animal breathe, a blow of air from in front, and he saw the bull's dorsal fin rise several hundred yards ahead.

Jake grinned. 'There you are. What did you think? You think old Jake would just go away if you stayed under long enough?'

He glanced at the deck where the crew had carried Penman back to the stern and one of them looked up.

'He's hurt pretty bad,' he said. 'I think we need to get him to a hospital.'

Jake ignored him and went back to the wheel. He increased speed a little. The orca was barely moving now, just floating and making feeble movements with its flukes. Jake shut the throttle right down, judging the moment so that the *Seawind* could drift up alongside. He reloaded the rifle, and stepped out the door. He paused for a moment, and was struck by how peaceful everything seemed now. The pain in his head had receded. All around, the high wooded hills of the point and the mountains inland rose to a clear sky. The water of the cove looked like a painting, barely disturbed by a ripple, deep and green and soothing. Ella was dead, Jake knew that, and she had gotten what she deserved. He guessed he was going to have to face some questions when he got back, maybe he'd even go to jail, but he didn't regret what he'd done. If he looked ahead, beyond the orca, beyond the finger of the jetty that poked out into the cove, beyond the strip of pale beach, he could see a glimpse of white in the trees where Bryan's house stood in the clearing.

Jake went down to the bow. It was time to finish this. Just lean over the side and put a bullet in the orca's brain. He waited as the *Seawind* drifted closer. He wanted to look into the bull's eye when he pulled the trigger.

Unexpectedly, with a smooth and almost silent passage, the orca vanished, slipping beneath the surface.

Jake ran to the side, the rifle raised, but he couldn't see anything. He leaned over, and squinted against the light, peering into the depths, trying to see beyond the reflection. He knew the cove wasn't too deep here. The ground fell away rapidly from the shore then levelled out for a hundred yards before dropping

334

away again into a deep hole. But right where they were it couldn't be more than ten fathoms or so.

He thought he saw something. He looked harder, and far below, resting on the seabed, a vaguely familiar form took shape. He leaned further over the rail trying to make it out. His throat felt tight and there was a hammering of rushing blood in his ears. The object became clearer, and a suspicion formed in Jake's mind. He caught his breath.

At the back of the *Seawind* Penman had come around, though he was groggy and his head felt as if he'd been hit with a sack of cement. The others helped him to sit.

'Where's Jake?' he mumbled groggily.

Someone jerked a thumb towards the bow. Penman leaned against the rail, and turned to spit bloody phlegm overboard and as he did his vision blurred a little and he felt sick, but even so he was sure he caught sight of a great, dark shape flash past, travelling like a locomotive beneath the surface of the water. He thought he glimpsed patches of white, and then in the blink of an eye it was gone.

He turned a puzzled look to the men beside him. 'I thought I saw . . .' He shook his head as his voice trailed away.

From towards the bow they heard the sound of erupting water and then a gigantic splash and the air was filled with a spreading fan-like wall of spray which dispersed to rain down on the deck, shot through with sunlight so that for an instant a hazy rainbow appeared above the *Seawind.* They heard the pattern of droplets hitting the surface then once again it was quiet, save for the ripples that slapped gently against the side of the boat.

All of them, except Penman who couldn't move, rushed to the side, but the water was settling and all they could see was the mirror image of the hills and woods.

Finally, one of the men went forward to look for Jake, but when he came back he shook his head, mystified. Jake was gone.

CHAPTER FORTY-TWO

Ben Harper looked towards the surface when he heard the sound of the screws as they bit, making the water boil and churn and from below he watched puzzled as his boat sped away, digging a deep furrow in its wake.

Minutes earlier he'd been searching among the craggy rocks that formed a landscape of small canyons and holes in the area. He'd been working his way in a grid pattern and now he was close to where the seabed fell away sharply at the beginning of the channel. The bottom of the boat was visible a hundred yards to his right, a broad white marker on the surface. Something caught his eye and he looked down at a narrow crevice twenty feet below. Behind his mask his expression creased into a puzzled squint as he peered across the distance, trying to make out what he saw. He could see an indefinable shape protruding from the crevice, perhaps part of a larger whole, but without his glasses he found it difficult to distinguish what he was looking at from the surrounding rocks. He wondered what had caught his attention, and then as he moved and the angle altered, sunlight pierced the depths and something flashed. He thought he saw what might be a metal clasp and maybe wire. He checked the time, and his gauge, and saw that he was almost out of air.

It was then that he heard the launch start and when he looked it was speeding away. He looked down again at the thing that had attracted his attention and made his decision. He had time for one quick look. He swam down and when he reached it he saw that he'd been right about the wire and clasp. The bundle was caught in between some rocks. Whatever it contained had been wrapped in canvas and secured with the metal wire and clasp. He put his hand on it, but couldn't feel the shape of what was inside, then grasping it he tugged to try and free it. It was stuck fast, but he adjusted his grip and tried again. He was aware of how much oxygen the effort was costing him. He stopped, and checked his gauge which now showed empty. One last time he tugged, and the bundle moved, breaking off a jagged sliver of rock where the wire had caught fast. Once free of its resting place the bundle felt heavy, and it sank and rested on the bottom, and as it did Ben ran out of air. He gulped and kicked for the surface, the long shape lying inert below him.

It appeared to be about the size of a man.

CHAPTER FORTY-THREE

Judge Walker sat behind his desk, clearly taken aback by the events of the day. 'Jesus H Christ,' he said. He got up and went to one of the tall windows that looked over the square. Outside the sun was low in the western sky and the statue of Oliver Wake cast a long shadow in the twilight across the dusty grass. 'I don't know what the hell has happened to this town lately,' he commented in a voice weary with resignation. He thrust his hands in the pockets of his pants. 'You know how many people I had before me in court yesterday? Fifteen. Fifteen for Christ's sake! I never had that many cases to hear in one day in all the years I've been doing this job. Hell, I don't think I've had fifteen cases in a month before now.'

The judge looked at Matt and Baxter, and as if he couldn't find any words to express what he felt he just shook his head.

'You know Russ Williams arrested Kyle Perrit this morning? Got him locked up in a cell over at your office.'

'Kyle?' Baxter said. 'I didn't know about that. What's he done?'

'He took a shotgun and blew out a window at Bill Hodgiss's house. Could've damn well killed somebody.'

Baxter was astounded. 'Kyle did that? Him and Bill Hodgiss have been buddies for thirty years. What the hell would he do a thing like that for?'

'Seems Bill rented out his boat to bunch of sports fishermen from the mainland. The deal was if they caught a fish Bill stood to take a share of whatever they got for it, plus the eight hundred dollars a day he was making renting his boat. Kyle claims there was a school of four hundred pounders out there and the way he tells it he was about to harpoon one when Bill cut across his bow.'

Judge Walker shook his head in disbelief. 'Thirty years of friendship. Gone over a goddamned fish! Now this.' He folded both hands on his desk and broached the subject it seemed as if he'd been avoiding. 'Will somebody please explain to me what the hell is going on around here?'

The judge already knew what had happened out by the cove, what he didn't know was how come Baxter and Matt had been there. It was Baxter who explained what they'd learned, firstly from Jordan Osborne and then from their conversation with Kate and Evan Little. When he came to the part about Evan Little hearing shots and a boat in the cove that night the judge frowned. Then Baxter went on to relate the theory Ben Harper had come up with.

'Are you trying to tell me that you think Ella and Kate are somehow both mixed up in this together?' the judge said. 'Did Harper find anything?'

'He ran out of air,' Matt said. 'But he made three dives without coming up with anything.' In fact when they had gone back to pick Ben up from the water he'd confided to Matt that he had seen something just before he'd been forced to surface. He'd claimed he didn't get a good enough look at it to be sure what it might be, though he'd given Matt a vague description and idea of its size. The words he'd used were that it was 'some kind of canvas bundle wrapped in wire'. He wouldn't be drawn any further than that until he could go down again and bring it to the surface which he planned to do in the morning. Matt had asked him not to mention it to Baxter for now.

Judge Walker's eyebrows knitted together in a puzzled frown. 'What did Ella have to say about all this? You're her lawyer Matt. Seems a little odd you being out there looking for evidence that would convict your own client?'

'She doesn't know, Judge.'

Judge Walker contemplated the seeming paradox inherent

339

in Matt's actions that day, then he picked up the copy of Jerrod Gant's statement that was on his desk. 'So, right now there's still no other hard evidence against Ella or anybody else, except for this. Seems like Gant may have been telling the truth all along. You think Ella was in the house that night?'

'I guess we won't know that until somebody talks to him,' Baxter said.

'Any sign of him yet?' But neither Matt nor Baxter had made any progress on that front. The judge shook his head. 'And now Jake's gone too.' He let that hang for a moment, but nobody seemed keen to comment. The crew of the *Seawind* had related everything they'd seen and heard, but they couldn't, or wouldn't, speculate as to what had become of Jake. He'd simply vanished.

'I asked Ben Harper to take a look around the shoreline in the morning,' Baxter said. 'Maybe he fell over the side or something.'

The judge appeared unconvinced, but he let it go. 'All around I'd say this is pretty much a goddamned mess. Question is what do we do about Kate and Ella now? I guess we ought to place them both under arrest on suspicion of murder. Let the state boys find Jerrod Gant and sort this thing out before anyone else gets hurt.' He looked at them both, waiting for any objections, and when there were none, he sighed. 'Where are they now?'

'I talked to Doctor Laine a little while ago,' Baxter said. 'Kate had a few cuts but she's okay. She went home, but Anne's keeping Ella in overnight to keep an eye on her.'

'Well,' Judge Walker said resignedly. 'Might as well leave it until the morning, I don't suppose they're going anywhere tonight. I'll call the state attorney's office tomorrow and get them to send someone over here.'

CHAPTER FORTY-FOUR

Ella was sleeping when Matt arrived at the clinic to look in on her. Anne Laine took him inside her office. 'Helena's sitting with her.'

'How is she?'

'She hasn't said anything coherent yet. I don't think she's aware of what happened. She's in shock, and she took a nasty crack on the head when she fell, but I think she'll be okay.'

Matt detected a hesitant note in her voice. 'Is there something you're not telling me?'

'No. Well, it's just that she did say something.'

He wondered if Ella had made some semi-conscious confession. He recalled her pale features after Baxter had hauled them both aboard Ben's launch. Her hair had been plastered to her skull, her lips had a bluish tinge and her flesh had a waxy texture. He'd thought she was dead until she'd begun coughing up sea water.

'After she was brought in, she kept saying your name. Over and over. I guess she was delirious.' Anne paused. 'The chief told me what you did out there, you know. That was pretty brave.'

'He would've done it if I hadn't gone in first.'

'Maybe.' She pursed her lips thoughtfully. 'But the chief is a good swimmer.' He wondered how much Baxter had guessed, and what he'd told Anne. When he didn't say anything she smiled. 'Do you want to see her?'

'No, I just wanted to make sure she was okay. I should get going.'

'Do you want me to tell her anything when she wakes up?'

He shook his head. 'No.' What message could he leave? That she was about to be arrested?

After Matt left the clinic he went back to his office. It was growing dark by the time he unlocked the door and the first thing he saw was the light blinking on the machine, and when he played back his messages he heard Ruth Thorne's voice.

'I just called to make sure you hadn't forgotten about Charlie,' she said hesitantly. 'But I heard some things about what happened today, and I guess you might be tied up so don't worry about getting back to me.'

He groaned, and checked the time then picked up the phone and called her number. He remembered that the ferry company had told him Charlie wasn't working that night, but he hadn't yet told Ruth about that. He figured she'd made a mistake about the day. She answered almost straight away.

'This is Matt Jones, Ruth. Can you talk right now?'

There was a pause, then she said in a low voice, 'Hi, Mr Jones. Matt I mean. Charlie's taking a shower. He's getting ready to leave.'

'He's working?' Matt asked.

'Sure. Don't you remember?'

'Yes, I remember.' He thought quickly, wondering what was going on. 'Look don't worry about it, it's taken care of. I'll call you when I know something.'

'Are you sure this is still okay?' Ruth asked sounding worried. 'I know you have a lot on your mind right now.'

He was almost tempted to tell her that she was right, he did have a lot on his mind, but he'd made her a promise, and she deserved to know what her husband was doing when he was supposed to be staying over on the mainland. For now he didn't tell her that Charlie wasn't even scheduled to be working that night, since he didn't know what that meant, instead he reassured her again that he was on top of it.

He called Ben next at the inn and while he waited for the call to be put through to his room his eye fell to the desk calendar beside the phone. A date circled in red reminded him with silent irony that the election to decide who would be the next mayor of Sanctuary Harbor was due to be held the next day. Before he could think about that any further Ben came on the line and Matt asked him what time he was planning to leave the harbour in the morning.

'First light. Around five thirty.'

'I'll meet you at your boat,' Matt said. There was a pause then Ben asked him a hesitant question.

'Did you say anything to Chief Baxter about what I saw?'

'Not yet. Let's wait until we know for sure what it is.'

'Okay. See you in the morning.'

After he'd hung up he went down to his car and drove out to where Ruth and Charlie Thorne lived. On the way he reasoned that he didn't know what else he would have done that night anyway. It was a long time until morning, and somehow he didn't think he would sleep even if he had the chance.

Matt sat in his car along the street from the Thornes' house, waiting for Charlie to appear. He was thinking back to his conversation with Ella in the cemetery. She'd accused him of having narrow vision, unable to accept that sometimes life wasn't a black and white issue. He thought she had been implying that Bryan's death had been an accident and the dumping of his body somehow able to be explained. She had also implied that she hadn't told him the truth because she had known how he would react.

He wondered about that. If he was right, Ella had thought he would never condone concealing a man's death. But Kate and Ella obviously believed their actions were in some way justifiable. Were there any circumstances where he might have agreed with them? A few weeks ago the answer would have been unequivocally no. But now he wasn't so certain.

He recalled the feeling he'd had in the cemetery, that he was missing something. And Ella's expression before she'd left, the words she'd spoken – 'You're so sure, aren't you, that you have this right,' – seemed to give the lie to his theory. He'd had the same feeling later that night, when he'd run down to the cove from his house and stood on the sand looking out at the water. Something that was staring him in the face, but for some reason he was blind to. Perhaps tomorrow, when Ben made one more dive, all of his questions would be answered.

Across the street a door opened and Charlie Thorne emerged from a house carrying a duffel over his shoulder. He paused briefly to kiss his wife, then Ruth watched him go and closed the door, and Matt wondered if she was thinking this might be the last time she played out this ritual of domestic routine.

Matt followed at a distance as Charlie Thorne drove out to the ferry dock near the processing plant, a little way out of town. When he reached the parking lot Charlie locked his car, and it occurred to Matt that maybe he had switched shifts, and that he was working after all, but Charlie didn't board the ferry. Instead he headed for a car parked on the edge of the lot, and after a quick surreptitious look around he got in the passenger side. A moment later the car pulled out and Matt allowed it a head start before following, though since he'd recognized it the moment he saw it he could guess where it was headed.

The car took the route towards the point, which avoided going back through town. Only the driver's head was visible as if Charlie was keeping his head down to avoid any chance of being seen. Matt wondered how long this had been going on. He felt sorry for Ruth Thorne having to learn that she was right about her husband cheating on her, but he thought that she seemed like the kind of person who would deal with the situation and put it behind her, then get on with her life. It occurred to him that maybe he could learn a lesson from her.

He pulled over when the car in front turned off the road and vanished along a track between the trees. He sat thinking for a while, and then he got out and started walking towards the house that was set back in the woods.

It was past one a.m. by the time Matt arrived back at Ruth Thorne's house. He'd been home and called her from there so she was expecting him. There was a light on in the window and she opened the door before he could knock. She wore a robe wrapped around her, her hair looked as if she'd quickly dragged a brush through it, her face was scrubbed pink and shining. There was no sign of the slumped shoulders or resigned weariness that characterized defeat. Matt knew as soon as he saw her that she would be okay, and he thought she'd been right when she'd said once that she deserved better than a husband who cheated on her.

'Come on in,' she said. 'Coffee's on. You look like you could use some.'

They sat at the kitchen table and Matt told her what had happened after Charlie had left the house, and though she appeared stoically unsurprised to have her suspicions about her husband confirmed, when she learned the details she was angry.

'That bastard better not show his face around here again.'

Matt doubted that he would. He allowed her time to give vent to her feelings, but she wasn't the type to feel sorry for herself. Before he'd drunk his coffee she was questioning him about the practical details of obtaining a divorce, and he reassured her that it would be a simple process.

'I want to thank you for your help,' she said when eventually he rose to leave.

She showed him to the door, and the way she was handling all this made him decide to tell her something he'd been planning to leave until the morning. 'I found out something else tonight.' He related what he'd discovered, and as she listened she realized the implications, including the fact that before long the entire island would know about Charlie.

'Well, at least something good will come out of it,' she said finally, which Matt thought was a pretty good attitude for her to have under the circumstances.

After he left he drove home with the intention of trying to snatch a couple of hours' sleep before it was time to go and meet Ben Harper. By the time he got there it had started raining. Fat heavy drops hit the windshield, exploding like small bombs, and when he got out the car he could feel that the wind had changed. The breeze was cool and quickly gathered strength. One minute there was a rustling sound in the tops of the trees, and the next a strong gust came up the hillside whipping up dry debris on the woodland floor and then the tops of the trees were buffeted and began to tremble as if in fear of the approaching storm.

Matt raced for the porch as the rain came down in earnest. Great drops of water hit the dusty track making small craters, and then as he hit the steps the heavens opened and in minutes the track was a mass of surface puddles. It was impossible to see more than twenty yards from the house even with all the lights on. The sky was dark with cloud and on the ground the rain turned everything grey. The wind picked up and shook the trees like a giant hand. Inside Matt lay down on his bed and closed his eyes, listening to the storm outside. He tried to sleep, but his mind refused to shut down, and a constant parade of images and questions kept him awake until in the end he gave up, and spent the next couple of hours sitting in the kitchen drinking coffee while the storm blew itself out. It built to a rapid crescendo, the wind howling through the woods, rain lashing the walls and roof like some furious creature trying to gain entry, then as quickly as it had begun it abated as the front passed through.

'You look like shit,' Ben announced when Matt arrived at the dock in the morning. The sky was turning from black to midnight blue, the stars fading as night gave way to another day. The wind had changed again, and the air felt thick and warm. Steam rose from the wet ground and evidence of the ferocity of the storm lay all around. Crates and lobster traps and assorted debris had been picked up and tossed randomly about.

'I didn't get a lot of sleep,' Matt said, eyeing the scuba gear already laid out on the stern deck. Ben unhooked the bow line and stepped aboard.

'You ready?'

'As I'll ever be.'

Matt climbed aboard, and other than the half second it took him to notice that he didn't break out in a cold sweat or fall in a quivering heap on the deck, he hardly registered the fact that

346

he'd left behind the comfort of dry land. He joined Ben up top as he swung the launch away from the dock and headed for the mid-channel marker, and when they were clear he opened the throttle. The motor growled and as the stern settled back into the water the bow rose and they quickly gathered speed, planing over the placid harbour until they hit the swell beyond the heads.

As the sun came up and the sky lightened, the sea was coloured with a shifting palette of blues and greens. It took them just a few minutes to reach the entrance to the cove, where Ben used landmarks that he'd noted from the previous day to position the launch in roughly the spot where he'd last dived. He checked on the depth sounder until he found where the seabed started to drop away at the edge of the channel, and then he hit the button that dropped the anchor.

'This is it.'

Matt helped him get into his scuba gear, and while he was sitting on the edge of the boat cleaning his mask Ben looked towards the shore several hundred yards away, his expression creased into a thoughtful frown.

'What is it?'

'Look on the rocks there. That driftwood was all washed up by the storm last night.'

The rocks were covered all along the shore with a mess of seaweed and rubbish that had been dumped high above the current water line. As well as driftwood Matt could see plastic containers, floats and the odd broken lobster trap. All the detritus lost or dumped by fisherman in the waters around the island. It wasn't a pretty sight, but there was always a lot of debris after a storm.

'What of it?'

'Whatever it was I saw down there yesterday,' Ben said. 'It's likely to have moved and we're right by the edge of the channel here.'

They exchanged looks, but it seemed there was nothing else to say until Ben went down to take a look. He slipped over the side, and when he was in the water he pulled his mask down

347

and put his regulator in his mouth, then gave the thumbs up sign and a moment later he vanished.

Matt could only wait.

He was unable to keep still, and he paced back and forth across the small space of the stern deck, repeatedly checking over the side to see if there was any sign of Ben returning, but the water was murky from all the sand and silt that had been stirred up by the storm and he couldn't see beyond a few feet below the surface. He felt a mixture of dread and anticipation. One thing that had become inescapably clear to him after saving Ella from the wreck of the *Santorini*, was that he was in love with her. But whatever the consequences might be, before there could be any hope for a future between them, Matt had to know what had happened to Bryan. Perhaps then they could talk and she could explain her side of it and then maybe, just maybe they could move forward from there. But if Ben came back empty handed and Ella maintained her silence, there would be no answers and this would remain between them forever, a barrier they could never hope to cross.

He had to wait an agonizing twenty minutes before Ben finally surfaced. Matt helped him into the back of the boat and waited impatiently while he took off his mask.

'Did you find it?'

Ben shook his head. 'It's gone.'

Somehow Matt thought, he had known this would be the outcome. Despite everything he experienced a glimmer of relief that had nothing to do with the law, or with himself and the way he felt about Ella, but was purely about her. This was the evidence that could have convicted her of a serious crime and earned her a long prison term, and it was gone. He felt suddenly tired.

'You're sure?'

'Yeah. I took a good look around. The storm must have carried it into the channel.'

'It couldn't have just been moved somewhere else?'

Ben shook his head. 'It was too heavy. It felt like it had been weighed down with something. The currents couldn't have moved it more than a few yards, and I've looked in every nook and cranny down there. It's gone Matt.'

As if he had an inkling of what this meant to Matt, Ben allowed him a few moments to himself while he busied himself taking off his scuba gear. Matt stared across the ocean, surprised at the depth of the hollow emptiness that he felt.

'What now?' Ben said eventually.

'I guess we look for Jake.'

They raised the anchor and headed for the point to begin the search along the shoreline. As they motored along at a slow pace they scanned the rocks and tiny bays for any sign of a body amidst the flotsam. They tried the other side of the reef, staying well clear of the cliffs and finally when they hadn't found anything they went into the cove.

At one point Ben thought he saw something caught up in a sunken tree trunk twenty feet down and he put on a snorkel and mask to take a closer look.

Matt watched him swim down then lost him among the mass of shadows and half defined shapes that lay beneath the surface. He sat on the rail to wait, nursing the sense of defeat and melancholy that had descended over him. Though the launch was anchored close to shore he felt as if he were all alone, St George some deserted island he'd happened upon. The only sound was the call of gulls and the pounding roar of the sea as it thundered over the reef and crashed against the rocks at the foot of the cliffs on the other side of the cove. Out in the bay the water lay unruffled like a sheet of glass, the reflected woods so real that after a while the senses began to be deceived by the illusion and it was almost possible to believe land and water had merged as one. In the distance lay the dark finger of the jetty, and behind it the squat shape of the boathouse. Matt was mesmerized by the motion of the swell, by the hypnotic images around him, and slowly without deliberate thought or effort, something that had bothered him, but which he hadn't been able to put his finger on, took shape.

He was startled when Ben broke the surface just a few feet away.

349

'Shit, don't do that,' Matt said, his heart leaping. 'You find anything?'

'Just a rotting log.'

Matt helped him back on board and pointed to the jetty. 'Take us over there. There's something I need to look at.'

Ben steered for the beach and cut the motor as the launch drifted towards the jetty. Matt stepped ashore and tied the bow line. The strip of beach was littered in both directions by the mess of driftwood and other rubbish that had been washed ashore. Across the bay the dark shape of the dead orca was visible, though it looked sunken now, as nature absorbed it slowly back into the earth.

Matt went back to the old boat shed, and pushed open the door, though he already knew what he would find. He stared into the empty space for a few moments, and when he turned around Ben was watching curiously.

'What is it?'

'I'm not sure.' Twenty yards away, he spotted a chunk of wood lying on the sand. When he reached it he saw that it was in fact not just a piece of wood and he bent down to examine it. One side was painted white, and the boards it was made up of were jagged at either end where they'd broken.

'What does this look like to you?'

Ben gave it no more than a cursory glance. 'It's part of a boat. Maybe a crabber.'

'That's what I thought.' Matt looked out at the bay, and then back at the boathouse. 'Every time I came here something bothered me, but I couldn't figure out what it was until now. It's the boathouse. It's empty.' Ben looked at him uncomprehendingly. 'Think about it. Bryan lived just back there in the woods. This is his jetty, that's his boathouse. So where's his boat?'

'Maybe he didn't have one.'

'He was a fisherman. What fisherman have you ever heard of who didn't have a boat? Besides, what else would he keep in there.' He gestured back towards the old wooden structure at the end of the jetty. Matt felt as if he had an itch he couldn't scratch. Something about this was important. He didn't know how or why, but he felt that he was right. He looked down at the piece of wreckage, and then his gaze turned out to the cove as if the answer might be there.

An image of the *Seawind* took shape in his mind as she had followed the orca into the cove. And now Jake too was gone. His gaze travelled back around the shoreline to the remains of the dead orca along the beach.

An idea began to take shape.

'What is it?' Ben asked, watching his expression.

'I want to run something past you,' Matt said.

CHAPTER FORTY-FIVE

Matt turned back to the beach where a small group of people stood waiting, and started towards them. Out in the cove, where the mirrored images of the surrounding hills and trees were painted on the surface, Ben Harper's launch lay at anchor close to a dragger that had been brought in from the harbour following Matt's call to Baxter earlier that morning. Judge Walker and an officer in the uniform of the St George police department stood alongside Ella. Her mother was also there, as well as Anne Laine who had insisted on being present to look out for her patient.

As Matt wondered how much longer Baxter would be, his cruiser appeared at the end of the track that led through the woods to the road. He got out, and Kate Little emerged from the passenger door. Ella watched as they approached, her attention fixed on Kate, her expression difficult to interpret.

Further back a small knot of onlookers had appeared, curious to see what was going on after news had spread in the harbour, and they gathered together where they'd parked their vehicles at the edge of the trees. Another of Baxter's officers stood close by to keep them back as yet another truck appeared and a man and a woman climbed out.

'What's this all about Matt?' Judge Walker asked when Baxter had joined them.

Ella and Kate had done no more than offer one another guarded nods. Ella was still pale, though otherwise she appeared to be okay. Matt noticed that she avoided looking at him.

'Sorry to drag you out here Judge, but I think I know what happened the night Bryan Roderick vanished. And I think everybody here is going to be surprised when you learn the truth.'

Kate and Ella exchanged uneasy looks, but Matt thought he saw something else in Ella's expression; he thought she looked puzzled, but not by anything he'd said.

'I should start by saying that Bryan is dead,' Matt said. 'But I don't think it was Kate or Ella who killed him.'

This time they both stared at him, and though Kate appeared the more surprised of the two, it was clear that both of them were taken aback, and it was only right then that he knew the theory he'd formed that morning as he and Ben had trawled back and forth across the cove was probably right.

'Before I say anything else,' he went on, addressing them directly, 'I need to ask you both a question, and in light of what I've just told you, I need you to answer me truthfully. My guess is that ever since Bryan vanished the two of you have each independently assumed that the other was responsible for his death. Am I right?'

He looked from one to the other, but neither of them spoke.

'You don't have to worry about incriminating each other anymore. Like I said, neither of you killed Bryan. Whatever you may have thought.'

It was Ella who finally broke the silence, her eyes fixed on Kate. 'You're right. I thought Kate had killed him.' And then Kate slowly nodded too, though she appeared completely bewildered.

It was the final confirmation Matt needed. He looked at Ella and he thought she had already worked some of this out, or at least suspected. 'Did you know?' he asked.

She shook her head once, slowly. 'Not exactly, but yesterday I felt something was wrong. Kate said something that didn't make sense to me. But I didn't get a chance to ask her about it.'

'Hold on here. I don't understand this,' Baxter interrupted. Both he and the judge were totally lost. 'Why would the two of you think the other one had killed Bryan?'

'I think I can answer that. They were both out on the point that night.' He looked at Ella. 'My guess is you saw each other out there. Tell me if I'm getting any of this wrong.'

'You're not wrong,'

'I think Kate left her house when she heard shots in the cove. Am I right?'

Kate looked around at them all. 'Yes,' she admitted at length.

'What happened then?'

'I went down through the woods, and I saw Ella. It was dark, and a little scary out there. I got quite a fright.'

'You didn't speak?'

'No. We just saw each other for a second.'

'And what did you do then?'

'I went home.'

He could see that she was reluctant to say too much, still uncertain if this was some kind of trick, so he speculated as to what had happened next. 'For the rest of the night you lay awake wondering what Ella had been doing. You kept wondering about those shots you heard. Maybe you were worried about Ella. You knew how she and Bryan felt about each other. You knew he'd been giving her trouble over the election, and you knew the kind of person he could be, and so in the morning you went down to his house and you found him gone. Is that right?'

'Yes.'

'Did you know then, or did you think you knew, that he was dead?'

'No. I didn't know what to think, but I suppose I had a suspicion that something might have happened to him.'

'That's when you decided to clean up the house?'

'I did that for the reason I already told you, because I didn't want anybody to know I'd been there.'

'And when did you decide that Bryan must be dead?'

'A day or two later, after I heard that he was missing.'

'And you thought Ella had killed him?'

'Not at first. Maybe I suspected something, I'm not sure. But then I heard the talk, and I put two and two together.'

354

'But you didn't say anything?'

Kate took a moment before she answered. 'No. I didn't say anything.'

'And for her part Ella kept quiet about seeing Kate that night too,' Matt said, turning to her. 'You knew that Bryan had beaten Kate before, and so after you saw her and you heard Bryan was missing, you assumed she'd killed him. My guess is you thought it was some kind of accident, and you thought that if Bryan was dead then he probably had it coming. Am I close?'

Ella met his eye, and after a long pause she nodded. 'You're close.'

Matt held her gaze, waiting to see if she would say anything else. He knew there was more, but he hadn't worked it all out yet, and even if he had he couldn't prove it. But she stared back at him silently. She glanced at her mother, and something passed between them that he couldn't interpret, but Helena appeared troubled.

The sound of another vehicle arriving dissolved the moment, and then a car door slammed and they heard raised voices as the officer keeping back the growing crowd tried to stop Howard Larson getting by.

'Let him come,' Matt said.

Baxter signalled the officer, and Howard came down the slope towards them. As he drew nearer he looked at the boats on the cove and then his eye ranged over the group, pausing on Ella and then fixed on Matt.

'What the hell is going on here?' he demanded.

'Nothing that's any of your business, Howard,' Baxter said.

'The hell it isn't. I'm making it my business. This is about Bryan isn't it? People have a right to know what's happening. Are you finally going to arrest her?'

'You can keep your voice down Howard,' the judge cut in. 'This isn't an election speech you're making here and whatever you may think, you really don't have any business here.'

'I'd like Howard to stay, Judge,' Matt cut in. 'As a matter of fact this does concern him in a way.'

Howard looked at Matt as if he was surprised at finding

support from that quarter, and then his surprise changed to wariness.

'I was just explaining to everyone that it wasn't Ella who killed Bryan.' Matt paused to let Howard absorb what he was saying. 'Looks as if Jerrod Gant wasn't exactly telling the truth about what he saw that night.'

'Gant?' Howard looked around, as if he expected him to appear.

'He isn't here if that's what you're wondering. As a matter of fact I don't have any idea where he is, though when he turns up I expect we'll find out where he's been hiding. What did you do? Put him up in some motel on the mainland? I bet he's there right now, watching cable with a six-pack at his side, eating take-out pizza and fries. Who's paying for it Howard? Is that on top of what you already promised him? What exactly *did* you promise him Howard? Did you wipe out the rent arrears he owes you and tell him he could relocate his business to one of those new units you have planned for when the marina gets built? Is that what it cost to persuade him to lie for you?'

'I don't know what the hell you're talking about,' Howard protested.

'Is that so? I wonder what Gant is going to say when he does turn up? You think he'll tell us it was all his own idea to make up the statement he gave the chief here? Maybe when he finds himself looking at some jail time he'll think twice about that. What were you going to do, have him change his story after the election was over? Have him suddenly decide that it was dark and it could be he made a mistake about what he saw after all?'

'This is all a lie. You can't prove a single word of any of this.'

'Maybe not yet. But I can prove that you were out at Jerrod Gant's house the night before he made his statement. And I can prove that Gant wasn't even on St George the night Bryan disappeared.'

Matt noted with some satisfaction that even Howard was surprised by this last piece of information.

'I guess he forgot to tell you that.'

'Is this true?' Judge Walker asked.

'It's true.'

Matt explained how he'd found out. He related how the previous night he'd followed Charlie Thorne back to the Gants' place after Lucy Gant had picked him up at the ferry dock. 'Ruth Thorne suspected her husband was cheating on her, and she was right. But he wasn't staying over on the mainland the way she thought. Instead, whenever Gant was away from home working on one of the other islands, Charlie was spending time with Lucy. Lucy told me about Howard going to the house, and both she and Charlie admitted that on the night Bryan vanished, Jerrod Gant was away working for a guy on Lucia. There was no way he could've seen anything. He made the entire story up.'

Howard looked trapped. His anger had dissipated, replaced by uncertainty and the first flicker of fear.

'Looks like you should start thinking about a new career Howard. Somehow I think your political ambitions just went belly up. Or maybe you'll get elected spokesman for your cell block.'

Howard paled and fixed him with a look of pure malice. 'I don't have to stay and listen to this kind of crap. You can speak to my lawyer.'

He wheeled around and went back towards his car and Matt watched him go, grinning a little and thinking at least he'd derived some satisfaction from all of this.

Before anyone could say anything else, a shout attracted their attention. On the launch out in the cove Ben Harper waved his arm.

'I think the show is about to start folks,' Matt said.

On the deck of the dragger a man operated a winch. To the east, a line of cloud hung over the horizon, its edge marked by great sooty brush strokes that extended to the sea as another front slowly advanced towards the coast of Maine.

Ella and Kate stood side by side at the end of the jetty as close by a shape broke the surface of the water and Ben Harper in scuba gear raised an arm and passed a line to the man on the dragger who hooked it with a gaff. The line was fixed to the winch reel and once Ben was out of the way the hum of the machinery started as the slack was taken up. The line snapped taut in the air, and rivulets of water dripped to the sea.

Matt explained how the realization that Bryan's boat was missing had prompted an idea earlier that morning. He said that after witnessing what had happened when Jake had harpooned the orca the day before, it had struck him just how intelligent orcas were.

'That orca appeared to lead the *Seawind* into the cove, which gave the others a chance to escape. And then judging by what the crew heard and saw, maybe it turned the tables on Jake.' He pointed along the shore. 'Ben thinks the dead orca he found in the cove probably belonged to the same pod. It died from pneumonia, but Ben found bullet scars on the dorsal fin which isn't all that unusual, but there was one wound that he thought might have been recent, though the body is pretty decomposed now so he can't say for sure. He thinks the pod probably came into the cove the same night Bryan disappeared, hunting fish they'd herded in past the reef.'

Out on the water the line was being winched slowly in. Matt watched for a moment before continuing.

'We already know that Bryan had been drinking that night, and earlier he'd had a fight with Ella on the dock, so he was probably in a lousy mood. We also know that the Rodericks had a habit of shooting orcas if they got the chance. I think that's what happened that night. Bryan saw the orcas in the cove and he got his rifle and went out in his boat.'

'The shots Carl Johnson heard?' Judge Walker said.

'That's my guess.'

Just then something broke the surface of the water and was slowly hoisted into the air. When it was almost clear Ben shouted for the winch to be switched off. Matt looked at Ella.

'Bryan's boat,' he said.

It had been a fourteen foot crabber, with a large outboard motor on the back which was still attached, though it was draped with seaweed. It was this that had ensured that the boat had sunk to the bottom and stayed there when it had gone down. One side of the boat was smashed, the wood splintered and crushed where massive force had been exerted and a good two thirds of that side was missing. Part of it was what Matt had found on the beach earlier.

It took a minute or so before the eye could make sense of all it could see. As well as seaweed what was left of the boat was part-filled with mud and sand that had partially buried it when the storm had churned up the seabed the night before. But gradually as more detail made sense it became apparent that there was something inside the boat. Something shapeless, but impaled on a jagged section of planking. And then as the eye focused on this image, and filtered out what was around it, the shape of it began to make sense, and then automatically the eye sought clarification with some familiar aspect, and it seemed that what hung limp at one end, gray with mud except where a flash of white showed through, might be a head, and the white a section of skull.

Ella drew a sharp breath.

Matt looked at her. 'It's Bryan.'

CHAPTER FORTY-SIX

What remained of Bryan's boat was hauled aboard the dragger and both it and the body it contained were taken back to the harbour. The body would be examined to establish the cause of death, but Matt had little doubt about what had happened. He figured Bryan had seen the sick orca and had meant to finish it off, but before he could reach it another member of the pod had intervened to protect it, perhaps the bull Jake had harpooned. He imagined an eight ton animal rising out of the water with the speed and power of a locomotive, and how easily it would have flipped a small boat. Maybe when it had crashed back into the sea it had landed partially on top of the crabber, and in the resulting wreck Bryan had fell or been forced on to a section of jagged planking. He probably wouldn't even have known what had hit him.

When the dragger headed back to the harbour, Ben offered Matt a ride on his launch, but Matt said he'd see him back in town and he joined the rest of the group on the beach as they headed back towards their vehicles.

Judge Walker shook his head incredulously, still hardly able to believe how everything had turned out. 'Damndest thing I ever heard of.' He turned to Ella. 'Things must have been tough for you these last weeks.' His eye drifted towards Kate. 'Course if you two had both told everything you knew from the start, maybe things would have been different.' There was a slight note of censure in his voice. 'Anyway, I'm glad it's settled now. You and your mother need a ride back to town?'

Ella glanced at Matt. 'You go ahead Mom, I'll be along in a minute.' Helena hesitated, her expression still troubled. 'Go on, I'll be right there,' Ella urged her gently.

'I'll take Kate home,' Baxter said to Matt. 'You want me to come back for you?'

'I think I feel like a walk. I'll see you later.'

'Okay.'

As the others headed back to their vehicles Matt and Ella were left alone. For a moment neither of them spoke, then they started off side by side, a slight distance between them.

'I didn't get a chance to thank you for what you did yesterday,' Ella said.

'Forget it.'

'You don't just forget it when somebody saves your life.' She paused, and laid a hand on his arm. 'Thank you.'

They continued in silence for a while. Matt wasn't sure how to broach what was on his mind. In the end he thought she knew what was coming and was waiting for him to say it.

'There's something I didn't mention back there,' he said eventually. He kept his gaze focused straight ahead, even when he felt her look at him. 'I let everyone assume that the reason you didn't say anything about seeing Kate that night, was to protect her, but that's only partly true isn't it?'

'Yes,' she admitted quietly.

'It hasn't occurred to anyone to wonder what you were doing out on the point that night.'

'Why should they? Now Bryan's been found.'

'The thing I didn't mention was that Ben found something out near the channel when he was diving yesterday.' He looked into her eyes, but he couldn't read what she was thinking.

'What was it?'

'He wasn't sure. He went down to take another look this morning but the storm last night had moved it. He thinks it went into the channel. But it was some kind of bundle, wrapped in wire and weighted down.'

He was certain that she knew what he was talking about, and he was equally certain that whatever that bundle had contained was the real reason that Ella had been on the point. It was what Carl Johnson had seen hanging off her davit, and it was the main reason she had kept quiet about seeing Kate Little that night, even when she herself had been accused of murder. It was also what stood between them. The bundle was gone. Nobody would ever know about it if she chose to remain silent, but by doing so she would be shutting the door on him.

He thought she knew that, but he also knew what her answer would be.

In the end, she made the barest negative movement of her head, and though her eyes clouded with sorrow, she turned away and he stood there and watched her go.

CHAPTER FORTY-SEVEN

The election had been postponed after the revelations surrounding the discovery of Bryan's body. It was three weeks
before it was finally re-scheduled, by which time a new hopeful
had surfaced to replace Howard, who had dropped out and was
keeping a low profile. So far Jerrod Gant hadn't returned to
the island, and Matt wondered if he ever would. The new candi-
date was the island's only other lawyer, and a long time associate
of Howard's. He declared himself to be in favour of the marina,
and the development that would flow on from it. On polling
day Matt went to cast his vote. Both candidates were in the hall,
glad handing voters and wreathed in smiles. Matt took a voting
slip and marked a cross against Ella's name, then handed it to
the official at the booth. When he looked up he caught Ella's
eye across the room, and her expression faltered for a second
before she went back to the conversation she was involved in
with some people around her.

'Hey.'

He was startled by a voice at his side and he turned to find
Sally Brewster grinning at him.

'Why the miserable look?' She followed his gaze and understanding dawned. 'Don't tell me. I think I can guess.'

'How are you Sally?'

'Aren't you going to go over and wish her luck?'

'She looks busy right now.'

Sally regarded him with a level gaze. 'You know, I ran into
Ella about a week or so ago. She was pretty cool towards me,

which isn't like her, so I asked her what was wrong. Anyway she didn't admit it but I got the feeling from a couple of things she said that she thought there was something going on between you and me. I don't know where she got that idea, but you might like to know I put her right.'

'I doubt that it was of much interest to her.'

'If you think that you don't know much about women. If she didn't care, how come she was acting so off-hand with me? Think about it,' Sally said. 'I have to go, I'm on a break. I just came over to vote. I'll see you later.'

As Sally left he glanced over at Ella again, but she had her back to him.

On the way out of the hall he met Baxter, and they walked down to the coffee shop together.

'So, who do you think will win?' Matt asked.

'Hard to say. I guess people have had a chance to take a long hard look at themselves recently,' Baxter mused. 'But you never can tell.'

Sanctuary Harbor was a changed place since the bluefin had briefly turned it into something akin to a gold-rush town, Matt thought. Though visibly it remained the same, there were people who still weren't on speaking terms. People who'd been friends and neighbours, for years. Even families had become involved in bitter disputes that would take a long time to heal.

Matt didn't want the island to change. He'd come there to start a new life, to get away from what he'd become, and he still thought St George was the right place for him to be. He knew that nothing stayed the same for ever, and that with fishing declining it was harder for people to make a living. He just hoped that didn't mean the island had to become a tourist resort where the year round residents were reduced to acting as service providers for a whole new community of wealthy summer people. But whichever way it went, he thought he'd probably stay. At least for a while.

He asked Baxter if he'd seen Kate Little lately and Baxter shook his head. 'She went back to New York a couple of days ago.'

Matt wasn't sure what to say. He guessed that Baxter had discovered that he cared a lot more about Kate than even he had known himself. 'Did you see her before she left?'

'Yeah, I ran into her one day. She said that she and her husband were getting a divorce.'

'Did she say if she thought she'd ever be coming back here?'

'No, but I don't think she will,' Baxter said. He looked away, across the harbour. 'I don't think she felt as if she fitted in here. I guess she was probably right.' They reached the coffee shop and paused outside. 'You spoken to Ella?'

Matt shook his head. Baxter hesitated as if he were about to say something, but then he changed his mind. 'Come on, I'll buy you a cup of coffee.'

Matt and Henry sat on the porch and watched the clouds rolling in from the east as dusk fell. It had grown noticeably cooler. Sheet lightning appeared in silent flashes far out to sea. When a truck appeared along the track through the trees, Henry got up, and put out the butt of the cigarette he'd been smoking.

'Looks like you have company. I'll leave you to it.' He breathed deeply. The scent of pine was sharp in the evening air. 'It'll rain soon. Better shut your windows tonight.'

'You don't need to leave, Henry,' Matt said.

'I'm kind of tired anyway.'

The old man went down the steps and paused to speak to Ella as she got out of her car. She was wearing jeans and a white shirt, and her hair was tied back. After a moment Henry raised a hand to bid her good night. Ella approached and at the bottom of the steps she smiled uncertainly.

'Hi. Can I come up?'

The moment he'd recognized her truck Matt had felt his throat constrict, and a feeling as if a band had been tightened across his chest. 'Help yourself.' He offered her a seat, then a drink, both of which she accepted. His feelings towards her were complicated, but he tried to sound as if he wasn't too surprised to see her. 'I've got beer or wine. Or coffee if you prefer.'

'A beer would be good. Thanks.'

He went inside and re-emerged carrying a couple of bottles of Millers and two glasses. He sat down opposite her, and while he poured their beers he noticed the slight flush to her cheeks that lent her a colour like the faded pink of a rose at the edge of a dusty road. He smiled and raised his glass and she did the same.

'How did the election go?'

'The result won't be in until later,' she said.

'Well, you got my vote.'

'Thanks.'

He waited for her to tell him why she had come. She appeared to be trying to find a place to begin. Eventually she looked over and met his eye.

'My mother told me to do this three weeks ago. Actually she said it before then too.'

He could believe that. He'd thought a lot about the events leading up to the day Bryan's body had been recovered, and why later on the beach, Ella had chosen not to tell him what it was Ben Harper had found. He knew it was because she was afraid of what his reaction might be, but he didn't think she was afraid for herself, or for Kate as he'd once thought, which didn't leave too many other possibilities. He was aware that she was watching him, maybe wondering how much he'd already guessed. There were slight furrows in her brow.

'You know don't you?' she said at last.

He picked up his beer and took a sip while he considered how to answer. 'I think I know some of it, but not all.'

She sighed. It was a long exhalation of things she'd kept to herself for too long. 'I came here to explain it to you. I realized that if I didn't I'd always regret it, I'd always wonder about us.'

She began, in a quiet voice, to tell him the whole story. Now and then she met his eye when she paused for a moment, but for the most part she was looking backwards, her eyes focused inward on images only she could see. She started by describing her father to him, painting a picture of a quiet man, a stoic fisherman who liked to spend long periods of time alone. He was always that way, she said, but he was also a gentle man, and a good father and husband.

He began to noticeably change after Ella's younger brother died. The loss of his only son affected him deeply, and even when she was very young Ella had sensed the depth of the grief that her father kept locked away somewhere inside himself. It seemed as if a part of him had withdrawn from the world.

'I suppose I was looking for reassurance when I started trailing him around on the docks. I didn't consciously try to replace my brother, but maybe kids know things instinctively. Anyway, I became daughter and son all rolled into one. Or at least that's what I tried to do.'

It was only as she grew older that Ella began to appreciate that her father was ill.

'I think he suffered from chronic depression all his life. But he would never admit it, or see anybody about it. It got worse as the years went by. My mother said there was always a part of him that she never knew. There was a lot of himself, what he was thinking, that he didn't share with anyone. I don't think he knew how. But the way he dwelt on Danny's death wasn't natural. It became too much for him and eventually he started drinking, which is something he'd never done before, and that made his mood swings more erratic.'

She went on to describe how her father's introspection turned to occasional violence when he'd been drinking. It was a secret kept within the family over the years.

Ella paused and looked at Matt, her expression a plea for understanding. 'He wasn't a bad person. This wasn't some bad tempered drunk throwing his fists around, my father was a sick man. But he wouldn't let us get him help.'

She related the events of the night of the February storm when her father had drowned, when everything had finally come to a head. She'd received a call from her mother late at night, to say that Ella's father had been drinking and they'd argued. He had hit her hard enough that she had fallen and cracked her head against the stove, and horrified at what he'd done her

367

father had fled the house, raging with the voice of a man whose sanity had finally been tipped over the edge.

'When he got like that he always blamed my mother for Danny's death.'

Ella had met her mother at the dock. The harbour was lashed by the storm, the seas pounding the wharf, and her father's boat was gone.

'They found the wreckage in the morning, by the cove,' Ella said. 'But there was no sign of his body.'

That night she'd left her mother to go back to the cottage where she lived to fetch some clothes. While she was away her father had returned. He was wet through, shivering with cold, and his eyes were fixed with a glazed expression of madness. He'd attacked Ella's mother, who had defended herself with a cast iron skillet. The blow she'd aimed at him struck his head and killed him.

'I never knew what had happened. By the time I got back she had hidden his body in the garage. She kept her secret for six months.' She shook her head, the gesture almost one of disbelief. There were tears in her eyes and she paused to wipe them away.

'After the funeral she dug a shallow grave at the end of the garden, and one night she wrapped his body in a tarpaulin and dragged him out there where she buried him.'

She fell silent. For several minutes neither of them spoke until eventually Matt asked the question that he knew she was waiting for. 'Why didn't she tell anyone what had happened? From what you've told me, it was self-defence.' He couldn't prevent a hard edge from creeping into his voice, and her eyes snapped to meet his.

'I can't give you a simple answer to that,' she said. 'It was partly that she was frightened. My mother comes from a very traditional background, where a wife does what her husband tells her to do, where family problems are not aired in public. She was taught that a woman's role is to support her husband no matter what. Nobody knew what my father could be like. He only ever drank at home, or when he was alone on his boat. My mother was afraid that she wouldn't be believed, but she was also confused. She felt guilty and ashamed, as if what had happened was really her fault. But she also loved my father, and I think in her grief she wanted to blot out what had happened. I don't even think she was really aware of what she was doing.'

As Ella tried to explain, Matt's reaction was almost automatic. He had heard this story before, in a thousand different guises as people tried to explain away their actions, to abdicate responsibility for something they had done. And he knew this was why until now, Ella had never felt she could tell him all of this.

She went on to explain the rest, much of which he'd already guessed. Her mother had suffered a stroke not long after the funeral, and after that progress towards recovery had been unnaturally slow.

'It was as if she didn't want to live.'

Ella had always suspected her mother was troubled by something other than grief, and as the months went by and her mother's health failed, Ella became convinced that unless she discovered what it was her mother would die. Finally she persuaded her mother to tell her the truth.

'It was too late by then to tell anyone what had happened. I couldn't see what good it would do to put my mother through all the questions she would face, raking up the past, so I decided to move my father's body. To bury him at sea, where he would have wanted to be. So that my mother wasn't reminded of how he'd died every time she looked out of the kitchen window.' She paused and when she spoke again her voice was leaden. 'The rest you know.'

It had grown dark. Their beers remained on the table in front of them, untouched since Ella had begun her story. Matt could no longer see her face properly in the shadows of the porch, but he knew that she was watching him, waiting to see what he would do.

He understood why she had kept silent, unwilling to risk putting her mother through the rigours of an investigation that would have laid the secrets of their family bare. She would have destroyed her father's name, and ultimately she would have been taking a chance that her mother's story wouldn't be believed, in which case her mother would have faced a prison term. Matt wondered what he would have done if she had told him all this when Bryan had first gone missing, and the answer was that he didn't know.

His whole life had been shaped by a day a long time before when he'd almost drowned in Stillwater Cove. When Paulie had died, the character traits that had set Matt off on a mission of vengeance were already in place, and for a long time he hadn't questioned what he was doing. If he'd heard a story like this from people he didn't know when he'd still been working as a prosecutor he would have brought a charge of murder. Innocent people didn't bury their husbands in the garden or dump their weighted bodies in the ocean. He still didn't know if he had the right to make a judgment that he didn't really believe was his to make. This was an issue that ought to be decided in a court of law, but if that happened people would be hurt regardless of the outcome, and in the end he believed things had occurred in much the way that Ella had related them.

But most important of all he wasn't the same person he had been six months, or even two months earlier.

He knew without asking that if the same set of circumstances arose again, Ella would repeat her actions. It was her nature. Just as it was her nature to empathize with Kate Little even though she had believed Kate had killed Bryan.

'There's no evidence of any of this to convict either you or your mother,' he said at length. 'It doesn't matter what I think.'

'No, you're wrong Matt. It does matter.'

He knew what she was asking him, what he had to ask himself. Could he love her knowing all that he did about who she was?

He rose at last and wordlessly he went to turn on a light, and when he came back Ella was standing at the top of the steps. He looked at her, her face half in shadow, and thought how beautiful she was.

'It's getting late, I think I should go,' she said.

Inside the house the phone started to ring. Matt ignored it. 'Why don't you stay awhile.'

She looked at him for a long time.

'Is that what you really want Matt?'

'It's what I want.'

The phone was still ringing.

'Are you going to answer that?'

He hesitated, unsure if she would still be there when he came back, then he went inside. When he returned a couple of minutes later she wasn't where he'd left her, and for a moment he thought that she had gone until he saw her leaning against the porch rail.

'That was Baxter. He wanted to tell me the result of the election. You won. Congratulations.'

He went over and put his arms around her. She leaned her head against his shoulder, and Matt knew finally that everything would be all right.

EPILOGUE

The orcas swam in close formation as they moved towards an unsuspecting minke whale in the cold waters off the coast of Nova Scotia. A male was at the front, and close by swam a female, and further back was the old bull whose body bore the scars of his long life. Behind his dorsal fin the presence of the broken shaft of a harpoon showed in the lump of scar tissue that covered it. The bull was weak. A young male and a female swam close to him, never straying far from his side. An infection had set in, the latest in a string of ailments that had troubled the bull after the pod had left the gulf, but this one was more serious. The harpoon point had worked its way further into his body towards his vital organs, and now the bull was feverish and his strength was rapidly failing. He did not take part in the hunt any longer, but relied on other members of the pod to feed him.

The minke was an adult, and almost as big as the old bull. It didn't hear the orcas until it was too late. The animal was too big for them to kill quickly. The orcas positioned one of their number at each end of the minke. A female seized the whale's flukes, while another held it by its long pointed snout. The minke was unable to move and knew that it was doomed. It sounded a deep moan of anguish. The lead male of the pod attacked first, swimming underneath and ripping at the minke's genital slit, flaying open a strip of the thick blubber. An oily bloody film seeped into the surrounding water. One by one the pod attacked as the helpless whale was held fast. Each time the whale shuddered and low moans echoed in a haunting death cry through the deep waters. The orcas at fluke and snout were replaced by other members of the pod, so that they too could take their turn, and gradually the minke was stripped of its outer layer of blubber. Only after some time of this torment was enough flesh exposed that the lead male orca was able to bite into the minke's body cavity. He ended the whale's ordeal by seizing its great beating heart and tearing it out, spewing great clouds of blood into the surrounding water.

The old bull ate a few chunks of the rich blubber that were brought to him, but he was unable to keep the food down. When the pod continued on its way, all but the bull gorged, he swam with increasingly feeble actions, often supported by the other orcas.

During the night, the old bull dozed, and when the sun rose in the morning he was dead. The orcas all took their turn to swim alongside, rubbing close to the animal that had led them for so many years. They held him afloat for another day, reluctant to take their parting.

And then at dusk they at last released his body to continue on their way.

The dead bull slowly sank into the depths of the ocean.